THE
HANGED
MAN

EDITED BY P. N. ELROD

❖

Dark and Stormy Knights
Strange Brew
My Big Fat Supernatural Wedding
My Big Fat Supernatural Honeymoon
Hex Appeal

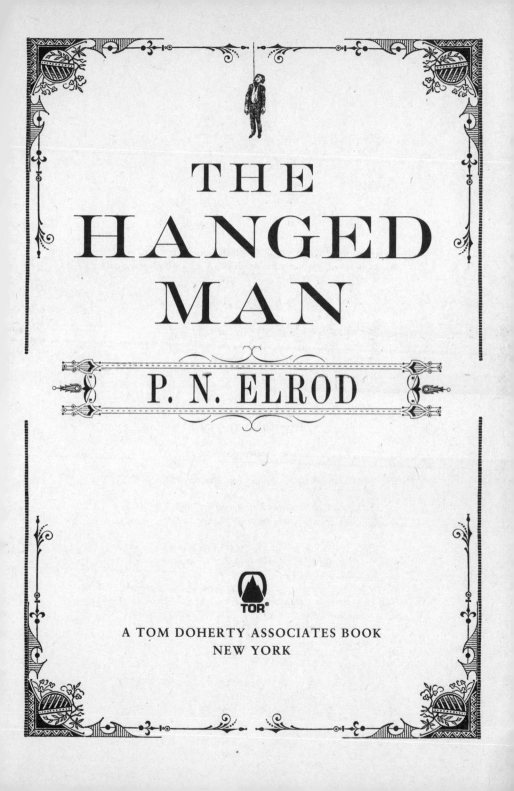

THE HANGED MAN

P. N. ELROD

A TOM DOHERTY ASSOCIATES BOOK
NEW YORK

THE HANGED MAN

Copyright © 2015 by Patricia Elrod

A Tor Book
Published by Tom Doherty Associates, LLC
175 Fifth Avenue
New York, NY 10010

www.tor-forge.com

Tor® is a registered trademark of Tom Doherty Associates, LLC.

The Library of Congress Cataloging-in-Publication Data
is available upon request.

ISBN 978-0-7653-2971-4 (hardcover)
ISBN 978-1-4299-4664-3 (e-book)

Tor books may be purchased for educational, business, or promotional use. For information on bulk purchases, please contact the Macmillan Corporate and Premium Sales Department at 1-800-221-7945, extension 5442, or write to specialmarkets@macmillan.com.

First Edition: May 2015

Printed in the United States of America

0 9 8 7 6 5 4 3 2 1

For Mickee

ACKNOWLEDGMENTS

Heather Fagan,
Dan Hollifield and Lindsey Burt-Hollifield.
High five!

THE
HANGED
MAN

PROLOGUE

In Which Vital History Concerning Her Majesty Is Revealed

When informed at the age of ten that she was likely to be queen of England, it was reported that Her Royal Highness Princess Alexandrina Victoria of Kent replied, "I will be good."

What she actually said was, "I will *do* good."

Sometime in 1835—it is a well-kept secret—the sixteen-year-old princess escaped her highly managed routine and spent two weeks walking incognito among commoners. The revelation of how ordinary folk lived and died made a profound impression on young "Drina." She resolved to improve the lot of her people, especially that of women.

During this taste of freedom, she met the dashing Lord Arthur Godalming, who was in the right place at the right time to rescue her from street ruffians. It was love at first sight for both, and when she became queen two years later, iron-willed Victoria defied custom and changed law so she could marry a peer rather than a prince.

The love match of Victoria and the Lord Consort Arthur marked the beginning of a new era of enlightenment for England.

Her progressive policies, particularly the historic "Time of Women" Equal Franchise Act of 1859, which granted voting rights to women, changed the world.

The young monarch made her childhood declaration a reality.

Victoria's empire now circles the globe, but the brass and

steam progress of the Industrial Revolution disturbed dark forces. Reason and science were in vigorous conflict against fear and superstition. The empress could not ignore the fact that something was supernaturally rotten in the state of England. In 1847 she called for the creation of a new department within the Ministry of Science.

This special branch, Her Majesty's Psychic Service, dedicated to investigating all matters supernatural, employs the psychical gifts of those who serve in it to protect and preserve the realm.

Here follows the story of one of her agents.

CHAPTER ONE

In Which Miss Pendlebury Is Called to Duty

LONDON, ENGLAND,
CHRISTMAS MORNING 1879

No commonplace death would require Alex's presence at such an ungodly hour; calls to the house of a Reader at two in the morning were never of a social nature. She girded her emotional barriers for the possibility of brutal murder and sent up a silent request that it would not involve a child. Those were the worst, though, of course, none were ever pleasant.

Someone rang the front entry bell just as she was about to put out her candle and attempt sleep. Mrs. Harris, the housekeeper, was away visiting relations for the holiday, taking along the page and the maid, so Alex herself slipped downstairs. She did not bother with slippers, throwing a blanket about her shoulders against the chill.

A man's looming form showed through the door's frosted glass panels. He was too tall to be Sergeant Greene, who must also be away visiting family. Everyone had a holiday except herself, the luckless fellow sent to fetch her, and death.

She used her candle to light the gas sconce, instantly brightening the foyer. Wary for problems, she slid open a discreet drawer in the foyer table where she kept a revolver.

Clutching the blanket to her throat, Alex threw the bolt with her free hand and opened the door to the freezing night.

"Miss Pendlebury," said the tall man on her step. "You're needed."

The stranger held out a folded paper and, after his initial glance, looked at some point above her head, politely not noticing her state of dishabille.

He did not mistake me for a housemaid, she thought, sliding the drawer shut on the revolver. *Why is that?* Not from the blanket or what was visible of the nightdress under it. Then she remembered that no respectable servant would venture forth barefoot and without cap or dressing gown. Only the master or mistress of a house would do so. This was Baker Street, not Grosvenor Square, therefore the master or mistress of a house were not above answering their own—

She cut that thread of thought and took the paper. Scrawled in pencil was a Harley Street address and the name of the detective in charge of whatever investigation was presently taking place. Inspector Lennon, the toughest of a surly lot . . . he'd be in a fine temper getting called in at this hour. He'd want things wrapped up quick to have the coming day free for Christmas dinner with his family.

Alex had a surfeit of relatives herself, but no intention of dining with any of them. A cold supper, hot cocoa, a good book, and sweet solitude by a crackling fire suited her better. That, and not being called to Read a suspicious death.

She abruptly noticed it was sleeting, rice-size beads collecting on her caller's shoulders and hair. "Oh, you must be frozen. Come in, Lieutenant." She stepped back to make room for him.

"Thank you, miss, don't mind if—" He got that look they always get. "Beg pardon, but how did you—?"

His regulation boots below his heavy ulster, hat tucked under one arm, and ramrod posture had given him away as a military man. She'd taken those in with her first glimpse, hardly aware of the process between observation and conclusion. While he could have been a sergeant, she added in his general manner, the cut of his hair, his carefully trimmed moustache and, of course, his accent, placing him as a scion of an upper-class house who had found a place in the Service. Whether he'd volunteered or had been transferred over as punishment for some infraction such as passing the port in the wrong direction at dinner, she did not know or care.

It would do no harm to add to her reputation; Alex preserved the mystery and made no reply.

"I shall return directly," she said, pointing to a chair where he could wait.

"Yes, miss. They asked you to hurry, if you'll pardon my saying."

"They always do, but the dead are a patient lot, I think."

"Yes, miss," he somberly agreed, this time not reacting to her knowledge that a death was involved. It was, after all, her trade.

She did not rush upstairs, but once there made a speedy toilet. Not knowing whether she'd be indoors or out, she prepared for the worst: long woolens under her winter knickerbockers, a wool waistcoat over a wool blouse. Her new cycling boots that went up to her knees took forever to button, but once done, she was ready for anything.

Alex descended the stairs smartly, pulling on gloves. Her driver rose, his mouth agape for an instant before he clamped it shut and assumed a studiously blank expression. She placed him as one of the vast number of males who still found females who chose to wear practical clothing to be an amusing (or even shocking) novelty. *Punch* printed many a cartoon in reaction to the transformations in fashion.

"Please, sir, we've had the vote for decades. Accustom yourself to fresher progresses" was the caption of one showing Lord Nelson's statue swooning at the sight of two respectable ladies in trousers strolling Trafalgar Square. Alex bought several postcards of that one to share with a few female friends who would appreciate the humor.

The emancipation the Equal Franchise Act gave to women had been the law of the realm for twenty years, but some men still grumbled about it, predicting the downfall of the British Empire—if not the end of the world—depending on the depth of their prejudice. So far, neither had happened, but Alex knew many lived on in hope, if only to have the satisfaction of saying, *"Hah! Told you so!"*

She took her cape-topped ulster from the hook by the door and allowed her visitor to help her on with it. When he offered he was simply showing common courtesy. Had he required similar assistance, she would have done the same. It would not have been easy; he was dashingly tall while she was little more than a few inches over five feet in her boots.

"Thank you, Lieutenant . . . ?"

"Brook," he said. "Attached to the Service by special order," he added.

That covers a number of sins, she thought. *And by whose order?*

Alex transferred the revolver from the foyer table drawer to her coat pocket, which raised an eyebrow on her escort, but it, along with a notebook and other odds and ends, was part of her normal kit when on duty. Though not strictly required to carry one, all Readers who dealt with criminal cases had to learn the use of firearms. Many times she'd been called to parts of London as dark and dangerous as any jungle, and she liked having the solid weight of a Webley on her person.

She donned her fore-and-aft hunting cap, tying the earflaps under her chin, and wrapping a muffler about her throat. Whatever awaited tonight, she would not suffer unduly from the cold.

Brook held the door. She almost threw him a salute in passing to find out if he'd return it out of habit. That would be inappropriate humor, given the situation. Instead, she went out, then locked up.

Their conveyance was an ordinary hansom, not the unadorned closed carriage the Service favored. Her driver was much too finely turned out to pass as a London cabbie, though.

I will have to send word upstream about that.

There was a fresh crop of New Year recruits to train, and none of the upper-class ones, including their hide-bound instructors, had the least idea how to blend into the vast background of commonplace London life. Brook was evidently one of them. A cabbie with an Eton accent? Quite ridiculous.

Alex climbed in, pretending to overlook the lieutenant's offered hand. Yes, definitely from some high stratum. His mother, or more likely his nanny, had taught him nice manners. Well and good. Alex appreciated nice manners. Had she been in a dress she would have accepted help, but the ease of movement her cycling costume allowed abrogated the need.

Brook put on his hat and touched the brim, and the cab rocked as he climbed up to the driver's seat.

She pulled shut the half doors that would protect her from some of the wet, and heartily wished for a more sheltering conveyance. Sleety wind stung her face as they trotted north along Baker Street, then cut right onto Marylebone Road, heading for the northern end of Harley Street.

London was usually clogged with all manner of vehicles, but not at this hour of night. Their trip was miserable, but brief. Brook pulled the horse up just short of the house. There was a hospital ambulance already waiting in front, and two men hunched in its lee, smoking cigarettes. They couldn't remove the body until she had a look at things.

Even in this weather, a few idlers hung about, hoping for a glimpse of something interesting or to earn or beg a copper. A constable kept them at a distance. Every window with a view of the street had one or more faces in it, taking in the show like theater attendees in private boxes.

How long has this been going on?

She preferred to arrive at the scene of a death as soon as possible, nearly always before the ambulance. Things were easier to Read when the residual emotions were uncontaminated by intrusive traffic or eroded by the passage of time. There were strict rules of preservation in place now, but not everyone followed them.

Investigations had a pattern: discover a body, notify a doctor or a constable depending on the circumstances. If there was *anything* suspicious about the death, clear the area and send for a detective from Scotland Yard and a Reader from Her Majesty's Psychic Service. Tonight, Miss Alexandrina Victoria Pendlebury happened to be the closest.

Lieutenant Brook dropped down, one of his heels slipping on a patch of ice. He grabbed the hansom and kept his balance. This time she accepted his hand as she emerged.

"Have a care, miss," he advised kindly.

Would that be for the sidewalk, or for what waited inside the house?

She was familiar with the locale, often cycling along Harley Street, taking the air when the weather was temperate. The house was part of a row of impressive structures, each four stories tall with three dormers at the top, each made individual by the use of different colors of brick. They were wonderfully respectable and, despite high rents, much in demand by members of the medical establishment.

This one's wide door with frosted glass panes was very like her own. It was also noteworthy for being between two large bay windows, one for its own building, the second belonging to the neighboring house.

The lower facade of number 138 was of fine white stone with a faux Roman arch trimming the fanlight window. The metalwork screen on the fanlight, the elegant iron fence on either side, and the brass knob in the center of the door were all nearly identical to the front of her own house, but on a grander scale.

The keystone of the arch had a distinctive carved head, like a death mask, emerging from its surface. That was new. She'd have noticed such a thing on her last jaunt here some three weeks ago. Prior to that, the building had been vacant for about a fortnight. So the new tenant had been here less than a month and had money to spend on exterior decorations.

She wanted to ask who lived here, but that could wait. The Service was strict about investigative process and rightly so. They caught more criminals that way.

Inspector Lennon opened the door. Gaslight spilled out, catching on specks of sleet flying past. "Finally," he growled, looking her up and down. "Get inside and get on with it."

Despite tangible results that came from Readings, Lennon

maintained a broad skepticism tinged with contempt for those with psychical talent, but followed official procedure to the letter. One could not lodge a complaint against that, however poor his manners.

"Good morning, Inspector," she said, mounting the three steps and entering, unruffled at being addressed like a lazy scullery girl.

"Nothing good about it, Miss Pendlebury, as you'll find out."

"Please, no information. Just tell me where." She removed her muffler and cap, stuffing them into her pockets, then took off her gloves.

"Upstairs, last room on the left."

Unbuttoning her ulster, she had a quick look around, unsettled by the similarity of the house's exterior to her own. The foyer was somewhat different, this one paneled in dark, shining wood, not bold, cheery wallpaper.

To her left was a sizable parlor with chairs and tables along the walls. The draperies on the bay windows were closed. The parlor obviously served as a waiting room. She could assume a doctor owned the premises, and that he might be a bachelor or widower. A framed print on the wall extolling the virtues of Dr. Kemp's Throat Elixir supported it. No lady of the house would have *that* up in even the public receiving areas. It was frightfully common.

"Where are the servants?" Alex asked.

"The whole lot's back in the kitchen." Lennon nodded toward a door under the stairs that must lead to that area. "We got them clear soon as may be."

She heard voices and clamor: someone sobbing, someone else clattering about with pots and pans, probably seeking solace in the familiarity of work.

"Inspector, would it be possible to have a cup of tea for me when I'm done?"

He grunted and looked at Brook, who had shadowed her inside. "My men are busy. You see to it."

The lieutenant might have wanted to watch her at work, but said, "Yes, sir," and went off. Imagine that: a member of the upper class fetching tea. The Service was a great leveler. To his credit, Brook gave no indication the task was beneath him. Sergeant Greene, born and raised in Whitechapel, would have balked, but only because he'd consider it woman's work.

Alex left her ulster on the banister and climbed the stairs with Lennon a few steps behind. He was a big man; they creaked under his boots. His hard gaze would be on the back of her neck, suspicious for any sign of weakness. She'd heard from others in her department that he took pleasure in intimidating them. He never said a word, letting a hard stare do the job of breaking their concentration. Complaints were lodged, but never went far. What could one say that would not sound like childish whining?

Ignoring his presence, Alex opened to the atmosphere of the house.

It was, surprisingly, buoyant.

Most doctors' offices had quite an awful mix of hope and despair, the latter being the natural result of patients getting bad news about their health. The darker, heavier feelings tended to be stronger, soaking into the walls like a case of damp. Those could be dispelled easily. Sometimes simply airing a room was sufficient. However rare sunshine was in English weather, especially in winter, there was always enough to scour most places of old emotions.

She reached the landing and focused on the left-hand door at the end of the hall.

Move slowly, test the way.

Sometimes there were nasty emotional jolts lingering near a death, the psychical equivalent of stepping on a nail. So far she picked up a general feeling of shocked disbelief, deep grief . . . and horror.

She'd encountered those before, the normal residue left by those who found the body. People tended to have the same emotions when death paid a call. While she could not say that she was used to such, they no longer overwhelmed her. On her very first case she'd opened up too quickly and fallen over in a faint. The instructor had been prepared. Alex struggled awake to the burning sting of smelling salts in her nose and was sharply told to show greater care for herself. She got no more sympathy than a medical student fainting at their first anatomy lesson.

Of course, those students made a *choice* to become doctors or nurses. If unable and unwilling to handle the necessary requirements of their art, they could find another occupation. Alex had been born to this particular work. As with others possessing psychical talent, it ran in her family, and she had been blessed (or cursed) with a particularly strong ability. Her choices had been to learn to control it or go mad.

Perhaps I'm mad and no one's noticed yet.

She always thought that just before looking on a corpse. It was a tired observation, long bereft of its feeble humor, its very weariness a comforting affirmation that she was in her right senses.

She paused before the door, which was ajar. The gas was on within and strange shadows swung lazily on the hall floor. She pushed gently forward to see what cast them.

The taint of night soil hung heavily in the air, turning her stomach. In all the stories and books she read for pleasure, none of the writers ever made mention of this noisome aspect that attended the discovery of a corpse. Either they'd never dealt with death themselves, or deemed the subject indelicate.

Alex kept handkerchiefs in a jar of rosewater on her dressing table. Just before leaving on a call, she'd wring one out, tuck it into an oilcloth pouch, and tuck that into a pocket of her waistcoat. She retrieved the one she'd taken tonight, holding it to her nose, then pushed the door wide.

It was a room for a gentleman, furnished with a big bed and a reading chair by the window. There had been a fire in the grate; a few coals glowed but offered no warmth. A window was raised high, and the air was freezing.

Otherwise everything was normal, except for the man's corpse hanging from the gas chandelier in the center of the room. His back was to her, which made it easier. However they died, she avoided looking at their faces. After burnings and drownings, hangings were the worst. The last one, with its bulging black tongue, bloodshot eyes popped wide, and horrifically elongated neck would last her a lifetime.

Alex had no need to look, anyway.

Her job, God help her, was to *feel*.

A suicide? The chandelier must be singularly sturdy to hold such a weight. Then she noticed the rope was looped over the same large hook in the ceiling that held the light. The hook had been driven deeply into a support beam hidden by plaster, certainly strong enough to carry out an act of self-destruction like this.

The chief grotesquery was that the gas yet burned. The body, so near to the source of light, cast a deep shadow upon the floor and walls. The man's gray head was against one of the glass globes. While still alive he must surely have flinched from the heat. *Why* had he lighted the gas? Why not that candle on the bedside table?

While death occasionally possessed a macabre humor, it was never kindly, particularly with suicides who hanged themselves. The bowels and bladder had given way, which accounted for the bad smell. The rose scent in her handkerchief could not wholly overcome the reek, but it kept Alex from retching.

His bare feet dangled loose and vulnerable under the blue nightshirt. A draft created by the open door stirred its pale folds; otherwise the corpse was quite still. His slippers were next to the bed, which was rumpled from occupancy. Had he crept under the covers to stare at the ceiling until unrelenting hopelessness caused him to rise and end his torment?

While it was not outside possibility, there was a false note to the terrible scene before her. Several, in fact.

If he planned ahead enough to bring a rope, why bother

going to bed? There was no need to mislead the servants; as master of the house he had only to shut the door and attend to his repugnant undertaking in private.

Why undress for bed? While she had encountered suicides who stripped naked to meet their Maker, most kept their clothes on. In one case, the lady put on her wedding dress and reclined prettily on a chaise lounge while a draught of laudanum took her into the next world.

Why choose such a long, painful death by strangulation? If he had been a doctor then there would be better choices in his medical bag. Laudanum, morphine, or heroin were painless and just as effective.

Well, the initial discovery was out of the way, time to get on with the rest of it, and there, perhaps, find answers.

Murder victims tended to be surprised, terrified, or enraged, leaving those feelings behind in the wake of an attack removing them from life. Those who passed due to accident often left nothing at all, if their death was sudden enough. She'd encountered that in the aftermath of a train wreck. A great number of the dead hadn't known what befell them and all that remained were their poor broken bodies. Most of the emotions she'd gotten had been from those whose work was to remove and attend the dead. It had run to ghoulish humor. Ugh.

Suicides, though, had weeks, months, even years of despair and anguish about them. It built up like silt in a river. It bogged them down, trapped them, tortured them until they finally succumbed willingly to end the pain.

But hanging was a singularly agonizing way to die. It always took longer than expected. The pain, shock, and helplessness usually left an imprint of emotion as harsh as any violent murder.

Alex opened herself a tiny bit more, bracing for the worst.

But nothing came.

Which was *not* normal.

She opened still more, eyes shut, and cast about like a

hunting hound. There was the discordant rasping shock here in the doorway. That would be from the person or persons who had found the body.

A servant had found him, male, his valet or butler. The horror and sincere grief were profound, but not the same sort one got from a relation or a spouse. A calm fellow, he'd likely seen death before and recognized it readily enough. A relative might immediately take down the body in an attempt to revive it or to conceal the self-slaughter, but this one had been left as found. The man was clearly dead—nothing to do but alert the authorities.

As for the room's late occupant—odd—there was no trace of melancholy at all, which puzzled her. Why, then, had this man killed himself?

No emotional residue presented itself to answer. The only feelings here were of self-satisfaction, a sense of accomplishment, anticipation—not at all what she'd expected.

If not suicide, then murder?

But she found no trace of that either, unless that satisfaction belonged to the perpetrator. Not likely, for the emotion was well attached to the general atmosphere of the room, imprinted there by its most habitual occupant.

The man had not killed himself, nor had he been awake to resist an attacker. He'd passed unaware. Considering the agony of such a death, that was just as well, but it was impossible that he could have slept through it. Had he been in a drunken stupor?

The attacker had left no sign of himself behind. Not one hint remained of anger, jealousy, love, hate, or any of the myriad emotions that drove one human to take the life of another.

That was impossible. There was always *something;* an action as intense as murder always left a stain. She'd never been at a scene of violence that did not have motivational emotions lingering about. They lay like shards of broken glass, and one could follow them to the source if it was a fresh enough trail.

But no such trail existed here. Had there been a psychic

cleansing, then it would have removed the latent emotions of the dead occupant as well.

Opening her eyes, Alex shut down the inner mechanism of nature that others ironically called her "gift" and switched to her cultivated talent for observation.

A chest was at the foot of the bed, nearly under the chandelier hook. The dead man's right ankle brushed against the chest's side. Supposedly he stood on it, secured one end of the rope to the ceiling hook, then stepped off.

It would have been difficult to lift an unresisting body up high enough to slip a noose around its neck. Even to loop it first, then hoist the body up using the ceiling hook as a pulley would require a strong, strapping fellow. Two would have found it easier, but she could not think how one man could have erased his psychic spoor, much less two.

No shoe prints or scuffs were visible on the bare wood of the chest. A few swipes with a gloved hand would take care of that.

First things first: How had the killer gotten in and out?

The window was the likely point of entry. Perhaps the late tenant enjoyed fresh air; some hardy sorts left their windows wide open, even in this weather. She crossed the room. The latch was unengaged. He could have left it cracked and an intruder took advantage of it.

"What are you about?" demanded Lennon. He'd been quiet during her psychical scrutiny, which was now clearly over.

"Checking things," she said, peering at the sill. It was wet from sleet melting on the relatively warmer surface of it and the floor. Had there been footprints left by an intruder, they were lost now.

He grunted and joined her. If the stench bothered him, he gave no sign. "You think someone done for him?"

"Yes. Despite appearances, this is a murder."

"That what his ghost told you?"

"Inspector, you are well aware that I Read only the emotions left by the living, not the dead. What I found tells me that this poor man did not kill himself. He was somehow rendered insensible, then hung up like a Christmas goose at a butcher's."

"Who done for him, then?"

"I can't tell. There's no psychical trace of the killer."

"Meaning?"

"Whoever did this left no muddy footprints for a Reader to follow. He's psychically invisible, and that's impossible."

"Your whole Service is impossible, and yet here you are."

"Which is your good fortune, Inspector. This is something new; you'll have the credit for it."

"Keep your credit. You can't see him? Then how do you know anyone was here?"

She shook her head. Trying to explain the emptiness to him would be like describing light and color to a blind person.

"If you think someone topped him, show me real proof, Miss Pendlebury."

That might be a problem. There was no city soot on the outer sill to hold footprints either.

"My missus should clean this well," grumbled Lennon. "Someone could have got in and out this way, but he'd have been seen. Someone in the street would have noticed a ladder where it shouldn't be. There's idlers about. We questioned them, they didn't see anything."

"What about a misplaced mountaineer dangling from the roof like a great spider?" she asked. "People aren't likely to look up in this weather."

"There's that," he conceded. "Though anyone at a window across the way would notice. But at this hour and in this dark—"

"Otherwise the only entry and exit is the room's one door."

"Unless you think there's a secret passage behind the fireplace."

"I should be most surprised if there was." The layout of this house was similar enough to her own, and hers had no such feature.

"You're minded that it's a sneak-thief?"

"If not a thief, then a sneak with murderous intent and the intelligence to arrange this to be taken for a suicide. I suggest sending someone observant to examine the roof, otherwise this horrid deed may have been done by a member of the household or one letting in a murderous confederate."

Lennon's eyes narrowed and his jaw worked as he grunted agreement. He had not risen through the ranks at Scotland Yard by being a fool. While showing unflagging contempt for her psychical talent, he never discounted her observational skills.

Again, she cast about, searching every corner, every item in the room.

The table next to the bed held a water carafe and a glass on a little tray. Neither had apparently been used, but a clever killer would have tidied things.

Alex went to the bedside to examine the carafe. There were potent soporifics without color, though they were often detectable by taste or smell. If one wanted to render a person insensible, then a large amount would have to be dissolved in the carafe—and when would the killer have an opportunity to do that?

"You think there's something nasty in his water?" Lennon asked.

"It's too uncertain. How could he be sure his victim would even take a drink in the night? Or when?"

"Too true, but I'll collect it in evidence."

Someone had silently entered the room and—what? Injected the man with some substance? If so, then the sting of the needle had not wakened him. The medical examiner might find the puncture, giving lie to this being a suicide.

"What makes this murder, eh?" pressed Lennon.

Alex checked a drawer in the bedside table. Inside was a pocket watch and a Bible. She had to forsake the scented handkerchief, needing both hands. She took a deep breath, then picked up the watch and used the small key on its chain to wind it. A quarter turn and no more, so he'd wound it before retiring, read a bit of his Bible, then put out his candle, just as a thousand other men might do.

"What suicide troubles to wind his watch?" she asked.

"Force of habit," Lennon countered. "I've seen queerer stuff. What else?"

Her pent-up breath puffed out as she put the items back, and she did not get the handkerchief to her nose in time, catching a whiff of the stench—and something else.

She bent to sniff the man's pillow.

Sharp and astringent, no more than a whisper of it remained, and that was well masked by the stronger smell of night soil, and further diluted by the freezing air blowing in; this death might well be ruled a suicide but for that.

"Got you," she said, pointing and stepping back to make room for the inspector.

He shot her a suspicious glare, as though expecting a trick, then bent and breathed in.

He snorted, but not dismissively. "Now *that* is interesting. Let's have another opinion, just to be sure. Brook! Up here on the double!"

Brook must have been at the foot of the stairs. He charged up in quick response to Lennon's bellow, but stopped short in the doorway to stare at the corpse, and lost much of his color.

"In here, man," Lennon snapped. "That beggar's past harming aught."

Brook visibly braced himself, assuming the carefully blank expression again, and came forward.

"Put your beezer to that pillow and tell me what's there."

With puzzled reluctance, Brook did so, then straightened. "It's . . . like a hospital?" he hazarded.

"Yes, something you might notice in a hospital," Lennon prompted.

"Not carbolic or vinegar. . . . Pungent stuff."

"You'd think so. Ever have surgery? Of course not. I have, and when you're facing a jolly fellow in a black coat with a knife in his hand you'll bless the stink of this poison. It'll turn your belly over after, but better than being awake when the cuttin' starts."

"Ether," Brook said. "Of course."

"Just so." The two of them looked at the body and back to the pillow. No need to explain to Brook; he'd clearly grasped that foul play had been involved.

Lennon said, "Once they clean him up, they'll find ether still trapped in his lungs. Anyone will be smelling that off him for days. When I come back from getting cut, my missus had the windows up, complaining how it filled the house just from my breathing."

Lennon's emotions were starting to contaminate the scene. He was excited, interested, and eager to press forward, having embraced Alex's conclusion as his own. Nothing left but to find the murderer so far as he was concerned. She was pleased with the validation but resisted the temptation to thank him for it.

He opened the drawer and fingered the deceased's pocket watch, showing its face to Brook. "Make a note of the time and that the smell of ether was detected on the pillow by the three of us. Then make an inventory of all the items in here, starting with this bauble. Mind you get everything down. I won't have some sticky-fingered servant claiming anything went missing while I was on duty."

Brook produced a notebook and a pencil and wrote as instructed.

"Did the butler find the body?" she asked.

"The valet," said Lennon. "He was doing the last rounds before turning in, making sure the windows were shut and the gas off, saw the light under the door, and looked in. Apparently it was unusual for his master to be up so late."

"A steady fellow?"

"Seems steady enough. What's that to do with anything?"

"You can thank him for keeping the room untouched. I should think he may have had some police training at some point."

"We'll stand him a drink at the nearest pub, then. Brook, make a sketch of the room while you're at it. Come along, ghost-catcher." Lennon went out.

"Sketch?" Brook echoed. "I'm no artist." He looked at Alex a little helplessly. "Do you draw, miss?"

"Not that sort of sketch," Alex said kindly. "He wants a map of the room, approximate dimensions, placement of furnishings, window, door, and the body."

"Oh. I can do that. Thank you, miss."

"Two copies, if you please. One for the Yard, another for the Service. As identical as possible."

Alex caught up with Lennon at the far end of the hall. He held a lantern and had a door open. Narrow stairs lay beyond. He bulled up, the lantern's pale light dancing drunkenly on the plain walls. She knew what would be next and cursed him. He'd take great enjoyment grumbling about the delay if she went to fetch her coat, and she refused to give him the satisfaction. She followed him to the servants' floor. To judge by the clothing left out, the females of the household had the whole of it, and it was quite nice. Only two to a room and at one end was the unheard-of luxury of a water closet. That must have cost a few pennies.

Lennon searched with no regard for the occupants' privacy until he found a bolted door that opened to the roof. Any other time of the year Alex would have delighted in such a lofty expedition, but not now.

She eased out in Lennon's wake, shrinking from the cold despite her woolens.

Ice coated everything and the wind cut like a fury.

Directly opposite was a low wall that divided this house from its neighbor. To the left was a flat space with lines strung between a braced pole and hooks piercing the main chimney. Such washing as was done on the premises would be hung here in the more clement months. Alex stepped carefully across to the low wall that overlooked the back. Below were the mews and an enclosed extension leading from them to the house, its windows lighted, probably the kitchen and quarters for the male servants. A constable paced back and forth in the small yard below.

She oriented toward Harley Street. The roof over the servants' rooms slanted up and blocked the view. Above its line, oppressive gray clouds reflected back what little glow the city possessed. The smoke from countless fires rose to combat the falling sleet, sinuous black and translucent silver writhing and twisting about each other in the sky like silk rags.

Footing was slippery. Lennon proceeded with much care toward the house's main chimney, which stood out from the lesser ones like a brick obelisk.

Alex tottered toward him and found it necessary to grab his arm to keep from falling. He glanced down at her with amusement and held the lantern so the light fell on one corner of the structure.

The chimney was black with years of soot from London's thick air. No need to clean something only the servants would see. The corners, though, had some interesting blemishes.

"Rope marks," said Alex, forgetting the cold for a moment. "There are fibers caught in the brickwork."

"I'll have a man collect 'em. Mind your feet." He made his way toward the low slanting roof, dragging her along, since she still had hold of his arm. He seemed unaware of her weight. He peered at the roof, which had a dusting of ice over its dark surface.

"Someone's been here, I think," she said.

"Let's be certain." He held the lantern out.

She took it, thinking he wanted his hands free for climbing.

"Your pardon, I'm sure," he said, grasping her around the waist and lifting.

Alex yelped.

"Never mind that, what d'ye see?"

Far too much. Until now she'd never minded heights. "The

other side of the roof, the dormers coming out from it—" The street far, far below.

"Any tracks?"

She made herself hold the lantern steady. "Yes, someone's been here. No boot prints, but lots of smears in the soot between the dormers."

"Good enough." He shifted and set her down. She staggered a bit. "Steady now, you're just startin' to be useful. I couldn't have boosted Brook up like that."

"I'd have paid to see you try."

He snorted and took back the lantern. "It seems we *are* after a human spider. He tied a rope to the chimney, went up, over, and down to the window. That's a lot of effort even without ice. Why not break through a door during supper? With everyone in the kitchen no one would have heard. He could have hidden until the place was quiet, done the deed, then nipped downstairs and out to the street afterward when they were asleep."

"He may have been unwilling to wait all night. He might not have a familiarity with the routine of the house. He left the gas on in the master's room, too. Forgetful, or did he want the body to be found more quickly?"

"And how the blazes did he get up on the roof in the first place?"

She broke away to check the dividing wall of the neighboring house, gesturing for Lennon to bring the light. "More disturbance in the dirt. He climbed over here. When it's daylight you can send someone to backtrack farther."

"What, no mystical horripilations from beyond?"

"There's nothing to sense. He would not have lingered long enough to leave an emotional impression"—not that he'd left one in the death room—"and the sleet and wind would have the same effect on his psychic trace as a wave on sand. If it warms into rain you'll be hard pressed to follow even a physical trail. Perhaps you better not wait for the dawn and get someone up here now."

He looked over the wall, but the lantern light did not carry far. "You know, you'd make a first-rate detective if you packed up the spook business."

The compliment surprised her. "I'll keep that in mind, Inspector."

"I'm serious. Everything you found is to do with what's in the here and now, not spook land."

She did not correct him with the term favored by Spiritualists. He was in a relatively good mood, no need to spoil it.

Lennon paced off the distance between the chimney and the roof. "He'd need at least seventy feet of rope and a bit more, so there's some left to string up the toff. Brassy devil, doing circus acrobatics in this weather."

"It would be nothing to a mountaineer or a sailor," she pointed out, willing her teeth not to chatter.

"You suss out if any of the household has been to sea, climbed Ben Nevis, or had recent dealings with such a bloke."

"It could be a woman."

"Then she's a proper Amazon and not a little tweak like yourself. It would take real effort to pull that big boy from his sheets and haul him up, so unless you notice a Brunhilde struttin' about lifting horses for sport, my money's on some strapping lad for the dirty work."

The inspector had mixed his mythologies, but she had to agree with him. "Are we done?"

"What? You chilly? An' this such a balmy night."

Alex shivered on the upper landing as Lennon bawled for the morgue attendants. They hurried past, bringing the long straw basket that would carry the body.

One of them muttered something about *bloody spook chasers* just loud enough for Alex to hear. She was always on guard against comments from the uneducated and superstitious about her trade. Her internal defenses were up; their emotions would not leak past and pollute her own. They didn't understand, didn't want to, and never would.

Lennon ordered each to the bedroom to smell the pillow

in situ. One claimed to have a cold, but the other confirmed the stink of ether.

"Good," said Lennon. "Remember that if you're called to give evidence. Brook, get his name and make a note."

That done, the four of them initialed the page as witnesses.

"Plain as pikestaff," said Lennon, summing up for the benefit of the morgue man who asked why he had to sniff some toff's bedding. "Person or persons unknown made entry and inflicted a dose of ether on the man as he slept. Some of it slopped on the pillow. They strung up the poor devil, neat as neat, expecting to draw a verdict of suicide at the inquest, which they won't get. Cut him clear and get him out."

With no desire to watch, Alex went downstairs, feeling sick and sad as she always did afterward. Only it wasn't afterward; more was yet to come, all part of the investigation. She would have no sleep tonight. Closing her eyes would only conjure images from the death room. Those would fade, given time and some meditative cleansing. Regrettably, given her trade, there would always be replacements.

The under-stairs door leading to the kitchen opened, and a slender man of middle years garbed in a robe and slippers stepped out. Taking him for the valet or butler—a person she preferred to avoid for the moment—she did not meet his eye. Her attention was instead fixed on a laden tea tray left on the foyer table.

She hurried to it, pouring a cup of the blessed brew with the same reverence another might accord a French brandy of noble lineage. Blessings on high, it was hot and strong, but not bitter. No need for milk, she drank it straight, glad of the heat.

"Please, miss, what's to happen?" asked the man behind her. His voice was hoarse and hushed from grief.

She shook her head in reply, not wanting to think about the hours to come when she would sit with each member of the household and Read their various feelings. That was invasive, exhausting, and uncomfortable to her, but necessary. Murderers were the most vulnerable when the shock—or guilt or triumph—was fresh. If any here was or had aided the killer, she would discover it, pointing to the most suspicious or discounting the innocent. It was almost impossible to lie to a trained Reader.

Alex had studied cases where the murderers showed and felt no remorse, even considered what they'd done to be a good job, though she'd yet to encounter one. This might be her first.

If so, then she would look for that which wasn't there, but . . . later. Another cup of that wonderful tea, sweetened with an excess of sugar, would brace her up.

From the corner of her eye she was aware of the man's hesitant approach. "Miss, begging your pardon, but—" He stopped in his tracks. "Good heavens. . . . Lady Drina?"

She gave an involuntary start and nearly dropped the cup. She'd not heard that name in years. Years. Not since—

Alex rounded on him. Time slipped treacherously and dizzily backward as she matched his face to one in her memory. He was older, his thin hair showing gray, but the port wine birthmark on his right ear was unmistakable.

"Fingate?" she whispered in disbelief.

"Bless you for remembering, Lady Drina. It's myself, sure enough. How you've grown, if you'll pardon my saying." A crooked smile passed briefly over his drawn features.

"Whatever are you doing here?" she asked, and the question sounded foolish even as the words left her lips. She abruptly knew the answer, but her mind froze, absolutely froze.

"What I've always been doing, looking after—oh! Oh, no." His expression shifted to horrified dismay.

She stared up at the landing where the grunting morgue men were just beginning to descend with the heavily laden basket. It had no lid. A grimy sheet of stained canvas served as a cover, but it caught on something and began to peel away, revealing what was inside.

"They didn't tell you . . . ?" Fingate whispered.

She blinked rapidly as ghastly realization flooded in. Step

by step, the men lugged their burden closer to her, and she would see—

"Is it—? I . . . I didn't know it was . . . no one *said* . . ."

Fingate rushed forward, putting himself between, blocking her view. Against all rules of proper deportment that male servants must follow toward their female betters, he threw an arm around her shoulders and dragged her to the parlor. "There now, you've no need to see your poor father like that. In here—and for God's sake close your eyes."

CHAPTER TWO

In Which Cold Inquiries Are Made
of the Past and Present

There was hell to pay when Lennon was informed.

As a relative of the deceased, Alex should never have been allowed anywhere near the house. In a case of murder, family members were always the first suspects.

Her psychical observations would be discounted, the room sealed again until another member of the Service arrived. Of course by now the scene had been emotionally contaminated by the coroner's men, by Brook and Lennon, and by Alex herself. A very experienced Reader might make sense of the mess, but each passing second meant the dispersal of latent emotions—including those of the servants who had yet to be questioned. Given time, some suspects could cover their reactions, masking their feelings as well as the most adept actor.

Murder disguised as suicide was complicated enough, but the procedural breach put Lennon in a fury, which he aimed at Lieutenant Brook.

"I'll not be responsible," he roared. "If you bloody Service people can't keep track of your own, then it's not my fault when things go wrong."

Alex sat numb and silent in the parlor, out of the direct line of fire, finding Lennon's reaction to be more comforting than if he'd taken her hand and offered sympathetic condolences. Though his anger clouded this part of the house, it was a good thing. He'd stir people up, get them moving, see to it they found out who had murdered her—

God, I can't get my head around it. It's too grotesque.

She choked at the rose scent of the handkerchief and threw it away. The smell clung to her hands. She clenched them into fists and hammered them once on the arms of her chair. Only Fingate, standing protectively over her, noticed, but made no move, just a soft humming sound of distress.

Alex glanced up at him, noting other minor changes the years had made. His soft brown eyes were sad and full of pity for her. Her control slipped and she felt a wickedly strong slap of anguish and grief from the man. It was unintentional, but the purest emotions could bowl one over; he was in great pain from the death of his master. She took a breath, eyes shut, and had to imagine a lead barrier clothing her like a suit of seamless armor. It was the first exercise in self-preservation she'd taught herself and the most reliable. She steadied out and squared her shoulders.

"We must get outside," she said. "All of us." The last thing the next Reader would want was a fellow member of the Service failing when it came to basics.

No one heard. Lennon was still on a rampage.

Alex raised her voice to a strident, cutting level. It felt unpleasant to speak, was unpleasant to hear, but she repeated her statement as an order, and this time it got through even to Lennon. He was in charge of the investigation, but she was the senior member of the Service here, and ultimately her authority trumped his.

This was the first time she'd ever used it. She wondered if he would comply. She locked her gaze on him and hoped he'd fall back on duty and training.

Apparently yes. He shut down and turned to the servants. They'd crowded into the entry, drawn by the row and to get a glimpse of the remains being carried out in a basket. Fingate had spared her that, bless the man.

"Everyone *out*," rumbled Lennon. He wasn't shouting, but his size and tone made it seem so. People fled through the front door into the sleety night as though the house were afire. Lieutenant Brook herded the last ones clear, pausing on the threshold.

Alex stood, forcing herself to be steady, and indicated to Fingate to precede her. He slipped past Brook. She followed, then Lennon, who slammed the door with a bang.

Strangely, he had her ulster over one arm. He glared at her as though not pleased at being caught doing a kindness and thrust it at Brook, then stalked over to one of the mystified constables to pass the word up the ranks about the disaster.

Brook came to her, awkward for a moment, then politely held the coat that she might thread her arms through. It was so mundane as to be ridiculous. Alex fought down the treacherous ripple of hysterical laughter that wanted to break free. That was dangerously close to losing control, which would not do at all. She was in charge until someone else arrived.

She murmured gratitude to Brook and buttoned in, grateful to have silk-lined wool between her and the wind. The servants were not so lucky, huddling together with miserable faces, not a coat or cloak in sight. Fingate stood next to her when he should have been with them. No matter.

"Mr. Brook, please organize something with Mr. Fingate and get those people to shelter in one of these houses as quickly as possible. They are not to speak to anyone. Impress that upon them." She could trust that Fingate would know of a friendly neighbor who would lend their home to such a purpose and that Brook's official standing would smooth the way.

"Yes, miss," they said in unison. Suddenly working together, they exchanged unsure looks, but sorting credentials would have to wait.

They moved off, leaving her alone with the sleet speckling her face and clinging to her hair. She found her hat in a pocket and pulled it on, then her gloves and the muffler. Everyone had something to do, the world rolled on, and yet her father . . .

Mere yards away, shoved into the anonymity of a morgue wagon, his cold clay growing colder.

How could I not know his *emotional trace?*

Because she'd not expected it. Why should she? She hadn't seen him for ten years, not since he'd cut short her education in China and sent her packing back to England without a word to explain why.

Alex had been fifteen and adored him, but Father's odd reticence against answering her reasonable questions had left a lasting hurt. Until then, they had always been so comfortable together and talked about everything.

"Something's come up," was all he'd said.

Something more important than me, she'd finally concluded.

Ten years since she'd last seen him waving from the dock in Hong Kong, and in that time, not a letter, not a telegram. The thorny pain of being sent away like a discharged servant had been slow to root, for she had not wanted to believe it, but it burrowed deep and had grown strong. She'd consciously pruned it back over the years, but now it jabbed her, all over again, making her flinch.

Why did he not contact me when he got home?

Why had he not contacted her, period?

He'd been in London at least three weeks, perhaps longer, living less than half a mile away. Surely he'd have gotten in touch with his brother, her uncle Leopold, to get her address. *Why* had no one spoken to her of this? She wasn't on good terms with the Pendlebury clan, but Leo had always been polite to her and would have sent word.

She'd have to remain here until another member of the Service arrived, but once free she'd go straight to the Wilton Crescent house and make a holy terror of herself.

Damned Pendleburys, she thought, then more charitably wondered if Leo had simply not known his wandering brother had returned. That didn't seem right. Certainly Gerard would have—

Or not.

Alex did not fight the surge of old anger that rushed her. It was a familiar if tiresome companion.

If he'd not contacted his own daughter, then he might not have called on the rest of the family.

Why?

That question could only be answered by the inquiry into Lord Gerard's murder, but she was now banned from the case. *The next Reader will clear me, though.* That done, she'd get back into the middle of things—starting with Fingate. He'd been her father's valet for ages and would know everything. It might spare her the need to storm the Pendlebury sanctum.

Inspector Lennon accomplished what he was good at, making an ungodly row, stirring things around far more effectively than she'd expected. He took possession of the front parlor of the house next door, expediting Brook and Fingate's efforts to shelter the servants from the weather. Alex was included and dragged inside with them, but kept apart. Despite orders, there was considerable conversation going on until Lennon snarled a believable threat to clap everyone in darbies and set them back in the street if they didn't shut their bloody pie holes.

Their host, a sturdy-looking doctor named Millcrest, didn't seem to find anything objectionable about the irregular use of his home. His bearing and clipped manner marked him as ex-military. He set his staff to work making tea, and they hopped to it as though the fate of the British Empire hung in the balance.

Alex sealed herself within the leaden armor of her imagination to avoid being emotionally overwhelmed by the crowd. She would get through this part of things, get answers from Fingate, and then deal with the looming grief.

Or not. Her father's death was still an abstract concept. In her mind's eye he remained alive, active, and vital. She could hear his voice, see his smile, and almost feel his tall, reassuring presence next to her, as clear as it had been more than a decade ago. However angry she was that he'd sent her away, she had no reason to think she would never see him again.

Which was simply *not* sinking in. She was numb and must remain so for the present. Later, when alone and able to let down her defenses, she might succumb to tears, but not now.

She took a seat at the house's bay window to keep watch on the street. Fingate approached, silently offering tea. Constrained by Lennon's orders, neither could speak. It was cruel.

She accepted the saucer and its cup of sweetly fragrant jasmine, nodding her thanks to him. Fingate winked once, his somber gaze dropping to the tea, then he moved off.

Under the cup was a scrap of paper. Alex covered it with her thumb and continued as normally as possible, given the circumstances. It took a moment to shift things to make an examination without anyone noticing. The flimsy piece had been torn from the margin of a newspaper, about half an inch wide and an inch long. The message, written in neat pencil, was disappointing:

Cold duck, 9:00.

What the devil?

It appeared to be a dining or drinking appointment, being vague enough for either; it was meant to mislead others, but have a meaning she alone would appreciate.

It was too outlandish. To cast her mind back ten years to recall some incident involving Fingate and ducks was ridiculous. How could the man expect her to remember?

Duck—was it meant as animal, action, or drink?

Ducks swim and duck under water to feed. That covers both animal and action.

There were plenty of ducks in London. Most of the parks had ponds, and the ponds all had ducks. Did *cold* mean they were to meet at a park? If so, then which one?

What about vintners or poultry shops? Impossible, there were too many. He could just as easily written cold goose or beef or—

Cold *duck*. Any duck would be cold at this time of year, with some ponds frozen over, preventing them from swi—

The meaning came in a gratifying flash.

For decades the maddest members of the Serpentine Swimming Club met in Hyde Park for their Christmas morning race. There were always stories about it in the papers. As a child she'd walked with her father to one such event. Fingate brought a hamper with bread, apples, and cheese. She'd given bread to some wayward ducks, finding them of more interest than the swimmers. Fingate had picked apart his loaf to tempt the ducks in closer, but none would leave the water. They'd fled, quacking with indignation, when the swimmers dove in.

Alex had not witnessed the race for herself for years, finding the press of crowds and their emotions to be wearing. Why meet her there? Why not wait until things were sorted out, when they could sit for a proper talk?

She spared a glance toward Fingate, to let him know she understood, but he was no longer in the parlor, probably in the servant's hall negotiating more tea and seeing about sandwiches.

She slipped the scrap into her coat pocket just as a black landau rumbled to a stop next to the walk. Its front and back hoods were up, and a curtain covered the window set in the door. That should have been the conveyance sent to fetch her in the first place.

Not waiting for the driver to descend, a slender, competent-looking woman a decade older than Alex emerged, looking around with a stern face. Lennon hurried to put himself in her way, escorting her to the house next door.

Alex knew her: Mrs. Emma Woodwake. A widow, she was in charge of the psychical training branch of the Service and rarely ever called to do Readings. She was many rungs up the ladder from those out in the field.

Lennon returned a moment later, going straight to Alex.

"You're for it," he said, jerking a thumb to indicate the general direction.

Instead of the murder house, Lennon guided Alex toward the coach, opening the door and assisting her inside. He was a hindrance to balance with his great paw tight on her lower arm, and she dropped with a clumsy bump onto the thinly padded bench. The interior was cold and dark with the black velvet curtains in place. It turned to pitch when Lennon slammed the door and strode off, growling.

As she tumbled in, Alex glimpsed another passenger sitting opposite: male, wearing black trousers, a walking stick with a worn iron ferrule braced between his polished black boots. The rest blended into the shadows, including his face.

"Hallo? Who's there?" she asked.

On the seat next to the man was a bull's-eye lantern, as she discovered when he eased open its shutter. The beam of light fell on her, but there was enough ambient glow to fill most of the interior. Her mouth went dry as she recognized the imperious-looking fellow across from her.

"Lord Richard?"

"Miss Pendlebury," he said in greeting. His voice was soft, just enough for the confines of the coach. Any listeners without would hear nothing.

She matched his level. "Sir, I was not aware of my relation to the deceased, else I would have—"

"Miss Pendlebury, be assured that had we known, you'd have never been called. This was an oversight. There will be repercussions, but not directed at you." He fixed her in place with a chill and impersonal gaze. His eyes were a clear icy blue, but the lantern light stole their color so they seemed to be white, the pupils like black pits. "May I offer my condolences for your loss?"

The question, spoken in the same tone one might use for any mundane social inquiry, caught her off guard, and her breath hitched in her throat. Lord Richard Desmond was the head of the Psychic Service, so far upstream as to be unreachable. He reported and answered directly to Queen Victoria herself and no one else, not even the prime minister. Only the Lord Consort Arthur was higher up. For someone like that to unbend enough to offer Alex sympathy, however formally framed, took her aback.

"Yes, sir. Thank you, sir."

She had only ever seen Lord Richard this close on the day

three years ago when she'd been accepted into the Service. Shockingly tall, strongly built, a faint red tint to his gold hair, he did not look old enough to have been running things since 1848. When she discreetly asked, she was informed that the Psychic Service had been wrested into existence by Lord Richard's father (also named Richard) as an outgrowth of the Ministry of Science. Exactly how that happened and how he'd gotten the ear of the queen in the first place were not general knowledge.

That the son took over his retired father's duties was hardly worth notice. There were many families in more or less hereditary service to Her Majesty, after all—such as the Pendlebury clan, who'd been at it for generations. Uncle Leo did something at the Home Office. Her cousins held positions in other areas of service, and without a second thought she'd used family connections and the fact that she was one of the queen's many goddaughters to apply for her own place in the great machine that ran the empire.

Three years ago Lord Richard had personally welcomed Alex and five other nervous recruits, shook their hands, and presented them with the gold medallions that identified them as bona fide agents of Her Majesty's Psychic Service. Since then, he had been a rarely seen figure in the distance.

"Sir, if I may ask, why are you here?" Alex had expected her supervisor to deal with the situation, or perhaps *his* supervisor, but not the head of the Service himself. She was a small cog in the machine; just how bad were things to bring out the chief engineer?

"Mr. Jones is unavailable."

She didn't believe him. No need to tap into her ability to know that. It made no sense. "There's something serious afoot."

Lord Richard's expression did not change, but neither did he contradict her. "Every murder is serious. Please report your initial impressions."

"But—"

"I'm aware of regulations, but there is no reason to think

you had anything to do with the crime. Please report to me the same as you would to Mr. Jones."

So she did, beginning with her arrival. She felt as though another person had taken over to use her voice to speak. Alex recognized it as a means of getting through the unpleasantness without breaking down. That could come later, if it did come. For the present the emotional recusation was a comfort. She covered everything, even those horrid moments in the foyer until Fingate had gotten her away.

Lord Richard was silent for many long moments. Sleet ticked persistently on the roof and sides of the coach, and she felt the cold seeping into her limbs.

"I would hazard to think," he said, "that you are wondering why Gerard Pendlebury was posing as a certain Dr. Kemp."

"Indeed, sir, I want to know everything." She hoped Lord Richard would respond to that, but he did not. "I last saw him—"

"A decade ago in Hong Kong. I am aware of your personal history, Miss Pendlebury, but so far as your father is concerned, I have no more information than you and am also mystified."

"Perhaps my uncle Leo may be of help. He's the elder brother."

"Do you think your father communicated with him?"

She hesitated. "Not to my knowledge, sir."

"A carefully chosen phrase. Why do you use it?"

"My uncle is at the Home Office."

"A branch of government not given to sharing information."

"None of them are. Father was once attached to the Foreign Office. When my mother died, he resigned and collected me, and we traveled, usually calling on embassies. I believe he was an unofficial envoy of some sort—or so I concluded years later. I must stress that if his trips were of a sensitive nature, Father never said anything to me. Neither has my uncle."

"Do you think he would have not passed word to you about your father?"

Leo had his limits. "Family concerns come second to his

duty. I don't think he would, he is absolutely dedicated to his work."

"Your uncle could be accused of being overly diligent."

"Relations between myself and Father's family have always been difficult, sir."

Lord Richard's mouth thinned ever so slightly. "It is their loss, then."

Just how much did he know of her private life? She felt discomfited under the press of that unblinking gaze. A change of topic was overdue. "Sir, my father's valet may be of immediate help in this inquiry. His name is Percival Fingate. He's been in my father's employ since before I was born. He'll know everything."

"Of that I have no doubt. One cannot keep anything from one's servants."

She'd planned to be at the Serpentine at nine of the clock, but this would make it unnecessary. Lord Richard had the authority to question the man. Alex was certain Fingate would be forthcoming in her presence. If allowed to stay, that is. She would argue for it.

Lord Richard tapped the door with his cane. The driver climbed down. Instructions were given to fetch Dr. Kemp's valet; the driver passed the word, then returned to his bench. Shortly afterward Inspector Lennon could be heard bawling orders. A good deal of activity took place between the houses as the constables rushed about.

Lord Richard remained quiet, but Alex sensed his growing anger.

Both buildings were turned inside out. Fingate was gone. No one had noticed when. Alex guessed that it had been right after he'd given her that note.

"Why would he leave?" she wondered aloud.

Lord Richard said, "You tell me."

"I can't think why."

"Do so, Miss Pendlebury. It is your job, after all. Remove your feelings from the facts and tell me why."

She felt her face turn hot and red. "One might conclude he had something to do with the crime—which I will not believe. The man's character is above reproach."

"When you last saw him. Time changes people, twists them out of shape, turns saints into monsters, monsters into saints. You have no reason to assume—"

"Your pardon, sir, but neither do you. For all we know, Fingate might have been forced away against his will by the murderer and be lying dead in an alley hereabouts."

"Then he will be found." Lord Richard seemed to be un-used to interruptions, staring in such a way as to make her feel like a bird under the hungry regard of a cobra.

But she did not back down. "If Fingate had a hand in this then I want him brought to justice, but I believe him to be the same honest and loyal man I once knew. I would urge . . . prudence."

Who was she to make suggestions to the likes of Lord Rich-ard? He could twitch his little finger and swat her sideways into the Psychical Fraud Section to catch out mediums at séances.

In a mild tone he asked, "Is precognition one of your gifts?"

"Not that I'm aware, sir."

"Then the source of your recommendation would be . . . ?"

"My instincts, sir." She refused to feel foolish for stating the truth.

"Just so," he murmured. "I am inclined to trust instinct in most situations. Whether this is such a situation is yet to be determined. Why prudence?"

A good question, and the answer required cold logic. "If treated as a fugitive rather than as a resource, he could be hurt. Fingate is clever and capable and I'm sure he's aware that his departure will look bad. If he left of his own volition, then I have absolute confidence that he had an excellent reason." She was risking much on that confidence by not mentioning the note; she should do so now. She really should. He'd clearly planned from the start to get away and meet her later. "Perhaps Fingate has knowledge of a suspect. His temper is such that he would go after that person himself rather than wait."

"Seeking revenge?"

"Oh, no, sir. He would turn the other person over to the police. If he has taken himself away of his own accord, then he has done so as a hunter, not as a guilty man avoiding capture."

"Or a fearful man avoiding the fate of his master. It has been ten years, Miss Pendlebury, since you last saw him."

"Some people do not change, sir. Mr. Fingate is as constant as the north star."

"In which case, his motives are well obscured by fog."

"Which will clear, given time and more facts."

Good God, the man cracked a smile. It had the quality of an involuntary facial tic, but Alex was heartened by his response. He seemed to be listening. She kept quiet, taking care not to open herself to catch a hint about his internal feelings. The temptation was there, but it was unconscionably rude, and, if he sensed it, unforgivable. She had no idea if Lord Richard possessed psychical talent, but it was best to not test things.

"Or," he said, after some thought, "he is guilty and could not allow himself to be in the same room with a Reader once suicide was discounted in favor of murder. Or he knows who did the deed and is protecting that person. Perhaps he knew he would be unable to successfully lie to you and concluded his best course was to leave. There are a number of reasons to explain his actions."

She wanted to protest, to defend Fingate, but Lord Richard's tone, so soft that she could barely hear him, was speculative rather than accusatory. His colorless eyes were focused inward.

Then his attention was full on her again. "Whatever the causes, Mr. Fingate is required to aid the police in their inquiries. I will make sure Inspector Lennon understands that caution must be exercised in the search."

Tension that Alex had not been aware of left her shoulders.

"Thank you, sir." He was being inordinately generous, and though she was consciously not Reading the man, that did not feel right to her.

What *else* was afoot?

It was discovered that Fingate had apparently made his way home, packed, and departed via the mews, slipping past the constable on watch. Mrs. Woodwake lost his fading psychic trace in the lane behind the house. His modest quarters were stripped of clothing, papers, and money. So far as could be determined by the housekeeper, nothing else was missing. The man had efficiently cleared out and vanished.

Alex admitted that it looked bad, but Lord Richard held fast and did not change Fingate's status to that of a fugitive. That was a relief.

None of the servants had any idea where Fingate might have gone, agreeing that he was friendly, but not given to idle chatter. All of them had come to Dr. Kemp's house from the same agency and had excellent characters, confirmed by Mrs. Woodwake when she questioned each in turn. They thought Fingate was also from the firm; he had never said anything contrary to that assumption. He always addressed their employer as Dr. Kemp, never by another name. No, Dr. Kemp had no patients, he'd not opened for practice yet. He had no need for a practice; his money was from that throat elixir, didn't you see the sign in the parlor?

Alex remained with Lord Richard, the misery of the cold and her state of mind mitigated by hearing the reports as they arrived. In the lulls between, he questioned her about her travels around the world. She was certain he wasn't simply passing the time, but more likely fleshing out whatever information he already possessed. He was skillful, making it seem like ordinary drawing-room conversation, exactly what was not to be found in a chilly landau next to a murder house at four in the morning. Alex suffered it, though. For all its shortcomings, she was committed to her duty. If the head of the Service wanted to know about her, so be it.

W hen Alex was ten, her father swooped in to remove her from her mother's family. He and his wife had been estranged for a few years; Alex never knew why, though she suspected it was because the Fonteyns were manifestly unstable and given to drink. That's what had happened to her mother. Alex barely remembered her. She was a dim face and a babbling voice, supplanted by a succession of nannies and aunts.

Lord Gerard judged that none of the Fonteyns possessed the temperament suitable for raising a child and claimed his paternal rights. Later, Alex suspected a sum of money had changed hands to speed things and, given the mercenary nature of her maternal relatives, she was not particularly surprised.

For the next five years father and daughter had journeyed around the world—twice. Though at times dangerous, it had been a marvelous series of adventures.

Those came to an end one night in Hong Kong when an English messenger stopped at their house in Victoria, departing less than a half hour later. Though curious, Alex had not been privy to the conversation that had taken place between him and her father, but afterward she'd been told to pack. She was used to sudden departures, always traveling to a new place to learn new things. They'd been in China for nearly two years, though, and she'd not completed her studies with Master Shan.

Father had not answered her questions, which was unusual, just told her to see to the packing—which included that of her paid traveling companion, the fearfully proper widow of a Methodist minister. Mrs. Falleson had been stranded in Hong Kong after the death of her husband and had lost her enthusiasm for converting the heathen. The lady was happy to chaperone Alex if it meant a trip back to England at some point.

The last time Alex saw her father was on the steamship that would take her eastward across the Pacific. It was her second crossing, but this time she was bound for the United States, not Mazatlán, in Mexico. He saw to it that she and Mrs. Falleson were well accommodated and had more than sufficient funds and the means to get more, but never said exactly why they had to depart without him.

"I've business to see to first, my dear," was all he imparted to Alex on the topic. "Please do look after your companion. I fear she is no sailor."

He kissed Alex on the forehead, and then waved from the dock as the ship left the harbor. Alex kept him in sight for as long as possible, but eventually her tears and distance became too great and he was lost to view.

She initially thought Father would catch up with them in San Francisco and that they would wait there, but Mrs. Falleson had strict orders to get to England as quickly as possible, which was in line with her own heart's desire. Their choices were limited. The much-touted transcontinental rail line was yet incomplete. Mrs. Falleson refused to inflict a long, dusty stagecoach journey on herself and her charge, convinced they would be slaughtered by Indians or robbed by outlaws (and then slaughtered) at some point along the way. The contents of various newspapers validated her avoidance of that route.

They could take a slow steamship around Cape Horn, make a dangerous land crossing of Mexico, or court death in the fever swamps of Panama. Alex had traversed Mexico on her first trip around the globe, but in a large, well-armed party. Her accounts of that journey were enough to send her chaperone on a hunt for smelling salts.

Mrs. Falleson, after a number of prayers pointedly asking the Almighty for a solution, picked an unorthodox alternative that delighted Alex.

The Americans were an enterprising lot when it came to commercial exploitation of their inventions, even the more terrifying ones. The San Francisco papers had been full of stories about the triumph of air travel. Mrs. Falleson read of the many successful flights achieved by the Aerial Navigation Company, particularly those executed under the command of a certain Captain Lucius Miracle, whose surname offered a strongly symbolic appeal to her spiritual side.

Taking it as a sign from above, she and Alex boarded one of the lighter-than-air ships to skim (barely) over the Rocky Mountains and beyond. Though not the first females to make the trip, they were enough of a rarity that their participation was of interest to the newspapers. Mrs. Falleson was more horrified at having her name in a common rag than by defying gravity in a frail-looking gondola suspended beneath three balloons shaped like fat cigars.

The ladies boarded swathed in veils and heavy coats, having been warned it would be cold, and at her request the captain of the ship gave false names to anyone who asked. Alex did not understand until her chaperone explained that a proper lady should only ever be mentioned thrice in a paper: when she was born, married, and died. Anything else was simply vulgar.

Alex had heard stranger views expressed on her journeys and learned to discount them without offence to the speaker. A nod and a polite smile usually sufficed, and so it proved again.

Their air transport was wanting in comfort, but peerless in speed. They rode the prevailing winds far above the wilder portions of territories claimed by the United States. For three days and nights Alex clung to the gunwales, gaping in wonder at the changing landscape below. Her eyes stung from the chill, her face hurt from smiling so much, and she grew hoarse asking countless questions of the crew and the captain. Mrs. Falleson prayed a great deal, only occasionally pausing in her orisons to admire the view. Alex tempted her often with that distraction, having the idea that God might appreciate the respite.

Their airship landed in St. Louis amid fanfare that included a brass band and jugglers. Mrs. Falleson once more resorted to obscuring veils and managed to get them away unscathed and unidentified by the local press. She found a respectable hotel and there they rested for two days before boarding a slower if more sensible train for Chicago, another to New York, and finally a clipper ship back to a country Alex barely remembered.

In London, the remarkable Mrs. Falleson tearfully delivered her charge to the Pendleburys and departed to seek out her own family, never to return. Though they did sometimes correspond, those occasional letters did not entirely mitigate Alex's sense of having been dismissed again.

Thus ended her second circumnavigation of the globe, which put her ahead of all the adults in the Pendlebury clan, most of whom had never stirred from England unless one counted occasional trips to Balmoral Castle in Scotland.

It certainly put Alex ahead of the cousins of a like age to herself. She had nothing in common with them. What was normal to her was to them strange and worthy of ridicule. They teased her as a liar when the adults weren't around and otherwise treated her like an exotic and not terribly safe zoo specimen. Cousin Andrina (who had often been to Balmoral as a lady-in-waiting to Princess Alice and her daughter, Princess Charlotte) informed her that Alex's hiatus abroad was a disagreeable family scandal. It was on a level with Gerard marrying that unstable Fonteyn creature. Alex was told to keep both shames to herself and never mention her sordid history again.

Alex considered Andrina to be a great fool, but this was cruel and unnecessary. Cousin Andrina was wonderfully resentful and unreasonably jealous that she and Alex shared the same name and royal godmother. It didn't matter that the girls were two out of the hundreds of Alexandrina Victorias named after the queen, Andrina was always putting about that the honor was wasted on her odd cousin.

Revenge for Alex, if not prudent, was imperative. Circumstances suggested a suitable retaliation. She poured out her cousin's perfume and filled the bottle with gin. Andrina had no sense of smell, owing to a childhood illness, and the next day departed for a lengthy visit to Balmoral reeking like a drunkard.

There had been no repercussions since the prank could as easily been carried out by any of the other cousins—who were not talking. The only thing they abhorred more than Alex was a tattletale (and none them liked Andrina), so they closed ranks. Andrina, though, knew who was behind it, and from that point on ignored her cousin completely, thinking that a snub from a person of her social standing would completely crush her foe.

Nothing could have had less impact on Alex, who was unaware that she was supposed to be miserable. It proved to be an imperfect but workable resolution to both girls. They found ways to avoid each other and not speak at the dinner table.

Family disputes aside, Alex had written her father nearly every day, the first letters addressed to him in Hong Kong with "please forward" printed neatly on the envelope in English, French, and Chinese. She did not ask why she'd been sent away, reserving that question for the next time she would see him. She did inquire where he was and when he expected to be in England, then went on to describe the happenings of that particular day, certain that he would be interested as he'd always been.

Her certainty wavered as the months crawled on without a reply, puzzlement gradually giving way to hurt, and then anger. No one knew where he was, not even Uncle Leo, and no one seemed inclined to find him, though Leo made inquiries. Nothing had come of them.

A year after her return to England, a battered packet of unopened letters turned up, half a dozen out of the more than three hundred she'd sent. Someone had scrawled "return to sender" on the front in pencil and by some miracle it had found its way to her. It was not, so far as she could tell, her father's handwriting. They were some of the earliest, on stationery acquired in San Francisco. She'd opened each, reading the events within, recalling forgotten details, but not relishing them as treasured memories. They mocked her then-belief that being sent away was only a temporary thing.

Five years with Father, a total of twenty years without him, and now he was gone forever.

I t must have been quite an adventure," stated Lord Richard.

"Indeed, sir. The adventure of a lifetime." She'd left out much from her account, and everything to do with her family. Childish feuds between cousins could hardly be of interest to him.

"Beginning when you were only ten? There is the danger that ennui might overtake a person exposed so soon to such variety."

"I have thus far been spared."

Not strictly accurate. Alex loved traveling and it had been difficult adjusting to living a quiet, relatively predictable life. While Samuel Johnson's declaration that when one tires of London, one tires of life might be true for some, he'd never ventured farther than the Hebrides.

Besides, he'd not been plagued with a psychical ability for Reading or he'd have ended up in Bedlam.

Some of her Fonteyn relatives had done so or been secreted away elsewhere for their own good. The psychical gifts that ran in their blood sometimes had a malignant effect, hence the family reputation for brilliance mated with instability. Had Father not gotten Alex a measure of special training early on, affording her control of her talent, she might well have gone down the same path.

Mrs. Woodwake returned, climbing inside the landau to sit next to Alex. She nodded once in greeting, looking exhausted. "Pendlebury."

"Ma'am," she said, and nodded back like a schoolgirl to a

respected teacher. Woodwake had that effect on her. "Shall I leave, Lord Richard?"

"No." He looked at Woodwake. "Your report, if you please."

It was much as Alex expected. The emotional traces in the murder room were contaminated, so they would have to rely on the physical evidence. It was well there was a goodly amount, with more being gathered. On the roof, Inspector Lennon traced the intruder's tracks to an empty house along the row that had been broken into; Woodwake inspected the premises, finding only faint echoes of its previous occupants.

"You interviewed the servants?"

"Yes. Innocent, so far as I am able to ascertain. They're genuinely shaken, no one is hiding anything. They've no idea where Fingate's gone, either."

He looked at Alex, who felt an uncomfortable prickling under her arms. She should tell him about the note. It was not too late. She could talk her way out of any serious disciplining. Knowing where Fingate was likely to be hours from now was different from not knowing where he was at present, though she doubted Lord Richard would appreciate the argument.

Besides, it was now her turn to be questioned by a Reader. It was a foregone conclusion that Woodwake would sense a lie and any lie to cover the lie.

"Sir, I—"

Something struck the coach with a great deal of force, making a strange, flat percussive sound like a hammer on iron. Several more percussive somethings struck, shattering the glass window facing the street. The curtain twitched.

Lord Richard flinched and grunted, then Alex felt the brute force of his hand on her shoulder. She and Woodwake were shoved down to the narrow confines of the coach's floor with his lordship's considerable weight on top.

CHAPTER THREE

In Which Hokery-Pokery Is Judged to Be Useless

Alex felt a wave of rage that was not her own and another of fear not her own, the first from Richard, the latter from Woodwake, before closing herself off from the onslaught.

More things pelted the coach, tearing through the leather hood. She was certain they were bullets, but could not hear gunfire. The curtain and hoods were holed, the supporting hoopsticks splintered, but nothing penetrated below the sides. From the sound those were made of metal, not wood.

She smelled blood and realized Lord Richard had been hit. She tried to shift, but he snarled at her to keep down.

"I have my revolver, sir," she said, her voice strained, given the fact she could hardly breathe. "In my coat pocket . . ."

"Good for you; stay where you are. The driver is armed."

So it proved when the bark of a firearm put a stop to the hammering. The coach rocked as the man apparently quit his position on the bench.

His pistol barked twice more and men shouted.

The conveyance lurched forward. Once in motion it kept going, picking up speed, the horses' strength overcoming the brake. She heard more shots as they rocked away unchecked. Alex had a horrible feeling—this time, entirely her own—that matters were about to get worse. She pushed and squirmed, Richard ordering her to keep still, Woodwake getting in the way. Whatever was being used in the attack was directed at one side only, so she'd be safe enough. She hoped.

Alex wriggled her torso clear, kicking his lordship in the process, to judge by his curse, and pushed the door open. The sidewalk was on the move, or so it seemed from her vantage on the floor. The alarmed horses were trotting away from the uproar. Alex undid the buttons on her ulster and struggled to shed it.

"Get *down*!" Richard ordered and caught her by the back of her collar—the coat's collar, which was a bit of luck. He pulled, she pulled, and she was suddenly free. Her revolver was still in the pocket, but she had no time for shooting. She turned to face the interior and backed out the door, holding tight to the leather roof as they swayed along. The hoopsticks supporting it on this side were still intact and held her weight for an instant as she swung her right leg up. Her foot landed on a horizontal spot, then skidded awkwardly into the skeleton boot under the driver's bench. It gave her leverage. She boosted over and made a successful grab at the seat irons, then pulled herself onto the bench to pick up the reins.

Her instinct was to stop, but a bullet—or whatever it was—whipped by her ear like an angry bee. Men were giving chase or attempting to; the sleety glaze on the paving made it hazardous for attackers and defenders alike.

She released the brake, gave the reins a smart snap, and yelled at the horses. The animals plunged ahead. She sent up an incoherent prayer that neither of them broke a leg.

The slippery road was clear of traffic at this hour on Christmas morning. She risked a glance back, but darkness, their movement, and distance kept her from seeing anything. Best to assume the worst. Lord Richard shouted, but she ignored him and kept going. They passed Devonshire Street and were approaching Weymouth before she looked back again. No one seemed to be immediately behind.

Fortunately the horses were inclined to respond when she pulled on the reins, and slowed to the point where she could make a turn without tipping the landau. She went right, then right again, doubling north on Marylebone High Street. His lordship was cursing loudly enough that she could make out words even over the rumbling wheels and the ring of horseshoes. She urged the horses left onto Paddington with the idea of getting to Baker Street and a doctor. Harley Street was chock-a-block with physicians, but too warm a climate for the moment.

Warm? She was freezing up here. The sleet stung her face, clung to her lashes, and the cold wind hurt her teeth because she was grinning. Nothing to do with mirth, though her short huffing breaths might be mistaken for laughter rather than a reaction to nearly getting killed. She could still hear the heavy tearing sound of that missile passing her by a quarter inch. What could do that? A bullet crossbow? No, not enough velocity for the distance, but close. Ah, of course, it would have to be—

"Pendlebury, stop this damned thing at once!" Lord Richard's anger intruded on her deductions. She grimaced.

"Almost there, sir," she shouted back.

"*Where?*" he roared.

Paddington intersected with Baker Street. She eased the horses into the turning. They trotted smartly, heads tossing and bits jingling, apparently ready for another mad dash. She brought them to a stop, set the brake, and clambered down. Lord Richard was already out of the coach, glaring at her. Mrs. Woodwake crept out more slowly, looking rumpled and somewhat wild-eyed. More alarmingly, her clothing was bloodstained.

"What happened?" she asked, righting her hat. "Bullets and no gunfire?"

"Air guns," Alex and Richard said at the same time, then looked at each other, startled.

"How do you know about those?" he demanded.

"A member of my shooting club collects them." She pushed past Woodwake to get her coat—the sleeves were inside out—and the bull's-eye lantern, which had fallen off the seat. It was one of the "safe" models, and had hardly leaked any fuel. She sought and found lucifers in her coat pocket and lighted the thing, aiming the beam at Lord Richard. He had a thin streak of blood on one temple, but his left side was soaked.

Woodwake gasped and went to him. "Sir, back in the coach. At once. We must find a doctor."

"I'm all right." But his face was white and sheened with sweat.

Alex had seen that kind of shock when she'd crossed Mexico. Their party had been attacked by bandits, and a man hadn't noticed he'd been shot. He'd bled to death in the saddle denying to the last that there was anything amiss. She checked the house numbers, ran to the one she wanted, and yanked the bell chain until an annoyed-looking young man opened the door.

"You better be dying," he said, bloodshot eyes unfocused. His hair stuck out in a variety of directions, and he wore evening clothes that had seen better times. "Oh, Cousin Alex. To what do I owe the honor?"

"Wake up, James, I've brought you a shooting."

"Thoughtful of you. Half a minute—I recall you don't like me."

"I don't, but you are convenient. Now *help* us."

Showing no consternation or much speed, he quit the doorway to light the gas, calling to someone within to shift himself. "This is your lucky night. I've a houseful staying over. You might like one of *them*."

Woodwake struggled to prop up Lord Richard but he wasn't cooperating. "Get back in the coach and have the madwoman drive us back," he insisted. He held his left arm clamped tight to his side. Alex took his elbow.

"This way, Lord Richard, we're nearly there."

"We are not." But his legs gave out partway up the steps, and she and Woodwake were obliged to take his weight to keep him from cracking his skull.

"What is this place?" asked Woodwake. "Where are we?"

"Baker Street. Mr. Fonteyn is my cousin. He's an eye surgeon . . . and a bit eccentric." That was putting it charitably.

"He lets rooms to medical students, so there's bound to be someone here who can help." *If they're sober enough.*

James wakened sufficiently to lend a hand. He took Alex's place and dragged Richard into a parlor. "Where *shall* we put him?" he asked. "He's too long for the settee, and anyway, it's occupied."

Another young man in evening dress sprawled asleep on that object of furniture. He didn't stir despite the commotion.

"The floor, James," Alex said. "For God's sake, take this seriously."

They eased the patient down. James swatted at his clothes. "Damn, I've blood all over my suit. Haven't finished paying for it, either. Just what sort of parties are you attending these days, little cousin?"

"I'll explain later." Alex ripped her gloves off, knelt, and began unbuttoning Richard's clothes. Her hands shook. There was so damned much blood. "Blanket? Clean water? Bandages?"

"Try the kitchen, I think the water's still working. Don't know about the rest, that's the housekeeper's domain, and she went home ages ago."

"Mrs. Woodwake? The kitchen's toward the back. Open cupboards, Mr. Fonteyn won't mind."

"I might," he said. "Depends on the cupboard."

Woodwake nearly bumped into another young man as he came in.

"Your pardon, miss," he said politely, getting out of her way. He was also in evening clothes that looked slept in or—knowing James's habits and those of his friends—passed out in. "Fonteyn, some of us are trying to slee—" He gaped at the tableau of a half-conscious man bleeding on the parlor floor. "Good God, what the devil is this?"

"All yours," said James magnanimously. "Freshly delivered by my cousin Alex. That's Alex tearing away his clothes, by the way. Who'd have thought it? Well, don't stand there, get your kit and see if you can save him."

"What about you?" Alex snapped.

"I'm almost blind drunk and wholly useless. Hamish, however, is in somewhat better condition and just back from Nemley, where he learned how to be a first-rate army doctor. I'm sure they covered taking out bullets. Is that not so, old chap? Here, now, where's he gotten to?"

Hamish had vanished, but quickly returned with his bag and knelt opposite Alex. "I've never done a fresh bullet wound before. They only let us practice on pig carcasses."

"Well, if you lose this patient you can't have him for dinner." James slouched toward a liquor cabinet that was in disarray and a selected a bottle. "*Garde à l'eau,*" he sang out by way of warning, then drizzled gin liberally on the now exposed wound.

Alex squawked in irritation as she was splashed, Hamish crowed approval, and Lord Richard roared and bucked. Hamish was a big sturdy fellow, built for rugby, but had trouble holding him down.

"Keep still, sir, you'll make it worse," he informed his patient.

Richard's reply was unfit for polite company. He tried to pull his clothes back on. Alex forgot herself and the dire situation for a moment, staring in shock at the exotic pattern of blue tattoos covering the pale flesh of his torso. They coiled up from his lower regions, flowing over belly, chest, arms, and shoulders and apparently down his back. She'd never seen the like. Hamish was busy, but behind her James made a low whistle of surprise.

"Well, well," he said. "I never thought I'd ever s—"

Woodwake returned, bedding in one hand and a pitcher of water in another. "Bandages?" she asked James.

"No, thank you. Never bother with the things."

She shot him a look that he was long used to collecting.

"I know," said James with satisfaction. "I'm a great fool. Not a mere fool, but a great one." He pulled out a penknife and offered it. "Here, cut that sheet up, I'm tired of it anyway."

Using the knife, Woodwake efficiently sliced and tore the fabric into long strips, giving Alex the impression that she'd have preferred it was James. Alex lighted the room's one lamp, holding it close so Dr. Hamish could work. She smelled liquor on his breath, but he seemed up to the task. At least his hands were steady. Hers weren't. She fought to keep the light still.

He bathed the wound clean and probed with his fingers to locate the bullet. Richard grunted his discomfort the whole time, but managed not to yell.

"You're lucky, my man," Hamish pronounced. "It went under the skin, but above the ribs and out again. Nasty furrowing, be quite a scar if it doesn't go septic."

Woodwake left again, returning with a washbasin and soap, setting both on the floor next to Hamish, who thanked her. Alex moved out of the way so Woodwake could sponge the wound clean.

"Are you two nurses?" Hamish asked, wiping his bloody hands on a piece of sheet. "I must say, you're cool-headed. No fainting."

James gave a short laugh. "My sweet cousin there has dealt with more corpses than you've ever seen, and no, she isn't a mortician."

Hamish shot her a look and brought out a needle and silk thread from his bag. "Just a few stitches, sir. I'll be quick as I can."

"You're finished," Lord Richard announced decisively. His blue eyes regained their icy focus for a moment. "Apply pressure until the bleeding stops."

"That won't do, sir. Now lie still. I can give you some laudanum or—"

"Mrs. Woodwake, discourage this fellow from proceeding."

Alex did *not* expect Woodwake to stand and draw a gun from her coat pocket, but that's what happened. She had a revolver and a determined expression.

"Good God," said Hamish. "No fainting *and* quite mad. I like your relatives, James."

"Just one of them is a relation. I've no idea who the other two are. Alex does consort with some shady customers."

Alex was horrified. "Lord Richard, stop this! We're trying to help you!"

James snorted. "There's gratitude for you. Madam, I'll ask you to put away your pistol. I don't want holes in Hamish. He is my guest, after all. Hamish, put away your darning needle. You're outclassed for this bout."

Young Dr. Hamish was reluctant to give up, and addressed Richard in a reasonable tone. "Sir, a wounded man is like a child. You may not like the nasty medicine, but it *is* for your own good."

"Taught you that at Nemley?" Richard asked.

"Actually, my mother's responsible—"

Alex put her hand on Hamish's shoulder. "Doctor, if the patient is so reluctant then let him have his way. If he should pass out, you may reassess the situation."

"You put forth a charming argument. Very well."

Woodwake, at a nod from Richard, shoved her revolver into her coat pocket. Alex began breathing again.

Dr. Hamish checked Lord Richard's wound. "Not wise, sir. Not wise. You're still bleeding too much." He gathered sheeting strips and made a pad, pressing it to the damage. "You should have something for the pain."

Richard closed his eyes. "I've work to do. Miss Pendlebury, are the horses and coach in a condition to return us to our starting point?"

"Sir, *you* are in no condition to—"

"Yes or no?"

She couldn't believe his folly, but answered in the affirmative. "It is bound to be too dangerous, sir."

"I expect those who fired on us are gone by now, and my place is there sorting out the mess. We may require medical help if others were shot. Dr. Hamish, are you sober enough to come along?"

Hamish's face went red.

"Yes or no?"

"Who the devil are you, sir, to ask such things?"

James chuckled. "Hamish keeps a bull pup and bad manners brings it out. You're both well matched. Alex didn't introduce us, but I like you two. Refreshingly direct. Mrs. Woodwake? I'm James Fonteyn, how do you do? Welcome to my home, at least until I'm thrown out of it. When the landlord sees the parlor floor he'll bounce me quick enough. Alex, you'll have to do the honors for the big fellow."

Alex felt her face going as red as Hamish's. Coming here no longer seemed such a good idea. Even the more stable Fonteyns—and James was in that number—were subject to raving lunacy when the mood was on them. She resorted to chill formality for her employer's sake, well aware that it would only amuse her cousin. "Lord Richard Desmond, may I present my cousin on my mother's side, James Fonteyn, and his friend, Dr. Hamish."

"How do, your lordship?" James was unfazed, but then he never opened a newspaper unless it was a sporting journal.

Hamish's eyes went wide. He clearly recognized the name. "You're *that* Lord Richard? I do beg your pardon, sir."

"Oh, Hamish, don't be a bore. He's just a peer. Haven't you heard they're going out of fashion? But this fellow seems to be going out, period. Best see to him."

True. Lord Richard's already stark white face turned gray as blood continued to flow onto the floor. Hamish cursed, a trace of fear in his voice, and boosted the man over, pulling away the rest of his clothing. There was another bullet hole in the lower left part of his back.

James fell quiet, staring down, his expression now grim. Hamish probed the wound, got the bullet out, and stitched the damage with admirable speed.

Alex, intentionally distracting herself, noticed the blue tattoos covered Lord Richard's back as well, or as much of them as she could see under the gore. They tricked the eye, seeming to writhe under the skin as though barely trapped in place by its fragile barrier. There was something repulsive yet fascinating about them.

The lamplight dimmed, then Alex snapped alert, gasping in pain. James had her by the arm, pinching hard. "Not the time for fainting, my girl. That's past." He took the lamp from her, and one-handed lifted her up and dropped her into a chair.

She tried to move, but there was no strength in her legs.

He put the gin bottle in her hands. "Find something to do with that," he said, and turned to hold the lamp over the grim tableau. Lord Richard made some murmured objection; Woodwake told him to be still. Her voice was thin and strained.

Alex hated gin. She disliked the taste and effect of all spirits, but given the circumstances, a sip wouldn't hurt. It was disgusting, but the heat slithering down her throat braced her up. God, how she wanted fresh cold air. The room reeked of blood. It couldn't be helped now, so she blocked things out, raising that leaden armor again in her mind's eye. Her concentration was imperfect, but sufficient to carry her a few moments so she could rally.

Hamish and Woodwake tore another sheet up to fashion a bandage.

"He's staying here, not traveling to a hospital," he said. "Fonteyn, send one of those fellows upstairs to bring down a bed. I won't risk jostling him—" He froze in place, his mouth open in shock as he stared past Alex.

Four extraordinary apparitions stood in the entry.

By their general size and form they were men wearing identical black hooded cloaks and masks that covered all but their eyes; each held an exotic-looking firearm.

Air guns?

These were a type that she'd never before seen, heavy enough to require both hands. The stocks were bulky and wide, the barrels thinner than normal.

The men were lined up, facing her and the others in eerie silence.

They look like a firing squad, she thought, then understood with a sickening swoop of pure horror that that was, indeed, their purpose.

As one, they aimed their strange rifles at Lord Richard.

Anticipating the shots by a split second, Alex threw the bottle of gin at the closest. It struck his head with force. At the same time, her cousin James flung his lamp at another. Glass shattered, oil splashed, and by a miracle the flame went out.

In the sudden dimness she heard two soft *chuff*s, but further sounds were blotted out by the sharp barks of Mrs. Woodwake's revolver. Its muzzle flashes marked her shift sideways as she dodged the rifle fire that followed.

Only the damned things didn't really *fire*. They gave a kind of cough and spat bullets at a rate far quicker than anything else short of a Gatling gun. The slugs striking the walls and shattering the front windows made all the noise.

Alex dropped and rolled, hitched against the settee, encountering the man who had been asleep on it. He was awake now and apparently throwing things at the invaders, too. There wasn't much to hand; the last was a vase, to judge by the crash. He grabbed something else. It required a heaving effort followed by another, much bigger crash and a cry of pain. That must have been a table.

A bullet sheered over her head. She went flat and tried to get under the settee, but it wasn't high enough off the floor.

Where the devil had she left her coat and her own revolver?

Woodwake shot again, and Lord Richard bellowed something that sounded vaguely French. He was, impossibly, on his feet, grappling with two of the shooters. Even more impossibly, he won the contest, flinging the men to one side and seizing another two.

There were more than four invaders now. Alex couldn't be sure of their numbers—the only light was from the open entry—but hooded men crowded into the confined space as though rushing to board a train. They got in the way of one another; it might have been comical but for their air guns. Two began shooting randomly, others shouted, overcome by excitement. The mounting chaos was interrupted by a fearsome blast from the upper part of the stairs.

One hooded man screamed and fell away, and his fellows caught him and withdrew toward the door.

While they had the advantage of numbers and superior weapons, the roar of a shotgun fired in a confined space had a deleterious effect on their collective courage.

A second blast inspired a full rout.

Woodwake fired again, clipping a man, but he was yet able to run. Another kept his head and shot toward the upper landing, then into the parlor to cover the retreat. At his orders, the remaining men grabbed the fallen and their air guns and withdrew. Whoever was on the stairs either reloaded or had another shotgun ready; he sent two more blasts after them.

A short man in rumpled evening clothes clattered downstairs. He had a shotgun broken open, reloading on the run. He snapped it to and rushed out the door, but made no shot. He returned a moment later.

"Scattered like rats before a terrier," he reported. "They've no belly for a bit of rock salt, ha! I say, Fonteyn, who were they?"

"Damned if I know, they're—oh. Oh, God." James had found and lit a candle.

The room was wrecked, bullet holes everywhere, along with broken glass and furniture. A slick of oil from the shattered lamp mingled with Lord Richard's blood. He lay where he'd fallen in the melee, gasping for breath, more blood frothing at his lips. He'd been shot repeatedly; several more wounds marred his torso.

Woodwake and Hamish went to him, calling for light.

Other guests in the house cautiously came downstairs. The short man with the shotgun gave quiet instructions, wresting order and action from their bewilderment. Some were dispatched on errands within the house, others were sent outside to keep watch in case the attackers returned.

Another lamp was found. Lord Richard's breathing went from quick and labored to a slow, shallow sighing, then silence.

James pulled Woodwake away and took her place next to Hamish. They employed techniques used for reviving drowning victims, forcing air into the man's lungs and listening for a response from his heart.

For naught. Richard's flesh remained inert. He looked smaller lying there so still.

Mrs. Woodwake seemed in shock. She clutched the fullness of her skirts, as though to raise them for running, but there was no place to go.

Alex's composure, held together by necessity, began to crack. Her sight blurred, and she swiped at the tears spilling down her cheeks.

Eyes shut to stem the flow, she slowly drew a long breath, ignoring the taint of blood and gunpowder in the air. She held for the count of five and slowly released, letting the turmoil of her emotions go out with the exhalation.

Master Shan could never have anticipated her applying his training under these conditions.

Or perhaps he had. She imagined his serene eyes, a hint of a smile always in them and amid the fine lines of his face. What would he do?

Another deep breath and exhale.

He'd tell her to step up and bowl her best. Unlike many of his countrymen, he had a keen interest in cricket.

Eyes open, Alex went to work. Centered and in control, she moved toward the entry, her internal senses open for clues about the armed men. Emotions washed over her: fear, excitement, and a bright exultation from the act of killing. She pulled back from it as though recoiling from contagion. The feeling was so strong that it threatened to overtake her. She was well schooled to avoid that trap. Apprentice Readers often had a hard time, especially when it involved pleasant emotions. Such mad joy could be perilously addictive.

Then the calmer and stronger impression of Lord Richard's

feelings swept through her: fear, not for himself but for others. It had raised him to his feet to defend them. He'd not allow it . . . righteous anger, contempt for faceless cowards, sudden bursts of surprise as they shot him and finally a weakening as his body slipped past the point of return. She pulled back to avoid experiencing his death, but the last trace from his psychic spoor was, oddly, annoyance and exasperation. He knew he was dying and instead of a final prayer to his Maker he—

"Alex, wake out of it."

James was before her, concern on his face. She slammed her lead barrier between them before his emotions could intrude. That was enough Reading for one night.

"You're not all right, so I shan't inquire if you are," he said. "You will sit a moment. You will sit *now*."

His hand on her arm, not pinching this time, he guided her to the settee. She noticed its back was full of holes, as were the walls.

"We're lucky no one else was killed by those bas—bounders. Terrible shots."

"They were aiming high on purpose," she said. "Lord Richard was their target, not the rest of us."

James gave no reply, but glanced at the room as though to confirm her assessment.

Mrs. Woodwake, moving like a sleepwalker, drew the remnant of a sheet over Lord Richard's body. Dr. Hamish was still on the floor, and he looked ill. James went to what was left of his liquor stores and found an unbroken bottle and a glass. He poured and pressed the contents of the glass upon Woodwake and gave the bottle to the doctor.

"Get up, John. Drink to a fallen warrior, not a dead patient."

Hamish gave a great weary sigh and stood and drank, then handed the bottle back. "We need to find a policeman."

That snapped Woodwake out of her daze. "Absolutely not. This is a matter for the Psychic Service, not Scotland Yard."

"Bit late for that, ma'am," said James, nodding behind her.

Flanked by Lieutenant Brook and two wide-eyed constables, Inspector Lennon stood in the entry taking in the scene of battle with a great scowl.

Mrs. Woodwake had a barrage of instructions for him once she got his attention, and Lennon had an objection to all of them, apparently. His low rumblings were reminiscent of a lion with a bellyache. He never actually roared, but made his opinions clear.

The guests in the house were asked to stay on the stairs for the time being, until they could be interviewed. They retired, grumbling and full of questions. Dr. Hamish sat with them. He wore a black look and perhaps needed the company of friends.

Alex kept to herself on the settee, thinking it best to stay out of the way until called for; James joined her, taking a swig from the bottle.

"What the devil is going on?" he asked quietly. He looked to be a dangerous creature with his bloodshot eyes, hair a wild mess, and blood halfway up his arms and streaking his face, but his manner was composed. Events had boiled the fool out of him. "Who were those men?"

"I don't know," Alex whispered. "I was called to a case over on Harley Street . . . and . . . and things went wrong. Lord Richard arrived . . ." She faltered over her story. It was no proper report made to a senior in her department, but a rushed and disjointed muddle of random words, conjuring images she wanted to forget. Beneath it all, she knew she'd have to tell the whole thing later again and again and that there would be no ease in her spirit from it, no catharsis of release. This would be with her forever.

"What happened?"

"Father." She felt herself choking. "My—my father's dead, James."

"Gerard? When did he get back from—dead? Good lord . . . was *that* the case?"

She nodded. "I didn't know. Not until after. I didn't know. Murdered . . . and I didn't know it was *him*."

"Oh, my poor little Alex."

She used to resent him calling her that, but not now. He put an arm around her. He'd never done that before, not even when they were children. But she couldn't relax against him, couldn't allow herself to break down and howl her grief—she had none. She was numb inside. That wasn't right. She should feel something. That was her trade, feelings. Emotions of death and life and truth and lies—but belonging to others, not her.

"What's to be done?"

She shook her head. "The Service will deal with it. Why didn't he write to say he was home?" *Why didn't he write at all?*

"Are they connected?"

"What?"

"Your father's death and this attack. Are they connected?"

"I don't know."

"One did follow hard upon the other."

Indeed they had. She slipped free of his arm and went to Mrs. Woodwake, breaking in on what looked to be an increasingly tense exchange between herself and Lennon.

"Ma'am, I need to know—"

"Know what, girl?"

Alex repeated her cousin's question.

Woodwake glared at her, mouth tight, eyes hard. "I cannot answer."

"You must have some insight, ma'am."

"If I do, then this isn't the time or place to impart it to you or anyone else."

"But—"

"The matter is closed. Protocol was violated at Harley Street, accidentally, but there's to be no repetition. Miss Pendlebury, you are excluded from both investigations except as a witness."

"I can't be excluded!"

Woodwake rounded on her like Medusa, and with the same effect: everyone froze in place. When she spoke, her voice was low yet penetrating in the hush. "You will follow orders. I am aware of the unique circumstances of tonight's events and how difficult this is for you, but rules are in place for a reason. You cannot be involved." Her face softened. "Reverse things: If it had been my father, what would you be telling me this moment?"

There could be no argument for that. "May I know how things progress?"

"So long as it does not compromise the inquiry—inquiries."

Alex hated it, certain that she would be told nothing.

"I require your attention, please." Woodwake raised her voice, directing it at the others present. When they were looking at her, she delivered the startling order that Lord Richard's demise, indeed, all that had happened tonight, was not to be discussed with anyone.

"I rely on your discretion and loyalty to the crown," she said. "Until further notice this whole incident is a state secret. Anyone speaking of it will be prosecuted for treason."

This resulted in a near-collective gasp from those present.

Only James did not appear awed. He stood, still holding the bottle. "*What* did you say, madam?"

She repeated the order.

"That's mad," he drawled. "How the devil do you expect this lot to not talk? Everyone talks. First thing tomorrow someone will share a hint with his barber or her dressmaker, another will wink at an old school chum at his club or get to yarning over the port and in an hour it'll be in every paper in the land. You cannot possibly hope to keep *this* secret."

"I fully expect it to remain so, sir," she snapped. "Or will you accuse any here of being disloyal to queen and country?"

"Not disloyal, merely careless. Come now, you lot. Which of you has never dropped a word when you shouldn't? The more important the word, the more dire the promise, the faster it fell, am I right? You can't get more important than Lord

Richard. Unless it's the Lord Consort Arthur, God forbid. This thing's a proper blister, masked hooligans tearing through London and murdering men. . . . One word in the wrong ear and it's all up."

Mrs. Woodwake's glare had no effect on James, but the whole house seemed to hold its breath. "For the sake of Her Majesty's feelings, we *must* keep this quiet. I will *not* have the queen reading of the death of a dear friend and faithful servant in the paper. How do you think she would feel? How would your own mothers feel?"

The small crowd stirred, and frowns of anger for James subsided into a sheepish awkwardness.

"To a man, we'll swear on the Bible that this goes no further," said Hamish. "Is that right, lads? For the queen's sake?"

They responded, as loyal subjects must, with growls of affirmation and stubborn faces. "We know our duty," confirmed one, the others agreeing.

"I'm proved wrong," said James. "If you lot can keep such a secret, then the Empire is secure. Count me in as well. Swear on a Bible or this bottle of excellent whiskey, whichever you hold more sacred."

Woodwake and Brook looked appalled at the blasphemy, but Lennon was amused. Alex was too tired to show her disgust. James was incapable of being serious for longer than a minute, even with the shrouded body of a murdered man at his feet.

"I'll swear on both, if you don't mind, sir," said Lennon, stepping forward. He accepted the bottle and drank to the pact.

Alex spoke to Mrs. Woodwake, keeping it between them. "What about my family? My uncle needs to know his brother is dead."

The woman shook her head. "No. Not yet."

"He has a right to know, ma'am."

"He will be informed, but not yet. It's impossible. Until we know what your father was doing posing as Dr. Kemp, until we know how or if his death was connected to the attacks on

Lord Richard, you are not to speak of this to your uncle or any member of the Pendlebury family. The nature of a state secret is that it overshadows personal considerations. I realize this places a heavy burden on you, but you must find the strength to bear it."

How?

"You're all in, girl. I'm sending you home."

"It's just up the street at the end. I'll walk. I need the air."

"Not alone and not there. You're to pick up what things you'll need for the next few days and stay with your uncle's family for the time being."

Alex was initially too stunned to speak. "I-I can't. Your pardon, ma'am, I simply cannot go there."

"They're your family, of course you'll go."

"You don't understand . . . my dealings with them are not—congenial."

"A state of affairs you share with many others in the Service, including myself. Our gifts are often misunderstood by those closest to us."

"That's not it—"

"Are they a danger to you? Have they ever done you physical harm?"

"What? No, but—"

"Then you're to stay with them."

"I'll put up in a hotel or the Service dormitory with the apprentices. Either will be fine."

Woodwake leaned close. "Miss Pendlebury, put your feelings aside and consider that if someone murdered your father then that same person might have similar designs on your uncle or the rest of the family, including yourself. I want you there to keep an eye on them. There is safety in numbers. You should not be alone and vulnerable in a hotel, and you cannot look after your family hiding among the apprentices."

Alex went red. "Hiding? Madam, you've no—"

"I've every right," she said. "You're the only one in the

whole damned Service who can get under the Pendlebury roof without raising questions. You're keen to be on the investigation; this is as much of it as can be allowed. I'll arrange to have armed people on watch in case there's another attempt like this. Now for God's sake, do as you're ordered and see to your duty."

Woodwake's startling language and the force behind her words seemed to steal the strength from her. She swayed; Alex steadied her without thinking and felt a rush of feelings strike like the lash of a whip. The woman was on the edge of screaming from the turmoil within. Panic, guilt, terror, rage . . . held in check by sheer will, and there were cracks in that brittle barrier. Her greatest fear was that she would lose her tenuous control, break down, and fail to uphold her facade—and Alex was not helping.

She backed off, ending the contact. "Of course, ma'am. Whatever is required."

Woodwake shut her eyes a moment, composing herself. When she looked at Alex again they were softer and infinitely tired. "Go. However horrid, go be with your family. Whether you like them or not, you need them. I'll send for you tomorrow to give a report at the head office. Have a detailed account ready to hand in. Keep your wits about you and your eyes open. I don't want another body in the morgue."

Lennon put himself forward. "You hens done clucking? Right then, Mrs. Psychic Service, you were telling me my job on what to do with that toff doctor."

"Yes, Inspector. That case is now fully under Service jurisdiction. We will see to it and to this one here and you'll speak to no one about them."

"That serves me fine. The wife has a fine goose for our supper and I'll be pleased to enjoy it and forget this botheration. I won't grass on you. There's not a jack at the Yard who'd believe it, anyway. I'm off, then."

"Not yet," she said. "I would be most obliged if you would

escort Miss Pendlebury to her home. Mr. Brook, is your hansom outside? You'll take them, then return here."

Lennon had no objection to having a Service driver instead of a constable at his beck, even for a short time.
He crowded into the cab next to Alex, and Brook took them
up the street to her house.

It looked exactly the same as when she'd left, and that felt
odd. The atmosphere of serenity within was untouched by the
hideous chaos she'd been through.

*It's the same, but I'm different. The changes aren't appar-
ent yet, but they will overtake me.*

She decided to not think about them. Later would do. It
would have to do.

Not knowing how long she'd be, she told the men to come
inside to wait. The wind and sleet had died, but the damp cold
was the kind that sank into the bones and stayed. She unlocked
the door but Brook went in first, pushing past her. He had a
pistol in one hand.

Alex almost spoke to tell him not to worry, but changed
her mind as she remembered Woodwake's last order.

Lennon noticed. "There's a wise little tweak," he said. "Let
the big strong soldier do his job. He'll feel useful."

"Clear, miss," said Brook, some minutes later. "Leastwise
this floor. I should like a look upstairs if you don't mind."

She did not and stood with Lennon in the entry. When
Brook returned with a negative report she went up to her room.
It was as she'd left it, the bed unmade, nightclothes tossed on
the pillow, the sweet scent of rosewater lingering in the still
air. She wanted to burrow under the familiar comfort of her
own soft sheets and thick blankets and shut herself away from
this awful night.

She should have been allowed to stay in the sanctuary she'd
so carefully built here. She should have been able to convince
Woodwake to set Brook or some other man to keep an eye on

her. Forsaking this peace for the stifling atmosphere of Pendlebury House was wrong.

She'd be sent for tomorrow, though. Perhaps she could
make other arrangements by then.

Alex abruptly remembered Fingate and his cryptic message.

She gave a groan.

Bloody hell.

It wouldn't count for anything that she'd been *about* to tell
Lord Richard of her nine o'clock meeting in Hyde Park. Or
that she'd forgotten it until now, when it was too late to mention to Woodwake.

*I'll just have to meet him and get him to come along to the
Service head office.*

And hope that would be sufficient to keep her out of trouble.
God knows, being attacked by masked lunatics was a damned
good excuse, but Woodwake might not see it that way.

Alex removed her clothes. By the time Mrs. Harris got back
on Boxing Day the bloodstains would be set.

"It's too absurd," she muttered, realizing she never wanted
to touch those things ever again. She bundled them up and
shoved them into the inadequate wastepaper basket by the
small writing desk.

She spent some while in the washroom at the end of the
hall, scrubbing blood from her hands and trying hard not to
think of lines from *Macbeth*.

I should be weeping.

She was alone, she could allow herself to break down and
grieve for her father. The distress of the last hours were enough
to lay anyone flat for weeks. She'd learned that emotional in-
juries were every bit as damaging as physical wounds and
needed longer to heal. Some never healed at all, the poor souls
bearing them for life, bleeding out day after day.

I don't want to be one of them.

She'd have to release it.

But feelings were not like water from a tap to be turned to

flow and turned to stop. Perhaps actors could do that, and certainly self-serving criminals she'd met in the course of her trade were adept at conjuring grief in an attempt to deceive Readers or gain sympathy.

Alex could not call or force such expression. Her training at the Service and her lessons from Master Shan had taught her control and defense, lest the emotions of others take her over. It was of no help in dealing with her own. She'd shut down. At some point the barriers might lift. Or not.

"Just have to wait and see," she said to her reflection in the washstand mirror. What a sad face it was that looked back, almost a stranger's face, and she could hardly bear looking into her own eyes.

Changed into a practical calf-length woolen walking dress, with a carpetbag packed with necessities for the next few days, Alex descended the stairs, her steps tired and heavy. Brook met her halfway up to take the bag, and she gratefully let him.

Lennon had helped himself to the port she kept in the dining room cabinet, but she didn't mind. He was a guest, why shouldn't he? He finished off his glass, left it on the entry table, and jerked his head toward the back of the house.

"Something to show you," he rumbled, taking up a lighted candle.

She followed him to the kitchen. He pointed at the mudroom door, which opened to the mews behind the row of houses.

"You keep that locked?" he asked.

"It was when I left tonight."

"Check it. Both sides."

He held the candle as she inspected the lock. The flame blew out shortly after she opened the door, but lasted long enough for her to spot new scratches in the brass. She felt a tightness in her chest and pulled away.

Lennon struck a lucifer and relit the candle. "Floor."

Smears of mud, hardly noticeable unless you looked closely. Mrs. Harris would never have left without a last swipe of the mop. She took pride in having a pristine, mouse-free kitchen.

"You've had a visitor," said Lennon. "Brook and I went through the place again, cellar to attic. Near as we can tell, some cautious chap hid in the cupboard under the first-floor stairs. There's a bucket been overturned he could have sat on—"

Alex shot from the kitchen and up the stairs to see for herself. Her sanctuary violated—she wouldn't have it, by God.

The cupboard was general storage for that floor, where Mrs. Harris kept cleaning supplies and their attendant tools. Alex couldn't recall the last time she'd bothered to look inside. It was just steps from her bedroom.

When she'd centered herself, she lifted the latch and opened the narrow door, braced for anything.

Almost anything.

She was unprepared for . . . nothing.

Physical objects were tidily in place, except for the tin bucket resting overturned in the middle of the floor. She eased in and widened her internal senses bit by bit, seeking some trace of the person who had been there.

A closed space, someone sitting, waiting for who knows how long, there should be a remnant of emotion. Patience, impatience, excitement, boredom.

Nothing. It was an absence, a void.

"What'd the spooks tell you?" asked Lennon. He'd come up more slowly and, as before, held quiet until she was done.

"It's like what I didn't find at Harley Street. That same emptiness."

"Maybe he *is* a ghost."

"I don't speak to ghosts, Inspector," she said wearily.

"The other kind. There's human ghosts walking this world right enough. You see 'em but you don't. Beggars, street Arabs, moppets selling ribbons and violets, those poor devils with carts who shovel the road waste. They're there, solid as you or me, and no one notices them."

"But they *all* have emotions. Nothing is here. Nothing. Even animals leave emotions I can track."

"Do you now? Never knew that. Well, then, whoever was here is a cold 'un to the bone or one of those clockwork dummies from the seaside, put in a copper and he tells your fortune."

"Don't be ridiculous. Those things are in cabinets and have to be wound up."

"I saw one with legs once. He could stand, take off his hat and bow, move his head, give yes or no answers. . . ."

"But no walking around. No such thing could scramble over roofs and down ropes or pick locks—or need to rest on overturned buckets."

"So what we have here is a human ghost. There's some cold customers out there, little tweak. You've not been at it long enough to meet any and if you're lucky you never will. Maybe this one is colder than the worst of them. . . . He's done for your pap and it looks like he's after you. Service hokery-pokery's useless here. Eyes open and ears sharp, same as the rest of us."

Had there been no attack on Lord Richard, Alex would have completed her report and been released to come home . . . to . . .

The tight feeling in her chest increased until she forced it away. Panic wouldn't help. Mrs. Woodwake had been right; Alex could not be alone. Given a choice between the Pendleburys and a traceless killer—

"Time to leave, Inspector."

"Thought you'd never say."

CHAPTER FOUR

In Which Family Demonstrates to Be Inconvenient to the Case

Under Lennon's approving eye, Alex slipped a box of cartridges for her revolver into her ulster pocket and shifted the weapon to the reticule she now carried. She locked the front door, cognizant that it was not likely to keep out a determined threat.

She'd written a note for Mrs. Harris, extracting a solemn promise from Lennon that he would deliver it personally. Under no circumstances should Harris or any of the household return home until Alex came to fetch them. They could leave messages at her office. She slipped in a few crowns for their expenses.

Brook checked the street, announced that it *looked* to be clear, and hurried them into the hansom. He hoisted up to his perch and snapped the reins, taking them north, then doubling back and doubling again.

"Don't look as we're being followed," said Lennon. "Suits me; I've had all the excitement I can stand."

Alex, jammed against him in the small space, felt his body relax.

"You look all in, too." He produced a pocket flask and offered it.

"Inspector, I've had more drink tonight than in the last year."

"Best make up for lost time, then. Or are you one of those finger-wagging pledge-poppets?"

She accepted the flask and took a mouthful of something

foul that made her gasp, but the heat was welcome. "Not at all. It interferes with my abilities."

"Sounds a good thing, to hear others talk of 'em. Every spook chaser I ever met wanted to be rid of their abilities."

"I wouldn't be me without them."

"Sure you would, but havin' a different job or married off to some bloke bereft of all sense."

She glanced at him. Yes, there was a glint of humor in his eyes. "It interferes with my defenses," she added. Should she have mentioned that? Must have been the drink.

"So it should, leading to many a ruinous downfall or blissful engagement. That's how I caught my missus. I got her so jolly she was signing the registry book before she knew what happened."

Alex could not imagine what Mrs. Lennon might be like. Was she formidable and strapping as her husband or a meek-ish sylph who somehow found his unpolished manner appealing? How could that be?

Or was it because he was uncomplicated?

His selves, inside and outside, were identical. He didn't hide his feelings. While others concealed their inner self for the sake of social interaction, he didn't give a bloody damn what people thought of him. Alex hadn't appreciated his kind of honesty before.

She found it comforting, enough so that she unexpectedly dozed off against him, unaware of it until the hansom lurched. She snapped awake, hand on her pistol.

"At your ease, soldier," said Lennon. "Your man's making way for the fire brigade."

Brook pulled to the side of the road, slowing, but not stopping as a much faster fire wagon shot past, bell ringing, the big horses struggling on the ice-glazed street.

"Not the first or last call for them on a Christmas. That'll be another pack of bloody Germans setting fire to things. I ask you, what's the sense of bringing a tree into a house, sticking candles on every branch and lighting 'em? That's just begging for disaster. If they don't like a simple Christmas dinner the way we do it, they should bloody well leave."

"You want England for the English, then?" she asked. The E. for E. radicals were mentioned often in the papers, even *The Times*.

"There's something to that lot. With any luck they can send the riffraff back where they come from."

"Our ancestors were foreigners. William the Conqueror came from Normandy."

"Be sure once he set his foot down he didn't allow anyone else in. You know how close we came to having a German on the throne?"

Should she inform him that the queen was her godmother? Best not to; it would be boastful and pretentious, qualities she did not admire. Alex had heard the stories that German had been Queen Victoria's first spoken language, and in her youth she'd been introduced to more than one prince from that land. However, she'd chosen an Englishman for her husband, though he'd not been royalty unless one traced his ancestry back a few centuries. The young queen wanting to marry a lord had been quite a political crisis at the time, but she'd changed the law of the realm so love won out over custom. The match had worked splendidly. The royal couple were still pleased with each other, had produced four healthy, intelligent children, and the eldest daughter had provided heirs; the crown of England was secure for another generation.

Brook turned their hansom east to avoid the brigade, then south. Church bells tolled the half hour, making it five thirty by her reckoning, which Lennon confirmed with a look at his pocket watch.

"What a night," he said. "Be glad when it's over."

The statement could be taken as a declaration for himself or as advice to her.

They passed St. Paul's Knightsbridge. Her heart quickened with dread.

Just yards to go . . . a last turn and they were before 16

Wilton Crescent, the first of a curving line of fearfully respectable white facades, each nearly identical to its neighbor: same
doors, same transom grilles, sturdy iron fences lining the walks
along the lower ground-floor entries.

Lennon gave it a lengthy stare. "You come by your toff ways
straight, then, don't you?"

"I'd rather go to a workhouse."

"No, you wouldn't." Before she could get out he put a hand
on her wrist. "Listen up, little tweak, there's more afoot than
they're sayin'."

"The Service?"

"Don't pull a face, you ought to be feeling it, if that's your
trade. Me, I can smell it. There's politicking going on. Always
a rotten stink."

"You can't mean that."

"Bet your life on it, missy. Your *life*. Instead of taking you
into the fold where you're surrounded by other spook hunters and big lads like Brook, they've cut you loose where you
can be got at."

"Mrs. Woodwake would never do that. Besides, men will
be posted to watch this house."

"Not nearly enough if those chappies what done for Lord
Dickie come around, never mind that murdering ghost and his
bottle of ether. Makes me think of those stories about hunters
in India tethering a goat to tempt in a tiger. Maybe they get
the tiger, but he gets the goat first."

Having been on a tiger hunt, Alex had seen that for herself. "You think the two cases are connected."

"I couldn't say. Maybe those hooded blokes were following young Dickie all along and took their opening. But the
ghost that broke into Harley Street also tried for you. Why
do you think that is? Who would want to hang angel wings
on both you and your pap?"

She shook her head.

"You come up anything on it, see me first. Don't trust for

a moment that your precious Service won't toss you to the tigers if it suits 'em."

He believed what he was saying, but the *Service?* It was scrupulously honest, if necessarily secretive. Lord Richard was—had been—above reproach and insisted all those under him be likewise honest and honorable. They never employed frauds, the testing system was too rigorous. She'd vetted people herself, and would face a Reader tomorrow. That would clear things, perhaps allow her to keep a close watch on the progression of both cases.

Lennon continued, "They do some good, I'll grant that, and you're one of the good ones, but beware of rot under the shiny paint. For all their power, they got a bloody nose tonight. Instead of raising the alarm to hunt down a pack of hooded killers, that woman does the direct opposite. If someone had done for the head of Scotland Yard every copper in London would be turned out. There'd be no stoppin' us till we had the shooters in darbies or dead. Woodwake's running scared about something and it's got to be bigger than her chief getting served up to hell tonight. I tried to get her to drop a clue, but she wasn't having any. Her wanting *that* kept a state secret? Barmy."

"She gave good reason for it."

"Bah. I know her type. Thinks too much, just like you. Only your thinking has you meeting yourself coming around corners. She's got a wider view and keeps it to herself. There's a use for that sort, but they're dangerous."

He let go her wrist and got out with her. From his perch on the hansom where he could see trouble coming, Brook covered them as they went up to the door. Alex tried her old key and it worked. She thought she would never have need to use it and wasn't sure why she'd kept it on the ring after all this time. A sense of antic humor, perhaps, allowing her the freedom to present her relatives with a disagreeable surprise should she ever drop in for a visit. She had often thought of coming by, but had never acted on it.

The disagreeable surprise was all on her tonight, but she'd be safe here. Knightsbridge was a well-kept, quiet place, plenty of police about. Pendlebury House teemed with people: relations and who knows how many servants to see to their upkeep.

Lennon put her carpetbag inside the door. "Remember my words, tweak. You keep that pie hole of yours shut, your ears open, and your head down. Now go get some sleep. And . . . and I'm sorry about your pap." This last was muttered quickly and then he stumped off.

Well. What a startling man.

She locked the door and went into the ground-floor drawing room to look out the front windows. Lennon piled into the hansom and they clattered away east along the curve of the crescent. Despite the gaslights, the cold darkness swiftly stole them from sight.

Tethered goat. More like thrown to the wolves.

Her family wasn't that bad, not really. They had sheltered, clothed, and fed her. The adults had been . . . polite. She was fond of Uncle Leo. He wasn't at all like his brother in temperament, cold and aloof rather than smiling and affectionate, but there were enough physical similarities to remind her of Gerard, and that had been comforting. He had no time to spare for her or any of his family, but when she first arrived he'd not minded her sitting in his study so long as she was quiet.

When bad weather kept her indoors, she'd take a volume from Leo's collection of books and read for hours by the window, emerging only for meals.

His children were barred from the room, making it an even more attractive refuge. Andrina's reading tastes were for lighter material and her brother Teddy proved too active to be trusted. He was always getting into things he shouldn't, such as his father's Napoleon brandy—wasted as a casual libation for a thirteen-year-old.

Aunt Honoria was far too respectable and commanding to

be likeable, but initially saw to it her children behaved civilly
toward Alex. They were angels in her presence, which amounted
to a few minutes a day. She was fearfully busy with social ob-
ligations and granting her time to charitable events. At those,
she limited herself to a smile and voicing a sincere "Well done"
to the workers who had actual contact with the beneficiaries
of those many charities. She didn't like looking at the poor,
who were, after all, such an ill-favored, cheerless lot.

But she respected the rules of society and, as she'd done
every year since Alex moved out and (horrors) gone into trade,
Honoria sent an embossed invitation to Christmas dinner to
her niece. Each year, Alex sent her regrets, claiming that her
duties prevented it. Sometimes that was even true.

I can bear them for a few hours. She'd hide out in Leo's
study; they'd not think twice about it once the grudging greetings were past.

Alex hoped to avoid Andrina. With any good luck her
insufferable cousin would be off playing lady-in-waiting to
Princess Charlotte. What the royal family saw in Andrina was
a mystery, but she could be pleasant and clever when she chose.
Showing one face and hiding the other worked on the rest of
the world, but never on Alex, another thing besides the perfume
switch that Andrina could not forgive.

After lighting the gas, Alex rang the bell, confident that servants would be astir. Honoria ran a tight ship. If staff couldn't
be bothered to be awake and working by five in the morning,
they were welcome to find a position elsewhere. Many did.

Sure enough, one of the maids arrived, carrying a tray. She
nearly dropped it when she saw Alex.

"Begging pardon, I thought you were her ladyship."

"New here, are you? It's all right, I'm her ladyship's niece,
Alex Pendlebury."

The girl nodded, so she must have heard the name mentioned, and glanced at the tray.

"Better take that back. When Aunt Honoria rings again you
don't want to be late with her morning tea."

"Yes, ma—your ladyship. Shall I announce you?"

Oh, dear, the girl was too new to know the protocols. "Leave that to Mabrey. He's still here? Ask if he might spare me a few minutes."

Off the girl went. Alex took the respite to remove her gloves and hat and undo the buttons of her ulster, but not shed it. The drawing room fire was laid but not lighted, and the room chilly.

Instead of Mabrey the butler, Andrina swept in. She was already corseted for the day and in a sumptuous dressing gown, with layers of silk and ribbons and pleats in the French style. Her hair hadn't been seen to yet, and a long dark braid hung down her left shoulder. She was an uncommonly beautiful girl and knew it.

She stopped and glared, her lips going thin with distaste. "What are you doing here? And at such an hour?" she demanded. No greeting, despite the fact they'd not seen each other in several years. She got straight to the point with people she didn't like.

I should have gone to a hotel.

Alex was prepared, inspired by Lennon's opinion of German Christmas customs. "There was a fire in the building next to my house. It was too smoky to stay."

"There *are* hotels," she pointed out.

If not for her "gift," and the intervention of a loving father, Alex might have turned out just like Andrina. Or not. There was no denying they often thought along similar lines. She smiled. "And miss Christmas dinner with my family? Aunt Honoria has ever welcomed me to the table."

"Yes, she has a wonderful goodness of heart for poor relations."

"Is that the best you can do?"

"Have I misapprehended something? You work, therefore you must not have an income."

"It's a match to yours, Andrina, and you know it. I work because I like to do so."

"How could you possibly like mucking about with dead people?"

"They're better company than some I can name. Now before we draw blood I suggest you hear me out. It will be to your advantage."

Andrina sniffed, but chose to listen.

"I'll be pleased to not disrupt Aunt Honoria's seating arrangements at table today. If someone brings a tray to Uncle's study you won't even know I'm here."

Honoria, splendid in an obviously new morning dress, came in. "Why, Alex, what are you doing here? And at such an hour?"

"Her house burned down, Mother."

Lady Pendlebury gasped in horror.

"It did not!"

"That's what you *said*."

And just like that, they were back to being snarling schoolgirls again, engaged in yet another round of explosive tit for tat. Alex raised her hands and voice. "Enough!"

Andrina, standing behind her mother, beamed with delight. In the past, whoever shouted first lost the battle, collecting a reprimand from Honoria for not behaving as a lady should.

What a fool, Alex thought, deciding the judgment applied equally to Andrina for setting the trap and to herself for walking into it. "Aunt Honoria, my cousin's grasp of the facts is imperfect. The house *next* to mine had a fire. There's smoke all through my home, so while it airs I'd hoped to find a safe harbor here."

"Not burned down? You're sure? Well, of course you may stay as long as you like, child. It's been ages. We must catch up, but this is such a busy day. Have Mabrey sort things for you. You're a bit early for breakfast, but we'll sit down together and have a nice chat. Church is at nine sharp; we'll expect you to come with the family."

Mentioning her meeting with Fingate at the same hour would not be the done thing. Alex would come up with some

excuse. "Thank you so much. I'm sorry to intrude like this."
Very sorry.

"Nonsense, what are families for if not to give refuge when
one is in need? Mabrey, excellent timing. Lady Alex requires
a room for a few days. Have someone prepare her old one,
please, and add another place for breakfast."

Mabrey, the butler, hadn't changed much, possibly because
Aunt Honoria had ordered it. He nodded a silent greeting at
Alex. She smiled and returned the courtesy. Her old room?
While not the comforting refuge of Uncle's study, at least she'd
not have to share with her cousin.

When she'd first arrived they'd put the girls together, thinking they'd become friends. The instant they were alone for the
first time, Andrina made it clear she was in charge and Alex
was always to be subordinate. In two trips around the globe,
Alex had never encountered such bald-faced discourtesy before and laughed, thinking it was some sort of poor joke.

Andrina responded with name-calling and throwing a shoe
to assert her authority. It hit Alex lightly in the chest. She stared,
realizing that this was a variant of the sort of challenge that
duelists engaged in; Alex was pleased to provide satisfaction.

The next few moments were a bit of a blur, but she emerged
the unquestioned victor of the skirmish.

Master Shan's instruction included physical as well as mental training. Andrina had expected girlish tears, slaps, and hair
pulling, not being flipped head over heels, slammed flat to the
floor, her limbs temporarily paralyzed by knuckle strikes to
key nerve points. Her bloodcurdling screams brought most of
the household into the room. Once order was restored, it was
Mabrey who quietly suggested to her ladyship that a separa-
tion of the combatants might be the best for all.

After that humiliation, Andrina confined herself to subtle
verbal blows when her mother was out of earshot, as well as
keeping her distance: even now she withdrew as Alex followed
Mabrey from the parlor. He dispatched a footman to bring the
bag and a tweeny to lay a fire.

No impression of Alex's tenure remained, but upon moving out she'd taken everything that was hers. It was a stranger's room now, and she was comfortable with that. Certainly she was a stranger to her hosts. They didn't know her, couldn't possibly understand her. She was comfortable with that, as well. The more they knew, the more it could be turned into a weapon. Lennon's instincts were right, even if he was not conversant with how things worked under this lofty house's roof; keeping one's pie hole shut was ever a wise idea.

The tweeny scuttled out and Honoria's personal maid, who looked to be a sensible sort, unpacked the bag. Alex explained that she was too exhausted to take breakfast with the family, but absolutely had to be wakened at quarter past eight to go to church with them. The woman nodded. Would some tea be required then?

Alex had to admit that she missed having an army of servants to see to mundane needs. Her own household was small because she couldn't abide the conflicting emotions generated by a large staff.

The woman left, and Alex applied a buttonhook toward undoing her cycling boots. She'd been tempted to have the maid do it, but that meant physical contact and she was tired of keeping her barriers up.

Boots off, thank God. Her liberated feet seemed to breathe and expand. Next, her outer clothes, skirt, jacket, and blouse on a chair, then the corset cover, then the corset, which was painfully constricting by now. She'd experimented with several styles, needing something she could easily don without help. Her corset maker introduced her to a design that laced in the front, yet presented a smooth silhouette by means of a clever facing. Alex loosened it and climbed into the bed. The sheets were cold, but she hardly noticed through her flannel chemise.

She expected, considering the terror and strain of the last few hours, to be wakeful. Sleep rarely came easily. She often coaxed it with warm milk and dull books, and when those failed, put herself into a meditative trance in the hope of dropping off.

So it proved again. However tired she was, her mind refused to blow out the candle. Questions for Fingate, speculations about the morrow, mental images of her poor father's dangling feet, the death room, Lord Richard's blood on everyone, masked killers and their near-silent guns, her own home invaded—and mingled throughout were the emotions, hers and those imposed on her. Even a person without her Reading talent would be overwhelmed.

Shan tried to persuade her to adapt the traditional cross-legged sitting posture for meditation, but she got better results lying flat. Alex pulled the covers to her chin and went through the steps she'd used for years to still her racing mind. While bred and born to the idea that nothing could replace a good night's rest, when that eluded her, then a few hours of meditation would suffice.

She had no sense of time passing; it seemed but an instant later that Honoria's maid was shaking her awake.

Definitely a quarter past eight, the nearby church bell—she'd not missed its loud proximity—tolled.

Alex's head was clear. Her body was stiff and ached from not enough physical rest, but stretching helped.

A tray with tea, toast, jam, and a boiled egg was on a table by the window. She gulped a cup of the blessed brew between bites while washing up and getting her clothing sorted.

Her abused feet wouldn't go back into the boots again, but she'd wisely packed some plimsoles. Though wrong for church, a long black skirt would hide them. It was not precisely right for church, but more acceptable than the walking skirt. In the more informal congregations women could be found wearing female trousers, but not in the Anglican fastness of St. Paul's Knightsbridge and never on Christmas.

At twenty-five of the clock she was presentable and hurried downstairs.

The Pendleburys were gathered in the drawing room and

upon seeing them in their unrestrained finery, Alex faltered, for the first time feeling like a poor relation. Damn Andrina, anyway, for putting forth the idea. Alex had a generous income, but was in the habit of dressing like any young working woman of the middle classes.

"Really, Alex, you look like a parlor maid," said Andrina, who resembled one of the princesses she waited on: watered silk, buttons, ruffles, and other embellishments in a shade of pale rose that suited her complexion, a matching hat, shoulders swathed in fur. She was a vision.

Honoria was just as well turned out, as was Uncle Leo, who stood by the door in an astrakhan coat. He'd have a new suit under it. His wife would have insisted.

"At least put on a decent hat," Andrina continued. "Mother, have you something she could borrow?"

"Please, girls, no rows today," Honoria said, reaching for the bell pull. "I'll have Clara bring down that one I wore to the—"

"Aunt Honoria, I have a hat; please don't trouble yourself. It's not important."

"It *is*, my dear. You're a Pendlebury. One *must* keep up appearances."

"We'll be late," said Leo. "Hello, Alex. Remember me?"

His voice was so much like her father's she got a knot in her throat. Dear God, dear God, she would *have* to tell him about Gerard.

It can't be now.

"Yes, Uncle. It's so good to see you." For him, she was able to go over and kiss his cheek in greeting. He grunted and told her she looked *fine,* ending further discussion about her appearance. "Where's Teddy? We must leave now."

"Outside waiting for us," said his wife. "I wish you would tell him to stop smoking in the street. He'll be mistaken for a common loafer."

"I doubt that. Come along, no more time, come along." A footman held the door and the family filed out into a freezing gray, overcast day. Alex was last, not wanting Andrina behind her making faces.

Cousin Teddy, also in astrakhan, shoes polished, top hat at a jaunty angle, finished his cigarette and flung it away, drawing matriarchal criticism.

He shot a grin at Honoria. "One of the servants will get it. Cousin Alex! It's been too long. Finally weary of fortune-telling?" He took her hand and she made herself accept the touch. Her lead armor was firmly in place and having gloves on helped. Two years her junior, he'd been a ruthless snot of a boy when she'd arrived. Though more friendly than Andrina, he was also more open to doing mischief if he knew he could get away with it. He was clever enough to not take sides between Andrina and Alex, keeping his own pranks clear of the house.

Teddy had grown into a handsome man, though this morning his eyes were as bloodshot as Alex's. He'd been out on his usual Christmas Eve carouse, and probably had not slept. She smelled spirits on his cigarette-tainted breath. He'd have made a fine crony for her Fonteyn cousins. Teddy contrived to take Alex's arm as they strolled to church. She was unused to lengthy contact and on guard for a reprise of some childhood trick, but a small trickle of Teddy's cheerful mood filtered through. She would not allow more, else lose her focus for the problem at hand: how to get away to meet Fingate.

"I heard you were burned out of house and home; bad luck, that," said Teddy. "Oh, don't fuss, I know dear sister overdramatized things. Mother set me straight. Bad luck for your neighbors, what? Are they Germans?"

"I don't know."

"Wouldn't be surprised. I was out with Etchells Braddock and his crowd last night; must have seen the fire brigades a dozen times if we saw them once. You'd think Germans would be more careful with candles and trees, considering they have the ancestral practice of putting them together. Oh, I must sound a right nob, you do know what I'm talking about?"

"Yes." There was no danger that Teddy would ever over-estimate her intelligence.

"Well, I hope you'll stop a few days with us. What have you been doing with yourself?"

"Teaching."

"What, in a little schoolroom with girls, ribbons in the hair and giggling?"

"Young men and women, mostly. The Service has coeducational arrangements for some courses."

"There's luck for the lads, getting a chance to show off."

She fought the urge to disabuse him of whatever nonsense he'd imagined. Alex taught a number of subjects not found in public school. Few could pass the rigorous qualifications the Service demanded—you had psychical talent or you did not—putting females and males together was a necessity. Sometimes there were no more than four to a class. She was to be teaching tomorrow, helping a new crop hone their ability to discern truth from fact (the two often differed), but that might be changed in the light of Lord Richard's murder. By then the queen would have been informed and then the rest of the Service. How that would influence the daily run of things, she could not guess.

And Father's death. What about it?

Alex resolved, after her interview with Fingate, to not wait to be sent for and go straight over. She'd persuade him to come, too, or demand a damned good reason why not.

"Still at the Home Office with Uncle?" she asked Teddy, shifting the subject.

"Following in his footsteps, as expected. I can't talk about much of it, one half is too secret, the other half too dull." Teddy smiled at her.

She attempted to mirror him, but his statement had the quality of being a frequently repeated witticism, and she didn't find it witty.

"Just teaching at the Psychic Service?" he asked. "I thought you did more than that, laying murderers by the heels and such."

"We help Scotland Yard with inquiries."

"Call yourselves Readers or some such? How does that work?"

"It's not something easily explained. I'm awfully tired, Teddy. Was up half the night because of the fire business."

"And yet you're coming to church with us? You should have slept in."

"It's easier to agree with Aunt Honoria than disagree."

"Isn't that a great truth of the world? I tell Father we've the wrong people at the Home Office. If he wants to get anything done, send his men home and let their wives take over."

"Women work there now."

"A few. There's plenty of the old club men who worry that their lady comrades can't keep a secret, so you won't find a lady running anything that matters. The bearded dodgers don't want to chat politics with females, would rather kiss 'em, y'see."

"How shortsighted of them."

"The way the world works, my girl."

"Then change and improve it."

"Oh, things are fine as they are. You'll see that, in time."

Alex reflected that Teddy had grown from ruthless snot to predictable prig. Measured against her cousin James, the latter was preferable company. He was annoying, but never patronized her.

"You'd do well in the Foreign Office, y'know," he observed. "They could give you plenty of work translating documents. Father might know a few chappies who could offer you a place. It would be a jolly sight better than chasing fortune-tellers."

She'd rather do that than be buried alive in a damp basement slogging through tedious papers.

They reached the arched gate to the church. The street was crammed with carriages and there was a great crowd on the sidewalk.

"I see a friend I need to have a word with," she said, detaching from Teddy's grasp. "She may invite me to sit with her for the service, so please apologize to Aunt Honoria for me, I really must have a word."

Alex did not wait for a reply, but slipped off, went around two carriages, and dove into the many churchgoers, threading against their flow along Wilton Place. Her short stature was in her favor amid the stately march of the beautifully garbed pious. Top hats on the men and elaborate chapeaus on the ladies helped; she passed virtually unnoticed beneath their cover.

The crowd thinned; she was on Knightsbridge Street with the Arthur Gate ahead and no other Pendleburys in sight.

The gate was open and less spiritually minded sporting types passed through it, across Rotten Row and into the park. She blended better with this crowd, but they were raucous, having started their Yuletide celebrations early or continuing what they'd begun the night before.

When no less than three men in as many minutes grinned and approached her with a greeting of *'Ello, girly, you be wantin' some candy?* she realized she should have borrowed Aunt Honoria's hat after all. There were women in the park, but some of the solitary ones in plain clothing were apparently tarts.

Alex pulled the veil of her hat down, lifted her chin high, and fell in close behind a group of ladies taking the air, in quest of safety in numbers.

There was a risk that Fingate wouldn't see her, but the man was observant and smart. He'd be looking at every short woman in the park.

She cast about, checking anyone with the least similarity to his form and height. She couldn't count on spotting the port wine birthmark on his ear—he'd have something covering it—so she looked at men wearing mufflers, low hats, and even uncommonly long hair, on the chance he'd wear a wig as a disguise.

At least fifty men within view were similarly attired.

Cold duck, his note said, but is this what it meant? She worried that she might have gotten the clue wrong.

Chill drizzle clung heavily to the net of her veil. A light wind pressed the damp folds of silk against her face. She followed the women down to the bank of the Serpentine. At this point the lake was as wide across as the Chelsea Reach of the Thames. The water was a vile gray, its surface seeming to shiver in the wind. Ducks were about, along with a number of the park's mute swans, most ashore on the opposite bank, looking droopy and miserable.

People splashed about in the water, hooting and huffing as though it were high summer. Most ran in for a quick bath and rushed right back out again, dripping and shivering. Alex preferred a washbasin of hot water—who would not?—but was acquainted with the advantages of a bracing cold morning tub. It did wonders for appetite and energy, and gave a rosy glow to one's complexion, tightening the skin. She could not, under any circumstance, imagine herself to ever be mad enough to strip to a bathing costume and leap into December-cold water, but that's exactly what so many were doing.

A man wearing a several life-saving medals from the Royal Humane Society seemed to be directing things for the race to come. Hurrying about, he pointed to where two flags should be left in the water by some obliging boatmen. A hundred yards along, toward the Serpentine Bridge, was a long diving board extending out just above the water like a boat dock. Half a dozen men were lined up on it, wrapped in blankets; likewise three woman stood with them, all waiting for the race to start.

Alex hadn't known that women were allowed to participate, but when the Serpentine Swimming Club opened the race to nonmembers then it was no surprise that females had applied. That explained the size of the crowd and why groups of women were about: not merely to take the air, but to cheer their more adventurous sisters to victory.

The director called to straggling bathers to come to shore.

Men and a few women waded clear, quickly dried and wrapped up.

Mad. Quite, quite mad, the lot of them.

Alex withdrew from the immediate edge, thinking to head for the bridge. The higher vantage would improve her view, and it was a logical meeting point. Fingate might be there already.

"I say, Alex, hold up!"

Bloody hell. Teddy. Why isn't he in church? She couldn't pretend she'd not heard and waited for him.

"What are you doing here?" he asked.

"I needed to walk and to think."

"So you weren't really meeting a friend?"

"I'm sorry. I couldn't bear to be in that press in the church. You know I don't like great numbers of people."

"Yet here you are."

"It's different out of doors. Please, Teddy, I need to be alone now. Go back."

"I wouldn't think of it. You're much too pretty to be wandering alone with all these rough fellows about. I'll be your escort and so quiet you won't know I'm here." He started to take her arm. This time she evaded his grasp.

"No."

"There now, Mother wouldn't want us quarreling," he said with a good-natured smile. She'd seen it before and it usually meant a trick.

She backed away a step. "I don't give a bloody damn."

"What?" He was genuinely shocked.

"I need to be alone."

"You don't want that, you just think you do."

She pushed the damp veil clear of her face so he could see her eyes and thus have no doubt of her intent. "No one in Pendlebury House ever listened to me when I lived there, but by God one of you is going to listen to me now. Teddy, go back to church and let me have an hour's peace. I don't need your protection or company or anything else."

"Fine words from you on a Christmas. Always one for playing the queen, thinking yourself so much better than us with all your running around the world. Well, you're not having your way. I'm sticking with you through thick or thin. It's for your own good, you silly nit. There's a man following you."

"What?"

"When you flew away at the church gate this rum-looking savage took off as well. Made me think of a hawk after a mouse. I didn't like his look so I followed him. Lost him, but I found you, and you're not shifting me, so there."

"What did he look like?"

"As I said, rough sort, unshaved; who doesn't shave on Christmas morning?"

"His height, his form, what was he wearing? Give me details!"

"I don't have any, it happened too quickly. He was there and gone, but I might spot him again if we walk around. Why is a man like that following you?"

It was past nine. Fingate could be anywhere and if she turned up with company he might not meet her. He wouldn't know that Teddy was family.

But who's this man? Fingate in disguise?

Perhaps. He might think she still lived with the Pendleburys and anticipated that she would enter the park by means of the Arthur Gate. Aside from her not being able to stand them— which he wouldn't know about—there was no reason why she shouldn't continue to live with family long after she reached her majority. Many young women did, even when they had independent means.

The alternative was the ghost. He must know she was a Pendlebury and had been watching for her to emerge from the house. Lennon was right about his tethered goat analogy. That frightened her as few things could. When it came down to it, she was desperately vulnerable. So was Teddy. His only experience with physical conflict was on the playing fields of his school. He was no rugby forward, so that left cricket or fencing or—

Stop panicking and think.

"Have you a weapon?" she asked.

Teddy stared. "Why on earth should I want a weapon?"

"In case Hottentots attack, of course. Never mind, keep that walking stick of yours handy."

She opened her reticule, closed her gloved hand over the grip of her revolver, and felt better for it.

He saw and was appalled. "What are you doing with *that*? We're in *London,* for God's sake."

"Which is no safer than any other part of the world that has people in it."

"And I thought Andrina was one for dramatics. Put that away. You're making me nervous."

"Forget it and look around. Do you see the man?"

He gave the immediate area a hasty glance. "Can't say as I do. Let's go back to the house. A nice cup of tea and a slosh of brandy will set us both up and—"

"The devil take it, little Alex, what are *you* doing here?"

Though they'd been moving steadily toward the Serpentine Bridge and were on the watch, James Fonteyn appeared out of God knows where, falling into step with them. Alex nearly jumped out of her skin and had to abort a movement to bring her hidden revolver to bear.

"Go away," she snarled.

"Can't do that, as I went to a good deal of effort to get here. Actually walked. Walked every step from my digs to this if you can believe it. That's far too much exercise to be healthy." James did indeed look worse for wear, his eyes blurry and his nose red, but he was in his best coat and hat, and swaggered with a silver-trimmed walking stick. He was also shaved and couldn't be the man Teddy had seen.

She stopped to face James. "I can't talk to you, I have to meet someone and I must be alone to meet him."

"Oh, ho!"

"Don't be vulgar."

"Never, just curious, and you're not alone, you've company off your port bow, and he's in want of an introduction before he bursts."

That described Teddy with embarrassing accuracy. He eyed the intruder on their duet with the entrenched politeness of his class, which was clearly at odds with a need to identify the new fellow and thus present the appropriate social face.

Alex gave up and conducted the necessities that would allow two young gentlemen of the upper castes to exchange cordial greetings. She felt ridiculous, and this put her too much in mind of the last time she'd done it. She kept glancing around, dreading the sight of hooded men with air guns, yet hoping to spot Fingate. He'd not come within yards of her if she was lumbered with escorts. But if she shed her cousins, then she might be vulnerable to the ghost.

"James, why are you here?" she asked.

"Come to see the swimming race. One of my chums from the Elysian Club is in it. Thought I'd put a shilling on his nose just for a bit of fun. Happened to see you and thought I'd give greeting." He addressed Teddy. "It's a disgrace, Alex and I live on opposite ends of the same street and hardly ever see each other."

Teddy agreed it was disgraceful. "She should have asked you to put her up after the fire and saved a trip across town to Pendlebury House."

"Fire? What fire?"

"Her neighbors had a fire and she couldn't stay for the smoke. She's with the family at Pendlebury House until it clears."

James shook his head. "I never saw a fire, but then I was celebrating rather a lot last night. Could have been a war on and I'd have missed it. Alex, why didn't you come tell me?"

She'd been holding her breath, expecting her lie to be discovered, but James had saved things. "I did, but everyone was too drunk for sense."

James found that amusing. "Too true. Cousin Alex is being kind. My humble abode is crammed to the rafters with
medical students and they're all chaps and rather a boisterous lot. Wouldn't be appropriate having a female under my
roof even if she is my cousin. And the noise! I'm used to it,
but Alex likes her quiet."

"Strange how we've never met," said Teddy.

"Is it not? Different circles, I expect, but there should be
some overlap of acquaintances, always is in this town. See here,
Alex is *our* overlap."

Teddy liked that. "We're practically related, then. You
should come to my club for dinner. Let me invite you now,
here's my card. . . ."

James provided one of his own in turn, and Alex wondered
if something wholly regrettable would result from this new mix
of Pendleburys and Fonteyns. It would be her bad luck indeed
if they became best friends; they'd start comparing notes and
swapping childhood stories about her.

The three of them made it to the Serpentine Bridge, which
proved a perilous place to walk. The sleet from last night had
frozen on the cold stones. Ashes and straw had been thrown
down to aid the footing, but the only effective cure was sunshine. None today in that thick, dreary sky—it was the same
dull gray as the water.

They found a place by the rail and looked down the twisting length of the water. People who had gathered on both banks
to watch the race began dispersing.

"Drat, I missed placing a wager," said James. "That's what
I get for putting family above sport."

The contest over, the participants were emerging and wrapping up against the wind. Three were awarded medals from
the swimming club.

"First place to a female, by God! Wish I'd seen that mer-
maid splashing about. There's something to toast at your ladies club, Alex . . . Alex?"

She'd put her back to the view, separating herself from them to look at people on the bridge. She leaned close, whispering, "Keep Teddy here. It's important."

Fingate—she was sure of it, having spotted a man in a long coat behind a group of onlookers. He was the right height. She moved toward him, tugging off one glove.

He caught sight of her and pulled his muffler down, revealing his face. She felt a wash of relief, her own, though his was plain to see. He clutched a walking stick and used it to aid his footing as he navigated from one patch of straw to another.

"Bless you, bless you for coming," he said. "I'm so sorry."

The years fled and she was fifteen again and a bit in awe of Fingate, who seemed to know how to do everything. Traveling the most dangerous parts of the world or running an errand in the heart of London were all one to him, to be met with the same amiable face and outlook.

But a decade of life reasserted itself as she drew close. Alex saw the influence of time and hard living on him, along with a profound sadness in his eyes. His master and longtime friend was dead, and Fingate had obviously wept his grief while she had not.

"I am so sorry," he repeated, his voice unsteady.

She held his hand in both of hers, a gesture of friendship and trust she did not lightly undertake, given the risk of consequences to her emotions. "I know. It's all right. We must talk. They're after you for Father's murder."

"Murder. Yes. I knew he couldn't have—it's too awful."

"You must come with me to the Psychic Service and tell them everything you know. They've taken over the case from Scotland Yard. A Reader will hear you out."

"Impossible. I'd have gone there myself, but—no, I can't."

"Why?"

"There's no knowing who to trust. Your father was inquiring into something delicate for the Home Office."

"What would that be? Did Uncle Leo know?"

"There's no proof for it, but orders came from high up. His

lordship did not say how high. It was a close secret, because of worry about spies within the office itself."

Ridiculous, but she had to hear more. "We're in the open here. Let's find a quiet place away from the cold. Tell me everything and we'll—"

"Please, miss, you have to arrange a meeting with Lord Richard Desmond. Your father said he was the one man in England besides the Lord Consort who could be trusted. I know it's mad, but perhaps your uncle Leopold can clear a path. What's wrong?"

"Father knew Lord Richard?"

"They corresponded."

That explained how Richard knew so much about her and her history. But why was it possible for Father to write to an acquaintance and not to her? "I can't do that."

"Why not?"

"It's a state secret. Oh, bother that. Lord Richard was killed the same night."

Fingate's shock was genuine. She felt it through her contact with him, along with the rush of fear that followed. "How?"

"A group of masked men came to Harley Street and ambushed Lord Richard in his coach, wounding him with some type of air gun. I got him away, but they followed us and finished him off."

"Lord Richard was *there*?"

"As part of the investigation."

"Dear God."

Alex's mind spun rapidly with Fingate's information. A connection between her father and . . . so Lord Richard had not come because of her inadvertent violation in regulations. It simply wasn't important enough. But the death, the murder, of a friend, would bring him thundering in like a Zeus on a rampage. He'd already known the true identity of Dr. Kemp, so he must have known something about that investigation.

Who else at the Service knew?

"Have you had any encounter with or news of such men?" she asked.

Again, shock. "Oh, Miss, you don't think *I* brought them?"

"That's exactly what will be thought unless you come in and tell everything to a Reader. They'll know you're telling the truth and can move this forward."

"You're Reading me? Right now?" He didn't pull away, though.

"It's my duty."

He nodded, understanding. "Fair enough. It's best you don't have doubts."

"Very well. Now tell me: Who killed Father? Have you any idea? Why was he posing as Dr. Kemp?"

He shook his head at each question. "What he was working on required that he not be himself. You'd not have known him on the street—"

"*Why didn't he tell me he was home?*" There, finally out, and in a louder voice than she'd intended.

"He wanted to, but it was impossible. You know how it was with him, duty over aught else."

"Even me."

"And fair broke his heart, too, but as soon as he got in and got the names he was going to take a sabbatical, perhaps even retire."

Never to happen. "Got in where? What names?"

"Dangerous people, miss. He kept no papers on them, it was all in his head. You'll have heard of the Ætheric Society?"

"That's ridiculous. It can't be."

"There must be something to it, why else was he killed?"

"You tell me!" People looked at her. She felt her face go red. "I'm sorry, but I *must* know what's going on. You must come in. I'll make sure only people I know hear what you have to say. If not to the Service, then to Scotland Yard. The inspector who ran things last night can be trusted. His name is Lennon."

"No one can be trusted. His lordship must have found out something and they done for him."

"The Ætheric Society?" It was too absurd.

"They're more dangerous than anyone suspects. That's all he shared with me, and it must be true. He went to one of their meetings earlier that night, I don't know where, but he said he'd made progress and would be returning again soon. There was a woman helping him, but he didn't write anything down or repeat names. You know how he is . . . was. . . . Oh, God, this is so wrong. How could it have happened? The house was locked, I swear it was locked!"

She tried her best calming tone, hoping it would work. "Fingate, if we are to catch who did it, then come with me."

He was visibly torn between fear and loyalty. Having spent most of his life under the protection of another, content to follow orders, he was adrift and foundering on his own.

"If you don't, then what are we to do?" Alex felt his emotions engulfing her. His indecision flooded her, made her feel ill. She had to fight the urge to bolt. "I'll keep you safe. I promise."

"I know how to do that for myself, it's you I'm worried for; if the wrong people know you talked to me, they'll come for you." But he was teetering, just a little more weight in the right direction—

"Assume they do and have done so, Fingate. It's too late for warnings. We'll find a closed coach, make sure we're not followed, and I will get us to a safe place."

"Where people can't walk through walls?"

"What? You think that's how they got to Father?"

"We've seen stranger things in our travels, miss."

"This is London. People don't walk through walls, not even Ætherics." But that did describe the "ghost." He was solid enough, but to a Reader, he might well be incorporeal.

Fingate twitched, looking past her. "Those men, who are they?"

James and Teddy remained where she'd left them, though Teddy seemed ready to cross the distance. He looked eaten to the bone with curiosity, but James had somehow kept him in place.

"Cousins, one from each side of the family. The one on the left is James Fonteyn. He's annoying, but you can trust him. He lives at the other end of Baker Street from me at number—"

"You're on Baker Street?"

"Yes—and Father could have walked over any time he wanted. Did he not even look me up?"

Fingate was both shocked and ashamed, his emotions jumping to her like static electricity.

"Oh, never mind, we'll speak of it later. The other man is Teddy Pendlebury, Uncle Leo's son. I wouldn't bother with him, he's hidebound and unhelpful. Never learned how to listen."

Fingate wasn't listening, either. His nervous attention shifted; looking back the way he'd come, he gave a start. "Bloody hell, they're here. Stay with your cousins. I'll lead them away. It's me they want. I'll get word to you when I'm clear."

She glanced around him. Lieutenant Brook strode purposefully from the east side of the bridge. He fit Teddy's description of a "rum-looking savage" to perfection. He'd improved his disguise as a cabman. A shabby coat, beaten billycock hat, and chin blurred by emerging whiskers made for quite a transformation, too great of one to judge by Fingate's reaction.

"No, he's here to help." She held on to Fingate's hand, but he shook free.

"This was your father's, take it." He shoved the walking stick at her and darted away, slipping and stumbling.

Teddy and James ceased watching from afar and hurried forward. Teddy moved to intercept Fingate, and managed to lay hands on him. But Fingate executed a swift block and shift. Teddy gave a surprised whoop as he was deftly flipped forward in a full spin and landed flat on his back, to the startlement of passersby.

Alex had not been Master Shan's only pupil.

James shouted something and went to aid the fallen, but was more hindrance than help; Fingate did not look back and kept running. He made it off the bridge, cutting right to the path that led toward the Italian Gardens. There, even in winter, he could find cover in the dense growth of trees and bushes.

Brook charged in like a sight hound after flushed prey. He was much younger than Fingate and those long legs would eat up the ground, closing the valet's lead.

She'd promised to keep Fingate safe, and though Brook was Service and had been vetted by a Reader like herself, she did not know him. A remnant of Fingate's terror, of not knowing who to trust, clung to her, and though it was not her emotion, it raised the same physical reaction, the instinct to run or fight.

Alex chose to fight—or at least delay.

She put herself between and ordered Brook to stop.

"Sorry, Miss," he said. He changed course just enough to avoid her.

As he passed, she bodily launched herself.

She was too small to stop him, but few men could ignore eight stone of anything hitting them from the side. Alex struck him hard, wrapping her arms around him. For once, it was her own emotions that dominated the contact: mostly shock at the solid muscle under the concealing clothes. It was like tackling a mountain.

Brook was thrown off stride, of course, and she intended to hang on for as long as she could to slow him.

She did *not* intend for him to slip on a patch of ice and tumble over the bridge rail, taking her along.

Alex let go, but too late. She gave a short cry, cut off when they struck the freezing water with a great splash. The stuff went straight up her nose, filled her mouth, and what breath she had was lost to overwhelming, paralyzing cold.

CHAPTER FIVE

In Which Family Demonstrates to Be Useful to the Case

She thrashed in blind panic, reaching for the surface. Her fingers brushed slimy mud.

She pushed against it, tried to still herself enough to let buoyancy take her up, but her coat and skirts dragged in the current. Her chest hurt from holding out the water. She willed herself to not breathe, just a few seconds, another few—she had to find light and swim toward it.

But the day, so dark, the murky water the same color—

Mud again.

She put both hands into it and shoved as hard as she could away.

Bubbles. Air slipping from her mouth, floating free.

Follow them.

She reached, kicking, and could not quite catch up to them. But it was getting lighter. . . . Just a little farther. . . .

She slipped into a strange limbo where the desperate need for air ceased to drive her. Her lungs were empty; the next breath would be water, but her body desperately held off from that action. Instinct told her she had but a few counts of her laboring heart before that changed.

The bitter cold numbed her flesh, her mind. She'd perish from it, not drowning.

Then the water rushed in. She choked, gasped, more water painfully clotted her lungs. She ceased moving. A tiny ember of thought, that it was over and she'd see her father soon, winked and went out.

Something brutally strong seized her arm.

Such single-mindedness.

The emotions were simple and clean: worry, desperation, triumph. She didn't want them, but couldn't break the contact.

Triumph . . . relief . . .

Someone shouting in her ear. She was too listless to respond, just wanting sleep. If they'd only go and give her some peace.

Alex's nose, no, the whole front of her face ached, as though someone had struck her with . . . she didn't know what. So did her chest, constricted by a hard and heavy weight.

She rolled on her side, coughing. Water spewed, and again it hurt, hurt, *hurt* up inside the front of her head and deep in her chest. She gasped and gagged until more air went in than water came out. Her throat . . . an utterly revolting taste in her mouth.

Gradually, she became aware of being surrounded by people, and a man asked repeatedly how she felt. She waved him off, shivering uncontrollably.

She struggled through the shreds of emotions, fighting them as she'd fought the water. Which were hers, which were Fingate's, which belonged to others . . . ?

"Still on this side of the veil," pronounced a familiar voice.

A cheer went up, along with applause.

She rubbed her blurred eyes. Lieutenant Brook?

He knelt next to her and was the source of one set of emotions. She felt his gladness as a physical thing. Soaking wet and shivering, he had no mind for his discomfort, and was focused wholly on her. There was a warmth in his soul such as she'd sensed in Master Shan and a very few others: no pretension, he was as presented.

Which was greatly comforting. She'd trained to avoid embracing the feelings of others—too addictive—but this one time could do no harm.

"A blanket," he bellowed, standing. "Quickly!"

Lying on muddy ground, surrounded by concerned onlookers, she lost sight of him. In a break in the forest of trouser-clad legs she glimpsed two excited youths pushing through with a long wicker basket. It looked just like the one the ambulance men used to carry her father.

She choked and tried to get up, but well-meaning rescuers held her down.

The man in the medals who had directed the swimming race was one of them; he and two others lifted Alex into the long basket with little effort and tucked a blanket over her. She bucked and would have screamed, but her voice had been stolen by fresh panic. She was weak and—it hardly seemed possible—colder than when still in the lake. Her teeth chattered, fit to snap.

The helpful man, part of the Royal Humane Society and thus trained in the saving and resuscitation of the drowned, put a calming hand on her forehead. "There now, missy, settle down. You're safe."

Her armor was gone, but his warm reassurance flowed over her like balm on a raw wound. Her panic faded. After so many years of protecting herself from unwanted feelings, this was a day of revelation.

"Brook—where's Brook?" she demanded, her voice thin and raspy.

"That was no brook, my girl," he said, "but a great big lake you went into."

"The man who fell in with me."

"Which one? No matter, they're seeing to them all."

All?

They carried her, an odd floating sensation, to the Society's receiving house on the north side of the Serpentine.

A fit-looking matron took over her care and keeping, shooing the men away from the females-only area. She delivered Alex from the dreadful basket. In a remarkably short time Alex's soaked clothes were removed, and she was bundled into a long tub of unexpectedly hot water. Her skin puckered

with painful gooseflesh, then abruptly smoothed as the heat
took hold. It was better than any blanket. She'd never been
so deliciously warm before. She tried not to moan, but one
leaked out.

"There now, it's all right," said the matron. "A doctor's been
sent for. How do you feel?"

"Bloody awful."

"No surprise in that, my dear. Such a nasty shock."

Alex was not done coughing. She felt the wet bubbling in
her throat and whooped and wheezed into a bucket. When it
was all out, the woman gently washed her hair, reminding Alex
of some of the kindlier nannies of her childhood.

"Thank you," she whispered.

"Came that close, did you?"

A simple question and yet so much to it as Alex realized
just how easily she'd given in to death, fighting one instant,
ceasing the next, with no transition from one to the other. She'd
wanted peace, rest, to be left alone—but not forever.

The matron smiled down at her, as though able to follow
her thoughts.

Or my feelings.

Not all the psychically gifted were in the Service.

"I almost—"

"But you didn't. The Lord spared you for another day, so
there's a use for you yet. Never doubt that."

Years ago, Master Shan had expressed a similar outlook.
Alex had been in a low mood, desiring a cure for her ability
to Read. She did not *want* to learn to live with it. He'd been
gently adamant that she should. It had been a struggle; never-
theless, he managed to persuade her that she and it had a
purpose.

Alex hiccupped and felt hot tears. "Oh, not this. Not now."

"What better time?" The matron patted her hand. "It's
perfectly normal, dear. Have it out now while there's no one
about to tell you to stop. I won't mind."

Alex couldn't hold off her reaction; sobs shook her small

frame, even as part of her mind looked impartially on, analyzing.

Weeping for myself, but not for Father. I didn't die; he did. I'm mourning for the living.

Her analytical side decided she was indulging in self-pity because she was thinking too much. She shut that side down, recalling Inspector Lennon's comment about meeting herself coming around corners. His deep rough voice seemed to sound right between her ears. He'd show her budding self-pity to the door—or rather kick it through headfirst, a strangely comforting image.

The storm was intense but brief, and when it passed, the matron, God bless her, brought a cup of strong tea and a warning that it was hot.

"Do you get many in here?" Alex asked. The tea stripped the taste of the lake from her throat with a single sip. She nearly gulped the rest, suddenly thirsty.

"Too many by half. Some don't know how to swim well, get tired and sink, then there are the poor souls who throw themselves off the bridge, hoping they'll be gone by the time they reach the sluice at the end. That's why we're here. They said you jumped in, is that true, dear?"

"It was an accident. If he'd not slipped on the ice . . ."

"Oh, you've not done one of those lover's leaping acts of desperation, have you?"

Alex coughed again, clearing her throat, and handed back the teacup. "Absolutely not. Please, would you see if he's all right? His name is Brook. Tall, with a moustache, hasn't shaved today."

"If it'll settle you down, of course." But first she helped Alex from the tub, wrapped her in a Turkish towel, and sat her before a large iron stove. "Dry your hair, dearie."

The matron soon returned. "That first young fellow is fine, and so are the others. They're getting sorted out and their clothes dried. He's like to get a medal for this day's work, being the one who got to you first. Said you were limp as a water weed when he pulled you to shore. I let them know you're coming along just fine."

Alex had underestimated Brook and, influenced by Fingate, had unfairly judged him. Recalling Brook's concern, his unabashed warmth, she grimaced.

"There now, half the swimming club saw you go in, they weren't going to leave you. Several people jumped in to help, including a doctor—oh, here he is."

Looking like a theatrical ghost with a blanket wrapped Turkish-style around his body, a towel draped over his head, and his feet bare, James Fonteyn pushed through the door. He cast about with brief curiosity before spying her. For once he presented a serious face.

He came over, eased onto a chair next to her, and took her hand. She was tardy getting her armor up and caught a wretched tug of his guilt and worry.

"You look a right mess," he said. "I've never seen you so dreadful and that's saying a lot."

The matron lost her kindly expression.

Alex found herself responding with a feeble laugh that threatened to devolve into more coughing. "You jumped in after me?"

"Certainly not before, as I've better sense than to do such appallingly ridiculous acrobatics. My suit will never recover. *What* were you thinking?"

Devil take it. Now they'd demand explanations, not just James but everyone. It was bloody inconvenient.

"Doctor?" said the matron, moving closer.

"Thank you for the reminder. Her pulse is steady enough." He let go of Alex's hand, where he had indeed been pressing a thumb to the right spot on her wrist. "The patient is alert, but I'll hold judgment on her sanity until she can answer my question."

"It's a state secret," Alex said, looking at him steadily, and for the first time saw her cousin at a loss for words. A sweet moment.

"To do with the party last night?" he finally asked.

She nodded.

His expression shifted back to its habitual self-satisfied lines. "Oh, that won't serve at all. Reports will be written, witnesses interviewed; there's a few fellows without who claim to be with the newspapers, though one is with *The Times* and I wouldn't put that in the same class as the *Police Gazette*. Shall I mention policemen as well? They've a station just behind this place. They want to make sure you weren't drowning yourself on purpose, as suicide is against the—" He cut himself off, mouth open in honest horror. "Oh, my God. I'm sorry, Alex. I forgot. I'll stop babbling. Infernally stupid of me."

She chose not to speak, lest she damned his eyes.

"I'll make them go away, shall I?" He hurried out.

The matron shut the door firmly. "Calls himself a doctor?"

"He *is* a medical man, and my first cousin—and is usually far more foolish than that."

"Good heavens. How?"

"Will the police question me? I don't want my name in the papers."

"Of course you don't. The police are only here in case you're in a despondent state of mind, but if it was an accident, then there's no need."

James returned a short while later, damply dressed, apparently too impatient to wait for his clothes to dry. His great coat was fine, he'd shed it before leaping in.

"My hat's dented, but I want a newer one anyway," he told her.

"Bother your hat, is Mr. Brook all right?"

"He's bursting with good health and energy for his morning tub."

"Please, James, be serious."

"No, sorry, none today, thank you. He wants to see you as soon as is decently possible. I'll put him off for longer if you like. While it would be entertaining to see how you manage things with a colleague while looking like a water rat, it would be better to receive him after you're dressed and on your feet."

That was uncommonly sensible of him.

"The newspapers?"

"I worked a miracle, little cousin. I was brilliant, even inspired. The curious have been routed. The story will have mention in several London journals; that can't be helped. A Christmas swimming race is of minor interest, but a daring water rescue involving several participants and a helpless maid of tender years is something else again. Mr. Brook was modestly loath to have mention in the saga, so I provided the press with false names, and gave full credit to Mr. Ashburn Poultreen of the Royal Humane Society for recovering a schoolgirl of fourteen years, six months, who had fallen in by accident. Miss Violet Kettle of Basingstoke is now safe and well in the bosom of her family, thanks to his heroic efforts."

It could have been worse.

"Much as it went against my desire for fame, I downplayed my part and provided a false name as well. I've my reputation to protect. Can't have eye surgeons leaping into the Serpentine, it might cause a patient to blink in dismay, and that would interfere with a proper ocular exam. Don't you think so, Matron?"

The good woman ventured no opinion. "More tea, miss?"

"Please. Are my clothes dry?"

"Not nearly. You need to rest, give yourself a bit of time to get past it. Doctor, it will be best if you leave now."

"People are always telling me that. One of these days I'll sort out why. And if no one has mentioned it before, I want to express my appreciation on behalf of the family for looking after my soggy cousin." He presented a genial smile to her, along with five gold sovereigns.

She gasped, staring at them. "Oh, sir, I couldn't!"

"You most certainly can or I'll lodge a complaint. Not sure where, but it will be lodged. If you don't want it, then donate it to the Humane Society."

She gave him a shrewd eye, surrendered to the largesse with a soft "thank you."

"James?" He was well off, as were many of the Fonteyns, but the princely sum—not to mention the generosity—startled Alex.

He continued as though she'd not spoken. "If you're in a hurry to leave, I'll send someone to fetch clothes from your house. Boodles Churchill is here with his fiancée and they have a carriage to take us to Baker Street. She can find something appropriate if she has access to your digs."

"I lost the key, my reticule—"

"Was recovered. You dropped it when you tackled that big fellow; he's looking after it, so I suppose he's forgiven you for assaulting him. That was a magnificent block, by the way. Learn that in your travels? Oh, there I am rattling on, but I am curious why you thought it necessary. He was doing quite well before you decided to bring him down."

"Mr. Brook slipped on the ice. I didn't plan any of this, just wanted to delay him."

"Well, he was quite keen to catch up with that chap who ran off; who was he? Looked familiar."

"Fingate, my fa—damn you, James!" His blather had neatly undermined her defenses.

Across the room, the matron gaped at the outburst, apparently not used to refined young ladies expressing anger in such terms.

"I don't recall anyone of that name, but give me time," James said, unfazed and cheerful.

"You know very well who he is," she whispered.

"State secrets, little cousin. I'll have a chat with Boodles's fiancée. Stay warm and do what you're told for the next hour. It won't require effort, all you need do is sit there for a bit. Think of England," he added brightly.

Instead, she thought of bouncing some object off the back of his head as he left, but nothing suitable was within reach.

A second cup of tea helped, easing her sore throat.

"There's another man wanting to see you, Miss," said the matron. "Says he's your cousin Theodore. That first being a doctor was one thing, but this side *is* for females only."

"Assure him that I'm fine and will talk to him when I've rested—"

Teddy poked his head in. "Hallo, sorry, but had to see you, Alex. There's going to be the devil to pay when Mother finds out about this."

"Then don't tell her." Good God, she'd nearly died and he was worried about what Aunt Honoria would think? Alex knew him to be a sometimes charming fool, like James, but harbored a small hope that it was a simple front he presented to the world. But no, he was a fool through and through.

He eased the rest of the way inside, looking nervous. "I say, there aren't any undressed females about?"

"Hoping to see some?"

Teddy flushed a gratifying shade of brick red. "Really, now! I've been worried sick for you—"

More likely worried over the scandal had she drowned.

"Are you all right?" he demanded. "Whatever possessed you to jump in?"

"It was an *accident*."

"Who was the fellow you were talking to? He nearly took my arm out of my socket, the little bas—that is to say—I'm bruised all over. Who was he?"

She felt inordinately pleased about his damage. "Please, Teddy, don't ask questions. There's an inquiry I'm working on with the police and I'm not allowed to discuss it until it's resolved."

"Surely with family you can drop a hint or two."

She'd already had too much familial faux pas with James. "I'm sorry, I cannot, no more than you can discuss your own work."

"The two are hardly comparable. Now who was that fellow on the bridge? The one who ran away? Oh, don't make a face, I have to *know*."

"Honestly, I can't."

"That other fellow who fell in won't say a word, either. Why didn't you say he was with you? I took him for a ruffian."

"He was the one you saw following me?"

"Yes. Had I known he was a policeman in disguise I'd not have chased after you from church to protect you from him. Of course you had no way to tell me, so I suppose that's hardly fair."

Correcting his assumption about Brook's occupation would serve no purpose. "I appreciate that you tried to help."

"You're welcome. But your reaction when I told you—someone else must be following you, someone who is not a policeman."

That was a perceptive guess. She had to head him off. "I deal with criminals, Teddy. I have to be cautious. It's only good sense."

"But carrying around a firearm, really now!"

"Where is it?"

"With that policeman. Mr. Fonteyn gave him charge of it, which is only right. He'll keep it safe, I'm sure. Whatever shall I tell Mother about this—this . . . incident?"

"You don't tell her anything." She raised a hand to quell objections. "Our names won't be in the papers, so she need never find out. You'll just spoil Christmas dinner for her and Uncle Leo." Andrina would find it entertaining, and Alex did not care to provide *her* with any such distraction.

Teddy made noises to indicate he was thinking it through and then finally agreed. "That would be for the best. She'll be annoyed enough that I didn't sit with the family in church. I suppose I can say I saw a friend and had to chat with him, borrowing your story, as it were. What shall I say about your disappearance?"

"That I could not bear the crowds. Aunt Honoria knows my dislikes. I won't be there for dinner, so give her my regrets."

"You *can't* avoid dinner."

"Of course I can, I'll not show up. It will be better for all concerned. I have to go to the head office at the Service and put in a report."

"Ridiculous. Your employers will forgive you for having a respite after such a terrible misadventure, especially on a holiday. Come home."

She decided not to remind him of the perils she survived when traveling with her father. Most of those dangers were wholly preferable to dinner with relatives. "I'm to be called in today regardless. I expect a message is already waiting for me at Pendlebury House."

"Then you send a message right back that you're not going. Father will sign it. They'll have to pay attention to him."

"Most kind, but the matter is closed. Besides, I didn't bring anything suitable to wear."

That sank in. He blithered a bit, then said brightly, "Borrow a frock from Andrina."

She gave him a look.

He had the decency to wince. "Never mind."

"Just find Mr. Brook and make sure they're taking good care of him. He saved my life; afford him the appropriate respect and honor he deserves."

Teddy might have offered more argument, but the matron put herself forward. "Sir, I must ask you to leave. The lady wants care and rest." She guided him toward the door and threw the bolt the instant he was on the other side.

She and Alex each breathed a sigh of relief.

"Sorry," said Alex.

"It's good to have family about, but some of them do get underfoot. I'll make sure no one else comes in."

Taking advantage of the respite, Alex's busy mind turned to how she'd come to be here in the first place. Where would Fingate have taken himself? What had Father been investigating? What awaited her at the head office of the Service? She'd have to get to the bottom of this nonsense about the Ætheric Society.

No time to waste, then.

She stood and performed the undignified gyrations necessary to dry her hair: bending double, her head upside down, swaying one side to the other, shaking and combing through with her fingers. The result was an untidy tangle, but a few pins would keep it hidden under a hat.

The matron answered a knock at the door, exchanged a few words, and accepted a carpetbag from someone. Alex recognized it as one of her own and padded over. It contained not only dry clothes and her best wool cloak and hat, but undergarments, stockings, walking shoes, her brush, comb, hairpins, and a bottle of hair pomade that would smooth the wild disarray on her head.

She vowed to make the acquaintance of Boodles Churchill's fiancée and treat her to a lavish tea and some shopping.

The dress was not one Alex would have chosen for an interview at the head office. The blue was too frivolous, the fabric too rich, but the hat matched, as did the gloves. The ensemble was better suited for social calls, but it would have to serve for now. With the matron's help, she dressed and stuffed her damp clothes into the bag.

At the door, Alex hesitated.

"What's wrong, dearie?" asked the matron.

"Whatever awaits outside. That's what's wrong."

"Lord bless you, is that not the truth?"

After imparting her sincere gratitude to the matron (privately resolving to write a letter to the R.H.S. praising her), Alex left the sanctuary of the women's side and entered a sort of lobby. It had a lofty ceiling, dim in the winter gloom, and the gas was alight. Benches were placed along the walls, and a plain receiving desk was in the middle, but no one manned it. Several people were about, all strangers. She expected James and his friends to be there, perhaps Teddy still lingered. She didn't like him, but he was familiar.

No relatives in sight. That was oddly disappointing.

Brook, his cabman's clothing the worse for wear but dry,

detached from a group and hurried over. He seemed on the verge of reaching out to her, but checked himself. He did take her in, head to toe, his eyes strangely intense. Her barriers were back in place, so she could not tell if he was anxious or angry. Certainly he was entitled to the latter.

"You're all right, Miss Pendlebury?" His tone expressed concern. She could deal with that.

"Thanks to you, Mr. Brook. Are you restored, no ill effects from immersion?"

"They looked after me marvelously fine."

"Thank God for that. Mr. Brook, I am deeply, deeply sorry to have caused you such hazard and distress and am very grateful. You saved my life. I shall never forget that. Thank you."

His fair skin went pink. "I'm glad I was there to help, but would be gladder still to have possession of an explanation."

"I did not intend we should fall in."

"So I was informed. I felt my foot slip and then it was over and gone for us both. May I ask why you impeded my pursuit of a wanted man?"

"If I may ask why you did not make yourself known to me sooner. I assume the Service delegated you with the task of keeping watch on Pendlebury House?"

"They did. My round was up at noon. The next man will wonder where I've gotten to; I hope the horse and hansom are where I left them on the crescent."

"If not, we'll find them." Alex was chagrined. She should have noticed their presence, but Teddy had distracted her with his chatter. "Is my cousin about? Either of them?"

"They left. Dr. Fonteyn seemed to be in a hurry about something and said he'd be in touch. Mr. Pendlebury insisted I persuade you to return home. He was much in earnest about it."

She was not surprised, but it still stung. Teddy would have to be at the dining table so as not to offend his mother and whatever guests she'd invited. James must want to get back to whatever bacchanal he'd planned prior to her invasion of his house. She'd nearly drowned, but God forbid they should hang about. Had Alex died, then might they have been upset for a time, but not for long.

The flow of frivolous life must return to its normal course. *But not for Father.* The thought jabbed her, knife-sharp. Teddy could be excused, he didn't know, but she'd thought James might be more considerate. On the other hand, he had jumped in to save her. She should have thanked him for that, and would have had he not hared off.

"Are you all right, Miss Pendlebury?"

She was a breath away from a harsh complaint, but smothered it. The shortcomings of family were her cross to bear, not Brook's. "They can do without me. We must get to the head office. Mrs. Woodwake may have sent for me already."

"Yes, Miss Pendlebury." He took the carpetbag from her, gathered a bundle of his own from a bench, and followed as she briskly launched into the cold again.

B rook's hansom was where he'd left it along Wilton Crescent commanding a view of Pendlebury House. Anybody would assume the driver would be waiting to be called to one of the houses. While it should have been in the mews behind the trees banking the crescent, it was so common a sight as to be invisible. Little wonder she'd not noticed.

Behind the hansom was a coach, and two men Alex recognized as Service emerged as she and Brook crossed the street. Dressed as cabmen, they were alert, but lacked a certain tension of manner she expected to see. News of Lord Richard's murder must still be a secret, even within the walls of the Psychic Service.

They had orders she was to report to the head office as soon as possible. One took up post in the hansom, the other handed Alex into the coach—her long skirt and cloak were impediments to agility—and Brook followed after with the bags, settling them on the floor between.

She relaxed marginally when they were away from the crescent, proceeding along Upper Belgrave. This was Uncle Leo's daily route to the Home Office. They would travel a bit farther to get to the Service's offices, which were next to Scotland Yard.

"My question, Miss Pendlebury," said Brook.

"Question?"

"Why did you interfere with my catching Fingate?"

Why indeed?

"My answer wants for logic, Lieutenant. He took fright at your approach and I . . . I caught it."

"You caught fright," he said, his expression neutral.

"I caught *his* fright. Did they explain about Readers and how we work?"

"You sense the emotions of others and the residual of emotions they leave behind."

"Yes. When my internal defenses are down, the feelings generated by others can be overwhelming. Fingate was terrified and did not know who to trust. I was trying to convince him to come with me when your approach set him off."

"Sorry, miss, but I had orders."

"Not your fault, but singularly bad timing. Another moment and I'd have brought him around. We'll have to wait until he contacts me again."

"You'll pardon my curiosity, but when I came up you didn't look frightened."

"Readers learn to conceal emotions. If you don't know whose they are, it's best to keep them hidden."

"If you were so fearful, why did you not run yourself?"

She shook her head. "That's an acquired foolishness. I learned to fight rather than run from a threat."

He responded with a ghost of a smile. "Next time I'll give you a wider berth."

"I hope there will not be a next time, Mr. Brook."

"Indeed, Miss Pendlebury. Once was sufficiently damaging."

There was that warmth of spirit again, strong enough that it filtered through her barriers. She pushed aside its distraction. "You followed me from the house?"

"At a prudent distance. I planned to stay clear of you at the church, didn't want to intrude on the family, but you went haring off toward the park. Lost you in the crowd. Couldn't think why you did that, though now I believe it was to meet with Mr. Fingate."

"That was my intent, yes. Before running away last night he passed me a note on where to meet."

"You did not mention that then."

"We got rather busy. By the time I remembered—well, I know I'm going to be hauled over the coals. Had I brought him in, the situation would be different. Just have to deal with things as they are and hope they improve. I'll make a full report and mention you did your duty. You went above and beyond in your actions to preserve me. I hope you'll get proper recognition for that."

"Really, now."

"I mean it."

"I would prefer to forget it altogether—not my most shining moment, falling off a bridge."

"Nor mine." Alex was not keen to report; she'd look like a fool. There was a possibility of disciplinary action, but they'd not dismiss her. Good Readers were rare, and she was one of the better ones. "How long have you been with the Service?"

"A week. They gave some instruction in protocol, lectures on investigations, and yesterday was my first day of active duty."

Good God. Greener than grass. "Where were you prior?"

"I'd rather not discuss that, if you don't mind, Miss Pendlebury. This is where I serve now."

"Offended someone?"

He hesitated, eventually offering a wry smile. "I got noticed."

"In a good way or bad way?"

"I'm still sorting that out."

"What sort of experience do you bring to the Service?"

"Ample."

She verged on giving in to annoyance, but for his smile. A person must be forgiven for wanting to preserve their privacy; she certainly put effort into keeping herself apart from others. She had but a handful of friends, none outside the Service; like her, they had various quirks due to their psychical talents that had to be tolerated. Social gatherings tended to be an extension of work, with talk centered on whatever was going on at the time. Usually it was interesting, but Alex wanted to try ordinary chat about ordinary things. A simple conversation about weather that did not involve working out how long a corpse had been exposed to the elements would make a pleasing change.

As for anything approaching courtship, she'd found that impossible. Some men were too curious about her Reading ability, others discounted its existence, and the rest were unsuitable for one reason or another. Human relationships relied on pretense and lies, and one could maintain neither with a Reader.

She rather liked Lieutenant Brook, but Sergeant Greene would return on Boxing Day as her usual driver. Brook would remain a colleague to be nodded at as they passed in the halls, though perhaps a bit more, for having saved her life.

"Your cousin had me keep this for you," said Brook. He pulled her mud-smeared reticule from his bag. Her revolver was still in it.

"Thank you again, I'm glad to have this back." She slipped the firearm into her cloak pocket.

"Yesterday I'd have found the idea of a lady carrying one of those around to be a bit of a shock," he said.

"And today?"

"A necessity. That attack last night—well, you should have a spare."

What an enlightened sort.

"I've also this for you. . . ." He drew a walking stick out. "Never saw one like this before. Certainly unique-looking."

Her father's cane.

She'd been too distracted on the bridge to recognize it, but the memory rushed back sharply. The stick had been a gift from some South American dignitary, made from a type of wood that was almost as hard as the iron ferrule. The handle and intricately wrought wide collar were silver, its detailed, one-of-a kind crafting by a master smith.

Only yesterday her father's living hand had carried it.

Blinking, she pulled off her right glove and—

The imprint of him remained. She shut her eyes and felt his presence like a solid thing. He was next to her, warm, caring, proud, his love tinged with worry. It washed over her soul like a sun-warmed wave. Whatever his actions, wherever their travels had taken them, his love for Alex had been the force that kept him moving. If he hadn't found help for her . . .

I might have become like Mother or turned drunkard like most of the other Fonteyns.

That had been the unspoken threat over much of her young life. He'd all but obsessed on it, looking for some way to *save* her.

Alex drew back, opening her eyes. How much of that was from the cane and how much dredged from her memory?

They were too closely blended. For all she knew it was wholly from memory and only wishful thinking made him alive again.

But he was gone, the door between shut. He was never to return, and she was truly an orphan. All that remained were echoes in her mind of his voice, glimpses of his face, a thousand memories of travels past, and nothing for the future but grief. Her limbo of waiting was ended, cruelly ended. No chance to say good-bye, he'd said that on a pier in Hong Kong a decade past. In London he could have walked just a few streets over and knocked on her door. *Why* hadn't he done so? If he loved her that much, what could possibly be more important than seeing his only child?

Tears fled down her cheeks. She dropped the cane.

"Miss Pendlebury?"

"It was Father's. He's . . . something of him lingers."

"And it is not enough."

"No. . . ."

"I'm so sorry."

Alex dug blindly through the reticule for a handkerchief. One should be there, she always had two or three. . . . Had she forgotten, how could she forget anything so fundamental as a bloody handkerchief—

Brook offered her one of his and she realized she'd been speaking aloud. She must sound like a lunatic, but he merely looked concerned.

Alex accepted his help and snuffled and dabbed her eyes.

He abruptly shifted from the bench opposite and sat next to her. More shockingly, he put an arm about her shoulders. He must not know that most Readers did not like to be touched, the flow of emotions . . .

Such as came to her now.

Brook's concern was deep, sincere, mixed with compassion and sympathy. He'd known loss, understood what she was going through and what was needed. The touch from . . . well, if not a friend, then a caring stranger made it easier.

"I could say it will be all right, but I know it is *not* all right," he murmured. "It's perfectly awful."

She stopped fighting and let the grief come. Alex could never have dropped her barriers with any family member, nor even with her few friends. She had a facade to preserve, but with this man, as with the matron, it was safe. He would not think less of her or treat her differently after.

Alex sobbed and wailed and Brook held her and said nothing more.

CHAPTER SIX

In Which Miss Pendlebury's
Christmas Luncheon Is Interrupted

She'd recovered by the time they left Victoria Street to negotiate between Westminster Hospital and Westminster Abbey. One would think the miserable cold would have discouraged revelers, but there was a fair amount of traffic.

"I am again obliged to you, Mr. Brook." Her voice was rough and husky. Her bout with sorrow combined with nearly drowning left her barely able to breathe.

"Pleased to have been of assistance, Miss Pendlebury." He was back on the opposite bench, none the worse for wear, proprieties restored.

No pretension from him, not at the moment, but even the most honest people eventually gave in. Lies were like vents on a boiler, preventing explosions during social interactions.

"I hope you will feel better," he added.

"You're very kind." She *did* feel sharper than before, determined to square her shoulders and press forward. She found and pulled on her gloves, smoothing the fine leather to each finger before making a fist.

"If I may venture to ask . . . is it always like this in the Service?"

"No. Not at all. We do our work, same as anyone, it's just things have changed. I don't know what's to happen with Lord Richard gone."

"Do you think it will be disbanded?"

What? "I should hope not. That would be a terrible mistake. The queen herself called for it to be put together. She'd not allow it."

"The idea disturbs you."

"The Service is vital to criminal investigations. We're instrumental in solving hundreds, if not thousands of crimes every year."

"The general impression is that its contribution is a peripheral part of any inquiry. But last night they didn't do anything until you arrived."

She was glad he noticed. "We foster that impression. You won't see much of what we do mentioned in the papers. People are uncomfortable with us yet. We've found it's more tactful to give full credit to the police."

"There is opposition to the employment of psychical talent, though."

"Brought on by ignorance and superstition. Old fears run deep."

"In these modern times? In England?"

"It's no exaggeration, Mr. Brook. There are backward pockets of humanity all over the world who—well, I daresay you'll get some history during your training. There are a number of books in our library that cover the topic, unpleasant as it is. Acquaint yourself with them. Whether you have a psychical talent or not, you will be subject to guilt by association. Don't be shocked if someone spits on you or worse."

"They'll get paid back if they try."

"You *can't*. We're servants to the greater good, whether they know it or not. I don't wish to encourage a state of affairs of ourselves versus them; such divisions only lead to more distrust. You may find it better to impart to the curious that you simply work in the civil service. Conversely, the only thing worse than hostility brought on by baseless fear of the Service is unquestioning acceptance."

"I did hear something of that. Such enthusiasm is preyed upon by spiritualist tricksters who-who—"

"Pretend to have a telegraph to the Almighty?"

He nodded.

"Beware of them as well, Mr. Brook. Misplaced adulation can too easily turn to loathing if they're disappointed in some way. Many bear a perilously high regard toward those with psychical talent. It's a shock to find we're just as human and vulnerable as everyone else."

Their coach passed through the short arched tunnel opening into the mews entrance of Her Majesty's Psychic Service. It and the iron gates gave the building the look of a medieval fortress, though it had been constructed less than thirty years ago. She had expected to be delivered to the front door. Perhaps this was the first sign of change marking the end of the Desmond dynasty.

One of the porters closed and locked the gates, retiring to a tall, coffin-shaped guard's box just within. His right coat pocket sagged from a heavy weight. A pistol of some sort, she thought with approval. With masked lunatics carrying strange air guns capable of multiple and nearly silent fire, it was only prudent to be prepared for another attack. Many of the staff were ex-army. How much did they know of events?

When Brook handed her out, she noticed an inordinate number of people around, more than on a normal working day. There was a worried tension in the air, but it lacked the heaviness of anger and grief as one might expect if they'd been informed of events.

There was also something missing from the yard.

"Lord Richard's coach is not here," she whispered to Brook.

"Mrs. Woodwake was keen to keep things quiet. A conveyance full of bullet holes would demand attention and explanation. Easy enough to hide one, there's plenty of mews about, but where would they take *him*?"

"Any number of places for a general postmortem, but there are fewer choices for an investigation conducted by the Service. We have staff for that, but news of that nature is impossible to keep secret for long. Too many perceptive people about."

"She must have put the fear of God into them. It worked for me," he admitted.

The Service's austere facade was echoed within: plain walls and doors with numbers on the lintels as an aid to navigation. Some had printed signs stating the name of the department or the occupant, others were unadorned. It was either madly inefficient, or intended as a test to see how quickly a new member could memorize things.

The ground-floor walls were white, the first floor's were pale green, then pale blue, and the color of the top floor Alex did not know; she'd never been that high. There were rumors of a palatial suite with hidden staircases leading to secret passages and tunnels, one going under Whitehall to 10 Downing Street, another to New Scotland Yard, and a third having a small train with tracks leading straight to Buckingham Palace. Completely absurd, of course, such things required maintenance and lots of it, and it was quite impossible to expect members of the staff to keep that great a secret. Still, the stories were amusing to impart to new recruits to test their credulity.

Alex made her way to the front reception room and asked for messages.

"Just the one," said Mrs. George, who supervised a busy desk and had no sense of privacy, at least for others. "Woodwake wants you in her office. What did you do?"

"I invaded Egypt and they're very annoyed about it."

"Who is? Them upstairs or the Egyptians?"

"Both."

Behind her, Alex heard Brook make an odd noise. It might have been a laugh, but if so, he turned it into a throat-clearing sound. Mrs. George looked him up and down, unimpressed. She was as hard on new recruits as any drill sergeant. Her eyes narrowed at the sight of Brook's disheveled disguise and she started to speak.

"Mrs. George?" Alex headed her off. "I'm frightfully hungry, is there anyone who can do sandwiches for us?"

"There's better than that in the dining hall, a proper Christmas dinner for those called in."

"I haven't the time. I'll eat after I see Mrs. Woodwake."

"You won't have an appetite then. She's in a state, I know the signs. Go have a bite now than later. Anyway, she's down in the cellars with some botheration, has been for hours. Something's brewing, but they won't say what. There's no harm if she gets the news of your arrival a quarter hour late. Go on, off with you." She turned her back on Alex's objection.

"That would be that," said Brook, following Alex.

"She's a bastion of common sense."

"Does she have psychical talent?"

"Not that I know. Some people here have to be ordinary sorts."

"Like me?"

She glanced at him. "You are not ordinary, Mr. Brook."

Evidently possessing self-confidence, he did not invite her to elaborate on the compliment.

She liked that.

The dining hall was in the east wing. Halfway there, she smelled the food and her stomach rumbled joyful encouragement. Thankfully, there was enough ambient noise to make it unlikely so indelicate a sound had carried to Mr. Brook's ears.

The hall was a quarter full of people lingering to talk over the remains of their luncheon. She knew the majority of her colleagues by name or by sight, but didn't stop to give greeting, heading straight to a long table holding a surprisingly large amount of food. While normal etiquette demanded that Brook seat her and then fetch her a plate, this was a working situation, and she was pleased to pick what she liked.

Not trusting her voice to have lost its rasp, she pointed and the servers gave generous portions of a traditional Christmas feast. Aunt Honoria would have *tsk*ed, but Alex was ravenous. Apparently so was Brook, who carried two plates and saw to it the surfaces of both were layered high.

A waiter, well acquainted with Alex's preferences, brought a pot of tea and cups to their table. "You're looking most elegant today, Miss Pendlebury," he remarked. "Everyone's dressed up for the holiday. Makes a change, though it's a shame to have to work."

Brook shot the man a look. At a restaurant or private house the staff were silent and spoke only when addressed.

Alex hoped he would catch on that the Service was a great leveler and a certain amount of camaraderie was inevitable. "Thank you, Sutherland. It's kind of you to notice. Do you know why everyone's here?"

Sutherland poured tea that was almost as black as coffee. "Not a peep. I had to be here regardless, but word came to get the kitchen staff in and start cooking and keep cooking until Mrs. George says otherwise. They're not happy, but they're getting paid well for it, so that should be all right. I don't know what's going on, but it's got to be something big, and big things are not good things. Not for us, they're not. There's worry hanging in the air; you don't have to be psychical to feel it. Cut it with a butter knife, more like."

Alex offered agreement and attacked her food in a manner that would have horrified her aunt. Aunts of a certain type, she thought, *should* be horrified at regular intervals.

Brook, following her lead, ate like a soldier at mess. They didn't talk. Alex was glad of the respite, though she noticed his interest in their surroundings. A trio at the next table were in deep discussion about metallurgical stresses, and the tallest of them, his back to her, was busy defacing the white table cloth with penciled calculations.

"Who's that?" Brook asked, his voice low.

She matched his tone. "Mr. Alexander Humboldt Sexton, and why he's been called in, I cannot imagine. He's usually on the other side of town with Professor Crookes working on psychical sciences."

"On what?"

"The department seeking to find out why some are gifted and others are not. One section is trying to develop the means of artificially reproducing the same gifts, though I don't see how that could be accomplished by a machine. Another section has hope of being able to detect ghosts, though. Crookes is a physicist and has some interesting theories on residual imprintings."

"And Mr. Sexton?"

"A metallurgist and engineer with a smattering of chemistry. I expect he's there to design and build such machines, but he got involved with the Service because of his interest in magic."

"Good heavens, he doesn't think he's a wizard, does he?"

She nearly choked. "I meant stage magic. The same illusions you see at a music hall are employed by mediums to hoodwink the gullible. Mr. Sexton is keen to discredit them and studied all their tricks. His favorite ploy is to attend a sitting and then introduce considerably more spiritual activity than the medium planned for. He's been too successful. Most know him by now and forbid his entry, though he has gotten around it with disguises. He was doing that sort of thing on his own as a hobby, got noticed by one of our investigators, and invited to join to train recruits."

"That's jolly."

"Indeed. He gives the most amusing lectures, you should attend one. What raises gooseflesh in a darkened room looks quite silly with the lights on."

"When's the next? Perhaps we could—" He stopped as a woman, moving fast, approached their table and came to a rocking halt. She dropped a thin pale hand on his shoulder, preventing him from rising.

"Stay," she directed in a flat voice, as though speaking to a dog. Her whole focus was on Alex, who was too surprised to do more than gape up.

An abrupt silence enveloped the hall as everyone became aware of her presence.

"Miss . . . ?" began Brook, who seemed uncertain who to address, the woman or Alex.

At the next table, Mr. Sexton turned around and blanched. "Belt up," he whispered urgently. "And don't move."

Alex had never seen her before but instantly recognized her from thirdhand descriptions. She tried not to shudder, but could not completely suppress the reaction. Her first instinct was to bolt from the room and keep running.

The woman's uncommonly short hair was as pale as her skin, and stuck up in spiky clumps from her skull. Her intense eyes were black as soot with no boundary between pupil and iris. Unfortunate, as it made her look like a madwoman.

According to rumor, she was indeed mad, and had been so since girlhood, when her particular gift had manifested, wresting away any ordinary dreams of life she might have possessed. She gave a false impression of youth with her quick jerky movements, but her eyes were old.

They now narrowed as she shifted her hand from Brook's shoulder to point at Alex. "I'm Sybil. You're the traveler's daughter," she stated, her tone still flat, the words tumbling forth almost too fast to be understood. ·

Alex's racing heart nearly stopped.

"The traveler's journey ended. But I didn't see until too late. I'm sorry." She suddenly looked at Brook. "I could say it will be all right, but I know it is *not* all right. It's perfectly awful." Her voice deepened as she quoted him exactly, down to inflection and pauses.

His jaw sagged. "How did—"

"Not now," said Sexton urgently. "Let her speak."

Sybil spared him a glance, then focused on Alex. "Speak and be silent, see and be blind. Someone blinded me. They did, they did, they did theydidtheydid. The traveler almost saw, but one there and not there, stopped him. You will-will-will, I can't see what you will. They block the forward, not the backward, they can't take that from me. What's done is done, but it's useless, frozen in past time and-and-and-and forward flow goes into blankness. I *cannot* do what I must!"

As she spoke, Sexton made haste to write down her jumble of words.

"Traveler's daughter—" Sybil's voice thickened and her accent changed to that of Inspector Lennon. "Keep that pie hole of yours shut, your ears open, and your head down."

Alex gripped the edge of the table so as not to fall over.

"Good advice and he can't see, but maybe he does, no one's asked him, but he's right, he's right, he's right, will be right. Head. Down. Soon. Everyone. They're going to-to-to—everyone. They won't let me *see* it, damn them! I can't even see *them* in the past. There's a mirror in my face, looking backward, and it's a blackness where they are."

It was wrong to interrupt the flow, but Alex had an abrupt flash of memory of Master Shan and what he might say. "Then what's *next* to their blackness?"

Sybil's eyes closed. "*Clever* tweak . . . hah! Got you! Red curtains. Mirrors. Mirrors facing mirrors, facing me." Opening her eyes, she bent toward Alex. "Break them. Break all of them and damn the bad luck, think of England!"

With that declaration, she slumped and her expression relaxed. She appeared to be a bit less mad. Her gaze fell on the second plate of food Brook had brought and she gave a great smile of delight.

"Oh, how kind! I'm famished!" she said, and then slipped onto a chair, seized a fork, and began eating, oblivious to all else.

Sexton finished his hasty scribbling, then stood, his face grim. A finger briefly to his lips, he signed for Alex, Brook, and anyone close by to rise and back away, which they did.

The three of them retired to a spot near the windows. Alex found herself trembling. She, along with nearly everyone in the room, had a wary eye on Sybil, who continued her meal with no small gusto. Somebody must have had the presence of mind to send for Mrs. Woodwake, for she and another woman cautiously approached the table.

Sybil noticed them. "Hallo, ladies. I've had something of a seizure. It must have been a really *good* one!"

Woodwake was unflappable, merely smiling and nodding. "Well, that's progress."

"I feel wonderful! The lad with the squarish face wrote out much of it, I think." She gestured vaguely at Sexton's vacated table.

Woodwake moved dishes and utensils out of the way and gathered up the tablecloth. "I'll make sure it gets our full attention."

The woman with Mrs. Woodwake had the look of a caretaker about her, and placed herself behind and to the right of Sybil, who resumed eating.

Woodwake came over, clearly in a dark mood. "Pendlebury, where the devil have you been? Never mind, I'll get your report later. Mr. Sexton, are these your notes?"

"Yes, ma'am. Every word. In Pitman."

"I don't read shorthand." She spread the cloth on another table and stared at squiggles that passed for writing. "Translate and make sure to repeat *how* she said it, not just the words."

Sexton did so, running a long finger along each line.

"What's that 'pie hole' business about?" Woodwake demanded.

Alex went cold. "It's just something a friend said to me."

"Recently?"

"How could she have known?"

"That's not your concern. When was it said to you?"

"Last night, after the—incident in that house."

"What about the part of something being perfectly awful? What's the greater context of that?"

Now Alex felt a blush coming on. "That was-was a friend . . . offering comfort for my loss—and it was said in confidence."

"When?"

"About half an hour since. Is she also a telepathist?"

"Not your concern. I shan't repeat myself on that point."

Woodwake addressed the others in the hall, raising her voice to reach the corners. "Who else did she speak to?"

No one stepped forward.

"The three of you, then. Mr. Sexton, come with me and transcribe. You two will not discuss this with anyone. Pendlebury, to your office. Mr. Brook, who else was with you?"

"Only myself and Miss Pendlebury, ma'am."

"You've three plates. Who were you expecting?"

"No one, ma'am. But there's only two—" His eyes widened as he looked past her to Sybil, who was still wolfing down her Christmas dinner on the third plate. His skin faded to a sickly green tone. "Apparently that lady, ma'am."

"Interesting. You weren't aware of it, were you?"

He shifted uncomfortably under her gaze. "Mrs. Woodwake, I'd prefer not to—"

"No doubt. Stay with Pendlebury. And for God's sake, no long face, you've done nothing wrong. It's quite encouraging." Mrs. Woodwake folded the tablecloth, thrust it at Sexton, and departed with him hurrying to keep up.

Keenly aware of the interested scrutiny of everyone in the hall, Alex considered returning to her interrupted dinner. If that fierce-looking caretaker hadn't been present, she might have dared it. Sybil had, until now, only been another rumor, one that Alex discounted as an exaggeration. Now that she was over her initial fright, she was intensely curious to speak to her.

"Who is she?" asked Brook, pitching his voice so it wouldn't carry.

"A Seer." *Why did she come to me?*

"I'm sure you'll explain that shortly."

Giving Sybil a wide berth, they found a table away from the other diners. When Sutherland came by with a fresh pot of tea, he made no effort to engage in conversation. Like many of those on staff, he knew when topics were not to be discussed. The look on Woodwake's face certainly had put the fear of God in everyone; conversation was subdued in the great hall.

Sybil finished her repast, rose, and left with her companion, apparently unconcerned by so many watching her smallest move.

"The exhibition, Miss Pendlebury, is concluded," Brook said.

"One would hope."

"Who or what is a Seer?"

"An improbability. Not wholly impossible, just improbable."

"How could she know what I said to you in the coach?"

Alex hesitated. Woodwake had made it clear this was a sensitive subject, but some general knowledge couldn't hurt. Brook would learn about it if he delved into the building's library. "It's to do with her Talent. I have a gift for Reading; Seers can see the past, present, and future—not necessarily their own or in order. A certain kind of precognition is common enough in some. For instance, knowing when one might get an unexpected letter from a friend, or taking an umbrella instead of a walking stick when going out on a sunny day. Is that not what you have?"

His mouth snapped shut into a thin flat line.

"When you took that extra plate of food to the table I thought you were just very hungry, but you weren't aware of it, were you?"

"This is about Sybil, not me."

Alex considered pressing him, but understood how that felt. Most of those born with a psychical gift did not want the special attention it brought them. She gave a short nod and returned to the other matter. "Seers are rather more than precognitive. Something special and . . . frightening."

"How so?"

"Think about it—seeing the future? Would you really want to know what's to happen? Especially if it was something awful."

"But people want to know their future. Fortune-tellers make their living from it."

"Their predictions are always general in nature. They can't tell you that at half past three next Tuesday you'll encounter a man with a wooden leg. But some Seers are able to do just that, if it's important enough. The future is in flux. The past is fixed, but all that's to come is in constant motion. Any action we take at any given moment influences our future. If you choose to walk home by one route, perhaps nothing happens. If you take a different route you could trip and twist your ankle. That's two possible futures. Now imagine the countless choices made by everyone."

"It's what we do, it's ordinary living."

"Now imagine being able to see *all* those choices in your head at the same time."

"Impossible."

"The word is 'maddening.' The mind cannot hold it all. I suspect the more gifted one is, the more unstable one might become."

"But why is she here? Shouldn't she be in a hospital?"

"I expect she's able to predict things that are useful, providing one can correctly interpret what she says. She's obviously being well looked after. Her clothes are clean and tidy, her face and hands washed. She's luckier than many." Involuntarily, Alex recalled a wisp of memory of a desperate, ragged-looking woman with matted hair and wild eyes. She was curled in the corner of a brick-lined room, hugging her knees, crying for a bottle of gin, crying like a child.

Mother. . . .

Then someone, one of the Fonteyns, had grabbed Alex by the arm and dragged her away, scolding. The family had taken care of her mother as best as could be expected at the time. The links between psychic abilities and madness were still being explored—or discounted—by the scientific community.

To most people, including her mother's family, madness was a shameful weakness of character to be hidden behind closed doors. They'd kept it a secret even from Gerard. He'd been in a towering fury about it, too, once he discovered the truth.

However estranged from his wife, he said he should have been told. He had bellowed it so loudly that young Alex heard him on the other side of the house. She'd hidden under her bed, thinking he was angry with her because Mother had died. But when he came upstairs, he'd coaxed her out and hugged her close and said it was time to go on an adventure. . . .

"She wants you to break mirrors," said Brook, returning her to the present. "That was specific."

Alex forced the memories back into their box. "She mentioned red curtains, too."

"Do you know of such a place with both?"

She shook her head, feeling a little sick. "If there's anything to it, I expect I shall find out."

"Is that not the nature of predictions? To come true?"

"With countless variables keeping the future in flux, not necessarily. I've read somewhat of the theories involved. If an event is large enough, important enough, its impact on the future might be such that a Seer sees it across all the variations. For instance, a war. If she sees thousands of military funerals, she should be able to backtrack to the cause of the war and perhaps prevent it. Oh!"

"What?"

"Improbable, but not impossible."

"*What?*"

"Think of the advantage it would be to a government if one could glean a glimpse of the future from a Seer."

"If one can sort out the nonsense from her babbling."

"Indeed. This is disturbing, but it makes sense. What if our government—"

"Please. It's too terrifying a speculation. The prime minister or the queen herself relying on a fortune-teller?"

Alex raised an eyebrow. "No more so than Scotland Yard relying on Readers to guide investigations. Such a thing was once impossible, but here we are. Why not a Seer to help in making decisions? No wonder Mrs. Woodwake wanted no questions or talk."

"Too late now," said Brook. He finished his tea. "Mind you, if this is true, that woman is exceptionally dangerous to foreign nations. They wouldn't want an outsider becoming privy to their plans."

"If they're aware she exists. For all we know, they could have their own Seers."

"Now you're going from the terrifying to the monstrous, Miss Pendlebury. The governments of the world influenced by such women, all playing a vast and mad chess match?"

"It is possible," she said in a quiet tone. "It need not be mad, but for the good of the country. Think of the last forty years since the queen took the throne. They've been the most peaceful in English history."

"But we've armies in place throughout the empire. They deal with skirmishes all the time."

"Yet no major wars. Not like stopping the Armada or defeating Napoleon. Our last great battle was at Waterloo."

"Attribute that to excellent diplomacy."

"We didn't have diplomats in place when the Americans were in the middle of that slavery war. English mills were howling for cotton from their southern region and urging us to side with them and lend aid."

"Which we did not."

"It was a close thing, though. What would the outcome have been if we'd allied with a slave-holding nation in a war against the northern half of America?"

"I expect life would be much the same."

"Not if our respective fathers had participated in the fighting and been killed, changing things for their families. Neither of us would be here."

Brook gave this some consideration. "Perhaps it's better to not worry about might-have-beens and focus on what is at hand."

She decided he was right. Just thinking about it got her overwound. How much worse was it for Sybil? Was that even her real name? "Sybil called my father 'the traveler.' I think it confirms he was doing work for the Home Office."

"How do you come to that conclusion?"

"Fingate told me. He said it was something delicate. . . . I probably shouldn't say more until I've spoken to Mrs. Woodwake. We should go now."

He rose and saw to her chair and gathered the bag, along with her father's walking stick, and followed her out.

A lex's office door was open, its usual state. She shared with three other Readers and people were constantly in and out. Miss Heather Fagan, the youngest and newest of their group, and thus relegated to working on holidays, was at her desk. She was a pretty girl with sharply defined features, fair skin, stubbornly curly dark hair, and remarkably bright clear eyes. Those were focused on a large, complicated machine on the desk before her. It was black, box-shaped, and looked heavy, producing a clacking noise as Heather's long fingers stabbed at small disks on stalks extending from the main body.

She bounced to her feet and gave a wide smile as Alex and Brook came in. "Alex! You must see! It finally arrived!"

Her excitement struck Alex like a large happy puppy. It made a change from darker emotions, but she had to brace herself to move forward. "Your new toy?"

"This 'toy' will be a revolution, you mark me. Oh, Hallo, Mr. Brook. What a shambles you are. Been working?"

"Yes, Miss Fagan. It's been interesting."

Alex was glad to be spared from making another introduction, but wondered how the two had come to meet. Heather would doubtless inform her later; at the moment the younger woman was too distracted by the machine. The floor around her desk was obscured by the remains of a crate, drifts of excelsior, and crumpled newspaper. A hammer and jimmy, weapons used in what had clearly been a violent assault, were on Alex's desk.

"It was here when I came in," said Heather. "Just arrived on one of the freight airships—all the way from America."

"That great beast? What it must weigh!" Alex had no idea what the conveyance cost might be, only that it would start at "exorbitant" and go up from there. Heather came from a wealthy, not merely well off, family. When the Service did not apportion money for her obsessions, she used her own. That she'd chosen swift but expensive air travel over a slower and less risky steamship was typical of her natural impatience.

"I'll never have to bother with ink and pen again," she said.

"You've had typing machines in before," said Alex. This one looked like those made in England, perhaps less aesthetically pleasing with most of its works showing. The thing would the very devil to dust, if it lasted more than a week.

"This one's *much* better; the Americans have perfected it." Heather twisted a roller on the top, releasing a sheet of paper. "Look at that! It's like having your own printing press."

Alex cast an eye over the sheet. "Certainly an improvement over your handwriting."

"It's not as fast as writing something out, but I expect to improve with practice, rather like learning the piano. Once I know where all the letters are I shall type-write everything."

"You'll only ever be able to work on reports here. You can't possibly carry this to an investigation." Alex attempted to lift one corner and barely shifted the behemoth.

"Trust you to find the weak point in a marvelous invention, but I've thought of that already. I shall take notes as usual but type full reports here. Of course, once I'm proficient I'll be finished in half the time."

"Unless you're tempted to add in more details."

"Bother you! This is so much better than the other machines. It has upper- and lowercase letters, and you can see the paper as you type. Such an obvious thing, that. After all, one really should know where one is in a sentence." She put a new sheet of paper in, the roller executing a complicated thread-ing maneuver, then haltingly typed the alphabet.

Brook watched with interest. "The letters are jumbled on the-the—"

"Keys," Miss Fagan said, now typing numbers, which were set out in order along the top row. "The letters used the most often are in the middle where the strongest fingers may strike them—or so I've read. I must disagree with the placement of the letter 'a' though. My little finger slips right between it and 's' and gets stuck if I don't look."

"It's noisier than pen and ink," Alex pointed out, going to her own desk.

"I *like* the sound. Makes me feel as though I'm *doing* some-thing. And my hand doesn't get cramped from holding a pen for hours. The ends of my fingers are a bit numb, but that's better than a cramp." She noticed Alex assembling pen, ink, and paper. "What are you going to write?"

"A scene report." Alex wouldn't get much of it done, but she could make a start. She shifted the hammer and jimmy out of the way.

"I'll help! You dictate and I'll type."

"Another time? Please."

Heather's enthusiasm faltered. "What's happened? Oh no, someone's died."

Readers really should have separate offices, thought Alex. "It's a scene report, of course someone's died."

"Someone you *know.*"

It was impossible to hide anything from a Reader. Alex gave up. "Yes."

Heather abandoned the machine and came around, reach-ing out, but not touching. "Oh, Alex, I'm so sorry. Who?"

"I'm not allowed to talk about it. Not yet."

"One of ours?"

"I'm not allow—"

"Is it to do with what's going on? With everyone getting called in today? I had to be here, and it was quiet until a few hours ago. No one seems to know why and they're annoyed about it. Mrs. George organized a Christmas dinner, but that's not the same as being home with one's family."

Depends on the family, Alex thought. "I expect we'll find out soon enough."

Mr. Humboldt Sexton rapped on the doorframe to announce himself. "Hallo, all. Miss Pendlebury?"

Time to face consequences. "Yes. I'll go along now. What sort of mood is she in?" Alex quit her desk.

Sexton blinked as he moved out of her path. "Um . . . distracted? I should tread lightly."

"Who? What?" demanded Heather. "It's to do with what's going on, isn't it?"

"Can't really talk about it, Miss Fagan, sorry." He turned to Brook. "Hallo, we've not been properly introduced. . . ."

Alex left them to it and hurried down the hall and up one flight of stairs. She noticed, with strange irritation, that the blue of her dress clashed with the pale blue walls. Why would something as silly as that even come to her notice?

Because what awaits is likely to be unpleasant and you want the diversion.

Fair enough.

Woodwake's door was open. Alex knocked on the frame and went in.

"Close that, if you please," said Mrs. Woodwake. "Turn the sign."

A card hanging from a string tacked to the wall outside bore the declaration *No Interruptions,* which usually meant a Reading was in session. She flipped it around and softly shut the door.

CHAPTER SEVEN

*In Which Miss Pendlebury Makes
a Decision and a Discovery*

The office was the same size as Alex's but seemed larger with a single desk and occupant. The one tall window looked out on the Thames, visible through the bare winter branches of the trees on the Embankment. The river was the usual dull brown, its flat flow supporting a variety of boats and barges. To the right was a glimpse of Westminster Bridge. Woodwake faced away from the view, which put her figure in silhouette. She gestured at a chair opposite the desk, and Alex took it, aware that the light from the window was full upon her. She used such methods herself when interviewing people in the aftermath of a crime. Reading involved more than sensing another's emotions; one had to study their features. The least twitch of the mouth, the slightest tilt of the head, any number of things helped to reveal what lay behind the eyes.

It wasn't quite as bad as she'd anticipated. Delivering her report had a strange cathartic effect, lifting a portion of weight from her shoulders. Alex kept to the essentials of cold fact about the Harley Street murder room and did not allow emotion to color her narration. Now did she mention getting Fingate's note, and the reaction was as she'd expected. Woodwake demanded to know why she was hearing of it only now.

"I am sorry, ma'am. I was about to inform you and Lord Richard in the coach when the shooting started. I didn't remember again until much later when I was on my way to Pendlebury House with Inspector Lennon."

"You should have sent a message to me about it."

"Yes, ma'am. No excuses. I should have done that."

"Did you then meet this man, this suspect in your own father's murder?"

"He did not do it, and yes, I did meet him."

"Where is he?"

"I don't know."

"Please explain why."

Alex did so, recalling in detail the conversation on the Serpentine Bridge. She stressed the fact that Fingate was in the throes of a profound fear and not thinking straight. "I entreated him in the strongest terms to come with me to the Service offices. . . ."

Then she had to relate the incident of tackling Brook and the nearly fatal outcome of that debacle. Alex tried not to feel too much the fool. It had been an accident, after all.

There was, however, some satisfaction to be had at seeing Woodwake's jaw drop.

Alex expected a question or comment at that point, but neither came. She continued, touching on, in the briefest terms, the conversation she'd had in the coach with Mr. Brook. This fleshed out the context around Sybil's word-for-word echo of what he'd said.

"Is her name really Sybil? Or is it a title taken from the Oracle of Delphi?"

Woodwake shook her head, not as a reply, but in exasperation, and ignored the question. "I am not happy with you. Consider that to be a great understatement. You could have been killed."

"But I was not, thanks to Mr. Brook."

"*He* could have been killed. What if he'd been injured in the fall? You've a responsibility to your colleagues as well as to the Service. You took it upon yourself to meet with this Fingate, putting yourself and others in peril. I'm not talking about your near drowning, though that's bad enough. Those bloody madmen with air guns are still out there and so is this 'ghost' that you could sense only by his lack of a trail. By your account he murdered your father and was lying in wait in your own home, yet you slip away alone—"

"I had to. Mr. Fingate—"

"Will be located in due time by the police."

"I think not, ma'am. He is singularly resourceful."

"I'll grant that, but you are not thinking things through."

"Progress was made. I *Read* him. He spoke the truth. My father was inquiring into something delicate for the Home Office—those are Fingate's very words. He was told the only person he could trust was Lord Richard. Father impressed upon Mr. Fingate the necessity of trusting no one else, and that is why he's hiding. At some point he will contact me again, I'm sure of it. He knows I work here; this is the most likely place to get a message to me."

Woodwake gave a ladylike snort. "I suppose the man cannot be blamed for obeying his master, but he should have had the wit to stay with you."

"He was overwrought about Father's death and the Ætheric Society. One of the last things Father did was go to one of their meetings. Some woman was helping him—or so Mr. Fingate related. We must find where this meeting took place and who this woman might be."

"If not for the fact that a man is dead—"

"Two men, ma'am."

"Yes. Two deaths. If not for . . ." She shook her head. "It's utterly absurd. The Ætherics are a joke, a bad one."

"But what if they're not? What if there *is* something dangerous about them?"

"We are aware that the Ætherics are rather more than what they present to the public, but they're no threat except to themselves."

"But if so, then why is the Home Office interested in them?"

"Perhaps they're concerned with members of the government being subjected to blackmail, should any be foolish enough to join that so-called society. Some particulars about it are . . . distasteful."

"More than my Reading a room with my father's corpse hanging from—" Alex stopped. Anger would not progress things.

Woodwake frowned, but not unkindly. "I am sorry for your loss. I know this is difficult, but be aware that I am trying to protect you. Extraordinary events have overtaken us, and until we have a better idea of what's behind them, I must be cautious. It will be a trial to your patience and inclinations, but it is necessary."

"Is learning additional information about the Ætherics likely to be a danger to me?"

"Girl, you should have read law."

"I might have, if not for this damnable 'gift' of mine."

"And if not for mine, I should have . . . Well, I'd be anywhere in the world but here, and glad of it."

There were far worse places than a dim office by the Thames, but Alex knew better than to gainsay her.

Mrs. Woodwake shot her a look, as though picking up the thought, then shook her head. "All right, reports in the general press about the Ætherics may mention scholarly papers on esoteric topics. Members don robes and enact commemorative rituals celebrating 'High Masters' passing down great wisdom from some location in the Æther, wherever that might be. They enact elaborate magical rituals as well, which is enough to dismiss them as silly eccentrics. They don't hide any of that."

"So I've read in the library." ˙

"At first and even second glance, they are ridiculous. The only danger they present is embarrassment to themselves. Some members boast their association and thrive on the notoriety, while others are secretive, lest they suffer socially or financially from it, though the latter is unlikely. Ætherics tend to give preference to the wealthy when it comes to invitations to their meetings."

"That would describe my father's impersonation of

'Dr. Kemp,' posing as a physician made wealthy by a patent nostrum."

"So it would seem. Now, we move to things that are not in the files. Miss Pendlebury, just how worldly are you? Notwithstanding your travels about the globe, what do you know about the nature of men?"

"I don't understand the question."

"Men have appetites and desires, and even beloved fathers are not immune to the demands of the flesh."

Alex gaped at her, too shocked to draw breath.

"The hidden side of the Ætheric Society are the special meetings that take place in private houses. Those gatherings are open to a select few who have the means and mind to pay for certain services that are there rendered."

"Services? Like a brothel?"

Woodwake grimaced, her ears going pink. "Exactly like a brothel, but dressed up in robes and with chanting. I am inclined to think that your father made a visit to the Ætheric Society for a baser purpose than to act as an agent for the Home Office."

Understanding came in a flash. "I won't believe that!"

"It is a more logical conclusion than them being a threat to queen and country. To save face in front of his manservant your father gave him to think he was investigating something important. It sounds better than to admit attending a Christmas Eve debauchery held by a bizarre remnant of the old Hellfire Club. As for this woman he mentioned, one could consider that she was hired for the occasion, though I've heard that some female members of the Ætherics are known to voluntarily fill such roles as required by their . . . rituals."

Seething, Alex had to fight to keep from leaping up to strike the woman. She'd not been this angry in years. "How dare you?" she finally whispered.

Mrs. Woodwake remained silent, watching with a calm eye.

Alex pulled into herself, slamming the rage down and

thinking, thinking. There was more going on here than this woman casting aspersions on the character of Lord Gerard Pendlebury. Woodwake was Reading her, of course, and the process often involved provoking the one under scrutiny.

"This is a diversion," she pronounced, strangely reassured. "You know what's true and what is not about Fingate's story."

"I know that you believed him and if you Read him accurately, then he believed his master, but that doesn't mean Lord Gerard was being truthful with him or that there's anything more sinister afoot."

"Begging pardon, ma'am, but there *must* be or my father would never have been murdered. You made mention yourself of blackmail. That could well be the 'delicate matter.' Why else would Father adopt such an elaborate disguise?"

"The answer to that will doubtless be discovered in due course. Be confident that our best people are looking into everything concerning this case. The house servants, the neighbors, anyone your father had the least association with as Dr. Kemp, are under full scrutiny. We *will* find who is responsible."

Alex picked up on the truth of that statement. While it was heartening, she was still annoyed over Woodwake's attempt at provocation. *I should have seen it coming, but then I'm used to delivering, not receiving.* There was nothing more to be gained on that subject, though. Time to try another direction. "What about Lord Richard? Are the cases connected?"

"I cannot talk to you about it. You are removed from the first because of your relation to the victim and from the second because you are a witness. It would be a conflict of interest for you to participate in that investigation."

"But you're also a witness."

"I am, and therefore I am also off the second case."

That was unexpected. Considering her temperament, Woodwake would have insisted on being in the thick of things or knowing the reason why. Alex tried to come up with any name in the Service's limited hierarchy who would be senior enough for the job. "Who's taken charge of it, then?"

"Not your concern or mine."

"It is being seen to, is it not?"

"Of course it is."

Woodwake again spoke truthfully and with impatience, but Alex sensed something hidden. If she'd been the one conducting the Reading, she'd have pounced on it. A less direct approach was required.

"With regard to my father, Sybil called him 'the traveler,' and if she is a Seer, then that's important. Of all the people in this building, *I* am the one she sought out and spoke to."

"That's not your—"

"If it's not my concern, then it certainly must be yours. Allow me to help. That's why I'm here."

Woodwake's lips parted as though to reply. Alex's barriers were down and she felt an unpleasant emotional twinge from the woman, like an instrument out of tune. Woodwake was not merely uneasy, she was deeply frightened. That was unexpected, and at odds with her outwardly cool manner. It lasted but an instant, then she regained control. "I am aware of that. But for now, other business must be sorted out first. There's the matter of your delay in reporting that message from Fingate."

Alex couldn't believe she was still considering such a minor issue. *It's another diversion.*

"You will face disciplinary action on that, but not today. For the present, I require that you make your written report—in detail—and do what Sybil told you in regard to keeping your head down and mouth shut."

"And eyes open."

"Don't press me, girl. *Think.* The unknown person who killed your father was waiting in your home for your return. He is a real threat to your life. You must impress upon yourself that you are in danger and like to remain so until he is caught."

"I am cogent of the danger, ma'am, but I want to find him."

"Of course you do, but my duty is to keep you safe. Reason things out. If his purpose was to kill you as well—then why? So far as he knew, he murdered a man named Kemp. You've no connection to *him*. Therefore, he knew Kemp to be Pendlebury."

"But why kill Father? He'd been away from England for years."

"So far as you know."

"Indeed. But if so, then why kill me? Ma'am, is there *any* information from the Home Office yet on what he was doing? I don't ask for details, only to know if there's been progress."

"It's too soon to say."

Which did not answer the question. "Will you let me know when there is progress?"

"I will consider it, providing you do as instructed. Do not disappoint me. Finish your report, then take a coach home to Pendlebury House and stay there. We'll have at least two men on watch at all times."

"If it's a question of my safety, then is this not a far better place for me? I've no wish to put my uncle's family at risk by my presence, and I expect those men can be used elsewhere. The apprentices' dormitory will have a spare bed."

Woodwake pinched the bridge of her nose.

"I can be of use here, especially when you break the news about Lord Richard. I'll be one of the few who won't be in shock."

"W-what?" She looked up.

Alex felt a wash of . . . panic? She wasn't sure, the emotion was too fleeting and instantly smothered. "Has the queen been informed yet?"

When the woman's face flushed a deep, dangerous red, Alex knew that she'd pressed too far and had been caught out. The Reading in this session was to be one-sided. Woodwake stood and pointed to the door, apparently too angry to speak.

Alex left and hoped it didn't look too much like a flying

rout. It felt like one. She made it downstairs before realizing she'd been holding her breath and had to hang onto the stair rail to recover. Her head felt squeezed, turned inside out. An ordinary interview wouldn't have that kind of effect on her; Woodwake was just bloody intimidating. But for all that, what had her so afraid?

Anything to do with Lord Richard.

Why?

Cold logic led Alex to wonder if the woman had aught to do with his death. Such fear . . . of what? Being discovered? Alex had dealt with that on more than one murder case. The guilty were always terrified of being found out.

However, it was highly improbable. Woodwake had been in the coach with the first attack and equally vulnerable to being shot along with Lord Richard and Alex. The second attack at James's house was more questionable. The hooded men had focused their fire on Richard, but aimed more or less over the heads of everyone else in the room, at least until others in the house began firing back. Woodwake had done so. Had she hit any? Yes, certainly one, perhaps more. Alex had been busy ducking.

Absurd. Mrs. Woodwake's loyalty to the Service was above question. Some other reason lay behind this oddness.

Might she have had a personal attachment to Lord Richard? Something stronger than the friendship of colleagues? If so, then she was more likely to be engulfed by grief, not fear. She'd want that kept private, but was it enough to account for that level of fear?

And I dared to Read her, spoke in that manner to her. Alex would be lucky if she still had a place here come Boxing Day.

If I am dismissed, then what?

She couldn't and would not think that far ahead. First the report, then—

Not to Pendlebury House. At least not directly. There was a special line of inquiry she wanted to make about those air guns, and getting there wouldn't be too great a detour. It was direct disobedience to orders, but bother that. No one would blame her for trying to turn up useful information.

A deep and distant clarion sounded, carrying through the walls. Tolling from Westminster, Big Ben gave the hour to anyone within hearing: two o'clock. The short winter daylight would be gone altogether by the time she finished writing that report. She did not care for the idea of a coach trip after dark, either. Best to postpone one and expedite the other.

Alex had her plans sorted by the time she returned to her office.

Sexton was gone, along with Mr. Brook, which was disappointing, but Heather Fagan remained, still playing with her new toy. She'd removed a flat spool that trailed a black ribbon halfway across the office to the window. Alex knew the ribbon held some import in the printing operation.

"Problem?" she asked.

"Just seeing how it works," Heather replied. "I should have ordered extra ribbons. It will be a bother when this one wears out of ink." Much of that substance had transferred to Heather's fingers, so it wouldn't be long. "I might be able to roll another ribbon in if I can find similar-size ones made here."

Alex's desk was as she'd left it, but now her father's walking stick lay on it. She'd not left it there. The carpetbag with her damp clothes was in the corner out of the way. "Where did Mr. Brook get to?"

"Off to the bog, I expect. Not that he said it in so many words, but I got a bit of anxiousness from him."

Alex had attended to that necessity on her way back.

"And Mr. Sexton?"

"Who knows? He was unsettled, but not showing it much—rather the way you are now. Peeled your skin, did our Mrs. Woodwake?"

"It wasn't so bad, just a report."

"That you can't talk about."

"That I can't talk about."

"Well—rot on it. There's too many secrets in this place. Everyone wants to know why we're here and those at the top aren't sharing. Much more of this waiting and there will be a mutiny."

Alex debated ordering a pot of tea. The interview with Woodwake, the day's harrowing events, and lack of sleep were catching her up. She was about to ring for one of the pages when her attention caught on the walking stick's sliver trim: a detail that should not have been there.

An extra band had been added; indistinguishable in style from the original work, it stood out to her eye. There had to be a reason for her father to make such a change.

She found her gloves and pulled them on, not wanting another emotional jar, and picked it up. A swift and firm twist caused the stick to separate into two parts. The additional band hid the seam. The upper portion was hollowed out, and within the cavity was a scrap of paper rolled tight to fit. She coaxed it free with a letter opener.

"What's that? A calling card?" Heather asked.

"Apparently." Alex fitted the two cane parts together again.

"Clever place to hide things. I've an uncle with a stick that serves as a sort of elongated brandy flask. He likes to think no one knows about it."

On one side of the card was a name in the delicate cursive script favored by the finer printing shops, *Rosalind Veltre,* on the other, in pencil, *25 Grosvenor Sq. 8:30—"Masters Impart."* The writing was not her father's.

Alex forgot about tea, slipped the stick under the papers, and made her way to the file rooms. The main room was long and narrow; a line of card drawers took up the center and banks of files lined the walls. All of Alex's investigation reports were here, along with all the others conducted by her colleagues. The service was a great one for keeping detailed records.

She opened the card drawer for "V" and with considerable satisfaction found one for Mrs. Rosalind Veltre, her name neatly printed at the top and under it the numbers to indicate which file report contained her information.

The lack of content in the file sheaf was a disappointment:

ROSALIND VELTRE, b. 1851, London. Res. 3 Hill Street, Mayfair, London.

Widow of Thurman Veltre, Esq. 1840–1875, burst appendix, interred Highgate Cemetery.

Began attending séances 1876, approx. Favored those held by "Madam Szakaly." See file #M272.

Member of the Ætheric Society, 1877, approx. Attends public lectures and private parties.

Attached to the page, a clipping from *The Times* proved to be Mr. Veltre's obituary. He had been a solicitor with Veltre, Veltre and Caldershot and was survived by a number of relatives.

Mrs. Veltre would have to be well off to afford such a fashionable resting place for her husband and thus be of interest to the Ætherics. It was clear how the lady's path had taken her to them. Bereaved widows were bread and dripping for thousands of mediums plying their trade throughout England. The Psychical Fraud Section was always busy.

Should Woodwake be correct that the private parties were some form of debauch, then was Veltre a hapless victim gulled into acceptance or a willing participant? Alex had no illusions about her sex being passive when it came to certain activities of the body. Women were just as easily tempted by the demands and desires of the flesh as men.

But this was pure speculation. It was a capital mistake to weave possibilities out of imaginings, not facts, and there were few of those as yet. Rosalind Veltre was a cipher. *Why had Father been interested in her? What if she had not been helping him? What if she had aided in bringing about his murder?*

There was but one certain way to discover that.

Alex made note of the address, shut the file drawer, and held the briefest of inner debates about mentioning this to Woodwake.

Not in the humor she's in.

Woodwake would send someone else to question Rosalind Veltre and see to it Alex was physically hauled away to Pendlebury House.

No, thank you.

Alex had places to go first.

Mr. Brook was in her office again, combed and shaved, wearing a proper suit with a well-cut frock coat and polished boots, and carrying a top hat. Alex stopped in the doorway, taken aback by the transformation. He looked the gentleman and stood when he saw her.

"Miss Pendlebury."

"Mr. Brook. Heading home?"

He showed puzzlement.

"You've been on duty since last night," she reminded.

"So have you."

She took her cloak from a peg behind her desk and settled it on her shoulders. Her reticule was where she'd left it, heavy with the pistol inside. "I'm about to leave. Mrs. Woodwake ordered me back to Pendlebury House."

"Then I'll escort you."

That wouldn't do. She wanted a driver who wouldn't question her detours. "Most kind, but I don't think—"

"Alex!" Heather spoke from behind her typing machine. More parts had been liberated from it. Her face was smudged with ink, her hands black as a coal miner's. "Mr. Brook would like the pleasure of escorting you home. He would be greatly disappointed if you denied him such a small boon."

Brook cleared his throat. "Uh-hm, that is to say . . ."

Alex felt herself flush pink, possibly a florid red at the implications behind that boon. They'd been talking about her.

Heather, a forward young lady, was much given to speaking her mind, however socially awkward it might prove. She possessed a hearty disdain for consequences.

But I do not want a gentleman caller! Certainly not now.

Heather arched one eyebrow and fixed her with a glare. Alex instantly recognized the threat. Heather had picked up on her swoop of panic and would inform Brook about it unless—

"Thank you, Mr. Brook. I would welcome a little quiet company." There, a conditional compromise. He could not possibly expect more, given the circumstances.

Brook fetched Alex's carpetbag. "What's happened to the walking stick? I left it propped against the wall."

"You left it on the desk," said Heather, whose attention was back on the machine. "Alex was fiddling with it."

"But I—" He bit off the rest, looking uncomfortable.

Another precognitive occurrence?

"Interesting," said Alex, echoing Woodwake's assessment.

"Not to me," he muttered.

If he hadn't left it there, she'd not have found the calling card, not as quickly anyway.

"What a deuced inconvenience," he added as they went downstairs.

"I feel the same way about my so-called gift," she said.

"But you have control of yours. The devilry about mine is not being aware of it."

"Manifested early, did it?"

"No. Last year I took a knock with a polo mallet, fell off the horse, and haven't been the same since. That is, I recovered in body, but this . . . it started just afterward."

"Unusual. Most people are born to it, but a few are made."

"I'd like it unmade. More than once I've thought of giving myself another clout to see if it would cure me, but I might wake up and be even worse off."

"It takes time to adjust."

"So I've been told."

He did not seem in the right mood to suggest that with training he might learn to control the ability. Another day would suit better.

Mrs. George still commanded the reception area, which was crowded with people demanding to know when they were to be allowed to leave.

"It's been hours," complained someone at the back.

"And it may be hours more," she said with the weariness that comes from repetition. "Until then, make yourselves useful and do something else besides this botheration."

Alex took the lead, going around rather than through them—and stopped dead.

Sybil, minus her caretaker, stood with her back to the front entry. Pale face consumed by an unsettling grin, she put a finger to her lips. "Pie hole *shut*," she whispered.

A number of thoughts on how to deal with the situation galloped through Alex's head. She fell back on instinct and nodded. "Ears open, head down?"

"Yessssss!" Sybil responded, mad eyes bright. She stepped back, bumped against the doors, and walked out, backward.

Unlike the incident in the dining hall, no one seemed to have noticed her presence.

Alex followed, half terrified, half fascinated. She wanted to bolt, she really did. The woman continued to walk backward, negotiating a step down to the sidewalk as though she could see it. She continued along, heading toward the street. Alex rushed to catch her up.

"I'm sure it's much too cold," she called out. "You've forgotten your coat."

"Haven't got one. They keep me like a hothouse orchid, but I want to have a walk. This is *fresh*!" she declared, stretching her arms. She'd stopped inches short of a low stone balustrade that served to separate the Service's entrance from the public sidewalk.

Brook looked to Alex for some hint of what was needed, but she was at a loss. Getting Sybil inside seemed the thing to do, but how to accomplish that did not suggest itself. The woman was in the throes of an unsettling giddiness. That could change in a blink. Reason and respect might work.

"You'll be able to stay out longer with a coat. I know where we can borrow one."

"What color? Oh, never mind. I like this!" She turned slowly in place. "Yes! What's *next* to the blackness, traveler's daughter. You were clever to suggest that. Can't look for long or *it* will know. I saw what's reflected in one mirror, just-just-just the one."

"What did you see?"

"Not enough, of course. It's never enough or it's too much, each a tiny bit different and all bad. You told him how it is." She pointed at Brook.

"I should like to hear more," he said. "Over a cup of tea?"

"Whiskey's better. The traveler's daughter will need some soon." She looked past him toward a muffled and cloaked man strolling their way from the south.

Alex started, wishful hope making her think it was Fingate for an instant, but this man was taller with a different gait. He gave them no notice and turned for the entry, not in a hurry, but not wasting time, yet another member of the Service called in on the holiday.

"Bad news," said Sybil. "Very bad news."

From the pocket of her dress she removed a small pistol and, showing no hesitation, shot the man squarely in the back.

CHAPTER EIGHT

In Which the Law Is Violated. Several Times.

The weapon made a businesslike snapping sound, like dry wood breaking. His momentum took him a few unsteady steps, then he toppled and lay twitching.

Alex gasped in horrified shock and froze, training forgotten.

Brook surged forward and took the weapon from Sybil. It proved to be a single-shot Derringer and God knows how the woman had gotten it. Weapons were kept in Service offices, but locked up.

The man's cloak had flapped wide when he fell. Grasped in his right hand was the gleaming shape of a strange-looking pistol with a long thin barrel and a bulky tube above the trigger.

"Head down," Sybil intoned.

Gaping at what must be a smaller version of one of those deadly air rifles, Alex felt blank lunacy seize her. She responded: "Ears open?"

"No. Head. Down. They're here." Sybil abruptly dropped flat.

Brook grabbed Alex. For the second time within four and twenty hours, she experienced the shock of a man throwing himself over her body.

The air whooped from her lungs, curtailing immediate protest. She struggled to move, but he had her pinned, face to the cold walkway. A scant foot from her nose she saw a piece of the pavement the size of a shilling vanish in a tiny cracking

explosion. There had been no sound of a shot, but the rico-
chet was distinct enough.

Air gun.

Bloody hell.

They were behind the questionable cover of the knee-high
balustrade, which was better than nothing, but bullets began
smacking into the barrier like horizontal hail.

"Back inside," said Brook. "I'll cover." He shifted from
her, rolling once and pulling a revolver from his coat pocket.
Between themselves and the doors lay thirty feet of open
space. It might as well have been thirty miles.

"You've five shots and that Bulldog is only good at close
range," Alex said. She got her own revolver, a breakfront
Webley, from her reticule. "Where are they?"

"Can't tell, no sound, no muzzle flash or smoke." He
flinched as a bullet whizzed overhead, shattering a glass panel
in one of the entry doors. Someone ventured to look out. Brook
bellowed a warning. Another bullet followed, breaking more
glass, and whoever was inside ducked away with a curse.

A pause came in the hail strikes; Alex risked peering between the fat columns supporting the top of the barrier.
Amazingly, people strolled along Parliament Street unaware.
Carriages rolled past, carrying revelers. She heard drunken
laughter and song. When a hansom heading north cleared the
entrance to Downing Street across the way, a bullet winged
off the pavement. She sighted along the barrel of her Webley,
waiting for the shooter to show himself around the corner.

A shot pocked the stone barrier above her head.

"Two of them," she said. "The near corner of Downing and
to the right, behind that tree."

Sybil added, somewhat muffled: "Head. Down."

"It's impossible," said Brook. "We can't shoot back with
the street so busy."

"We use that. They hold fire when something's in the way.
Wait until both are obscured and run."

"Head down, down, downdown*down*," Sybil insisted, peevish.

"Or perhaps not."

"What?" he asked.

"She wants us to stay here. She can see the future, perhaps—"

"Miss Pendlebury, I have little confidence in that."

"Fell off the horse and haven't been the same since," Sybil told him in a scolding tone.

"Then again . . ."

"Hallo out there!" called someone from the building. One of the doors was open a crack.

Alex forced herself to keep low. "Mrs. George! We're being shot at!"

"We worked that out, dearie. Help's on the way!"

Brook yelled the probable location of the shooters.

"I'll pass the word," she said. "Mind you, there's—"

They missed the rest when a number of bullets slammed into the remaining glass panels, shattering them. Mrs. George squawked and removed herself from the area.

More than two were engaged in the assault now. Where the devil were they?

Alex's heart gave a leap of hope when she saw three men threading through the trees from the Richmond Terrace end of the building . . . until she realized they weren't Service, but wearing hooded cloaks, carrying their peculiar weapons at the ready. She suspected the rifles were not as accurate as their noisier percussive cousins and that closer range was needed. She and her companions had no cover from that direction.

But from her angle the three were apart from passersby. Alex brought her Webley around, sighted, and fired at the closest man, who strode forward boldly, his rifle up and aimed right at her.

She'd missed, but he stopped in his tracks, apparently surprised at a show of deadly resistance. That made her second shot easier, and she did not flinch. He dropped, and his two companions faltered in their forward progress, staring at him.

Brook's short-barrel Bulldog gave a loud, sharp bark for its size. He also missed, but the noise had a discouraging influence; they began backing away.

Alex sighted on one of them, but a different pistol above and to the side spoke first. He staggered, giving a surprised grunt before falling. Several upper-floor windows in the Service building were open, and people fired from them.

The third fellow coolly raised his weapon. No sound came from it, nor was there any sign of recoil. The only way to tell if it fired was when a bullet struck. She shot at him, but he seemed unconcerned, perhaps counting on distance and her shaking hand to keep him safe.

It was a poor choice. Her next shot brought him down.

The people in the windows aimed at targets across the street, shooting over the heads of pedestrians—who, alarmed by the unexpected row of gunfire, began sensibly hurrying away.

Service members seemed to run out of bullets at once. Reloading would take precious seconds. Alex tensed and bolted, not for the entry—it was too much in the open—but toward the three fallen men. She'd get one of those damned rifles or die trying.

Brook shouted after her, but she was away, skirts held high. She made it to one of the trees and paused behind it to gauge distance.

The hooded figure around the corner of Downing Street stepped out and called an order to cohorts scattered along Whitehall. They snapped to and made a firing line, aiming at the Service building and the balustrade. If they had sufficient ammunition, it was a certainty that bullets would strike home between the squat columns. Brook and Sybil had no chance against that. Alex had two rounds left and was in a good spot to take out the leader of the assault. If he fell the others might run.

Unfortunately, he was also in a good spot to take *her* out. His rifle muzzle was pointed straight at her and if he fired, she did not hear, but something struck the tree at the level of her head. She braced her revolver against the trunk, allowed for distance and . . .

Too far to the right and too high to judge by the pockmark appearing in the building behind him.

Her last bullet. Again, she allowed for error . . . and missed.

He stalked forward, ignoring all else, shot after shot striking the tree or sheering past. She could stay pinned or be a moving target. The longer she delayed, the closer he got, the better chance he had to—

Then came the powerful and distinctive *crack* of a rifle.

The man's relentless forward progress stopped. He rocked on his heels.

The *crack* repeated, and he fell heavily in the middle of the now deserted street.

She knew that sound; there was nothing else quite like the no-nonsense report of an American Winchester.

The shot came from a top-floor window of the Service building. The shootist had command of the field and took full advantage of it.

The *crack* repeated many times, the authoritative sound echoing off buildings and sending civilian stragglers shrieking for cover. Cloaked and hooded men fell, one after another in the space of seconds.

Silence for a moment: even Winchesters had to be reloaded.

Three cowering survivors seized the pause to escape, running north toward Whitehall.

Alex completed her dash, grabbed an air gun, ignoring the groaning and bloodied man on the ground near it. She hurried back to Brook, who was yet behind the low barrier. She counted softly, estimating how long it would take the rifleman on the top floor to reload.

He was quicker than she'd hoped. Two more shots: the farthest runner stumbled forward and fell, then the second farthest. The last cast away his weapon, yelling and waving his hands in surrender, but kept going. His right leg went out from under him. Rolling in the street, he howled and clutched his backside through his cloak.

From the top window, the shootist boomed a triumphant *"Hah!"* It, too, echoed off the buildings.

"Bloody hell," Brook said, staring up. "Who's the madman?"

"Be glad he's on our side. That's Colonel Mourne."

"Good God."

"Wrath of God, more like."

"The Colonel Mourne is . . . is with the Psychic Service?"

"As an advisor."

"He's supposed to be the best shot in England."

"I think he proved that just now." She looked down. "Sybil? Are you all right?"

The woman, lying on her back on cold, wet pavement, grinned at her. "Now *that's* an outing!"

Colonel Mourne called to them. "You three fools in front, get inside. I'll keep the rabbits from popping from their holes—if any are left!"

Sybil immediately bounced up. "They're gone. No more rabbits!"

"You sure about that, missy?"

She adopted the tone of a petulant schoolgirl. "Yes, Colonel. Gone-gone-gone." Sybil spun once in place and abruptly wrested the air gun from Alex's grasp. "Silent death, but not today. Not for us—it's Christmas!" She whooped and spun again, laughing.

"Allow me," said Brook, attempting to ease it from her.

"You can't carry *this* in your pocket," she informed him and thrust it back at Alex. "Under your cloak, there's a good tweak."

Alex didn't know what else to do with the thing. She put the fat stock awkwardly under one arm, the muzzle pointing downward. Her cloak fell into place, covering everything.

Sybil gestured west. "Be in a place that isn't here—make yourselves useful and do something else besides this botheration." She gave an exact impersonation of Mrs. George.

"We have to go back," said Alex, picking up her reticule.

She fixed Alex with a look. "*You* go forward. *I* do what's backward." So saying, she trotted off, still facing them, to the entrance. She avoided the body of the man she'd shot, went up the step without turning, and vanished inside.

"Were those orders?" Brook asked.

"I believe so. But for me. You stay here and report. I'll find my way home."

"Excuse me, Miss Pendlebury, but I don't believe you, and I'm coming along." He got her carpetbag.

"Lieutenant Brook, you're witness to a shooting battle just steps from the PM's house, there's more than a dozen dead and wounded up and down Whitehall—Mrs. Woodwake is going to want to know what happened."

"She can hear it from Sybil and good luck to her. If you're leaving, then do so before someone comes to stop you."

Argument meant delay, so Alex set a smart pace toward Richmond Terrace. Porters now looked after the two wounded on that side; the third man had a handkerchief over his features.

"Is that one you got?"

She shook her head. "Not that I wasn't trying to kill them."

"You've done this sort of thing before."

"Not in London."

They put more distance behind, passing Scotland Yard. Several constables were about, staring north. "Wot's 'appened?" one demanded of them.

"Don't know," Brook answered.

" 'Ere, is that you, Miss Pendlebury?"

"I think so," she said, not stopping. "Have to go, Service business."

He looked dubious, but let them continue on. They crossed to King Charles Street and were out of immediate sight of the

Service building and the Yard. Alex slowed, her legs wobbling, sending her off course and into Brook. He caught her arm and steadied her.

"Easy," he advised.

Her internal barriers were up, but she had to deal with her own emotions, the chief of which was annoyance . . . until it was replaced by—*Oh, God, not now.*

She pushed violently away from Brook, made it to the curb, and lost her Christmas dinner to the gutter.

R efreshment?" asked Brook. He tilted a flask at her. She took a sip, rinsing vile acid from her mouth, then spat. The peaty-tasting drink within was of better quality than that favored by Inspector Lennon. A shame to waste it, but she was unsure of her ability to keep anything down.

Sybil said I'd need whiskey.

"Sorry," she said, handing back the flask. It was heavy silver, engraved with the letters *J.M.S.B.* She realized she did not know Brook's first name. Not that she would require its use, but knowing that sort of thing about a colleague-in-arms was only being polite.

"A perfectly understandable reaction."

"I've never, that is . . ."

"You shot people before," he prompted. "Not in London."

She puffed a laugh without mirth. "I was a girl, hardly fourteen. My father and I were in a large group crossing Mexico. It was wild country, no towns for miles, just a thin track the guides called a road and *banditos*. We had to make a run, shooting from horseback. I'm sure I got two of them, but I wasn't like this afterward."

"A younger mind has better protection against such violence. Does it feel as though it happened to someone else?"

"How do you know that?"

"I've had scrapes, nothing quite so exciting as this, though. If you're recovered, we should keep moving. Those attackers were after you and there could be more about."

"Theirs was a planned assault on the Service, not me. No one could know I'd be coming out the front doors chasing after Sybil; I certainly didn't."

"Unless they have a Seer who knew you'd be there."

"Good God." What a terrifying thought. She began walking, glancing about for hooded threats.

"Of course, it could have just been bad luck and coincidence. We followed her and simply got in the way."

"That first man . . . Sybil knew he was armed. However strangely she acts, there is purpose to it. She was there to stop him. Shot him in the back. Didn't even blink."

Brook sampled from his flask, then put it away. "That's the coldest thing I've ever seen, but if he'd gotten into the building with that pistol, a nearly silent weapon like that, no warning—it's unthinkable."

"She saved all of them . . . and us."

"Who *are* these men?"

Alex shook her head. "They attempted an organized attack. The first man was likely set to go in, kill and wound as many as he could, the others follow him—they'd have slaughtered everyone in the building. Nearly the whole Service destroyed in one move."

"Two moves. Lord Richard's assassination prompted the gathering of all under one roof in the first place. Someone knew what the reaction would be. But why the Service? Forgive me, but it's not that important."

"What?" She stopped, staring at him. "It most certainly *is*."

"I don't mean insult, but it's not as vital as the police. Why not attack them?"

"Policemen are more easily replaced than those with psychical talent. All our most experienced people might have been murdered. It would take years to recover."

"Therefore, the Psychic Service presents an obstacle to some greater plan."

"Greater plan?"

"There must be something larger going on. As you said,

it's organized, and such things do not come into being over-night. Long thought and planning has gone into this—and a good deal of money."

The Ætheric Society? They had wealthy patrons, but it was absurd. They were too small a group and had nothing obvious to gain from eliminating the Psychic Service. Medi-ums and their ilk would be glad to see the Service removed, but hardly the sort to band together. The nature of their ongoing business of fraud made them all rivals vying for the same customers. The Service was more nuisance to them than anything else.

"It could be a foreign government," she said. "They'd have the resources. But speculation is pointless. The wounded from that attack will be questioned. We'll make our contribution by—oh, dear God. I need a telegraph. This way!"

She rushed ahead, but he caught up and did not ask the reason behind her abrupt urgency. He must have come to the same conclusion.

Alex spotted an office across the road, ran over, and snarled upon seeing it was closed, the shades down. "Here!" She shoved the rifle at Brook and dug through her reticule for a small leather case. Within was her collection of skeleton keys. She tried one after another in the lock and hoped there was no bolt as well. The fifth key worked and she opened the door, quickly drawing Brook inside.

"Aren't those illegal?"

"Haven't the faintest idea." She went around the front counter.

"Well, this is. We've broken and entered." He appeared to be sanguine about it, though. How sensible of him.

"Just entered. We'll be gone soon without breakage. I'd be obliged if you would keep watch in case a policeman comes by to rattle the doorknob."

Someone had thoughtfully left a box of lucifers out, and she lighted the gas. A quick survey of the long room showed this to be a major routing nexus, with telegraphs for specific countries as well as a dozen machines with links to various other locations within England. She went down the line and found the one that connected to the Service offices. There had been debate in the government about the funding of such lines. A fearful number of politicians objected, arguing against the cost. More than one wag pointed out that if the Service was truly psychic, then they had no need of a telegraph.

The issue was resolved in a most astonishing manner by Lord Richard Desmond (senior), who paid for it out of his own pocket. Many questioned why he'd thought it important, many still did. Alex accepted training to learn Morse code as just part of the job.

The telegraph mechanism was not engaged, but she put it in order and made use of the one wired to the Service's telegraph office. She tapped the code to signal an incoming message, waited, tapped again, waited. . . .

It took a few moments before anyone responded. No one could be blamed for that, considering the circumstances. The place would be stirred up like an anthill.

When a response came, Alex tapped in the words STAND BY, grabbed pencil and paper from a desk, and wrote her note. Her Morse was adequate, but she knew she'd get muddled trying to spell everything in her head. Once started, she attained a fair speed.

She ended her message and waited for a reply. It was not the expected MSGE RCVD. Instead, the clicks commanded RETURN AT ONCE.

Alex hadn't given her signature, but someone had worked out the identity of the sender. Their code people were so good they could identify a sender's tapping style as readily as hearing their voice.

Mrs. Woodwake was probably looming over the Service operator, looking grim.

Better to err on the side of good manners.

FLLWING INQUIRY CNFRM OTHER HQS WARNED.

The confirmation came, and Woodwake repeated her order,

RETURN RETURN RETURN, as though she'd caught Sybil's peculiar speech pattern.

SORRY MSGE END.

Alex shut the mechanism down, putting things back as found, taking the paper she'd written upon, and turning off the gas. "Done."

"Dare I ask for details?" said Brook.

"Had to warn them that ours might not be the only Service office subject to attack. They might have come to it on their own, but I wanted to be sure. I wanted to ask if everyone was all right, but Mrs. Woodwake—we should go now. Someone will guess how close we are and come to retrieve us."

"Then lock the front and we'll leave by the back."

She made use of the key again. "They may not know you're with me. I want to keep it that way. You're to return and make a report, whatever's needed."

"You've no idea how ridiculous you sound," he said. "I'm staying."

"Lieutenant Brook, my actions have just now guaranteed that I will be dismissed. There is no point in you also being dismissed."

"They'll do no such thing. With an unknown group making bold attacks, the Service will need everyone they can muster."

"You might be safe, but I'm disobeying a direct order from Mrs. Woodwake—several, I should think."

"But you're obeying an order from Sybil, and if I judge things correctly, she holds a higher level of importance than Mrs. Woodwake."

"I doubt Mrs. Woodwake will see it that way."

"Nonetheless, I'm staying. Sybil didn't exactly include me, but neither was I excluded."

"I had the impression you didn't take her seriously."

"She is an impossibility, but since she saved our lives, I will accept the impossible for the present. Now, where are we going and why?"

They'd made their way, stumbling and bumping into things in the black recesses of the office, to a small chamber with a single window and a locked door. This one was bolted, but Brook remedied that while Alex tried her keys again. A moment later, they were outside in a narrow alley, the door relocked.

"We need to get to Mayfair, Berkeley Square," she said. "I want to consult an expert on air guns." She put the keys away and took the rifle from Brook. "He's in my shooting club and might have an idea where this was made. That could lead us to the ones behind the attack."

"Have a look at it yourself," he suggested. "If you spot something we could go back to the Service office and avoid further ire from Mrs. Woodwake."

What an excellent idea, she thought.

The rifle's general form didn't appear too different from others she'd seen and fired, except for the bulky stock, which was made of dark metal, not wood. She could find no maker's stamp anywhere.

"Custom made, expensive," she pronounced.

"No smell of gunpowder to it."

"They don't use powder. Compressed air propels the bullet, which no longer needs a cartridge. This is the air reservoir." She tapped the stock. "One of the problems is having a metal of sufficient strength to withstand the internal pressure of that compression. By the time it's thick enough to support multiple firings, the weapon might be too heavy to carry. I wish Mr. Sexton was here to give an opinion on the metallurgy."

"You seem to know a lot already."

"I know air gun enthusiasts. None have anything like this, though. Theirs fire only a few shots, and then the reservoir must be pressured up again by an attached pumping mechanism. I don't see any obvious opening for air to go in."

"How many rounds might this one fire?"

"I don't want to break it open just yet to see. It could blow up in our faces if we get that wrong. It has power, but lacks

balance. Distance accuracy is rotten, though that was fortu-
nate for us. However, if you shoot often enough in the right
direction . . ."

"I know." Brook removed his top hat and pointed out two
holes just above the brim where a bullet had passed clean
through. "It fell off when we ducked. Rather glad I didn't
have it on at the time. Not a large round to judge by the damage."

"There's probably a trade-off between bullet size and weight
against its effective range, but these are enough to kill." The
awful memory of Lord Richard taking shot after shot intruded
on her mind's eye for a moment. She blinked it away as best
she could, looking at Brook.

He put his hat back on. The hole in front was just center
of his forehead.

She focused on his eyes instead, truly noticing them for the
first time. They were a deep and merry blue. She quashed a
rush of warm awareness. She'd felt that sort of thing before
and it never ended well. Better to not let it get a foothold. Disappointment was inevitable.

She concealed the rifle under her cloak and led off again.
"I'm no expert, though. Best we get to one. This won't take
long."

They had the good luck to acquire a hansom and sorted
themselves within its confines: Brook with the carpetbag
squashed on his lap, Alex with the rifle pointed at the floor and
out of sight. She took advantage of the respite while it lasted,
closing her eyes and clearing her mind. The near-meditative
state was almost like sleep, but she remained alert to the gait
of the horse, the movement of their conveyance, the chilled
air . . . and Brook's solid body next to hers.

Undeniably pleasant, even with her barriers up. She could
enjoy *that* for its own sake and no harm done.

"We're here," said Brook.

She snapped awake, chagrined that she'd nodded off after
all.

He handed her out. "I should mention that we are not quite at Berkeley Square." The bare trees of the square were visible a hundred yards ahead, along with a few hardy strollers taking the afternoon air.

"Intentional. I've a call to make first and she lives on Hill Street."

Number three proved to be a tall structure on the corner of Hill and Farm. The entry was too grand for such a narrow street. Four Doric columns supporting a false balcony overwhelmed the doorway, but the step's chessboard pattern of black and white tiles was pretty. No light showed in the narrow windows on either side of the black-painted door.

Above the door was a faux Roman arch, the keystone decorated with a head like a death mask. It was a common enough embellishment, but the address used by "Dr. Kemp" also had one. They were, in fact, identical.

"What's the matter?" asked Brook.

A bit late, she got control of her features and offered him the air gun. She dug in her reticule for the Webley and the box of spare cartridges. She broke both open and reloaded.

He watched, one eyebrow up. "Are we to expect trouble?"

"I prefer to be prepared for it." She chose not to point out the coincidence of the keystone. It might be a chance thing, after all.

"Who are we visiting?"

"Rosalind Veltre, widow, member of the Ætheric Society, and possibly one of the last people to see my father alive."

"How do you know of her?"

"Her calling card was in his walking stick. I found a hidden compartment once I had a closer look. The precognition that compelled you to leave it on the desk instead of propped in the corner is what brought us here."

Brook's mouth twisted in a strange way, and he looked like a man who wanted very much to express something, but there being a lady present, he could not.

She smiled. "I won't suggest that you'll ever get used to it, but perhaps you'll be able to come to a working tolerance of such an ability. It's proved useful twice now."

He settled for a long sigh, which might have been taken for a soft groan. "Well, at least in the Service no one gives such things a second thought."

"That's it, see the bright side."

"Perhaps you will afford me the use of your revolver until we know the lay of the land?"

"Your Bulldog wants feeding?"

"And I am without reloads."

She traded her Webley for the air gun, again concealing it under the cloak.

Alex tried the door. Locked, but her skeleton key collection solved that, and they were soon in the kind of vestibule common to houses with multiple residents. A long hall extended ahead; its two doors on one side were closed. A staircase led up. The wood was polished, the floors swept. There was no indication where in the building they might find the home of Mrs. Veltre. A table on one side served to hold mail, and it was evidently up to a servant to sort whatever dropped through the letter slot. Two untidy stacks, the first for a Mr. Smoles, the other for Veltre, remained unclaimed from yesterday's post.

Most of Veltre's letters seemed to be bills from dressmakers, milliners, and the like. With a satisfying disregard to the woman's privacy, Alex ripped one of the bills open and examined the totals. An expensive establishment indeed—a single tea gown had cost as much as a year's income to Alex, who considered herself fairly well off. Even Heather would have thought twice, but the widow Veltre had ordered half a dozen. She could well afford to indulge eccentricities like those and the Ætheric Society, so why not have a private house and staff?

"Well, well," Alex muttered aloud, plucking out a cream-colored envelope and dropping the rest. It was heavy card stock; someone had used a pen with a fine nib, the writing fair and regular as engraver's art, and most important, it gave Veltre's full address. She was on the first floor. "Hand delivery for this one, I think."

She hurried up the stairs, hampered by the air gun, until shouldering it like a soldier on the march. Her skirts were a nuisance. Perhaps she could persuade Brook to stop at Baker Street so she could change to more practical and cleaner garments. Rolling about on wet pavement while dodging bullets had left its marks.

There was a single door off the stairs to assault, and she made a vigorous action of it, making enough row to rouse the heaviest of sleepers but getting no response. Handing the air gun to Brook, she used the skeleton keys again and pushed the door wide.

The dim interior was silent, the air still and clammy.

As he had for her home, Brook went in first. He left the carpetbag in the hall and swiftly paced through the flat, pronouncing it empty.

"Wait out here a moment," said Alex. "I'm going to Read."

She and Brook changed places. She removed her gloves and bit by bit lowered her internal barriers as she paced around, getting a feel for the place.

The general impression left by the resident was that of frustration and anger. This was not a happy house.

The front room with two tall windows overlooking Hill Street was comfortably furnished, tidy, and nearly as cold as the outside. She moved toward the grate. Within lay the remains of the type of ash one got from burning paper, not coal. What had Veltre been so inconsiderate as to destroy?

A writing desk held only invoices for more expensive dresses and hats. Those were stacked according to date. She kept track of her accounts. Little emotional trace remained, just a residue of annoyance. Alex felt the same herself when dealing with bills, though not to this degree. She picked up a silver letter opener and a thrum of anger left by the last hand to hold it almost made her drop it again. Perhaps bad news had come in a previous post and the letter was burned.

No sign of a bankbook or money box; there were just a few stray coins in the corners. Disappointing and oddly sterile. Not one letter or even a visiting card, though there were empty shelves where such might have been stored. The blotter was well used, so Veltre did plenty of writing, but nothing of it lurked in the alcoves. She must have taken it with her or fed it to the fire. Damn the woman.

Alex signed for Brook to come in. He did, closing the door. She moved toward the back, finding a small study littered with theater programs and magazines. The books, not many, were on esoteric themes of interest to the sort of eccentrics who patronized séances. A stack of pamphlets for the Ætheric Society lay on a table. Topics were varied, from the true origin of Atlantis to dreams as a means of communication with the High Masters, whoever they might be.

Each issue bore the motif of a black sun with two white eyes staring out from its face. She'd never liked that emblem; it seemed to grimly demand that one take it seriously, and she could not. Black rays extended from it and beneath was a phrase from no language she could recognize. Such declarations were usually in Latin, and she understood that the Ætherics had their own language, chants of power supposedly passed to them by their High Masters.

"That's interesting," said Brook.

"What is?"

"That sun face thing. It looks like the one over the door."

"You noticed that?"

"I noticed you. Gave you a turn when we were on the step. Why was that?"

"It was on the Harley Street house, a new addition to the entrance facade. If my father was looking into the Ætheric Society, he'd have joined them. Perhaps that thing is common to their members, a way of recognizing one another."

"Or he happened to see it here, admired it, and had one put on his house."

"No." She said that without thinking twice. "He never gave

a fig what a place looked like on the outside so long as it was organized on the inside. That was always Fingate's job. He will know for sure."

"You've no idea where he might have gotten to?"

"We could call on my cousin. I told Fingate he could trust James, but I don't know if he really heard me on the bridge."

"That would be Dr. Fonteyn?"

"Certainly not Teddy."

"Yes, the doctor is a steady sort."

She shot him a "What the devil?" look. "Steady? James?"

"He was at the Humane Society building. Checked me over along with the others who dove in for you, made sure we were—"

"James did that?"

"He's a doctor, why shouldn't he?"

Any reply would be too complicated and take hours. Alex reluctantly conceded that James must put the fool aside now and then, else he'd never have gotten through medical college. People behaved differently with friends and strangers than they did toward family, after all. She knew that rather too well, but it hadn't occurred to her that James wouldn't bother to put on a foolish front before others. One needed less protection from strangers than family.

She continued through the flat. A room with a bathing tub, a nice deep one, and a gas water-heating device above it—the woman enjoyed her comfort. The tub was dry. Alex opened a cabinet above the washstand and rocked back.

"What's the matter?" Brook asked from the hall.

"Just the unexpected." Not touching it, she pointed to a bottle of Dr. Kemp's Throat Elixir on the lowest shelf. "I didn't think it was real."

The label was a smaller version of the framed poster in the Harley Street house.

"May I?" Brook removed it, pulled the cork stopper, and sniffed. "Smells like flavored liqueur, has some mint in it. You all right?"

"Father went to considerable trouble and detail to present himself as Kemp right down to having this made up. One doesn't go to such lengths on a lark."

"Perhaps someone saw through it, recognized him as Lord Pendlebury. But why would the Ætherics want to be rid of either of them?"

"It need not be the whole society, just one member in fear of exposure would suffice. Mrs. Woodwake said that at some of their gatherings they indulge in activities that"—How to phrase it?—"would leave a person vulnerable to blackmail. If he thought my father presented a danger, then he acted decisively and with imagination to stage things. This Veltre woman might well have played a part and fled. Whatever inspired her departure, it was before the last post arrived yesterday."

"Long before your father was . . . Well." Brook did not complete his thought and Alex was grateful for it.

She went on, "Fingate said a woman was helping Father. It might be a different lady than this one, though. I wish to God she'd been here, I'd have throttled answers out of her. Keep looking—an engagement diary, names of friends, anything useful."

Alex crossed the hall to Veltre's bedroom; it was less tidy, the bed unmade and clothing strewn about. She had two wardrobes containing the clothing, boots, and shoes needed for every season and social event. A dozen hatboxes were stacked on the floor, each labeled, each containing a pretty bonnet.

The dresses were lovely and favored certain warm colors, but no trousers, no cycling or walking clothes. Veltre was a lady's lady, like Cousin Andrina. A pleasant floral scent permeated things.

Alex took down her remaining barriers to determine more of the woman's personality.

Appetite . . . unsatisfied, a longing for something, a need, a hole in her soul, anger, frustration, fear, worry, grief—a lot of that. The young widow desperately missed her husband. Alex pulled back. Her own grief was too fresh.

What could be determined without Reading?

Vanity, to judge by the cosmetics crowding the dressing table. No prints or paintings, a few photographs, family perhaps. The table by the bed held more pamphlets, theatrical programs, nothing of note or practical use.

No photographs of the dead husband were on display. She should at least have the wedding portrait somewhere, if one had been taken. Alex checked the drawers and cupboards, wanting to know what her quarry looked like, but for a vain woman, Veltre kept no images of herself. How annoying.

Ah—what was that between the bed and table? A reticule, apparently in recent use and shoved out of the way. Alex usually hung hers from a doorknob. She emptied the contents on the bed: house keys, coin and paper money, calling cards in a gold case, a pencil, but no paper or address book. Was the woman friendless, or possessed of an excellent memory for house numbers?

Why would she leave this behind? Just how hasty was her exit?

In a bottom drawer was the type of family Bible given as a wedding gift. Between the Old and New Testament was a section for births and deaths and pages where small photographs might be slipped in. One held a single image of the Veltres in happier times, she in a wedding dress and he in a morning coat. Unfortunately it was too small to show much detail of their faces. Alex memorized the woman's features as best she could given the limitations. For a woman obsessed with expensive clothes, the bride's dress was plain and modest. Perhaps she'd not been able to afford better back then and was making up for it now with her inherited wealth.

"The servants' door in the back is unlocked," said Brook. "That's careless."

Alex wanted a Reading of that. She moved past him to a small kitchen and scullery. It was in good order, clean, but the bread in the box was moldy.

She bent for a close look at the outer side of the door lock.

Just the usual scratches, nothing to suggest a breaking-in. She stepped into the back hall.

The icy pressure of the Serpentine seized her body and dragged her into darkness.

CHAPTER NINE

In Which Lord and Lady Hollifield Provide Information and Mince Pies

Alex fought frantically against it, breath trapped, chest aching.

"There now, you're all right," said Brook in a steady voice. Her eyelids shot wide.

Brook held both her wrists; his concern was as solid as a physical embrace. She tried to break free, and he instantly released her. "You fainted is all."

Not underwater. Not dying.

Deep breath. A gasp, really. A shaky series of gasps. "I nev—I don't faint."

" 'Fraid you did. Dropped like a stone."

They were on a level, she lying on a long settee in the front room, and Brook on one knee next to her. Her hat was gone and the top buttons of her collar undone. Good God.

Brook had a damp cloth in hand and put it on her forehead. She forced herself to remember . . . the kitchen . . . a door . . . the back hallway—the rush of utter terror had snaked through Alex and slammed her flat. "Faugh. I walked into that one like a green apprentice."

"Walked into what?"

"If-if an emotional imprint is strong and you're not braced, it's like stepping blind from a cliff. You get a nasty jolt. That one was . . . exceptional."

"What caused it?"

"Someone took Mrs. Veltre against her will. She was frightened to death, tried to fight but—did you smell ether?"

"I was busy getting you off the floor. Anything injured? You made quite a thump."

She took stock. "I'm fine. I haven't as far to fall as some people." Barriers restored, if brittle, she sensed his amusement. "What, no alarm? You're getting used to the job?"

"Plenty of alarm, I thought you'd been shot by one of those damned air rifles."

"Oh."

"It was a considerable relief to find you breathing and un-punctured."

He would have left that emotion behind, contaminating the area. She'd allow for it on a second Reading. "Have you much experience dealing with fainting females?"

"Not directly. I read a lot. Ladies seem to faint in books and in plays far more often than in real life. In your case I went with my instincts. Couldn't find any smelling salts, though."

"For which I am grateful."

With some caution, she sat up, found that standing was possible, and did so. She had collected a few more bruises but nothing worse.

"You're not dizzy?"

"It was a psychical shock, a bit different from a theatrical swoon."

He offered his flask.

She shook her head, lips going tight.

Gently eschewing his offered arm, she made her own way toward the kitchen. Doing up her collar, she was careful to block any emotions he might have left when he'd touched the buttons. She did not want to know what he'd felt. That would complicate things and . . . distract her.

This time Alex entered the back hall with more caution, slowly easing open her internal barriers. She separated Brook's fresh traces and sought the older imprint of sheer panic. The intensity of emotion was like an explosion, brief and devastating. Veltre had been surprised, fought desperately, and then

abruptly faded. Though no scent remained, Alex was sure the
smothering feeling was due to ether having been used. Her inner mind had linked the sensation to her next closest memory, taking her back to that ghastly immersion.

She proceeded down to a courtyard that served two more
buildings. The court opened to Farm Street. Veltre could have
been carried out and loaded into a conveyance after dark with
no one noticing. On Christmas Eve most people would be indoors at dinner.

Futile as it was, she was thorough, but the psychic scent of
Mrs. Veltre was long dispersed.

By his very absence, Alex knew who was responsible for
the abduction. There was no trace of him, not in the hall, the
stairway, or the door leading to the yard.

"It's the ghost," she told Brook, coming back inside. From
his puzzled look she realized he'd not heard of it yet. She explained.

"Someone with no emotions at all?" he asked.

"None that I can track."

"But everyone has emotions. We can't help ourselves."

"Inspector Lennon suggested an automaton without its
box, but only as a joke."

"I'd prefer to believe that than a man without emotions.
Perhaps he puts himself in a mesmeric trance or something so
it's impossible for a Reader to find him."

"If so, then it works too well. I've found all there is to find
here." But on the way to the front room Alex paused at the
bedroom door, staring in. "That's . . . that's not right."

She hurried back to the desk and looked at the receipts
again, noting the number of items and whether they'd been
delivered.

"I'm a fool," she muttered. "Tea gowns, hats, evening
gowns—look at the number of them, the prices."

Brook did so. "I didn't know fashionable ladies paid so
much for their things."

"They generally do not; these are outrageous and she's got two wardrobes for storage. Unless she's let another floor in this building, there's no room to hold all this."

"Perhaps she bought them for a girls' school or something."

"I doubt any academy has need of three dozen identical ball gowns. See the handwriting? These invoices are from different shops, but the writing is the same. The venues must be false, I don't recognize any of the names. No addresses, either."

He went through a stack. "She's done a good deal of shopping in the last six months. Where's her bankbook?"

"Not here. The money amounts are probably correct, but the items themselves are not what was purchased. This sort of substitution code is not a new invention, but I've not seen it for sums like this. Thousands and thousands of pounds, but for what? And why was she recording them in this manner?"

Alex remembered the heavy envelope she'd brought up. The elegant handwriting did not match the invoices. No matter. She put the letter opener to use. The single card within had that day's date and *8:30—"Masters Impart"* perfectly centered on its cream-colored surface.

"An invitation with no address," he observed.

"I think she gave that to Father." Alex located her reticule next to the settee and pulled out the worse-for-wear calling card.

"Is that what you found in the—"

"Yes, Father's walking stick."

He glanced at the card. "Twenty-five Grosvenor Square. We could walk over. A meeting, you think? The Ætheric Society?"

"It *could* be an ordinary gathering. Christmas dinner."

"And I'm the king of Siam. You're going to go, aren't you?"

"How can I not?"

"I'm sure there are a dozen good reasons you will ignore. You will still be lumbered with me as a bodyguard, though."

"Not lumbered, you're needed. It would be foolish to go alone."

"Again, I am relieved. But why not telegraph the Service

with this information and let them send in people? They could have half of Scotland Yard in tow."

"Because at this point we have no empirical evidence that my father's death is connected to the Ætherics. We have no evidence his death and the attack on Lord Richard are connected. One followed close upon the other, but the methods differed. For my father, someone went to much trouble to make it appear not to be murder. For Lord Richard it was a determined and prolonged attack until the objective was achieved, and they were untroubled by the presence of witnesses. The man had enemies, so the timing of the two events could be coincidental. I do not like coincidences, but this could be one. Invading a meeting of the Ætheric Society might resolve only one issue."

"And possibly get you killed if that murderous ghost-man is there and recognizes you. There's no doubt this Veltre woman was involved with the Ætherics and knew your father. For all you know, she betrayed him in some way. You said someone kidnapped her?"

"I know they did. It's mad. On one hand, a sly, stealthy murder, on the other, two violent, public attacks against the Service by hooded men with unusual weapons."

She focused on the invitation card, intent to get some sense of the person who wrote it, but only a general feeling of ennui came to her. That might mean the writer had the thankless task of filling out a large number of similar invitations. All to the good; she and Brook would be less noticeable in a crowd. She abruptly realized the light was going. The short winter day was slipping by. "Time to get moving."

She donned her cloak, hat, and gloves, shoving the invitation into her reticule. Brook collected all the receipts and put them in the carpetbag.

"Shouldn't we question the other residents in this building?" he asked, handing her the air rifle after she locked up.

"We can come back. I want to get this weapon to Lord Hollifield's house before tea time."

"*He's* your air gun expert?"

"The closest I have to one. What little I know I learned from him."

"Lord Hollifield? You're serious?"

"Well, *somebody* has to be the queen's brother-in-law."

Less than a two-minute walk away, but a vast social distance from Veltre's modest rooms, the frontage of Hollifield House took up a large portion of the northwest corner of Berkeley Square. Its red brick was complemented by fresh white trim, the proportions of the windows and balconies were pleasant to the eye, and Alex noted with relief that there was no decorative death mask–like head above the door. Now that she'd become aware of the damned things, she cast about at other houses, looking for more. None were to be seen, at least on this part of the square.

A liveried footman on post outside opened the door with the correct angle to his bow, neither too low to overstate, nor too shallow to insult. His smile was warm and welcoming. The Hollifield household was a cheerful one, and Alex fought an impulse to relax her defenses. However pleasant, she had to avoid distraction. This visit must be short and to the point, with them leaving before his lordship got too curious about her deadly artifact.

Rather a lot to expect, she thought.

A maid and another footman were on duty to take charge of coats and wraps, but Alex put them off and asked where his lordship might be found. She was about to give a calling card to the maid when Lady Lindsey Hollifield came to greet her newly arrived guests. She smiled hesitantly at Mr. Brook, not knowing him, and looked expectantly at Alex, who raised the veil on her hat.

"Why, Alex! What a lovely surprise!" her ladyship said with much affection. She did not extend her hand, being one of those who knew that Readers were shy about physical contact.

"I'm sorry to intrude, Lady Lindsey, but I need to see Lord Daniel on Service business."

"Oh, how boring for you. You're not intruding at all, child. We've had the house open all day for friends to call in, it's very informal. If you're not too pressed, I insist you have tea and a nice mince pie."

"Very kind of you."

"You'll do me a kindness. The cook went quite mad and made enough to serve everyone at Buck House twice over. This place will smell of cloves for a week. Now, please introduce me to this handsome and patient fellow."

Alex did the honors, giving Brook's rank in lieu of a first name.

"Oh, my dear girl, is *this* your young man?" Lady Lindsey looked enormously pleased at the idea.

Alex hadn't expected that question, though she should have; her ladyship always inquired whether Alex had set her cap for anyone yet. Where she'd gotten that phrase was a mystery, but she was far too fond of it. By heroic effort, Alex held a fierce blush in check and managed not to choke. "Mr. Brook is assisting me, filling in for Sergeant Greene today."

Brook, managing to grip his hat and the carpetbag in his left hand, touched a gloved forefinger to his forehead. A proper salute would have been inappropriate since he was not in uniform and her ladyship held no military rank.

Lady Lindsey was disappointed as she eyed the bag. "That is really too bad. I'd hoped that you'd come by to show him off and let me know you were eloping."

Dear God.

Brook kept his face neutral, but despite her defenses, Alex picked up that he was inordinately amused.

"Oh, well, there's time for that another day. Let's see where Daniel's gotten himself. The billiard room or the gun room; he does like his toys."

She led away, Alex and Brook keeping up with her brisk but graceful pace. Alex had been to the house many times after a shooting club event, but its size still astonished her. They passed room after room, each with a specific purpose, each decorated in the most perfect taste, some boasting paintings that would have been gratefully accepted by the National Gallery.

The place was full of brilliantly turned-out people. Lady Lindsey was no exception. Her dark auburn hair was beautifully dressed with diamond-trimmed combs. Her gown at first look appeared understated compared to others, but at second look a richness of detail emerged to delight the eye and stagger the household purse. She wore it and her diamonds with an easy buoyancy that few women of her caste could carry off. She would have the same self-possession had they been glass and herself draped in rags.

Alex was rarely ill at ease about her own mode of attire, but in this instance and in such a glittering crowd she felt shabby even in her best cloak. She would have been invisible on her own, but simply walking in her ladyship's wake drew attention. At least the cloak covered the battle scars adorning her blue ensemble, as well as the air rifle, which would have certainly caused alarm. She recognized several guests as longtime friends of the Pendleburys and was glad she'd pulled the veil on her hat down again. This was no time for social exchanges.

The Hollifields moved in somewhat more exalted circles of the nobility than the Pendleburys, but had always made her feel welcome. Being much closer to the queen by means of family connection (Hollifield having wooed and wed the sister of Lord Consort Arthur), they saw the inside of Buckingham Palace far more often than even Cousin Andrina.

Hollifield House itself was something of a miniature palace, boasting a dining room that could seat forty, though Lady Lindsey preferred smaller groups of twenty, as there were fewer names to remember, but today was an exception. In the ballroom an orchestra played a sprightly waltz for a score of dancers, and Alex felt a pang of envy for their carefree turns across the floor.

But more imperative matters were afoot. She could not allow herself distractions.

One importuned itself, nonetheless.

James Fonteyn was in profile just within the ballroom, speaking to—*Oh, corks*—Teddy Pendlebury.

She nearly blundered into Brook in an attempt to turn away and duck. Even under a veil and cloak her cousins would certainly recognize her and if not herself, then they'd know Brook for sure.

He glanced down at her, and then above and past. His mouth popped open, but she seized his arm and conveyed the urgency to keep moving.

Her gentlemen relatives appeared to have become the fastest of friends, which was no surprise since they shared hedonistic tendencies. Teddy was the stuffier of the two, being constrained by the demands of a stuffy job, but was an expert at keeping his pleasures apart from his duties.

James had no such constraints. Alex could easily imagine him leading a willing Teddy into gradually lower levels of depravity. Compared to some things she'd seen on her travels, the debauches would be mild, but enough to damage, if not destroy, Teddy's professional reputation. What was acceptable in China was a scandal in Belgravia.

Doubtless Andrina would find some way to blame Alex.

Oh, bother the lot of them.

Why her cousins were here was no mystery. Her ladyship was famous for her hospitality. Anyone with a title, honor, family connection, or some other distinction would be made welcome with or without an invitation, particularly on Christmas Day.

Alex and Brook were soon out of view of the ballroom, but she could not relax, expecting any instant to be hailed and then delayed by tedious explanations for her presence.

Lord Daniel was in the billiard room the next floor up, along with a number of other men. The gas sconces and fireplace blazed, and the balcony doors were wide open to the cold, which was the only way one might be able to breathe. The air within was exceedingly thick. The large chamber doubled as a smoking room and those present were taking full advantage, including his lordship, who had a massive meerschaum ensconced under his fierce-looking white moustache. His attention was on the green baize table as one of his cronies considered a difficult shot.

Lady Lindsey waited until ivory clacked against ivory, a ball rolled and vanished into a pocket, and a rumble of approval for the player's skill circulated through the audience. She then murmured in her husband's ear. Lord Daniel cast an interested eye upon first Brook and then Alex, gave a brisk nod, and excused himself to those close by.

"Hallo, Alex," he said as they emerged from the smoky reek. "Wouldn't have known you standing there covered like a rani in purdah. Why aren't you having a holiday? I'll have a word with Desmond about it. He runs his patch as though we're at war."

He didn't seem to expect a reply, so Alex made none. "I'm sorry to interrupt, Lord Daniel, but I'll keep things brief. May we speak in private?"

He put some thought into that and glanced at Lady Lindsey.

"The gun room," she said.

How convenient.

"Had to lock it for the duration," she explained, again leading the way. "There are children about and they do get curious."

"If they're properly trained, there's naught to worry about," said Daniel. "Most of 'em are and are welcome to look, but they have sticky hands. Drives poor Sebbings to the edge wiping jam smears from the glass cases, y'know. The place smells of vinegar afterward, makes my eyes water. Now where's the key?" He paused, slapping his pockets.

Lindsey rescued him, producing a key ring from a discreet pocket and unlocking the door. "Will you need me for this? I must be in ten other places for another three hours."

"Thank you, Lady Lindsey," said Alex. "And if I might make one small request? Please don't let anyone know I'm here. I saw many acquaintances and at least two cousins, and I've no time to spare for them."

"Certainly. It was lovely to meet you, Lieutenant Brook. I'm so sorry you're not eloping with our Alex." She winked at her husband and glided from the hall.

Lord Daniel made a noise to indicate amusement, then went into the gun room. He did not bother to ring for a servant, but found matches in his waistcoat pocket and lighted the gas himself, then looked at Alex with some expectancy. She brushed away her veil and again introduced Brook.

"What regiment?" asked his lordship.

Brook had a ready answer. "None, sir. I'm now attached to the Psychic Service by special order."

"Huh. That means you did something ingenious and helpful that offended someone. Not to worry, lad, I won't pry. If Dickie Desmond approved you, then you're all right. He's an arrogant bludger, but knows people. Alex is one of his better decisions, aren't you, girl? Now, what brings you to my roof on Christmas if you're not eloping?"

The gun room was not large, but packed with an astonishing array of weaponry, each wall having glass cases holding numbers of firearms within. The collection was a mix of antiques in prime condition and modern pieces. In the middle of the floor was a tall table covered with a thick felt pad to protect anything that might be brought out for inspection.

"This," said Alex. Indulging in a theatrical flourish, she swept her cloak aside and set the air rifle on the table in one smooth movement.

It brought about the reaction she'd hoped for: Hollifield's instant attention. He fairly rocked back on his heels and dropped his pipe. Fortunately, it bounced on the rug and did not break. His lordship stared at the rifle, then snapped his gaze up at Alex, his eyes wide.

"I apologize in advance, Lord Daniel, but I cannot tell you

how I acquired it. This is part of an ongoing investigation. I'm hoping you will shed light on its origins."

He threw a look at Lieutenant Brook, then back to the table, then to Alex.

"Have you seen anything like it before?" she pressed.

His lordship got past his surprise and shook his head. He cleared his throat. "What the devil have you got here?"

"You tell me," she said. "It's capable of shooting multiple rounds with deadly force. I've not the same experience as you do with air-powered weapons. It seemed best to have you see it and perhaps—"

Lord Daniel was now wholly immersed in examining the thing. His first act was to shift it around so the muzzle pointed toward an outside wall. Should there be an accidental discharge, the bullet would smash into plaster and brick, not his guests or the display cases. He went over its mechanisms, muttering a bit, grunting with satisfaction as he worked out where the ammunition went in and the means by which pressurized air was introduced to the chamber.

"Where's the crank?" he asked. "There should be a crank or handle or some whatsit to fit into this bit here." He'd unscrewed a plug set in the right side, revealing a hexagonal socket.

"Sorry, don't have one. What sort of crank?"

"Hard to say, but a good size, one third to one half the length of the piece. You lock it in place, turn it enough times and that's what pumps the air in. The longer the crank the more leverage you have, the more pressure you can store in the reservoir. Sturdy goods, this is. I've nothing but admiration for whoever designed and made it. This is miles ahead of anything I've ever seen." He replaced the plug and tried opening another. When it refused to yield, he held off from forcing the issue. "I think the rounds go in here, but they're part of the pressure lock. There should be some means of reloading. . . . Ah, here we go." He pressed an indented circle that Alex had missed before, and they all jumped when the thing made a long loud hiss as though protesting its treatment.

"What's happened?" asked Brook.

Hollifield seemed embarrassed. "Hmm. I've vented the pressure in the reservoir, I think. Probably just as well. Wouldn't want the thing to blow up, now, would we? Let's see if this will open. . . ." He tried the second plug and a great number of round metal balls scattered across the felt padding. "Right, pressure gone and unloaded. I hope you weren't planning to put this to use later."

"Not at all, Lord Daniel," Alex said, peering close. "They're lead slugs, no points to them."

"I expect they have to be round to feed into the firing chamber, but that's going to play hell with accuracy. If you want to shoot at a decent distance you need rifling; this thing seems to kick 'em out with brute force."

"They are highly damaging at close range."

"Useless for hunting, but perfect for killing people before they know what's hit them."

Alex bit back the temptation to inform him of the attack on Service offices. "I've also seen a smaller version of this, a pistol."

"Have you now? Well, that would cause a lot of damage if it's got even half the power as this one must. This . . . this is a terrible weapon, Alex. I do not say that lightly. Who gave it to you?"

"I'm not at liberty to say, sir. As it is, I'm likely in a good deal of trouble for showing it to you at all. If there is anything you can tell me about who might have made it, I assure you that it will be of great help to the Service and to England."

"Just how desperate is this? Should I speak to Desmond? Not that I've much influence on the young sharp, but he might bring me in unofficially if I insist."

Hearing Lord Richard Desmond spoken of as a young sharp and arrogant bludger would have been amusing a day earlier. Alex shook her head. "That won't be necessary, sir. Please, if you know anything at all . . ."

He grunted, frowning through his white beard, eyes

narrow with thought. "Well, let's do the obvious and look for a maker's stamp." He took a magnifying glass from a drawer and went over the rifle as carefully as a diamond cutter searching for flaws. During that time, Brook picked up the fallen pipe, gently placed it on the table, and made a quiet tour of the displays. Alex, already familiar with the room, sank wearily onto a settee.

There came a discreet double knock upon the door, then it was opened quietly, and one of the footmen entered, pushing a tea trolley in ahead of Lady Lindsey who said she required a short respite from her hostess duties. She dismissed him and sat next to Alex.

"Close your mouth, girl, or you'll catch flies. I know there's something up and it's got to be grim." She poured tea into a deep and delicate cup with gold edging. "Get this into you, dear; you seem to need it."

Alex accepted with gratitude and reflected that her ladyship must possess an intuitive side.

"Lieutenant Brook? Will you join us? I've something stronger than tea if you want it."

"Tea is fine, Lady Hollifield. Thank you." He took a chair opposite the ladies, along with cup and saucer and a little plate with one of the pies. He made an admirable job of juggling things, indicating he'd had practice at it.

This could almost have been a normal social visit, but for the murders and deadly attacks.

"What's that toy Daniel's playing with?"

"A new type of air rifle, m'dear," answered his lordship, still poring over the thing.

"That should keep you happy. Are you going to acquire it?"

"I should hope so, if only to see how the deuced thing works."

"Goodness knows where he'll store it," she observed to her guests. "I expect we'll have to convert another room to look like this one if he keeps on collecting. Eat, Alex, you're looking rough about the edges, if you don't mind my saying. Having a bad patch with your family?"

Alex relaxed somewhat. She had a great fondness for the Hollifields. Not only were they friends from the shooting club, but they were genuinely kind people. They'd also done considerable traveling, giving her much more in common with them than with her own relatives. "I was at Pendlebury House this morning. Cousin Andrina was her usual charming self."

Lady Lindsey was aware of the ancient feud. "Families can be difficult. It's a pity you girls got off on the wrong foot, but such things happen. She does quite well as a lady-in-waiting to Princess Alice and her daughters. They think she's charming."

Alex could not imagine Andrina, with her sour and condemning temperament, being pleasant to anyone, therefore she must be better at dissembling than Ellen Terry.

"Mr. Brook?"

"Yes, your ladyship?"

"Are you by chance connected to the Brookes of Park Crescent?"

"The name is spelled differently, but I expect I am, distantly. We probably shared a grandfather or great-uncle a hundred years ago."

Although he gave no outer sign of it, Alex sensed his evasiveness and reluctance. "Lady Lindsey, your cook has done an admirable job on the pies. I'm so glad to have a chance to sample them." She spoke the truth; the crust melted like butter on the tongue, surpassed only by the excellent filling, the sweet perfectly balancing the spice. "I hope we are not imposing too much on your time."

"Not at all. Things can run themselves for a few minutes. It takes a good three weeks to arrange a reception like this and I've been on my feet since dawn. I'm glad to see so many here to make it a success, but next year I may forego the excitement and have a quiet time in the country. But of course one can't, not really, given our place in the world. Daniel and I will have to polish up and get over to Buck House. Formal family dinner, you know. I hope I can stay awake through all the courses."

This seemed to require a show of amusement. Alex provided, but was distracted by a satisfied exclamation from his lordship.

"Cracked it," he announced.

"You found who made it?" Alex put her saucer and cup on the tray and went to the table.

"No, there's nothing I can find on that, which is damned peculiar. Work like this usually means someone wants the credit, but it's clean as a boiled egg. I had to think who might have made it against who could afford to make it. Those capable aren't in this country, but I'll wager my fortune that this is British made. This is Sheffield steel or I'm a codfish."

"Really, dear," said his wife. "There are some perfectly good foundries in Germany."

"Bah! They can't cook a proper sausage, never mind work steel."

"Well, please don't say anything at the palace. Your sister-in-law has relatives on that side over as guests. Someone told me her cousins Albert and Ernest from Saxony-Coburg will be there—with their wives. We'll be swimming in German speeches and tiaras for hours."

"Not if my brother has anything to do with it. Arthur's sensible about such time-wasting rot, but I'll behave. I'll talk shooting with them if I must. Where was I?"

"British made."

"Hah. Yes. So here's the problem: there's one fellow in England who is capable of designing *and* making a piece like this, but he's not got the money to do so. There's not many interested in air guns, so even when he has a likely project, no one's keen to back it. He came to me, oh, about two years ago with some plans, but his timing was wretched. We were just taking ourselves off to Egypt or Rome or someplace for the winter."

"Rome," said Lady Lindsey.

"Right, nasty hole, rats, ruins, forged art, and the worst food."

She shook her head, observing to her guests, "The man is a darling, but I am certain he only ever consents to leave the country so he may prove to himself the superiority of all things English."

"Which they are. But never mind that. The visitor—I had no proper time for him. The plans he showed were a bit like this, but not quite as ambitious. The stock reservoir was smaller. Didn't hold so many rounds. I remember it had a crank attached, and I didn't care much for that. He's changed things—if it's the same fellow."

"A name, Lord Daniel, please," said Alex.

"Don't remember. Left a card, though. Polish mechanic, mad, of course, they're all mad. Heavy accent, couldn't take in half what he said, the drawings did all his speaking. Give me a moment. . . ." He poked and rummaged in a writing desk. "I know it's here, I keep running across it, meaning to write him to come again, but then one gets busy with other things. Surprised he's not returned on his own. Must have turned up a patron somewhere. Can't say I like the design—not being able to reload without depressurizing the reservoir? That's a flaw, but if it carries a hundred or more rounds—but *why* the devil would you want that many?"

"To kill people, I expect."

He paused. "Oh, well, yes, I suppose so. You know me, I'm more for target competition than anything else. But a hundred rounds for hunting—that's hardly fair. Doesn't give the game a sporting chance, takes the suspense out of it, reduces it to mere butchery, though there's some chaps who love their blood. Few of *them* under the roof today—ah, here it is." He produced a tattered card. "W. Nabadenski, if that's how y'say it. Didn't catch his first name."

"A London address," said Alex. It was on the other side of

the city. She and Brook might be able to go for a quick look and still get to the Ætheric meeting, but it seemed unlikely, especially after dark.

"If he's even there. That was two years ago. If it's his home he might be in, but if it's a workshop or factory he'll be closed for the day."

A good point. Tomorrow, in full daylight, would serve. *Or I telegraph Woodwake with this news and let her handle it.* That would be better. Let the woman know progress was taking place. Alex told him, "This is perfect, better than I'd hoped for; I can't thank you enough. You've been of enormous help."

"As much as all that?" Lord Daniel's eyes twinkled. "Am I to get the full story about this?"

"As soon as I know it myself—if I'm allowed."

"Don't worry about it. I can always pry it out of Desmond."

She looked away, not wanting to reveal any hint of Lord Richard's violent demise, and began collecting the scattered rounds, putting them back into the rifle. The bulky middle seemed to have the capacity to hold at least a hundred. "Is it gravity fed?"

"It would seem so. That puts a limit on your angle of aim. If you wanted to take out a bird or shoot down from a hill, you'd have to shift it level between rounds. That's another flaw. Be the devil to pay if it jammed."

Alex had noticed no tendency for jamming under repeated fire.

"Leaving without finishing your tea?" asked Lady Lindsey.

"I fear so, but it was lovely. Thank you so much, both of you."

Additional assertions that they had to leave were needed, but after stowing a large bundle of the tasty pies in the carpetbag, Alex and Brook were eventually allowed to depart. By request, to avoid any chance of encountering James or Teddy, one of the footmen bowed them out via a side door. They were on Mount Street with Hyde Park behind them and

Berkeley Square ahead. Just two streets north was Grosvenor Square. She was tempted to take a quick walk over to have a look at number twenty-five. It would have to wait, though; better to launch that campaign after making proper preparations.

"That was interesting," said Brook. "Not what one might expect."

"In what way?"

"A lack of pretension."

"They are lovely people. I like them better than my own fam—" Alex cut herself off. What business was it of Mr. Brook's to know anything like that? It did show her to what degree she'd let down her guard in the presence of friends. She cleared her throat and began walking east, crossing the street into the concealing shadows of Berkeley Square. The winter darkness was fully settled, and the cold eagerly rushed in to steal away the moments of warmth they'd gained.

"We need to break into another telegraph office," she said brusquely. "I'll get this information to Mrs. Woodwake. I think there's a place just along—"

She halted as a man unexpectedly emerged from behind one of the vast trees of the square's park, putting himself in their path. She had not sensed or seen him. Instantly thinking of the ghost Alex backed away in alarm. Brook was better prepared and had his empty Bulldog up and aimed, getting between her and the threat.

The lean, tall figure did not react, but held in place. "Put that away, Lieutenant," he growled.

"Identify yourself," said Brook, unfazed.

"Pendlebury will tell you."

She recognized the voice and her heart sank. They needed more time, the freedom to move and act. If she grabbed Brook's arm they could make a dash for it . . . and likely get only yards away before being brought back in disgrace. A number of mounted people were about, more than might be expected considering the day and the hour. They were there for her, of course.

Had she not been distracted by the wealth of good feeling at Hollifield House, she might have given greater notice to the street.

The man struck a match, lighting a small black cigar. The flame gave her a glimpse of a craggy lined face with a stubborn jaw and a long, cruel mouth. His eyes were as green and as hard as polished jade, a cutthroat's eyes, but by reports and action, he was unflinching in service to queen and country.

And he had saved their lives not two hours ago.

"Stand easy, Mr. Brook," she said. "This is Colonel Sebastian Mourne. He's on our side, God help us."

CHAPTER TEN

In Which Mince Pies Are Consumed

Mourne seemed unoffended by her observation and puffed on his cigar. "I knew you'd head here, Pendlebury. Took your time about it."

Alex noticed that the gas lamps on this side of the square had not been lighted. That was no oversight, not in this part of London.

"Get along, the both of you. In there."

He gestured at the sinister shape of a Black Maria that blended with the night. You'd have to be on top of the thing to see it. The metal door was open, yawning like a mouth into hell.

"Shift yourselves before some lunatic shoots you. You know the situation we're in."

Alex twitched her cloak aside to extend the air rifle to Mourne. "If you would, sir. I'll need both hands."

"Cheeky baggage," he muttered, accepting it, and there was a remote coloring in his tone indicating that he just might be amused. Briefly. Perhaps to the count of one.

She climbed in, feeling her way—it was pitch black—and tucked herself onto a narrow bench, sitting bolt upright. A drunken stink clung to the interior and she had no desire to accidentally touch any lingering emotions even with her gloves on. Her leaden walls were in place and a foot thick for this situation. She caught the hot metal smell of a dark lantern, which was an unfortunate reminder of Lord Richard's four-wheeler.

This moving box, certainly commandeered from Scotland Yard, was better able to protect its occupants from bullets, though that was cold comfort. It was still a transport for prisoners.

Brook sat next to her, then Mourne climbed in and secured the door. He gave a last look through the grilled opening, slid the shutter in place, and knocked twice on the front wall. They lurched forward. The confined area soon filled with the heavy smell of the cigar, which was an improvement.

"May we have light?" asked Alex, her gaze drawn to the cigar's intermittent glow, which was useless for illumination.

"No."

"You don't wish to examine the rifle?"

"Seen a dozen of 'em. When we counted bodies there was a weapon short and Woodwake knew you'd blagged it. There's only one expert in London on air guns you'd take it to, so I gathered some lads and set up a blind across from Danny's lair."

"Why didn't you stop us from going in?"

"Because as long as you were there you might as well get information. His lordship's more likely to spill to a pretty young thing like you than to an old goat like me. You are expected to report, in full, starting with how the devil you ended up out front and under fire with Miss Sybil."

Alex noted how he spoke the name, which indicated he had respect for the woman. Their interplay after the shooting . . . friends, certainly. Colonel Mourne was a harsh, forbidding sort and did not award his regard lightly.

"Is that her name or a designation?" she asked.

"What does it matter?"

"If a designation, then why not call her Cassandra?"

"Because no one believed *her* prophecies. We take everything Sybil says very seriously."

"She's a true Seer, then."

"And damn good at it, when she's not being blocked. Now get on with it."

Alex gave a swift recounting, beginning with Sybil back-

ing out of the building and ending with Lord Hollifield's re-
marks on the air gun.

"She wanted us to take it, sir," Alex concluded. "I'm not
excusing myself from disobeying orders, but after the attack
it seemed expedient to keep moving. Lord Hollifield provided
a name and address. If this Nabadenski designed these weapons, he might lead us to whoever is behind the attacks on the
Service."

"I expect he will, one way or another." There was a sound
of movement and Mourne rapped on the wall. Another sliding panel opened. He asked for and got the address from Alex
and repeated it to the driver, adding, "Have a rider telegraph
where we're going and that I want a flying squad to meet us
there. Make sure himself gets the message."

Their pace picked up, along with her heartbeat. She thought
they'd be going back to the Service offices. What in the world
was a "flying squad"?

Mourne returned to his place on the opposite bench. "Now
for the rest."

"Sir?"

"The two of you let yourselves into that flat on Hill Street
and spent a fair time there. One of my lads spotted you straight-
away."

"But we—" began Brook, who apparently thought better
of finishing and cut short.

"Didn't see anyone. I know. That's what you should expect
from those *I've* trained. Unless you fools were after some private trysting with each other, this missy gave that place a Reading. Why were you there and what did you find? This time
don't leave anything out."

Alex felt a sick heat in her belly for having been caught.
The prospect of dismissal had been easier to consider when
on the move and doing things. A lie of omission was still a lie.
The Service would not tolerate it. "Sir, I—"

"Your excuse is worth a tinker's damn to me. Report."

Next to her in the absolute dark, Brook shifted just a little.

Most unexpectedly, she felt his hand on her near shoulder. It rested there just for an instant, patted three times, then withdrew.

Good God. She almost said it aloud and was surprised she didn't. Even with her barriers up, she got his message of reassurance. One part of her was annoyed at his presumption, another part liked it. She wasn't alone.

She cleared her throat and pressed ahead with a full report of all they'd found in Veltre's rooms.

"Ætherics," the colonel muttered. "Bloody Ætherics and air guns."

She'd expected interest about the return of the ghost and the woman's kidnapping, not this. "Sir, a deeper investigation of them might provide solid evidence connecting my father's murder to that of Lord Richard and the attack on the Service."

"Evidence? We're past the point of needing that. If you'd come inside when you were told—never mind. Your running off to Danny may have saved an hour or so. Whether that's important or not remains to be discovered."

"What do you mean? Know you other connections?"

"Stew a bit, missy, and see how it feels."

"No, sir, I will not."

If he replied to that, then it was not audible above the rumble of the wheels.

"I have a right to know," she said, her voice far steadier than she felt. "As my father's daughter, I have a right to know."

"If they are linked, what of it?" he asked.

"Then we use that to find out who in the Home Office had him investigating the Ætheric Society and why. The death of one peer of the realm might be kept a secret, but not two, particularly when the second man is Lord Richard Desmond."

"Why should the first be kept a secret?"

"The nature of the Ætherics makes that a possibility. Mrs. Woodwake mentioned the prurient activities they indulge in at their private meetings. If my father discovered something embarrassing about someone in a position of power, then that person would want such discoveries buried. He or she could have arranged that 'Dr. Kemp' be killed and hope it be taken for suicide. Kemp was important, but not on the same level as Lord Gerard Pendlebury. Someone knew his real name. The killer planned an attempt on me the same night. There's no reason why I should be included unless—"

Alex did not want to voice it, for then it might become real.

"Unless . . . ?" Mourne prodded.

"Unless I also know the killer or the person behind him."

"Indeed? Do you know such a person?"

The idea was monstrous, yet it had been nagging at her since leaving Woodwake's office. "I-I have a concern that my uncle Leo might be involved."

"Do you?"

"A concern only. He works at the Home Office and so far as I know is wholly dedicated and loyal to the crown. But Mrs. Woodwake has been insistent that I should be at Pendlebury House. I can conjecture that she might be thinking along similar lines and wants me there to observe. The flaw in that is I would be in danger if . . . Oh, bother, that's entirely mad. Forgive me, Colonel. I'm short on sleep."

"And on evidence, but your reasoning's sound. That was one idea put forth at the war council."

"War council?"

"Which you missed. Make no mistake, there is a war on and you two survived the first skirmish. The attack on the Service was a major undertaking and we've no reason to think it's the last. That telegraph message you sent—Woodwake issued warnings to all Service offices. They're on the alert."

"I'm glad to hear it."

"As for your uncle—fratricide's not unheard of, what with Cain and Abel inventing the miserable business. If Leo topped your pap, then he'd have to top you, since you might Read something from him at a family dinner."

"That's not how Reading works."

"You and I know it, but those outside the Service think your lot plucks thoughts from their heads. Think how things might have gone last night if you'd not been called to Harley Street. Someone would have identified Gerard, and sent word to you, being next of kin. Once you're over the first shock, you'd have gone straight to Leo's house to break the bad news and he might have let something slip. But this ghostlike fellow who did the murder was to keep that from happening by killing you. Leo's safe from discovery by his niece the Reader."

Stated in such terms it truly was monstrous—and could not possibly be right. "I cannot believe that. Not Uncle Leo."

"What about the rest of 'em?"

"Impossible. Teddy's a boring prig but just as dedicated, Andrina would never risk her place as a lady-in-waiting, and Aunt Honoria thinks anything to do with the psychical is an affront to God, if not proof of madness."

"What about yourself?"

"*What?*"

"The possibility was raised."

"I've been cleared by Mrs. Woodwake," she said, her tone icy.

"Lucky for you, then."

Alex made herself calm down. Mourne was testing her in his own way, though it was pointless to trouble himself when he couldn't see her reactions. Perhaps he was something of a Reader himself, though she'd heard nothing of it in her time there. Theirs was an exclusive club and members all knew one another.

"What else was discussed at this war council?" she asked.

"Damn little that was helpful. I left them to it and went after you."

"What if," put in Brook, "what if Lord Leo himself sent his brother to investigate the Ætherics? He might have gotten orders to look into the business, but may have been reluctant to trust anyone but his own brother."

There followed a silence as Alex gave that unexpected idea

consideration. She didn't like her relatives, and had let emotion influence her thoughts. How unprofessional of her.

"Then Uncle Leo would have known where Father was and how to contact him. Why would he not tell me?" she demanded.

"It's called compartmentalization," said Mourne. "Is Leo one of those johnnies who doesn't talk about his work?"

"He was when I lived with them."

"There it is. He'd not tell you about Gerard. Probably thought you were in contact already. He'd not raise the subject at a family dinner."

"I don't *go* to family dinners," she snarled. "Aunt and Uncle are tolerable, but not my cousins. As soon as I was able, I moved out."

Mourne grunted. "Families. Best friends and worst enemies all at once. Can't fault you for wanting to avoid unpleasantness, but you might have learned something."

"Perhaps, but that doesn't explain why my father made no effort to contact me in the last ten years. Yours is an interesting idea, Lieutenant Brook, but it does not cover the facts. My uncle has an important place in the Home Office, but it is not that important. Someone higher up had charge of this. I have to find out who—"

"Devil take it—what is that smell?" asked Mourne.

She couldn't begin to guess which out of the mélange within these close walls had caught his attention.

Brook spoke up. "Mince pies, sir. Would you like some?"

"I certainly would. Haven't had a minute to stoke the boiler."

Lady Lindsey had been generous; there were plenty to go around. Alex managed another, though eating in the dark made it hard to keep track of crumbs and drips.

Mourne was pleased with the feast and made a low rumbling growl deep in his throat. It reminded her uncomfortably of a tiger, and not one held captive in a zoological garden. The last time she'd heard the sound had been on the back of an elephant making its way through tall grass. She and Father had been part of a hunt for a man-eater that had killed over a dozen hapless souls. She thought of the dozen and more men the colonel had taken down with his Winchester.

And the one he'd spared for questioning.

"What did you learn from the prisoner, sir?" She expected to be rebuffed, but he surprised her.

"They'd not got him talking properly when I left. Had to get a surgeon in to sew him up. Squealed like a spoiled toff until they put him out—which I was against. He'd have chattered quick enough if they'd given me a free hand. Woodwake's too bloody soft. He was our best hope. The other two are in bad shape, like to die. Good shooting on your part, given the circumstances."

The reminder gave her an uneasy pang. She abruptly lost her appetite for more mince pie.

"Here, you're not going to go sick on us about that, are you?"

"No, sir." *How can he see me in this murk?*

"Some do after a battle and there's no shame in it."

"Yes, sir." *Change the subject.* "Was anything helpful found on . . . on the casualties?"

"No papers, a few bob in their pockets, nothing else, not even a tart's calling card."

"Keys, watch fobs?"

"Some keys, of course, they have to live someplace. Don't know about fobs, could have used your eye there, girl. You see more than most."

"No laundry marks? Shop labels?"

"New clothes, the lot of them, with no clue who made 'em. Someone prepared for the possibility of these chaps getting killed or captured. We'll find who they are eventually. Woodwake called in the Yard, wants their lot to look at faces, see if they recognize any of 'em. Seems to think they're from the criminal classes, but she's on the wrong game trail."

"Indeed?"

"No thief or cutpurse could be bothered with that sort of work; there's nothing to gain in it. Same goes for any mad, murdering blackguard. He may have the temper to kill, but needs a reason. That line of shooters were drilled. They followed commands under fire and kept coming until we made it too hot for 'em over open ground. They're soldiers or I'm a Dutchman."

"Soldiers? But from what country?"

"Don't know yet. Could be anyone we've insulted in the last decade, which takes in a large portion of the globe. Could be our own; there's many discontented with how things are run on our own patch. They could be paid mercenaries. Plenty of those about if you know where to look."

"Colonel," said Brook, "if I may inquire . . ."

"Go ahead, lad."

"The Ætherics—they're an eccentric metaphysical group that hosts—uh—unusual parties. Certainly one or more members could blackmail others, but why on earth would they want an army?"

"Why indeed? It was also discussed. What do you think?"

"The equipping of even as few as twenty men would be costly. They were in nearly identical clothes, in the same hooded cloaks, carrying the same weapons. While Ætherics might have the money to kit them out, why do so? What return would they get from such an investment?"

"Destruction of the Psychic Service seemed to be the goal today. After the attack on Dickie Desmond all the eggs were in a single basket. If not for Miss Sybil shooting that first man— she saved who knows how many lives, bless her mad heart."

"But who would benefit most from its destruction?"

"Anyone with a secret to keep. The higher you go, the bigger the secret."

"There's no reading of thoughts involved, so you've both said. Secrets are safe enough. What if—" said Brook, "—what if the attack on the Service was a distraction?"

"Damn big distraction," said Mourne. "From what?"

"Lord Richard's death. Instead of investigating who would most benefit from his removal, we're led to think the Service itself is under attack."

"Which it was. If Dickie alone was the only real target, that puts a new face on it. But whoever is behind things sacrificed over a dozen men as a distraction."

"Sacrifice was never the intent. They expected to win. If Sybil hadn't anticipated things, hadn't shot that first man, the assault would have been successful. Who are Lord Desmond's enemies?"

"Enemies we guard against; let's instead ask who are his friends. That cuts things down. It'd have to be someone with deep pockets, which leaves me clear."

"Unless *you're* being paid well, sir."

Horrified, Alex held her breath.

Colonel Mourne suddenly released a boom of laughter. It was too loud for the confined space and she winced at the noise, but at the same time she opened her defenses enough to Read his reaction. It was wholly genuine.

When Mourne regained control of himself, he blew his nose and coughed to clear his throat. "I can see why you were transferred, Brook. Too cheeky and truthful by half. That's never gotten much respect in the army. The navy would have had you striped, whatever your station. Well, girl? Did I pass muster? No Reader worth the name would let that opportunity go by."

"Yes, sir, you did. We can trust you."

"Ah, but can I trust *you*? Don't bother answering, you'll show me."

"I'll do that now, sir."

"Will you?"

"Yes, Colonel. You said it yourself: the higher you go, the larger the secret. Or in this case, the more valuable. Nothing is more priceless than knowing the future. There's little to gain by destroying the Service, but it could be to someone's considerable advantage to kill or kidnap Sybil. Who knows of her existence?"

"Too many. Dickie had the influence to keep them quiet, but with him out of the way—but no, this is long planning. She started going off the rails weeks ago. We thought it was her bloody gift catching her up, making her even more mad, then worked out she was being countered by some outside influence."

"Blinding her from seeing the future."

"And playing holy hell with decision making. There's some who don't take a step forward without her say-so."

"Who?"

"Never you mind."

The prime minister, the queen herself? To have such an asset as a Seer and not make use of her was ridiculous. Alex knew her godmother would be open to anything that would preserve and protect the realm. She'd been the target of considerable criticism about the creation of the Psychic Service, but her foresight had proved correct, time and again. Those like Aunt Honoria, who had a horror of supernatural matters, politely overlooked the issue as one might for an eccentricity displayed by a wealthy and powerful relative.

Mourne continued. "If Miss Sybil had been in top form, Dickie would never have been caught out. Who knows but your pap might still—well, never mind. What's done is done, God help us."

"Which may be what prompted the Service attack. Yes, kill as many of us as possible, but find *her*. With her dead, whoever is behind these attacks can proceed toward some goal in happy security. But this is speculation. We must have more facts."

"We'll get 'em, missy. We've arrived."

Their wagon had stopped; the driver tapped twice on the wall between.

"I'll take a reccie. Lieutenant, you're heeled, you—"

"Out of ammunition, sir," said Brook.

"Are you now, and you still waved iron under my nose as though you meant business. Don't do that again. Here's my

shooter, see to it I get it back. You and Pendlebury stick here
and keep sharp."

Mourne opened the door, bringing a welcome flood of
fresher air. After the stuffy blackness, the ordinary night seemed
bright. Alex was not familiar with this part of London, but
knew from the smell they were close to the Thames. She expected great dirty buildings and a dearth of street lighting and
was not disappointed. They were not quite at the address,
though, but halted several numbers away.

In addition to their driver, four men on horses were along
for the expedition. The colonel issued orders. Each went off
in a different direction to reconnoiter the wider area for suspicious hooded characters.

Mourne departed south toward the river, walking briskly.
He was soon lost to the shadows.

The buildings were home to a number of businesses, some
with foreign-sounding names and few clues to what was made
or sold behind their walls. They were, of course, closed and
silent with no sign of a watchman or owners living on the
premises. It might be a busy place during the day, but seemed
as empty as the moon at this hour.

Which was wrong. London, being London, had a surfeit
of population to fill the streets. Even unfriendly, deserted ones
like this usually had a share of drunkards, prostitutes, and
thieves wandering through. What did locals know that kept
them away? Brook seemed to sense the oddness as well, holding himself alert and restive, though he was silent.

Alex decided she did not care for, nor was she suited to,
sentry duty. She was impatient and cold, but moving around
would make noise and possibly draw attention. She kept the
solid bulk of the Black Maria to her back and hoped this venture yielded fruit. That alone might (*might!*) mitigate her ignoring orders.

But in retrospect, it was ridiculous to hang expectations on
an old address even if the source was Lord Hollifield himself.

On a mere recollection he'd connected the air rifles to a visit from a self-proclaimed inventor. There might be a hundred such engineers roaming about with plans for making air guns with cranking mechanisms.

Which was the problem: someone had obviously executed those plans.

What a nasty yet appropriate word: *executed*.

She glanced uneasily at the tops of the surrounding buildings. *That's* where she should be, on the high ground—

What the devil?

Floating and silent, a vast rounded shape drifted over them, blotting out the gray sky. It was so unexpected a sight that she did not immediately take it in. Her first instinct was to duck, for anything that huge could not possibly remain aloft.

An airship?

Those were not permitted over the city; they caused too great a disturbance when people ran into crowded streets to stare. Sometimes one saw a ship in the high distance or moored in empty fields set aside for that purpose, but not over London and never so low.

Brook likewise noticed and to his credit remained quiet, though he was clearly just as startled.

Their driver quit his perch, reached into the wagon, and brought out the dark lantern. This one doubled its use as a signal lamp by means of an attached mirror. He lifted its gate, and the light flashed upward toward the ship. He blinked it in a set pattern until another light answered from above.

As the bulky ship maneuvered against the wind, the rumble of engines could now just be heard. This was a much larger, more improved craft than the one that had carried her over the hostile lands of the American territories; the lines were smoother, more graceful. With power for propellers it was not dependent on the prevailing winds for push. It was, just possibly, big enough for an Atlantic crossing.

Activity was afoot in the gondola; lights flickered and

moved about. Alex strained to hear orders being called, but the wind and engine noise prevented that. The ship was soon parallel to their street in an excellent show of deft piloting.

Then lines were thrown over the side and, most unexpectedly, men began sliding down them, as swift as circus acrobats. They had control over their rate of descent, some quicker than others, and shortly after a group of fifteen disembarked. They detached from the lines, which were rapidly pulled back up.

The driver signaled again. The airship continued south toward the river until intervening structures blocked it from view.

The men wore thick rugby pullovers, knitted balaclava helmets, leather gloves, and riding boots, every stitch and scrap in unrelieved black. Leather-and-glass goggles protected their eyes against the vicious cold and wind of the higher altitudes. They were armed with Webleys on lanyards, truncheons, and what looked like—if one could judge by the length and shape of the scabbard—throwbacks to a Roman gladius, also on lanyards.

Though hard to see against the black and in the dark, they were partially armored, too, with formfitting plates strapped to their chests and arms. Metal that was strong enough to stop a bullet tended to be too heavy to wear, but evidently this well-built lot had no difficulty with the burden.

The last man down, noticeably bigger and taller than the others, carried a captured air rifle, along with its crank, which hung from his belt. How he'd managed that and lowered himself one-handed on a hundred-foot line was a mystery.

One man alone was formidable enough. Collectively, they were terrifying.

"I would hazard to deduce," whispered Alex, "that *that* is a flying squad."

Colonel Mourne's lean figure emerged from the dark. The men snapped to attention.

"That was sharp work, lads. Finally got to use that training, what? Ready for a rat hunt?"

They murmured an affirmative.

"Right, then. I had a look, and there's an ambush ahead."
He cast a cold eye on Alex and Brook. "Anyone fool enough
to try the front bell will get a warm reception, so we won't
touch it. Whoever they are, they're set up to defend themselves."

"How many, sir?" asked someone in the back.

"I don't know, could be two or twenty. I'm going in to flush
'em out. Your objective is to capture if possible. We need prisoners to question, but if it's your life or theirs, don't hesitate.
You're more valuable, choose yourself every time. If they have
those special air rifles, it's twenty shots to your one. You won't
hear their fire. Keep your eyes open."

He then gave a concise description of the building. The front
wall, twelve feet high, made of stout brick, had a wooden gate
wide enough to admit wagons, locked of course. Inside were
a delivery yard and the building itself, which was three floors,
also brick with barred windows.

"There are only two openings in that wall for escape. You
six cover the mews in back. There's four of ours there already.
Tell them what to expect. You eight post up and down this
side to watch the gate. You"—Mourne nodded to the man
carrying the rifle—"are with me."

They slipped away. The ones remaining found concealment
in doorways and shadows and seemed to magically vanish in
the darkness.

"We'll come along," said Alex. "We can watch their back
while they watch yours."

"You trained for fighting?"

"I've seen my share. Practical experience, sir."

"That's jolly for you, then, but I trained these lads myself
and we all know what to do and when. You stick to Reading.
Let them do the heavy work."

"Yes, sir."

Her easy reply stopped him in midturn and he snarled a
curse. The man with him muttered into his ear. Mourne nodded and faced her. "I don't appreciate being lied to, missy, however keen you are to help. That ends or I'll toss you in the

wagon and lock the door. If you want to watch, you may do so, but keep clear and take cover if it turns hot. Brook?"

"Yes, sir, I'll see to it, sir."

"There's a man who knows the value of discipline." Mourne and his tall companion hurried on.

The snapping remark stung. Alex full well understood discipline; her life and sanity depended on maintaining it. She looked at Brook, frowning.

He shrugged. "You were going to rush in regardless, weren't you?"

"Not rushed. I'd have been careful. This excursion was not my idea. I was going to report and let the Service handle it, but we were abducted. Since I'm here, I want to be useful."

"So do they. And it will be better for all if we stay out of their way. The last thing they want is us in the middle, distracting them. You've practical experience, but they've drilled for it, weeks on end, in all weathers."

"How do you know?"

"One hears about special companies getting advanced instruction. Having an airship at one's disposal to deliver men, though, that's new. They're part of the Service?"

"Not that I've heard." Which was disturbing. She thought she knew all the gossip and rumors. This was an altogether different level of secrecy.

"It's one thing to have the police at hand, but this smacks of being a private army," he said. "I wonder if the queen knows."

Their driver wanted to turn the wagon to face away from things. "Don't need the horses in the line of fire if it comes to that," he added.

She and Brook aided in the operation, each taking charge of a horse, leading them around, backing and bringing forward. They made a good deal of noise. It occurred to Alex that they might be an intentional distraction, and she worried about snipers looking their way.

"If I might suggest," said Brook when the operation was completed, "we should take cover inside the wagon."

"I'd rather not." She did not care for enclosed dark places, even if they were armored.

"It's defensible."

"And a potential trap. I'd rather be a moving target."

He grunted agreement and they waited in its shadow, the bulk of the wagon between them and the south end of the street.

The driver stood in front of the big draft animals, hands on their noses to calm them. They kept trying to toss their heads, anxious about something.

"Did you notice if the colonel was armed?" Brook still had the borrowed pistol.

"Not that I could see."

"Doesn't strike me as a man who leads from behind."

"Indeed. How did he know so much about what's on the other side of that wall? He couldn't have climbed it."

"Probably found a ladder somewhere."

"Hardly the sort of thing one leaves abou—"

From the mews behind the buildings, a horse shrilled, alarmed over something. Had it been shot? Alex anticipated gunfire, but the nearly silent air rifles changed everything. What damnable weapons they were.

A dog started up, barking, then another dog and another. Some howled, angry and afraid at once.

The row was in the next road over. What was going on over there? Alex kept watch on the shadows where the flying squad men hid. If anything happened on this side, they'd confront it. She could see little of the building where Mourne had gone, just a slice of the wall and gate.

Then the voice of another animal added to the din. For all her ingrained self-control, she gave a start and so did Brook.

"What the devil was *that*?" he asked, then hurried to help the driver keep the horses from bolting.

The sound repeated, louder and closer, and Alex fought her instinctive urge to run.

It had come from their target building and was an impossibility. It could not, simply could not *be*.

But it came again and was unmistakable: the full-throated angry roar of a big game cat.

Hollifield said the Polish engineer was mad; was he mad enough to keep a pet lion?

The Black Maria rocked as the horses reacted. The driver and Brook had their hands full; they missed when the front gate burst wide open and dozen men ran out, some shrieking in what seemed to be blind panic.

The flying squad emerged like black phantoms to stop them.

This was difficult, for the fleeing men were hell-bent on getting away. They dodged, fists swinging. Whatever had routed them was a greater threat than the squad, and they were too terrified to organize much resistance. A swift attack with truncheons took out most. The one exception was on horseback; his mount was just as eager to escape. He rode low over its neck, clinging to the saddle and mane like a cocklebur.

They slammed through the squad and came tearing up the street toward Alex. Webley in hand, she stepped forward. There would be an instant to shoot the rider when they passed, but at point-blank range she'd surely kill him or hit the horse, neither an option she liked. Jumping in front of the charging animal to grab the reins was lunacy, though.

The decision was taken from her.

She glimpsed it, a flash of something large and lithe topping, then leaping down from the wall, landing heavily and surging forward in pursuit of the horse. It was a matter of seconds, not enough for her mind to accept what her eyes saw, but she brought her gun up in a futile attempt to stop a far worse danger. She got one shot off and certainly missed, for the *tiger* kept bounding forward.

CHAPTER ELEVEN

In Which Wild Beasts Run Amok

Bloody hell!" shouted Brook behind her. He abandoned struggling with his horse, fired, and also missed.

The driver bellowed at them to stop.

Alex ignored him; there was time for one more aimed shot, but she didn't get the chance. Something blurred at her hand like a striking snake. She cried out as the driver's whip lashed the Webley from her grasp. The same action upset Brook's aim and in that instant the tiger leaped at the fleeing rider.

She knew it would be efficient and brutal. Tigers bit down on the neck, strangling their thrashing prey to death.

But that did not happen. In midair, the great cat gracefully swatted the man clean from the saddle with one huge paw, then dropped onto all fours. The horse staggered at the buffeting from the attack, but kept going, ears flat, eyes bulging.

Brook got in front of Alex, sighting down his arm like a duelist, then flinched and cursed when the driver struck again with the whip, accurately plucking the gun away.

"Stand down!" he shouted. "Help with the damned horses!"

He had one by the bit, but the other reared and squealed, trying to break free. The tiger was not twenty feet away, looming over the fallen rider.

Alex's pistol had fallen under the wagon. She started to retrieve it when the cat roared again. Her knees turned to water, she couldn't help herself. No one could hear that and not be paralyzed by sheer primitive terror. She gulped it back, bitter and cold, and clawed for the weapon.

She shifted to face the tiger. Brook was next to her, staring in the same direction and feeling about for his dropped gun.

"Stand down, damn you!" The driver's anger stirred the horses even more; despite the brake being engaged, they began dragging the wagon forward.

The man had to be mad—or knew something they didn't.

She hesitated. The tiger looked right at her, down at the rider, who lay prone on the muddy cobbles, and back to her again.

It was purring. The sound was not soothing.

Alex put her hand on Brook's shoulder. "Hold a moment . . . I . . . I think it's on our side."

Brook forgot himself and cursed softly and urgently.

"It might be"—she struggled for a sane explanation— "trained—as for a circus."

"Trained?"

"A raja I knew in India kept several as pets. Perhaps—"

Two of the flying squad hurried up, going straight toward the tiger, which obligingly moved out of their way. They checked the stunned rider over, then went to aid the struggling driver. The great cat trotted down the street where others of the squad, unconcerned by its approach, were lining the conscious survivors against the wall.

One of the squad cried out and fell. No sound of a shot, but he looked to have taken a bullet. His prisoner broke free and ran, then unexpectedly dropped as well.

Already chary of snipers, Alex called a sharp warning, pointing toward the rooftop opposite. She saw the movement of something black against a slightly less black background.

Two more men were shot, along with their charges, before the others reacted. One shouted a command and they rushed across the street to press against the building's front. The sniper would have to lean out and down to get to them.

But he did not do that, and instead fired on the remaining prisoners. Those lying insensible jerked as they were struck, others attempting escape did not succeed. It was a bitter reprise of Colonel Mourne's defense of the Service offices, but he'd cut down armed men, not helpless captives.

Alex centered her aim on the darkest patch on that roof, fired, and made herself a new target. She heard the smack of a bullet hitting the road almost at her feet, and dashed for cover in a doorway on the same side. If she could pick the lock and get in and up to the roof—damnation, her reticule and tools were in the wagon, which was being led away. The displaced rider had been thrown into the back and the two squad men ran to join their comrades, Brook at their heels.

"Stay there!" he shouted as they passed.

Not likely, she thought, having spied a better vantage across the street. The sharpshooter continued to kill prisoners.

The big squad man who had accompanied Mourne raised the air rifle high and got off a silent shot. There was no way to tell if it struck. He attempted a second shot and failed. The gravity-fed ammunition must have jammed. He swiftly took cover behind the open gate.

She used the moment, hurried to the inset doorway and peered out. The range was bad for a revolver, but she could keep the sniper distracted. She used the building's corner as a muzzle rest. The resulting flash and recoil prevented her from seeing if she struck anything important.

The tiger roared, seizing everyone's attention for a few seconds, veered to the right, and leaped up. It gained the top of a protruding entry under the shooter's vantage, but could go no farther. Even its formidable claws could find no purchase to clamber up a bare wall.

The tall man emerged and ran across with startling speed, gave a jump, and grasped the top edge of the entry. Two of the squad each grabbed a booted foot and boosted him the rest of the way until he stood next to the tiger.

Alex saw movement above again and aimed for it, buying the squad man time for whatever his purpose. When her eyes cleared from the flash, she wasn't quite ready to believe them. He was flat against the wall, his feet on the tiger's massive head.

Back legs braced, front legs on the building, the animal pushed upward until the man was in reach of a windowsill. One forearm taking his weight, he smashed the glass with his truncheon, knocking enough clear to allow him to climb in.

She stopped gaping and fired again. The tiger quit its perch and stood with the squad under the cover of the entry. They all looked up, as though listening to their friend's progress through the building.

Dogs continued howling, the only sound she could hear above the blood pounding in her ears. She breathed shallowly through her mouth, straining her eyes, hoping for telltale movement. She had one bullet left.

A blurring of shadows on top of the building, a strangled grunt turning from surprise to rage, she glimpsed two men so caught in their fight that they had no mind for their high surroundings.

The larger one seemed to be trying desperately to fling himself from the height, while the other was just as determined to drag him back.

She emerged from cover, checking the other roofs for more shooters.

The fighters bobbed from view. Alex ran to one of the fallen men, a prisoner. He was stone dead and she pulled back to avoid accidentally Reading him. The next man was one of the squad; he bled from his upper side under one arm, caught in an area not covered by the metal breastplate. The bullet might have gouged against his ribs; she couldn't tell, but he was stunned and in pain.

"See to the wounded!" she shouted.

The squad members remained diverted by the progress of their man on the roof. Only the tiger looked her way, twitching its ears. Blast the beast, men were dying.

This time putting more force into her voice, her language and tone lashed like a master sergeant. She surprised herself at the vehemence. It had the advantage of gaining their notice. Even the damned tiger reacted. The beast gave a strange coughing growl, almost sounding disgusted, then sped from cover, loping across and through the gate.

The others spread out and pulled comrades to cover. So far as she could tell, given the circumstances, the armoring had accomplished its good purpose, sparing its wearers from fatal wounds. But there was plenty of blood and she worried about the tiger's reaction to it. Just how well trained was it—and how the devil had it come to be here?

A short, savage cry drew her attention back to the sniper's building. The two men were against the low wall, their rasping breath audible as they slammed fists like pugilists who'd forsaken the rules of the ring.

One gained an advantage unseen in the distance and dark, locked his hands around the other's throat, and then flung himself backward—over the wall.

The second man was dragged along, but managed to grab the edge, taking the weight of both for two heartbeats before his grasp slipped. They struck the entry roof with a sickening thud, and momentum carried them down to the street. Alex heard the muffled pop of bones breaking.

The flying squad man landed on his much larger adversary, who lay still. The man moved feebly and fell away, struggling for air, having apparently had all his breath knocked out. His clothing was torn from the fight, one sleeve gone from the sweater and the balaclava askew over his face. He groggily pawed at it.

"I'm with Colonel Mourne," she said, kneeling over him. "Let me help."

He wheezed and attempted to push her away, but she got past his waving arm and pulled the covering clear . . . then rocked so far back on her heels as to go completely over.

He tried to drag the covering into place but was too late. She'd seen his face and were that not proof enough, then the tattoos snaking over his bare arm confirmed it.

"Blast and damn," said Lord Richard Desmond, his pale eyes glaring at her. Then they clouded, and he collapsed, chest heaving as he fought to recover his breath.

Alex scrambled backward, awkwardly getting to her feet. In an instant she understood the appalling fear she'd picked up from Mrs. Woodwake; Alex felt it seize her as well. Impulse struggled with intellect, neither offering enlightenment for the impossibility before her. Hardly aware of the action, she raised her Webley, pointing it at Lord Richard.

He glanced her way and captured enough air to speak. "I'd rather you didn't."

She made no move, peripherally aware of the others as they dealt with less extraordinary matters. A man eased next to her and placed his hand over hers to gently persuade her to aim elsewhere.

"I'll see to him, miss," he said briskly. "Are you unhurt?"

His touch conveyed his confidence and exhilaration; the emotions engendered by battle were so strong as to sieve right through her shock. She was wretchedly vulnerable, her internal barriers a shambles. Alex pulled away, keeping hold of her pistol, for its anchoring weight was reassuring.

"Explain," she said distinctly and to no one in particular.

The man ignored her as he checked the body of the sniper.

Richard, able to sit up, muttered, "For God's sake, not now."

His comrade made a sound, as though in agreement, but suddenly staggered from a blow. The no-longer-stunned sharpshooter burst into violent movement, flinging the man aside.

Several squad members leaped in, truncheons swinging and slamming with wicked force. Despite the fall and broken bones, he threw off one after another, finally rising to his full height, standing a foot taller than the tallest. He had shoulders like a giant, and there was something wrong with their strange sloping shape.

Moving with unnatural speed, he slipped a massive arm around Richard's throat, lifting him. He struggled, but had no success breaking free.

The tumult brought the tiger back. It paused, seeming to take in the scene, then launched forward in a smooth, crouching movement, like a housecat sneaking up on an unwary bird. But the shootist turned in time to see, dropped Lord Richard, and foiled the attack by meeting the beast halfway.

Alex could scarce follow the melee as the two rolled and roared, the tiger clawing the shootist's back to ribbons, the giant strangling the cat with one hand and punching at its belly with the other. A chance reflection revealed the blade of a knife flashing amid the flying blood.

The great cat twisted and clamped its jaws on the knife hand, ending the torment with a savage shake that severed the man's arm below the elbow—but the giant's grip on the tiger's throat continued. Ignoring his own wounds, he raised it high as though it were no more than a kitten. The animal was weakening for lack of air, tongue thrust forward between bared fangs, paws flailing. It suddenly went slack as a dead thing.

The shootist dropped his burden and tore a gladius from a fallen fighter's belt, rounding on Alex.

At her first clear sight of his face, she froze, unable to accept the exaggerated simian features as anything but a grotesque mask.

But no mask was capable of changing expression. Wide lips drew back to show inhumanly large teeth. His red eyes seemed to snap with fire and glow with fury, but she felt nothing, absolutely nothing, beating against her internal senses. There was no emotion at all from that huge body, no hint of pain, no shred of anger. It might as well have been a wisp of fog—

A ghost.

Her heart faltered, recovered, catching up with her mind as it hurtled toward an improbable but inevitable conclusion. With no solid evidence, only surmise crossed with emotion, she knew beyond all doubt that this was her father's killer. However monstrous it appeared, it possessed the wit to creep in and—

The images in her mind's eye of what had followed in that

quiet Harley Street room were fleeting and vicious; she blotted them out, not wanting to see.

Lord Richard began to stir again. He groggily felt for his own weapon, but his belt had been lost in the fight. The giant uttered a short snarl as though dismissing Alex as a threat and turned toward him.

Half an arm gone, bleeding in pulses from the stump, it bore down like a machine, as inexorable and no more conscious of itself than a locomotive. Its fingers were much too long even on that huge knotted hand. Wrapped clumsily around the short sword's grip, they angled the blade to gut Richard like a fish.

While *he* was something unknown and inspiring fear, this bestial *thing* was an abomination.

Raising her Webley, Alex surged forward.

Her own hand was rock steady, a sure and certain extension of her will—and unlike the grotesquery before her, she felt rage. It roared forth from her small form like living flame as she fired point-blank.

Her last bullet crashed through its skull. Blood and brains exploded out the other side. The body spasmed forward, falling heavily across Richard. The blade struck hard, the point ramming between the cobbles an inch from his head. It stayed there, a truncated version of ancient Arthur's sword in the stone.

A dazed Lord Richard pushed clear of the madly twitching body, gaped at the quivering gladius, and then at Alex standing over him, smoke from her revolver drifting in the still, cold air.

"Explain," she repeated, this time specifically addressing him.

He tried that pale glare again, but this time she stared him down.

He finally nodded. "My word on it."

Brook loomed before her. He'd been one of those thrown

around by the all-too-corporeal ghost and was the worse for wear with his clothes torn and a swelling, blackening eye.

"Are you all right?" she asked, anticipating the same question from him.

"What about yourself?"

"Alive and standing."

Her gaze fell toward the tiger, lying on its side on the cobbles. It coughed pitifully, limbs and body shivering, dying in agony from all those knife wounds. The poor beast . . . she cast about for another gun to put it from its misery.

Limping, Lord Richard got to it first. Instead of keeping a safe distance, he knelt next to the wounded beast, putting a hand on its flank, bending close to one ear.

"Come on, you old fool, wake out of it," he ordered roughly. "Come on!"

It coughed again, opened its vast green eyes, and gave a long groan.

"I know, but you can do it. I still owe you five shillings. Don't let me get away with that."

The animal shuddered and seemed to shrink. Alex could not follow exactly what happened, for it was swift and dark and whatever it was that impressed upon her brain was quickly rejected. One instant there lay before her a dying tiger, the next Colonel Mourne was in its place, shakily sitting up.

"Dickie?" he said in a thin voice.

"You're back," Richard assured him.

"Blood, I smell blood." He gave a start, his hand sweeping across the front of his clothes, which were covered in the stuff.

"Most of it's yours. Give yourself a minute to remember."

"That's the worst, I do. What in God's name was that thing? All I wanted was to kill it, whatever the cost."

"I know. We'll find out later. Catch your breath." So saying, Richard straightened and followed his own advice, then moved on to check the others.

"Miss Pendlebury . . ." began Brook, but he seemed unable to finish.

"Indeed. The world's gotten just a bit madder. But they do seem to be on our side."

"So far."

At some point, Brook led her from the immediate area and indicated that she should stay until his return. She had no objection to standing quietly for the few moments. She wanted to think, but was unable to do so. Nothing, in all her varied experience of the world, had prepared her for such as this.

Brook came back bearing the carpetbag and her reticule, which he had to place in her hands. It felt heavy, then she remembered her lock picks and the box of cartridges.

Reloading her Webley did not require thought. She broke it open, ignoring the blood that had spattered her hands and sleeves when she'd blown that unholy beast into perdition. Clearing the chambers of spent shells, she shoved in fresh ones, noting, with a small portion of astonishment, that her hands did not shake. She thought they ought to, considering.

"You're rather composed," Brook observed.

"This is shock. Why aren't you screaming? I want to."

"What's the point? These other chaps . . . well . . . there they are. Knocked about a bit, but soldiering on, a whole side of the Service I expect few know about. I doubt we were supposed to see any of that. The question is, what will they do with us?"

A number of possibilities came to her, departing swiftly. "Lord Richard owes me his life. I will use that for all it's worth."

The ambulatory members of the flying squad searched the area to make sure it was clear; the Black Maria was brought back. They removed their one surviving prisoner, the squad's injured were loaded in his stead, and it departed for St. Bart's, the nearest hospital. The enemy dead, including the monstrosity Alex had killed, were dragged inside the gate and left on the ground. The men moved as though they'd drilled for such macabre work.

She did not participate. Alex lacked their physical strength and had no wish to touch the dead lest she Read their last moments. Her barriers were unsteady and brittle in the aftermath. Brook contributed by taking up the shootist's air rifle, which had fallen from the roof. The weapon looked much like the others, but she noted differences that begged for closer study.

A squad man by the open gate whistled sharply, motioning that they should hurry. They crossed the road with two other stragglers, entering the paved yard of a sizable building. Dirty snow was piled high in dim corners, shrouding the bones of cast-off machinery, broken crates, and other debris. The tall structure in the middle was cheerless, coated with decades of soot, and its iron barred windows might well have been bricked over for all the light the filthy glass allowed in or out.

One of Colonel Mourne's riders trotted past, his horse restive and snorting when it came close to the dead shootist. As soon as they cleared the gate, two men locked it and remained on watch.

Alex wanted a closer look at her kill.

She'd shot game before, to protect herself or to provide food, and afterward usually felt a letdown for taking a life, but not this time. Unconnected to any sense of revenge for her father, her heart swelled with a fierce pride of accomplishment. She'd removed something that was *wrong*, a thing that should not exist.

Though it wore outsize clothing, little about it was human other than its general form. The red eyes were faded and dulling, the large jaw sagged, and there was a flatness to the body she recognized. Call it soul or spirit, when that departed, the physical remains were strangely reduced.

Brook, not concealing his revulsion, said, "Seven foot tall if it's an inch. How could anything that big, looking as it does, slip around London unnoticed?"

"An excellent question. I would suggest powerful friends."

"Who could be friends with that?"

"Lord Hollifield. He directed us straight into a trap."

Brook shook his head. "He found an old address. He couldn't know what was here."

"He didn't have to, just see to it that we were followed or send a message ahead."

"He's your friend. Why would he wish you harm?"

She had no answer to that. The idea that Hollifield could be involved in this devilish business was absurd, unthinkable. *But not impossible, and if so, then something very nasty is afoot.*

"It makes no sense."

"We will find the sense, Mr. Brook. Obviously more information is required." She started to reach toward the creature, then hesitated. Her psychical barriers were badly in need of shoring up, but she had no awareness of the thing on that level; what harm could befall by touching it?

None, she discovered as she went through its pockets. All were empty.

"He had a knife. . . ."

"Over there." Brook was content to just point at the lower half of the arm the tiger had bitten off. One of the men had placed it in the general area of its original attachment. The unnaturally long fingers still grasped the weapon.

She pried them away with difficulty and examined the blade. Nothing remarkable: a folding clasp knife, and though large, such could be purchased from any number of shops. The maker was British. She would have liked a closer examination with a pocket lens, but such minutia could wait. She put it back and extended a hand toward the rifle Brook carried.

"This," she said after a moment, "is a conspicuously superior weapon to the one we took to Lord Hollifield. The air reservoir is heavier, so it would hold a more powerful charge, and there's rifling in the barrel, more accurate, as that creature demonstrated."

"But shooting its own men?"

"We've no proof that they're linked beyond being in the same spot at the same time."

"No proof, but possible. You dislike coincidences; so do I. But this thing . . . I've read about gigantic apes running loose in the depths of Africa—could this be one of them?"

"This is no animal. Not in the common definition of the word, anyway."

"Perhaps a human aberration, then, only this one was not displayed in a circus. It doesn't look intelligent enough to do what it did, though."

"This thing is not human. Look at the structure of its hands. Even the apes in zoos have a greater anatomical similarity to us than what we have here. This is neither fish nor fowl. Whatever their outward appearance, people and animals alike have feelings. This . . ." She removed one glove, stretching her hand forth, along with her internal senses.

Nothing.

"Well?" said Lord Richard, from a few paces behind her.

She'd sensed *his* approach and didn't jump.

"Like a hole in the air," she said. "I should feel something, but cannot. Yet the horse reacted to it."

"That'll be the blood, I expect. The smell of it is . . . not right."

She lifted her arm to sniff the stains there.

"You won't catch the difference."

"What is it, sir?" Unspoken was the thought *And what are you?*

If he picked up a hint of the second question, he ignored it. Despite his torn clothes and general disarray, he looked as imperious now as he did in the coach on Harley Street with his ramrod posture and frosty manner. "I cannot say. The one fact I know is that the instant I clapped eyes on the thing I wanted to kill it. Instinctive reactions that bypass thought are placed within us for a reason, usually to ensure our survival. You have my congratulations and gratitude for your timely intervention, Miss Pendlebury. I will not forget it."

"My duty, sir, though . . ."

"Yes?"

"I felt the same. This thing is *wrong*."

"Agreed. Have you studied it sufficiently for the present? Then come."

He led the way in. The building's double doors were apparently locked but a smaller one on the side was in use and gaslight dazzled her a moment when it opened.

The interior was bright, indicating that work went on here at all hours of the day and night. If not as tidy as a hospital, it had the same look of controlled efficiency and organization. Long rows of workbenches filled the barnlike space; machining apparatus and other tools she could not identify were everywhere. The smell of oil, hot metal, and sweat hung heavy in the stuffy air. The plank floor glittered with embedded brass filings.

"It's an air gun manufactory," she whispered, taking in sturdy bins holding long barrels and other parts.

"There's hundreds—thousands of them," said Brook.

To the left was a partitioned-off area. Wood walls about nine feet high framed it, but it was open at the top. Within were drafting tables covered with papers and other clutter.

In the center, bound tightly to a chair with his arms behind him, was the captured horseman. His back was to the door. His fingers clenched into fists and opened again as he strained against the ropes.

Mourne's lean form bent close; he spoke quietly to the prisoner, who kept shaking his head. Lord Richard remained without, close enough to listen, but not participate.

Alex spared them a single glance, then attacked a stack of unopened mail on a table outside, having spied something on top. With a rush of satisfaction she showed Brook the card she'd ripped from a familiar cream-colored envelope.

He read, "*8:30—Masters Impart.* Well, well. It must not be an exclusive gathering if that sort of fellow was invited." He nodded toward the office.

"If this was addressed to him, and I think it was. Look at his boots."

"What about them?"

"They do not match the drabness of the rest of his clothes. Those are a gentleman's boots. As for his hands . . . he's no laborer. Does a bit of writing to judge by the ink stains and—oh, bother this minutia; look at these invoices. Does the handwriting seem familiar to you?"

"Mrs. Veltre again—with an order for five thousand tea gowns?"

"We've found her dressmaker."

"What's this?" asked Richard.

She gave him a truncated report of the coded receipts they'd found at Hill Street.

"How did you know to go there?"

That was somewhat more difficult to report.

He was ill-pleased at the answer. "Why did you not pass this information to Mrs. Woodwake?"

"I discovered it after she interviewed me. She gave no indication that my father's death and-and yours . . ." She faltered, voice fading a bit. ". . . were connected. I wanted to be sure of things before bringing it to her attention."

"The truth, if you please, Miss Pendlebury. You knew she'd send someone else."

"Yes, sir."

"Whatever the outcome, there will be consequences for your ignoring orders."

"I know, sir."

"But not right now. Continue with what you're doing."

Before she could, Alex caught the word "regret" from Colonel Mourne and the prisoner raised his head and declared, "No, sir. Not one! If you had a shred of true honor you'd see to your duty as I have. England for the English!" he called out in a ringing tone as though it were a triumphant battle cry.

Lord Richard, battered and weary, reacted with a marked straightening of his already straight spine. On an altogether different level, Alex felt such a powerful wave of anger coming from him that she almost staggered from the force.

"Sir—" she began, but cut off when Richard raised a finger.

He left them, had a quiet word with Mourne, and took his place as interrogator.

Richard put one hand under the prisoner's chin, forcing him to look up. His lordship's full attention was in play; the man visibly trembled. Alex was glad not to be under the focus of those ice-blue eyes. They were intimidating enough when he was being friendly. Now, well, whatever it was, it looked intense and unpleasant.

However, she had endured and overcome that gaze. She was prepared to wait until he finished and could explain things.

But Colonel Mourne snorted and gestured for them to follow, muttering, "Get along, you two. Over here."

Flying squad men were busy throughout the place, opening bins and poking at machinery. When Mourne came to one of the long benches, he eased down with a groan of relief, abruptly looking old and tired.

He sniffed. "Lieutenant, any of those mince pies left?"

Brook obligingly opened the carpetbag and Mourne fell on the supplies like a starving man. Alex made use of another bench, pulling it close. A wave of cold fatigue seized her, stifling even her rampant curiosity as countless little aches and bruises began to make themselves felt.

Eyes closed, she slowed her breathing, creating a calm center within until the physical distractions subsided. When she could face things again, she opened her eyes to find both Brook and Mourne staring at her.

"Emma Woodwake teach you that?" asked Mourne.

"It's what I learned when Father and I were in Hong Kong. . . ." Treacherously, her control slipped and she gulped to keep from breaking into mortifying sobs. She would *not* allow it. "The man . . . the thing I shot—that's the ghost. That's what killed my father."

"You saying or asking, girl?"

"Both. What is it?"

"I've never seen the like before, but officially, things have gotten worse."

"What things, sir? Worse than Father's murder, worse than an attack on the Service, worse than what we've just been through?" She managed to keep her voice from rising, but her throat was tight.

"Yes. I'm deciding how much to tell you. I'll talk to a calm member of the Service, but not to an excitable outsider. Choose."

Brook took one of her hands and pressed his flask into it. "Drink," he ordered. "You're thirsty."

Indeed, she was parched, and she wanted water more than anything else, but choked down enough peaty fire to steady herself. The stuff had a more immediate and powerful effect than controlled breathing. She gave back the flask with a nod of thanks.

By then Mourne had finished off the mince pies and produced his own flask to wash down the last morsel.

Even with the rush of alcoholic heat making her head feel heavy, Alex plunged forward. "Lord Richard said he'd explain. He gave his word on it."

"Of course he would. He's a sentimental fool when it comes to pretty girls, and he should know better."

"This very morning he was shot dead right in front of me. Please don't say I was mistaken."

"I won't, though it's true. He was in a bad way for a bit, but it takes a lot to put a dent in our Dickie. I imagine there's times when he'd like it to take him away for good, but he wasn't killed. Not today."

He paused for another drink.

She recognized the kind of hesitation that preludes a difficult task. He'd speak in his own time, but perhaps a topic change and some small prompting would help. "I've seen tigers in India—but never ones with green eyes."

"How long were you in India?" he asked, giving her a sharp look.

"Several months."

"Get to see some of the stranger things their fakirs got up to? Listen to any of their stories? Doesn't matter if you did or didn't, what those johnnies flog to the crowds for begging bowl money ain't the real show. There's hardly a handful in the whole damnable country able to do it . . . and they keep it to themselves lest some raja wants 'em dead or chained up as a slave."

"Sir, of what are you speaking?" asked Brook.

"Nightmares, Lieutenant. Legends that are real and shouldn't be."

"Like the ghost?" suggested Alex.

"No, missy. Like myself and Dickie over there. You've got your ability to Read. Is it a gift or a curse?"

"Equal parts of both, sir," she said drily.

"I've heard the same from all of those with psychical talent. Some are born this way, others come to it late, and others acquire it. Dickie and I are in the last lot. He volunteered God knows how long ago; mine was against my will but I've made the most of it since. We serve queen and country, which is all that matters. Before you say you don't understand, don't bother. It'll come with time."

"This is ridiculous," said Brook. "Conjuring tricks. Magic lanterns. You can't ask me to be a part of such flummery."

"Too late for that, Lieutenant. You're square in the middle, like it or not. There is the psychical and then there is the supernatural, and for that there's no proof but your own eyes, but don't expect me to go the whole tramp. I'm all in."

With that, Mourne closed his eyes and took a deep breath.

Alex held her own, not knowing what to expect. Brook froze.

Mourne's features, his whole body, seemed to ripple like air over a hot oven. For an instant his form stretched in a wholly impossible manner, skin and clothes melding, changing color and texture. She glimpsed the supple, dangerous beauty of black and yellow stripes, deadly grasping teeth, and arresting green eyes set in a wide, flat skull.

Then it ceased and he was as solid as before, a savage-faced old hunter showing dour regard, as though expecting the worst.

"Rakshasa," Alex whispered.

"Close enough," he grumbled. He looked at Brook, who remained frozen. "Shape-shifting demon to you, Lieutenant, but leave off the 'demon' nonsense. I'm a man, same as you. Most of the time."

"Impossible."

"Believe your eyes or not, I'm too tired to do a full shift. Makes me hungry and we're out of mince pies. The tiger would be ravenous. He's fond of raw meat and sometimes not too particular where it comes from."

Brook glanced helplessly at Alex. "Shape-shifting demon?"

"It's from Indian folklore, a myth," she said, recalling what she'd read as a child. "Rakshasas are supposed to take any form and haunt graveyards looking for human flesh."

"That's the myth part, at least so far as I'm concerned," the colonel added. "Thank your lucky stars."

"How is it possible?"

"Any number of nasty things can happen to a soldier when he's off in a strange place. He might bring home a case of malaria to haunt him for life—or worse. This is what I brought back. There've been times when I'd have gladly traded."

"How did it happen?"

"I'm not giving my life story. Suffice that when I was much younger and more foolish I was in the wrong place at the right time and you don't need details. I'm all for females having an even footing with men on most things, but the rest of the tale ain't fit for a lady's ears."

Alex considered arguing the point, for she had read a number of books that were outside of what was thought to be "fit" for her sex. But it would be useless to press. Once a man got it into his head that he was being protective, there was no shaking him.

"Very well."

"Sensible girl." Mourne lifted his flask again, seemed to

think better of it, and put it away. "I came back changed, we'll leave it at that. So what is it? Gift or curse? I'll say along with you that it's both. What matters is we're on the same side."

She glanced toward the office. Lord Richard must have been making progress, for the prisoner appeared to respond to questions. That was a good sign, though his lordship did not seem pleased with the replies.

"Does . . . does the queen know?" asked Brook.

Mourne gaped with naked disbelief for a moment, then barked a short laugh. "*That's* your first question?"

"A reasonable one, I think."

"Of course she knows, though it's the Lord Consort who usually deals with us. He and Dickie's family have a long history. They haven't always gotten on, but times have changed. There's too many dangers afoot to be choosy about one's allies, but Lord Richard's always been bound to defend the throne, and I mean that in a literal sense."

"Is he also . . . a rakshasa?"

"No."

"What is he?"

"The official title is Queen's Champion, though you won't find it written down anywhere. As for how that came about, he'll tell you himself if he's so inclined. He's older than he looks, stronger than any half dozen of my men together, and it'd take more than a few rounds from some pop-gun toy to remove him from this life, the poor devil."

Alex could not imagine Lord Richard as an object of pity, though the memory of his bloody body on her cousin's floor was yet fresh. How had he survived *that*? She repeated the question aloud.

"Once upon a time, they called it magic," said the colonel. "Now young squibs like Crookes and Sexton are trying to explain us with science. Good luck to them."

Brook shook his head, a thread of helplessness in his tone. "Sir, this is impossible!"

Mourne was nettled, but he kept his voice low and even.

"Raise your voice to me again, soldier, and I'll have you transferred to the Hebrides. I know this is hard, but at least pretend a respect for what I've said."

"We're getting answers," Alex whispered. "Even if they are impossible. No more so than Miss Sybil, and you believe what she tells you."

"That's different."

"How?" demanded Mourne. "She pulls her prophecies out of thin air and you accept 'em over what you've seen firsthand? What you fought out there in the street? You laid fists on that creature. It was real enough to do injury."

Brook seemed about to speak, then shook his head. He tipped his flask and finished it off.

"Hold strong, lad. You might get used to the impossible. Right, let's move on to what's in front of us. We've been lucky. Miss Sybil foiled one attack and Miss Pendlebury saved us here thanks to a well-placed shot, but be certain the enemy will regroup once they know they've failed." He jerked his head toward the courtyard. "What do you make of that thing, missy?"

"It looks ape-ish," she began, then considered that Mourne would be after a useful summation, not a statement of the obvious. "But its actions indicate that it must have possessed human intelligence. It murdered my father, invading his home and attempting to make murder look like suicide. It invaded my home, perhaps to serve me the same way, but for some reason abandoned that task. I believe it abducted Mrs. Veltre and God knows whether she's alive or not. After Mr. Brook and I left Lord Hollifield it turned up on a roof here, ably handling an air gun. Mr. Brook does not like the suggestion of a connection between this business and his lordship, but I cannot ignore that he sent us to this address. However, the creature shot prisoners along with your men. Considering its apparent intelligence, I would suggest its goal was to prevent them from being questioned, rather than an inability to tell one side from another."

"Your two cousins were at Hollifield House," said Brook. "One or the other could have asked about our destination. His lordship would have seen no harm in informing either of them."

"I'll allow that James or Teddy could be involved, however unlikely that might be. But is it not more logical to consider that Lord Hollifield might be a member of the Ætheric Society?"

"The *Ætherics*?"

"Many members are of the upper classes. Whether they're there to hear lectures on metaphysical and theosophical topics or to enjoy a more prurient entertainment—"

"But he's your friend, Miss Pendlebury, and . . . and the queen's relation by marriage."

"All the more reason to keep his membership a secret and to silence a spy in their midst. That could explain my father's removal. Mrs. Veltre had some association with him, so she also had to be removed."

"Peace, missy," said the colonel. "You're making guesses. It'll be easy enough to determine if Lord Danny's mixed up in this."

"How?"

"We ask him. Our Dickie boy will do the honors. He has a way of getting the truth from people whether they like it or not. Try not to look too appalled, Lieutenant. Lord Richard may get his general orders from the Lord Consort, but he's bound by oath and honor to serve the queen. If her brother-in-law is up to no good it has to be sussed out for the safety of the realm. Wouldn't be the first time that royal relatives made a mess of things. Whatever you do, don't mention the Wars of the Roses—oh, there you are. About time. You look how I feel. Sit."

Lord Richard, accurately described by the colonel, found a bench and surrendered to its limited comfort. He was paler than before and pinched the bridge of his nose. "That was . . . not pleasant," he said.

"The lad has a stubborn eye."

"I've had better cooperation from dead mules."

"Was he drunk?"

"Not on spirits. He's a fanatic. It's typical for religion and politics and a few other vices. Their extreme views are without reason, like a fever sickness. Took an effort to get past that."

"What did you learn?"

"Nothing good. He's heart and soul with the England for the English mob, but confirmed that there's a group behind them directing business."

"The Ætherics?" asked Alex.

"They're also just a curtain covering deeper and darker things, a tool and a source of funding from fools who should know better." Richard turned his tired gaze on Mourne. "It's as you thought: the Order of the Black Dawn."

The colonel's chronic scowl deepened. "I wish I'd been in error."

The name was not familiar to Alex, but something about it instantly nagged her.

Brook shifted and muttered, "Those pamphlets we found."

"Ah," she said, catching the meaning.

"What do you know of the Black Dawn?" Mourne demanded sharply.

Brook continued, "Mrs. Veltre had Ætheric Society literature with the motif of a black sun on it. They're connected, are they not?"

He made a noise of disgust. "There's brass for you. Hiding in plain sight."

"What is this order, sir?"

"The nobs directing things, so far as can be told. The Black Dawn's worse than the Ætherics or the E. for E. louts playing at politics. Some hint of 'em started up about the same time young Drina took the throne. There were those who didn't want her marrying any German prince, must have been a dozen plots afoot to assassinate any man with royal blood daring to cross the Channel. Busy times. But she showed them all. Can't get more English than the Godalming tribe."

"The next time they surfaced," said Lord Richard, "was during the furor prior to the passage of the Equal Franchise Bill. Some thought it bad enough the queen wanted to give a vote to every man in her realm, propertied or not, but she insisted women have a vote as well. Predictions of chaos, revolution, God punishing us all for disrupting the natural order of things—it was a mad time. The Service had a different Seer then, a bit more focused, and he kept having a vision of a black dawn. Took us a while to sort out the meaning."

"Did some good," said Mourne. "Because of that we were able to foil another gunpowder plot."

"*Another* one?" said Alex.

"Along with assassination attempts on the queen and any number of politicians supporting the bill. The vote went through fair and square as it should and passed by a cat's whisker. Let's hope you appreciate the effort that went into it, missy."

"Indeed I do," she said, "but what *is* the Black Dawn?"

"From the little we know they're a pack of johnnies who don't want change of any kind. It can be bad for business unless it's a change that suits them. If you're a fella who makes his pile selling guns, then a war every few years is just the thing to keep you in country estates. But the queen's a great one for using diplomacy over force to defend her interests in the wide world. There's some as think women having the vote has to do with that. Pure nonsense. Females are just as bloodthirsty as men, given the right circumstances. The obvious answer is that our queen's brilliant at picking ambassadors."

"And consulting Miss Sybil?"

"There's that. Keep her name to yourselves from now on. There's a war on and the less said about our assets the better."

"The Black Dawn knows about her, since they appear to have a means of blocking her Sight," said Richard.

"Mirrors," said Alex.

"What about them?"

"She spoke of them to me."

"When did *you* get in to see her?" he demanded.

"Put your bull pup away, Dickie," said Mourne. "Miss Sybil slipped her keepers. Woodwake found her in the dining hall frightening everyone out of their appetites. Sexton had the wit to write down everything she babbled, but I didn't get a chance to read it. Tell his lordship the rest, missy, before he bursts a blood vessel."

Lord Richard snorted, but pulled himself back, looking a bit less terrifying.

"She . . ." Alex cleared her throat; it had gone tight. "She mentioned red curtains, mirrors, a blackness behind them, and that I should break them and damn the bad luck."

"That's all?"

She nodded.

"Well," he said, after a long moment. "It would seem that you do have orders. Good of you to share them with us."

"There's more, Dickie. These two have been . . ." Mourne then rapidly conveyed what he'd learned from Alex during the trip from Hollifield House.

To her chagrin, a now stone-faced Lord Richard ordered— but so politely that it sounded like an invitation that might be declined—Alex and Brook out of earshot.

"Whether one wears a uniform or not, a soldier's lot is not a happy one," said Brook.

"That depends on the trust one has in one's senior officers."

"Do you trust them?"

"I am conflicted on that point, Mr. Brook."

Alex could not determine which man had the higher ranking in the chain of command. Probably Richard, but the colonel argued with him like an equal, and his lordship listened. They kept their voices down but it was a forceful and rapid exchange.

While this went on, new people came in. A glance through the open door showed two coaches in the courtyard, each overflowing with Service members. Some were obviously there to augment the flying squad men, others she recognized as clerks and record keepers. Doubtless they would take the place apart down to the nails and sort through every scrap of paper looking for names. Alex opened the carpetbag and gave the senior clerk the now mince-smeared invoices collected from Veltre's home, explaining their code. He nodded and swept away to the office, calling orders to his staff.

"That was quick," Brook murmured. "The rider who shot past us must have found another telegraph station. A direct line to Service headquarters in this part of town?"

Just how many of those had Lord Richard set up? Alex recalled a story in *The Times* where a financier boasted of the extraordinary amount he'd spent on a single line running from his West End home to the Royal Exchange. He disliked venturing out in inclement weather and had paid dearly to avoid it. Richard's expenditure must have been a hundred times that. The outlay indicated tremendous personal resources. An intense curiosity about the man belatedly seized her. Who—and what—the devil was he?

As though sensing her regard, he looked her way just then and indicated that she and Brook should return.

"If the Veltre baggage kept the accounts for the Black Dawn," Mourne was saying, "no wonder they've been on the move. She'd know as much of their plans as any of 'em. If they thought she'd been spilling to Gerard—someone might have panicked, sent that beastie to deal with him. That doesn't explain why it was after the missy here unless there's another Pendlebury involved who didn't want to be rumbled by a Reader."

"Absolutely not," said Alex, before Lord Richard could reply. It was speaking out of turn, but she was already struggling to keep her annoyance in check. "We've been over this and I gave good reasons to exclude them. However, it has been years since I lived at Pendlebury House. Perhaps a belowstairs spy is within the household and feared discovery. Servants come and go. My aunt can be difficult. I should like a chance to Read any staff that—"

"*Now* she wants to go home," Richard put in.

"That place is not my *home,* but I'll do whatever is necessary to find who's behind this."

"I expect you will do what you please—we've had ample demonstration of that—but will you follow orders?"

She felt herself flushing red. They were never going to let her forget her lapse.

Mourne snorted. "Oh, turn her loose, Dickie. She'll do more damage."

"And possibly get damaged herself in the proceedings. If you hadn't stopped them, these two would have walked right into this place or been shot dead at the gates by that monstrosity in the courtyard. I think it was sent to kill her and Brook and instead began eliminating witnesses to the goings-on."

"That puts Lord Danny in the thick of things, y'know."

"I am inclined to think he's nothing more than a cat's-paw. I'll determine that later. For now, we must take action before the Order learns of this setback and either decamps or mounts a fresh attack."

"I'm all for it, what do you suggest?"

His lordship favored Alex with a wintry smile. "Ask Miss Pendlebury."

CHAPTER TWELVE

In Which Miss Pendlebury Acquires
a Dashing Disguise

They don't *look* like madmen," observed Brook. "You don't look like a madwoman. I've not gone mad quite yet, therefore we should not be doing this."

"They were easily persuaded," Alex conceded, "but it is expediency, not madness that brought them to their decision. They want information as quickly as possible. It would consume time to acquaint others for such an infiltration. I can think of none who could take our places. Perhaps Mrs. Woodwake, but she may not possess the necessary attire. Neither do I, but I know where to acquire it."

At that prospect, Alex allowed herself to enjoy a short but satisfying moment of pure malice. Within the darkness of their coach, Mr. Brook was spared from seeing any negative change overtake her features. He'd had enough alarming shocks in the last few hours and should have a respite.

Their Service driver held his horses at a smart clip through the nearly deserted streets, taking the most direct route possible to Pendlebury House. Four riders accompanied them as front and rear guards. All were squad men, armed and armored.

Lord Richard was keen to discover who was responsible for what he called "this bloody mischief," which explained his ready agreement to Alex's plan to attend the Ætheric Society event taking place at 25 Grosvenor Square at half past eight.

His spies would not be unprepared; Brook was both her escort and protector. Like the riders, he was now armored, outfitted by a flying squad fellow of similar size. The metal plates were bulky, but his heavy cloak concealed all. He now possessed two loaded firearms, one in his coat pocket and another strapped to his chest. A cleverly designed harness and holster held that revolver under his left arm, its grip within easy reach.

A captured air gun would have been handy, but such a distinctive weapon would only alert the enemy to the presence of cuckoos in the nest. Alex had her Webley and hoped it would not be required. Lord Richard thought they would be safe enough. Past gatherings of Ætherics were reportedly boisterous, but not violent. Attendees of their most private of private parties were well dressed and rendered incognito by means of masks and veils. Alex inquired how he came by his information and was told that "Blackmail can be a force for good, when properly applied."

She reasoned that he'd gotten a recounting from a luckless acquaintance.

The Grosvenor Square address was a puzzle, owned as it was by that fearfully respectable patron of the arts and bastion of the highest of high society, the Duchess of Denver, making it the most unlikely place to host an event of wild debauchery. Lord Richard informed them that the duchess and her household were wintering in the South of France, so she might have innocently leased the house to some member of the Ætherics, unaware of the possibility that unsavory proceedings might occur.

Or might she *be in the Order of the Black Sun?*
Disturbing thought.

Colonel Mourne's succinct instructions were in line with Alex's own plans: get inside, learn all that could be learned, and then get clear to report.

Eyes open, ears sharp, Inspector Lennon had told her. He'd likened her to being a tethered goat to lure out tigers for the Service. In this case, it was a Service tiger sending her forth. What would Lennon have to say about the colonel's strange talent? Being a sane and sensible man, the inspector could be expected to head for the nearest public house and remain there until he forgot the whole matter.

Brook peered around the leather flap covering one of the windows. "We're here."

Their conveyance slowed and stopped, but the front riders continued past Pendlebury House, circling Wilton Crescent, looking for but finding no hidden threats. Alex was out, key in hand, with Brook at her heels. She didn't breathe again until they were inside the dim entry.

The gas was low in the front parlor, but she corrected that and gave the bell rope a sharp pull. One of the maids appeared and, despite training, yielded to a bout of shock.

Alex distracted her by ordering tea. Mabrey the butler appeared, hiding his surprise rather better, and inquiring whether he might be of assistance.

"In due time," she assured him. "Where are the family?"

They were away at various celebratory functions. Mabrey gave a recitation of where each might be found.

Excellent. Alex would not have to explain herself to any of them.

"This is Lieutenant Brook, who is assisting me on a Service investigation. As you see, he's suffered a misfortune and is in need of attention. Do whatever's possible to improve his appearance and send one of the senior maids up to my room. We're in a great hurry, and I apologize for the imposition, but I assure you it is extremely important."

Mabrey, having developed a high degree of imperturbability from dealing with the demanding Lady Honoria, gave a dignified nod as though he understood all. Alex told Brook to ask for anything and to please excuse her for no more than twenty minutes.

She trotted upstairs, stopping at her old room to divest herself of the cloak and the worse-for-the-wear blue dress. Not bothering with a dressing gown, she crossed to the necessary, scrubbed the blood of combat from her hands and face, and then quickly tripped down the hall to Andrina's sanctum.

A candle served to light every gas sconce in the chamber. Little had changed since the day Alex sent her offensive and bossy cousin tumbling over the floor. Some surface trappings were different: favorite toys were gone, replaced by elaborately framed photographs of various royal personages, but the wardrobes remained. Four lined one wall and Alex invaded each.

Aunt Honoria's personal maid, who had seen to things that morning, appeared with a tea tray and biscuits.

"Bless you," said Alex. "Just on the writing table, if you please."

"This is Lady Andrina's room, Lady Alex," she cautiously informed.

"I'm giving my cousin the chance to serve our queen in another fashion." *Fashion indeed! Andrina will burst a blood vessel and serves her right, comparing me to a parlor maid.* "I need to borrow a frock. Something formal."

"Those will be kept in her dressing room, Lady—"

"In there? Capital. And please, address me as 'Miss Alex.' It's what I'm used to."

"Yes, Miss Alex. But—"

Alex barged into the adjoining dressing room. It had once been a communal playroom for the house children, but Andrina had annexed it. Four more wardrobes, shelves for shoes, boots, and countless other items of adornment filled the place. Where to start? There was so much.

"Best dress?" she prompted.

"There are several, Miss Alex. What sort of occasion are you attending?"

"A dinner." That would give her some flexibility. "Pearls, not diamonds. Modest neck. No train. Veiled hat."

The maid went to the second wardrobe. "Any of these might serve."

"Bring them out for a look."

While the maid did that, Alex attacked the tea. She was dry as dust, and this time took milk to cool it quickly. Not as quenching as water, but it revived her.

An old treasure box on a writing table abruptly distracted her from the tea. Years ago she'd salvaged it from the attic. It had been *hers* when she lived here. As a secure place for trinkets it was a disappointment; the lock was broken.

How odd that Andrina had claimed it, considering her contempt for all things to do with Alex. Their shared full name was carved on the lid, the result of hours of work by Alex scratching away with a penknife on a rainy afternoon. The dull wood now shone from beeswax polish. She touched it, her guard down, and a maelstrom of emotions swarmed her. She jerked back, feeling ill.

"Something wrong, miss?"

Many things. She forced order upon the turmoil, pinning each emotion in place like an etymologist mounting and labeling a specimen. Here was fear, there was loneliness, this one was vast frustration, and that one . . . a terrible internal pain like a bleeding physical wound: longing.

The box had layers of it, thick as mud built up over the years.

Alex's response was astonishment. She had no idea that Andrina kept all that in her heart. What an unhappy, empty woman; no wonder she obsessed over exterior show.

But this box also provided Andrina with a great and sly gloating pleasure. There was something unhealthy about it, repellent. What the devil was inside?

Internal armor back in place, Alex tried to raise the lid, but the broken lock had been repaired. Her picks or a hairpin would remedy that—

Don't be ridiculous.

Andrina's privacy was sufficiently violated with this raid on her clothes. Alex wished she'd not touched the box; she didn't want to know such things about her cousin.

The diversion did raise a potential problem Alex had overlooked. "Is there a dress Andrina has not yet worn?"

The maid pointed out several. After cautious testing, Alex determined the garments were imprinted more strongly with the fading emotions of the dressmaker (a cheerful sort) rather than her cousin. "I'll need a cloak, too. Something dark, just over waist length."

"Velvet, wool, silk, fur, or satin?" After tonight, the maid would certainly be looking for a new post, minus a character reference, but if the prospect crossed her mind, she did not seem concerned. Her internal calm was admirable. Well, if she was dismissed, there was a place in the Service for her; Alex would see to it.

Alex both marveled over and disdained the fine dresses; they were as far above her once-pretty blue ensemble as it was above a horse blanket. The effort and expense to make the exterior of such an unpleasant person attractive offended her.

But picking out the best of the lot imparted another great, warm wash of malefic pleasure. Andrina would be so offended that her things had been gone through like rags at a charity jumble she might throw away the whole lot. Alex enjoyed the thought for a brief, sweet moment, then got down to business.

The best was too ostentatious and would draw notice. She picked the next one, which was elegant without too many fussy trims.

Alex was soon buttoned into the heavy silk gown, which was the finest thing she'd ever worn in her life. The color was a faded mauve with a soft sheen to it, the lines simple, the trims abundant but not overwhelming. However wanting Andrina was in personal charm, she possessed excellent judgment in attire.

"It's as though it were made for you," the maid remarked. "You're just a bit taller than Lady Andrina, but it otherwise fits."

"The waist is tight." They'd had to take in her corseting to a painful degree. Alex hoped she'd not be required to do anything more strenuous than a walk.

"Gentlemen like a trim waist."

Alex had yet to hear a man, gentleman or not, express any such opinion. It had always come from females. One day she'd have to inquire into the why of it, and she was positive that her sisters in the greater world had got it wrong.

In less than the promised twenty minutes, which was a wonder since proper dressing for a lady could take hours, Alex descended the stairs, making adjustments to the matching kid gloves that reached to her elbows. She'd gulped more tea for her thirst, had two digestive biscuits to steady her stomach, and was ready for anything.

Under Mabrey's supervision, Uncle Leo's valet had worked some strange magic with a clothing brush and sponge. An almost new man again, Mr. Brook waited at the landing, face washed and hair combed. She was abruptly reminded of coming downstairs in her own home so early that morning, for he wore the same expression, mouth agape, eyes goggling, and this time he failed to collect himself.

"You—" He cleared his throat. "You look most dashing, Miss Pendlebury, if you don't mind my saying."

Theirs must be a collegial association, but there was nothing wrong with a bit of harmless admiration for a successful disguise. "Thank you, Mr. Brook. Your appearance is much improved."

"Wait a few days and I'll have a glorious blue-and-yellow bloom around this eye."

"It *is* rather swollen. Is your vision impaired?"

"Not a bit. Mr. Mabrey recommended the application of raw beefsteak, but I requested and got a mask instead. It will not be out of place at such a secretive gathering."

"Mabrey must have hidden depths."

"He liberated it from one of the footmen, a ginger Irishman. Why would a footman possess a mask?"

"I remember him. Rather fun, surprised he's still here."

"But a mask?"

"When the servants are off to one of their own fancy-dress balls he always goes as Dick Turpin. He claims it intrigues the young ladies. They don't mind so much when he steals a kiss since it is in keeping with the impersonation."

"Intelligent fellow."

"Or importune, depending on the lady's response to such a theft."

"One should always be considerate of the lady's feelings."

The intonation of that statement was such as to alert Alex to the existence of another level of meaning to the conversation. She became aware of Brook's amiable scrutiny and a hint of gentle hope in his eyes.

The hint vanished as he held the mask out. "May I impose on you for help tying it in place? The armor and small arms harness restrict movement."

Her agility was likewise limited because of the tighter-than-usual corseting, but she managed. He sat on a hassock, and she completed the operation.

"Will it pass, Miss Pendlebury?" He stood and turned, cloak swinging.

She decided he looked quite dangerous and was glad he was with her and not against her. She had a stray thought about Dick Turpin stealing a kiss. The prospect was more pleasant in consideration than in execution, given her inconvenient talent. Such intimate contact never failed to reveal the man's true feelings, and she'd ever found those to be a disappointment.

But might this one be different?

Heather Fagan had approved of him, and being a Reader as well, her opinion counted for much.

I'm taking too long to reply. He might get more ideas.

"It will do, Mr. Brook," she said briskly. "Let us proceed."

Mabrey materialized in the entry, his curiosity having overcome protocol. He let them out, not a footman, holding the door wide enough to obtain a look at the waiting coach. He might infer it to be Service, but would acquire no additional information. Lady Alex made a flying stop with a male companion, changed clothes, and departed without explanation.

Mr. Brook gallantly handed Alex into the coach; she required assistance with the full skirts. He took the opposite bench and tapped the roof with a walking stick he'd borrowed from a collection in the entry's umbrella stand. They lurched off.

"I won't be welcomed back after this," she remarked. "My cousin Andrina is rather particular about her things and does not possess a forgiving nature." Alex gestured at the gown.

"Remind her that her contribution is for queen and country."

"If I'm allowed. The secrecy level of this is far above even my uncle's post in the Home Office."

During the ride they checked their weapons. Alex's Webley was barely contained in a satin-lined reticule that came with the cloak. The outline of the gun was discernable if she held it wrong, and the weight of it, spare bullets, and her lock picks were obvious. She'd have to keep it at or below her waist.

Their forward escort dropped behind and, apparently alone, they proceeded along South Audley Street. Alex's heart began to swiftly thump. If they kept going north she could be in her Baker Street home in a few minutes. With that monstrous creature dead, it must be safe enough to return. She abruptly wanted to be huddled in bed with a hot water bottle at her feet and a coal fire warming the air. Lord Richard and Colonel Mourne could infiltrate the Ætheric meeting instead. They wouldn't think less of her—well, actually they would—if she chose not to go. She wasn't a soldier who had to obey.

But I volunteered; it's my idea.

And Brook would go in. She couldn't allow him to do that without herself along to protect him. He was capable, but too green.

They took the longer way, going anticlockwise around Grosvenor Square. Brook had an eye to the window and reported they'd just passed a Black Maria. "There seem to be a large number of men in the park. They're keeping behind the trees."

Colonel Mourne's flying squad . . . in case of trouble. That was reassuring. Unless—

"You're sure they're ours?"

"No hooded cloaks, but plenty of balaclavas and truncheons. It's just as well it's too cold for an evening stroll. The residents here would find it alarming."

"Indeed, mustn't have soldiers lurking in the shrubbery of the upper classes, however good the cause."

"But a location such as this?"

"Those hooded thugs attacked the Service just steps from Downing Street and Scotland Yard. I doubt they would blench at holding battle in Buckingham Palace if it suited their purpose. We must be on our best guard. I just wish this was a less formal event. I could conceal several more firearms in my walking clothes." At his look she added, "I don't expect they'll be called to use, I just prefer to be overwhelmingly prepared."

The coach stopped before number 25 and the driver swung down to open the door. Brook emerged and handed her out. Two coaches ahead of them likewise disgorged well-dressed passengers. With much relief Alex noted the women wore veils or masks. At any normal evening gathering a lady was expected to show her face. She belatedly pulled her veil down, hampering her view with black netting.

The house had a redbrick front and was vast, seven floors at least, plus the cellars. Gaslight showed through four well-spaced windows on either side of the impressive entry, indicating two to three large rooms in the front. Their foray might take more than the hour Lord Richard had allowed.

No decorative stone head over the door—perhaps the absent Duchess of Denver was not a member of the Ætherics after all.

Alex and Brook merged with the crowd from the other coaches. A doorman large enough to be a prizefighter blocked the way, allowing guests to pass two at a time.

"What is the word?" he rumbled, his face as grim as an overdue bill. He'd demanded the same of those ahead of her, but she'd not heard their whispered replies.

She leaned forward and muttered, *"Masters impart."*

He nodded once and let them pass.

No servants stood by to take their outer clothes; she and Brook followed the others.

The entry hall held to simple lines but was sumptuous in décor. The duchess had fourteen generations of English ancestry to define and refine her taste. Crystal chandeliers sparkled, the woodwork shone, the air was made light by the pleasant scent of hothouse roses—even Aunt Honoria would have approved.

The guests, however, were another matter. Alex instantly picked up on the atmosphere, which had the crackling heaviness that presages a lightning strike. They were looking forward to something, but there was a taint to it. She instantly thought of naughty children bent on mischief despite dire consequences should they be caught.

Being adults, they had no fear of a nanny spoiling the fun, though.

Just myself and Mr. Brook.

A music room seemed to be a gathering point. Chairs were set in close rows and someone in command of a podium lectured with much intensity about metaphysical matters. The audience appeared to be a motley of social stations. Psychical talent was no respecter of class and neither were those who preyed upon the curious. A shopgirl's halfpenny donation was just as welcome as a guinea from a noble, not that any crass collection bowl was in sight.

No one in that room was masked. Alex and Brook withdrew to the main entry and were accosted by another large specimen who, from his battered ears, broken nose, and scarring around his eyes, practiced the pugilist's art like his comrade at the door. He glared at them.

"That way," he said, pointing at masked and veiled people milling toward the back of the house.

"This gathering began long before the stated time," murmured Brook. "There's more than a hundred people here with more coming in."

"The Ætheric meeting is the cover for something deeper.

Did you recognize anyone of import back there? Neither did I. All the interesting ones will be incognito."

The crowd around them kept their voices low as they continued slowly along a hall. The cause for the congestion was a stoppage at a staircase, which was a narrow one intended for servants. In ones and twos, people descended.

Ears sharp, eyes open, Alex focused on as many as possible. While a mask obscured the face, there were other ways to identify people. Beards, baubles, modes of dress, carelessly displayed monograms, unconscious mannerisms . . . she fixed them in her memory and looked for the familiar. While it was unlikely she knew anyone, there was a chance of it. Someone had recognized her father and taken action. She'd destroyed the executioner; this foray might make it possible to remove whoever had given the order.

She held the reticule with her Webley a little closer.

Brook took the lead going down the stairs. Not gentlemanly, but the correct action for a protector. She had to mind her skirts, one-handed, making sure no one behind tread on them. Why couldn't Andrina have gone in for trousers? All the Paris designers were making formal styles now. Many of the less avant-garde ladies of fashion were wearing them, even to the opera.

At the bottom landing she heard (and felt) the deep measured beating of a large drum. They were in a long hall with a tall ceiling, unusual for an area below street level. Through a door, and then down another set of stairs, the drumming sound resonated through her body, quickening her heart and step. The crowd responded to it, growing restive, eager to press forward. If she and Brook had to make a hasty exit, it would be impossible.

Lest they become separated, she seized his left arm. Her internal armor was solidly in place, so whatever feelings he had did not touch her, but she couldn't help but pick up on the rising excitement that flowed around them.

The next landing opened to a large dim chamber, lighted

by candles and lanterns. The great weight of the house above was supported by dozens of squat pillars, and low benches had been built or placed around each. Cushions provided protection from the wood and brick, but those occupying the seating seemed too busy to notice.

Poor Mr. Brook stopped in his tracks, mouth open with shock.

Couples, trios, foursomes, and more were engaged in the sort of activities better confined to the privacy of a bedroom—or a Roman bacchanal, as enough spirits and wine were being consumed for the latter.

The old Hellfire Club had returned with a whoop, whistle and *hey, nonny-nonny* to a fresh generation.

"It's just an orgy," she said, though she blushed at having to use such a word. She'd read a lot. She'd also seen one firsthand in India when she and a group of friends sneaked away to look in on the activities of a local temple they'd been forbidden to tour. The revelries in that temple were nothing to what was going on under the Denver roof, though in comparison, these crude proceedings, though energetic, lacked imagination and grace. "Let's keep moving."

He bent toward her ear. "I'm getting you out of here."

"I'm perfectly fine. Ignore them and think of England."

"Oh, God."

A woman braced against a pillar with one man's head and shoulders concealed under her skirts and another ardently kissing her throat echoed Brook's words, but with more feeling. Alex tugged his arm, pulling him to one side.

She'd spied people leaving the main room via a door in a near corner. They appeared uninterested in the antics of others. No women were in the group, and their masks covered the whole of their faces. While they could be attending an exclusive party for men who preferred the company of other men, Alex thought otherwise. She perceived enough about their clothes to know they patronized the best tailors and shoemakers and employed the most careful of valets to keep things in order.

Their carriage and swagger spoke of confidence married to an equal measure of contempt for lesser beings. She recognized the genus: men of power who were in power.

But more importantly, shuffling along with them were a dozen other men in distinctive hooded cloaks.

"After that lot," she said in Brook's ear.

No need to tell him twice. He was all for removing them from the fleshy inferno. The doorway took them to a brick-lined hall, its arched ceiling blackened by the soot of decades. Many openings led off from it, and drunken celebrants tottered from one to the other at random, hooting and singing.

Another rough-looking guardian blocked the way to a sizable candlelit room where the hooded men were gathering. Again, she used the password and they continued through, being almost the last ones in. The door closed and the booming of the drum diminished. With that row going on there would be no eavesdropping from outside.

They filed toward a long table with more than a dozen chairs, some of which were occupied. The men did not interact with one another, holding themselves still and alert like faceless judges. It gave Alex a chill akin to the grave. Any of them could have ordered her father's death, perhaps all if they voted on it. With masks to hide human expression, there was no need to bother with human responsibility. One could make decisions for good or ill with the ease of a machine, free of conscience and morality.

She was the only woman present, and was noticed. A cloaked man wearing a half mask approached and addressed her, leaning close to her ear.

"My apologies, madam, but females are not permitted at this meeting. This way, if you would allow me."

It was pointless to fall into a fit of blood-boiling resentment. The Equal Franchise Bill had given women the vote, not access to private clubs, of which this must be the most private in the whole of the empire. Disagreement would bring discovery, and besides, he had been polite. Brook took his cue from her and they left. The man escorted them back to the hall, gave a little bow, and departed.

"That had the look of a staff meeting," said Brook. "While it might have been instructive, they're almost always dreadfully boring."

She nodded and moved forward past rooms hosting a variety of prurient activities, each louder than the last. Candles were only for the rooms, not the hall. She resisted the urge to brush her veil away to see better.

From the look of the bricks this subcellarage must have been dug out a century earlier. The planning and execution would be a prohibitively enormous expense, and how could it be kept a secret? But she recalled the fanaticism of the captured rider. If those in the Order of the Black Dawn had a tenth of that dedication a secret was safe enough, and if they pooled their money . . .

The drumming, somewhat mitigated by the wall between, bore into her head. Its insistent purpose was ancient: disrupt thought and awake the body, as effective at a sybaritic debauch as it was in war to work soldiers up for battle.

Clusters of amorous revelers slowed them, but no one stopped them from looking into the various rooms. Drink flowed freely, though in one strangely calm chamber Alex recognized the heaviness of opium and hemp.

Harried men slipped to and fro, carrying wine bottles in and bringing back the empty husks at an astonishing rate. This might be the largest den of iniquity since Caligula took power, but servants still had to run the place. Where did they find them and how were they kept quiet? Anyone desperate enough for this sort of work would be glad to sell his story to the first newspaper brave enough to print it.

But who would believe this?

"Over there," said Brook. "Something isn't right—"

The unholy entirety of place wasn't right; *what* had caught his attention?

Damned veil. She lifted it, trusting that her identity was safe in the murk, and instantly fixed on a trio ahead of them. A man and his shorter, burly companion had a woman between them and the three staggered erratically forward. They were in evening clothes and masked, of course, but the woman appeared to be in a desperate state compared to the other females present. Her hair trailed raggedly down her back, and her head drooped as though overcome by drink. Her wrinkled and ripped dress was stained, its once lush trims torn.

"Miss Pendlebury, that poor lady . . . whatever brought her to this, she should not be subject to whatever those two have in mind."

Alex had no doubt of what was in store. "We must be discreet. Use your stick to clout the man on the left, I'll deal with the other." She reversed her grip on the hidden Webley so she could deliver a sharp thump behind the ear of her target. Once he was down, she could disable him with knuckle strikes to his nerve points. With any luck others would assume he'd passed out.

She and Brook separated and rushed forward.

But before they could set to it, someone behind yelled a sharp warning. The men dropped their burden and turned as one, each with a pistol in hand. Alex stopped short and lashed an arm toward Brook. He froze, his cane halted in midswing.

The men likewise hesitated. Alex fought off a swoop of disgust as she recognized the one she'd been prepared to remove. That jaw, chin, his mouth . . .

"Dear God—James, how could you? And is that Dr. Hamish?"

"No names, please," said James Fonteyn. He ceased pointing his gun at her and lifted his mask.

"What the devil are—"

"Lady Drina?" The man who'd warned them came close, holding a lantern high. His disguise didn't cover the port wine mark on his ear. "You shouldn't be here!" said Fingate. "This is no place for a lady."

She was too angry for words, but intended to share a few

regardless. An open door on the right . . . ugh, it would be the opium den. She grabbed the startled Fingate and dragged him in, trusting that Brook and the others would follow. They did so, bringing the woman as well. Dr. Hamish had swept her up and now eased her down again on the bare floor. Brook, to judge by his stance, was still ready to club someone and blocked the way out. Their intrusion drew no notice from the languid inhabitants of the room.

"James—" she began.

"I *can* explain—"

"There's no explanation for such depravity!"

"Of course not, so give me the benefit of a doubt and consider that I'm not here for pleasure."

"Then why?"

"Staging a rescue, my dear. That woman the doctor is so carefully attending was being held against her will and we're trying to—"

Her mind abruptly leaped ahead without a logical progression of facts. "Rosalind Veltre," she said to Brook.

James looked pained. "Please stop blurting names. These wretches won't remember anything, but—"

"Bother that, no one can hear a word over that damned drumming."

"Such language, but you've a point. I expect you're on some mission for your employers, but I'm here out of the goodness of my generous heart. If we work together we might all get out alive."

She looked at Fingate. "You went to James after escaping from the park?"

"You said I could trust him, and so it's proved. I didn't want to draw danger to you by going to Pendlebury House."

Just as well. Teddy wouldn't have known what to do with him. "You knew of the card hidden in Father's cane?"

"It wasn't my place to read it, but considering the circumstances I thought I should in the hope of helping. I was sure you'd find it on your own. I didn't know what it meant, but

Mr. Fonteyn and his friends sorted it out and that's what brought us here."

"By many twists and turns," said James, "the Ætherics caught my attention last month. The Psychic Service wasn't doing anything about them, and the lads and I decided to look into things on our own."

"What happened last month?"

"One of our friends got involved. First séances, then metaphysical lectures, then suggestions that with modest donations he could be initiated into an inner circle where the real power lurked. They hinted that there was genuine magic to be learned if you got the right sort of instruction and had the inherent ability."

"Magic? Charlatans and stage trickery, more like."

"I know. So did he. The poor fellow went along with it for a lark but he must have been found out or learned things he shouldn't. His landlady missed him for the rent and came asking after him. A week later his body turned up in the Thames washed clean of anything a Reader could find. It was ruled death by misadventure, but Hamish and I rejected that. We began making inquiries and it put the wind up us. Why do you think we were so well armed when those hooded churls invaded my home?"

She'd been so busy that she'd not questioned it. When a Reading might result in the discovery of a murderer, having a weapon ready to hand was only sensible.

"When Fingate turned up after that dunking in the Serpentine we—"

"You were following me? Is that how you came to be in the park?"

"Well, yes, sort of, just a bit. That inspector friend of yours took me aside and gave me a few opinions on what he thought of the Service and that he didn't think they were doing all they could to look after you."

"Lennon did that?"

"Bit of a rough fellow, but sharp instincts. He reasoned that if some band of madmen could do away with two peers in one night without batting an eye, then they'd do for you just as quick. We had volunteers keeping watch at a safe distance, at least until you disappeared into the Service building. Of course, when the shooting started they had to get clear, and I don't blame 'em. While the lads were busy, Hamish and I got what story Fingate had to tell and we set about looking for Mrs. Veltre. Took us a while to find the woman's flat, and then she wasn't in. We learned a few things from street Arabs that led us to think she'd been kidnapped, so Hamish and I toddled over and infiltrated this party hoping to find clues. Had to bring Fingate along, he wasn't keen to be on his own."

"I'm not keen to be with company, either," he put in, distress overcoming his usually diffident manner. "Not here."

"I know, there will be billy-hell if we're caught. Some guards back there noticed us and we had to defend ourselves." He held up a white-gloved hand, which had blood on the knuckles. "Look what one fellow's nose did! I just bought these, too. When those lads wake up they'll be in a foul mood and tell all their friends."

Alex had heard enough. "Then *go*. You have no idea the danger you're in."

"Actually, I do, but you can't see my whey-faced cheeks in this light."

"Stop joking and leave. When you get outside go left. There's a Black Maria in the square. Go straight to it and tell them I sent you."

"Delighted to do so, but we may not get past the other brutes they have on watch. We're heeled, but I'd rather not shoot one."

"Do whatever is needed. You were going to anyway, weren't you?"

"Having permission takes all the fun out of it. You're coming along, of course."

"I'm not done here. Get her out. Quietly if you can, but out no matter what. What's the matter with her, Doctor?"

"Not sure," said Hamish. "Perhaps laudanum. There's another prisoner but we couldn't manage him and the lady both. Had to make a choice and she won."

"Another one?"

"We couldn't break the lock on his door, just peek through a grate. Nasty strange place they've put him, like something from an opera. He's tied to a chair in a room full of—"

"Where?"

"Back that way. A pry bar or a fireplace poker might remove that lock. He's wild, but looks weak as a kitten. Your man and Fingate should be able to handle him. Off his head with brain fever I shouldn't wonder."

"Who is he?"

"Don't know. Said his name was Benedict and he demanded that we kill him."

CHAPTER THIRTEEN

In Which Miss Pendlebury Reflects

My enemy's enemy is my friend," Alex muttered, feeling hopeful when the old Arab proverb popped into her head. If the Black Dawn found it necessary to hold prisoners, it followed that such unfortunates might be helpful to the Service. So far on this expedition she had learned much that was shocking, but nothing of use.

She again ordered James and Dr. Hamish to get Veltre away so she and Brook, with Fingate guiding them, could deal with the other captive.

Hamish was reluctant, but her cousin pointed out that "Alex has the bit in her teeth, just get out of her way and God help anyone who doesn't."

Such an exaggeration, she thought, but it convinced the doctor to take up his patient and leave. He departed, muttering about the hemp smoke addling them all.

Fingate's excellent memory got them through a perfect maze of halls. At each turn they paused to check for guardians, but none were there to give challenge.

"Is this not too easy?" she asked in a normal tone of voice. The drumming had faded, though it was still to be heard. "Shouldn't there be someone on watch?"

"Mr. Fonteyn thought so, too," said Fingate.

"Everyone's at that . . . gathering," said Brook. "How did you find Mrs. Veltre?"

"By accident, sir. The doctors thought serving staff would

know something useful. We followed them to catch someone to question, but came to this instead."

Fingate paused and adjusted the wick of his lantern to increase the light. They were before a "T" intersection. A length of string, ends tied to nails driven into the mortar, stretched across its opening. A sheet of folded foolscap hung from the string.

Neatly printed in ink, it read: Do NOT ENTER. VIOLATORS FACE DISMISSAL WITHOUT CHARACTER . . . OR DEATH. The last word was underscored.

Serving as a signature at the bottom was a skull over crossed bones.

Brook cleared his throat. "*That* is utterly ridiculous."

"I disagree, sir. A servant lacking a character reference lacks work. For some, death is preferable to ruin. Once Dr. Fonteyn saw that he insisted on investigating."

"He'd find it irresistible," said Alex. "As do I. Fingate, if you would, please," she added, with an encouraging gesture.

"Yes, Miss Drina." He ducked under the string, resuming the lead. "We were cautious, of course. Dr. Fonteyn had concerns about trapdoors and bottomless pits."

"He is fond of lurid reading."

"Then we saw three fellows loitering . . . here. They weren't part of the gathering to judge by their clothes. The doctors attempted to engage them in conversation, but were rebuffed and told to go back or know the reason why. Dr. Fonteyn took that as a challenge. It did not end well for them. We had to hide them, unbolted this door, and that's how we found the lady. Gave us a turn seeing a body lying there. She woke up enough to give her name when asked, then fainted again. While Dr. Hamish looked after her, Dr. Fonteyn and I dragged the guards through and shot the bolt on them."

"They're in there?" The stout door had grate set into it, but the opening was too high for her to see in. Brook obliged, taking the lantern a moment and holding it up.

"Three ruffians, dead to the world," he reported.

Fingate looked pleased. "They got a stern knocking about for their sauce. A dreadful place for a lady; I'll not feel sorry for them." He indicated another bolted door across the hall. "The man, Benedict, heard the row and called to us while we were sorting things. Dr. Hamish couldn't get much sense from him."

A large padlock of ancient vintage was in place.

"It's too big for my lock picks," Alex said. "Your walking stick, Mr. Brook?"

He gave the lantern to her and tried striking and then levering the hasp loose, but wood was no match for iron. He stopped before the stick snapped.

"We searched the men for a key," said Fingate, "and then Dr. Fonteyn tried to shoot the lock, but barely made a dent. A more powerful cartridge might have an effect."

The grate on this door was set lower, but Alex had to hold the lantern uncomfortably close to her head to get light through the opening.

The blood drained from her face and she retreated a step, nearly dropping the lantern. Fingate grabbed it in time.

"What is it?" asked Brook.

"I . . . I must get in there. Both of you . . . over there." Her hands shook as she got the Webley free.

"But the noise—" Brook objected.

The roar was impressive, so was the damage to the padlock, but it took another shot to defeat it. She wrenched it from the hasp and pushed hard on the heavy door. For all her want of hurry, she paused on the threshold.

In the center of the chamber, bolted to the stone-flagged floor, was a massive chair. A tall, thin man with a ragged beard was chained to it by his wrists and ankles, his head bowed forward; dark hair, hanging in strings, hid his face. He wore a dressing gown and slippers. His hands trembled, fingers twitching as though playing a piano.

The prisoner's eyes were closed and he took no notice of them, even when Brook shook him a little. He tested the chains.

"Miss Pendlebury, will your picks defeat these locks? They're smaller."

"Shooting's faster."

"And more dangerous. Noise and ricochets, you know."

"Let me try," said Fingate.

"You can crack locks?" asked Brook.

"Who do you think taught me?" Alex tossed the ring at Fingate.

The prisoner remained silent, fingers tapping empty air.

The chamber was swathed, ceiling to stone floor, in thick red velvet draperies. Little wonder Dr. Hamish had thought of the opera; they had the look of stage curtains. Alex's heart thumped. She cautiously approached the wall in front of the dozing man.

A few experimental delvings to find an edge and she pulled a long length of heavy velvet away to reveal a mirror under it. Her startled reflection floated in red-tinted shadows.

The mirror was enormous, four feet wide and twice as tall and encased in an iron grid like a cage which was bolted to the wall. Near the bottom the caging had a thick iron mesh door just over a foot square with a padlock attached. She could have slipped through such an opening, but not a grown man.

She twitched aside another sheeting of velvet and found another mirror, this one without a door in its cage. Alex and Brook worked their way around. The lantern's light reflected a dozen times over in cage encased mirrors that lined all four walls. They were well made, no warps or ripples in their silvery finish.

Sybil's cheerful command came fresh to Alex's mind: *Break them. Break all of them and damn the bad luck, think of England!*

"How the devil did they get these things down here and why would anyone bother?" asked Brook. "And these bars—?"

"Somehow they interfere with Sybil's ability. That must be worth much to anyone planning an action that she might foretell. Progress, Mr. Fingate?"

"A few more to go."

The man in the chair suddenly raised his head, blinking. He shook hair from his wild eyes. "Get out of here," he said in a high, strong voice. "Kill me and then GET OUT!"

"Let's get you out as well, old lad," said Brook in a kindly tone.

"Douse that light for God's pity!"

Fingate hesitated. "Sir, calm yourself and explain why."

"You won't believe me. More of them will come and then you'll die."

"Keep at it," said Alex, holding steady. The man was terrified, but it wouldn't do to catch it from him.

Fingate bent to the work, not easy when the captive began howling and thrashing against his bonds. "You'll be killed! Take the light away!" Weakness quickly asserted itself, though. He broke off, coughing and gasping.

"Who put you here?" she asked.

He shook his head.

"You're Mr. Benedict?"

"Probably, now please have the courage to kill me and then get out."

"Why do you want to die?"

"I don't want to, but I *need* to. You bloody stupid girl! *Kill me and get out!*"

Alex made encouraging motions at Fingate to continue, then returned to the walls, pulling the velvet away so she could peer behind one of the mirrors: solid brick, at least in that spot. "Why mirrors in a dark room? Why cage and cover them?"

"They'll see the light. You don't want them to see it."

"Benedict, are you a Seer?"

"I'm a conduit for hell. Will you *listen* to me? At least get that lantern out of here. They're attracted to the light."

"Who?"

"Oh, God, too late, too late! Run, you fools! Run while you can!"

"No one in the hall," reported Brook.

"Not there!" The man's gaze fixed on the mirror in front of him. "*That* one. It's seen this side and will come through. You can't fight, just run." Tears flowed from his eyes and his voice cracked. "*Run!*"

Alex went toward the mirror. Something seemed to be moving *in* it. Gooseflesh raised on her arms until she realized it was simply the kind of deception mediums used to hoodwink willing clients. The silver on the back must have been rubbed away, allowing whatever was behind it to show through the glass. The wall would have an opening and someone in the next room over was playing ghost, probably wrapped up in layers of gauzy muslin yardage.

With caution, she opened her inner senses to whatever might be before her. Just a crack . . . or the madman's emotions would flood in and overwhelm her.

Benedict shrieked, throwing himself around, hampering Fingate's efforts.

As she got closer, the mirror's surface silently *ripped*.

She shrank away, staring at the opening—

—and instantly recognized the enormous knotted hand with fingers much too long to be human that came questing out of the darkness.

A simian face, eyes alight with malice, appeared on the other side of the cage. Those iron bars now seemed as frail as straw. Without thought, Alex raised her gun and fired, pulling the trigger until she ran out of bullets.

Glass did not shatter. The missiles connected with a solid body, which swayed, but continued to press forward. The hand grasped at her through the bars, talons brushing down the front of her gown, shredding the silk to rags.

She'd gotten a head shot, though. The top of the thing's skull was gone, but the vast body kept coming, emerging from the impossible mirror and slamming hard into the iron, bending it. Two of the upper bolts set into the brick wall jarred loose. The great weight against the cage snapped the next two, and then cage, mirror, and the beast in between tipped and tumbled over.

Alex dodged barely in time. The glass was cushioned by the creature's body, but its own weight cracked it lengthwise in the middle.

She looked to the others. Brook had his pistol ready, but he'd clearly been caught flatfooted. Fingate was in shock, and the madman's head was bowed as though he were praying.

"Kill the light. Kill me," Benedict whispered. "This must stop. Kill me. Kill me, damn you."

Light . . . bloody hell.

She grabbed the lantern and barged past Brook. He followed her, dragging Fingate. They threw the bolt, but with the padlock gone could not secure it.

"You see?" Benedict cried from the darkness. "You *SEE?*"

W e won't leave him there," Alex pronounced.

"We just did," said Brook.

"I'll apologize to him about collective panic later."

Recovery of speech had been tardy in the aftermath of such a horror, but her racing mind made up for it. She'd worked out a plan long before her companions had caught their breath.

"Fingate, you can still crack locks with your eyes shut, yes?"

"My hands aren't steady just now. What in God's name was that?"

"We don't know, but if we keep the lantern away from the mirrors it should be safe enough."

"*Should* be?"

She broke open the Webley and reloaded. "Mr. Brook, I would be obliged if you would watch from the hall in case our noise has alerted anyone to investigate."

"I prefer to be in the room."

"Orders, Lieutenant. It's going to get much noisier and I need to move freely. Sybil gave me orders as well, and I'd rather have our escape clear with someone watching our backs."

Without waiting, Alex worked the bolt and eased the door open. "Mr. Benedict?"

"Fools and blackguards," he grumbled. "I'm surrounded by fools, blackguards, and monsters from hell's heart."

"No doubt. Has another of those beasts appeared?"

"If it had, you'd be dead by now."

"Why not yourself?"

"They need me to be able to come through. None safer from them than I."

When Brook had removed lantern far enough down the hall, she took Fingate's trembling hand and guided him toward the chair. The room was perilously black, her eyes creating phantom shadows where the mirrors stood. Or were they truly imagined?

"Are there more of those creatures in the mirrors?"

"They're *beyond* them, not *in* them—there's a world of the damned things. They bring them through, but with care. They pick only young ones, train them."

She kept her voice calm, the same as she would for a Reading interview, but the possibility of more such things running loose made her blood run cold. "Who does? Who might 'they' be?"

"Who might you be?" he returned.

"My name is Pendlebury and I serve in Her Majesty's Psychic Service. I thought I might break some mirrors. Any objection?"

"Er—not at all. But it will take time, whereas killing me would only take an instant and put an end to the whole issue."

"I'm going to make noise and there will be flying glass. Keep your eyes closed. You too, Fingate. Ready?"

Alex inched her way around the creature's body, slipping once on what she presumed to be blood, and felt for the mirror next in line on that wall. She put the gun muzzle between the bars and fired, the flash blinding, the sound making her ears ring.

Would that light and the noise bring more of the beasts?

The curtains must have been closed for a reason; she methodically made a full circuit and draped the things back again. Then one by one she returned the same way, shooting through the velvet. She reloaded twice, and a third time when the work was done. Her ears hurt and the pale pungent smoke clogged the air, making her cough.

Alex had a sudden urge to see the destruction, but held it in check. She felt her way toward the door.

"All done, Mr. Brook."

He did not reply.

The lantern was well down the hall, and Brook wasn't with it. His walking stick was propped against the bricks.

Not good.

She hurried forward, calling his name. Loudly. If the row in the mirror room hadn't brought anyone, then neither would shouting.

What had drawn him away?

Had another of those beasts taken him silently from behind?

She opened her senses again. Brook's emotional spoor hung lightly in the area by the lantern. He'd been alert and worried, but nothing problematic lingered. She'd have to trust that he'd left for a good reason and would catch them up. Her responsibility now was to get Benedict and Fingate to safety. She took the lantern.

Fingate had defeated the last lock and was helping the prisoner from the chair. The man was stiff and unsteady, but willing. This time he had no objections to light.

"Brave girl, taking on eighty-four years of bad luck," said Benedict. He staggered and Fingate supported him. Their reflections wavered in the glittering glass shards scattered wide over the floor.

She took a quick look at the dead beast. It was different from the one she'd killed earlier, far larger and naked, its rough flesh gray in the faint light. However, it was identical in regard to being a hole in the air. She sensed no emotional or psychical trace from it.

Her one instinct had been to kill the thing on sight. Granted, when faced with something so monstrous that was a normal reaction, but was it not more normal to flee in terror? That hadn't happened earlier with the flying squad. They'd gone after it like a pack of hounds trying to bring down a bear. None had hesitated.

"Can more of those creatures come through?" she asked.

"This gate's closed for now," said Benedict. "It will set them back; they won't be pleased with you. If you'd just shoot me it would end things for them."

"I'd rather shoot *them*."

Benedict paused his progress, smiling. "Oh! I *like* you! What an excellent idea."

His manner was all too similar to Sybil's. Would he start babbling strange predictions, too?

She helped get him into the hall, going back the way they'd come. "Who are *they*, Benedict? The men behind this? Have you names?"

"Only what I call 'em, which is not fit for a lady's ears. You think a carpenter gives his name away to his box of tools? I'm an instrument they use." His legs were stiff and dragged. "Ohhh, pins and needles, needles and pins, 'tis a happy man that grins."

"They've not taken good care of you." She took the walking stick as they passed and gave it to Benedict. Had Brook known they'd need it? Where the devil was he?

"The level of service in this establishment has dropped considerably in the last month. Maybe they found another me."

"Another Seer?"

"I'm not a Seer. I'm a Conduit."

"Conduit, then." *Whatever that might be.* "Like you?"

"No, silly girl, another *me*. There must be dozens of us out there. Poor fellows."

Fingate glanced uneasily at the man, then asked, "Where's Mr. Brook?"

"I don't know. We're on our own. Let's go back to the opium room. I've an idea. Benedict, what are those beasts? How many are there?"

"That's a good question. A positively gargantuan question. If there's dozens of me running about then there could be hundreds of them."

Dealing with mad people was not a topic covered in her Service training. It seemed to call for constant improvisation for half-understood subjects. "How many have been brought through in that room?"

"I couldn't say. They'd render me asleep for it. Otherwise I'd scream a lot and they didn't like that."

"The beasts or your captors?"

"Both, I expect."

"How many times were you rendered asleep?"

"Every night, of course. A man needs his rest. Whether they put me in the chair every night, I don't know. Whether they brought small ones through every time, I don't know. It's a bit like fishing, but you want a tiddler, not a monster."

"What are they called?"

"Ask me something I *do* know! And ask later, I'm bloody tired. I should be in bed. A lovely dreamless bed. With a nice cup of cocoa. Hallo, there's an odd smell. Who's burning rope?"

The inhabitants of the opium chamber were not disturbed by their second intrusion. A man smoking from a water pipe seemed amused, but only in a distant way.

Just as well.

"That one, Fingate." She marked out a likely fellow who'd fully succumbed to the narcotic. He'd slipped from a bench to the floor, eyes closed, mouth slack.

"What about him, my lady?"

"Get his clothes off. Mr. Benedict can't go about in just a robe and slippers."

Undressing an unconscious man proved to be a two-person job. She attacked the buttons; Fingate did the lifting and pulling. Benedict balked at removing his dressing gown in front of a female, and she had to promise not to look while he changed.

Though evening clothes often had the extraordinary effect of improving the looks of any man whatever his state or station, Benedict's transformation was not entirely convincing. His tangled hair and untrimmed beard set him apart from the mob. Fingate found a discarded hat that almost fit, and Alex filched a white silk scarf from its oblivious owner along with a half mask. When they'd finished, Benedict was as anonymous as they could make him, given the circumstances.

She was wobbly-headed from the hemp smoke and glad to quit the place, but halted short in the hall: the drumming had stopped. It seemed unlikely the revelry had ended. Out east, once such festivals got under way, it could be days before the celebrants yielded to exhausted satiation.

Alex held the reticule close, her other hand on the Webley inside. Benedict was steadier on his feet, but winded from the unaccustomed exertion, leaning on Fingate.

A troupe of servants with their arms full of empty wine bottles blocked the way out. Alex and the others were obliged to wedge against the wall to avoid them. As the men pushed past, a sudden brutal scrambling took place. Her reticule was torn from her hands, and two men seized her arms.

She instantly launched against them, kicking out as Master Shan had taught. Her skirts were a hindrance, but she caught one with a heel and he released his grip, cursing. Alex ducked and drove for a knuckle strike to paralyze the other man's arm, but he twisted and dodged, still hanging on. Two more men grabbed her, and she was suddenly smothering as they whipped a serving towel around her head. Blinded and short of breath from the damned corset, they easily pressed her face-first to the floor and tied her hands behind her. She kicked until they tied her legs as well.

"There now," said a not unkindly voice she did not know. "Ye've been rumbled. Take it like a lady."

Alex heard the sounds of the others struggling, but Fingate and Benedict had no chance against such numbers.

"Up with 'em," said the man in charge, and she found herself carried ignominiously along like a roll of carpet. "Those to the cupboard, 'er to the meetin'."

The trip was short, with few turnings and no stairs, so they were still far below the street. Though the drumming had stopped, the carousing continued. Drunken voices and laughter echoed unevenly in this brick-lined antechamber to hell.

Then a heavy door slammed and most of the noise ceased. In the comparative quiet Alex heard murmuring voices, all male, and shuffling as they moved around. She was pushed down on a chair.

"No need to be uncivilized," said a man. "Untie the lady. She can do us no harm."

"Beg pardon, your lordship, but you don't know 'er."

"As it happens, I do. See to it."

Her bonds were removed, and she tore the towel away herself. Her eyes adjusted to the brighter environs of a room crowded with men in evening dress all wearing full masks, all focused on her, and all silent. Along the edge of the crowd were a number of other mask-wearing men swathed in hooded cloaks.

She rejected their collective intimidation. After facing and killing another of those hideous beasts, mere men were nothing.

"The Order of the Black Sun, I presume," she said in the clearest voice she could muster.

No one moved. She picked up a thread of unease. Perhaps they expected her to weep with terror. They could wait till doomsday. She was far too incensed.

Her gaze fell on the one standing directly in front. "I'm deeply disappointed in you, sir. Deeply disappointed. What would Lady Lindsey say?"

The eyes behind the mask flickered, giving Alex the understanding that her ladyship was ignorant of her husband's activities.

Lord Hollifield slowly removed his mask and put it on the long table that took up the middle of the chamber.

Alex continued, "I took you to be a friend."

"I am grateful for that friendship, Alex."

"How can *you* be a part of this indecent flummery?"

"I've no need for flummery. Everyone knows everyone else, and I always thought that this lacked dignity. Gentlemen?"

Some hesitated and remained incognito, but a few followed his example. She recognized several faces, matching them to sketches and engravings that had appeared in newspapers. These were indeed men of power, both in politics and business. One didn't have to be a Reader to interpret what lay behind their cold eyes. She was to suffer the same fate as her father.

"Gentlemen, our cause is just, so we need have no fear. If you quail before a young woman such as this, how can you expect to prevail against more desperate foes?"

"Who might those be?" Alex asked in a reasonable tone.

His lordship responded in kind. "The misguided, the beguiled, the ignorant. You'll learn all about it once you're settled."

"Settled?"

"Out of respect for your station and service to the realm, you'll be taken to a quiet place in the country for a well-deserved rest. When matters are resolved elsewhere, you'll be released to live life in a much better, freer England."

"England for the English?"

"We're taking back our sacred realm."

A rumble of agreement went around the room. She looked for, but did not see Fingate or Benedict, and God knew what had happened to Brook. "Where are my friends?"

"Don't worry about them, they'll be treated well enough for their station."

Apparently no one had recognized Benedict. "You plan to use air guns and those revolting beasts to aid in your treason?"

"It is not treason. We're all loyal to our good queen, God save her, but it has become necessary to remove undesirables from our shores. Anyone who is not a true Englishman is to be transported out."

"What's a true Englishman? We're all descended from invaders. Where do you start? The Norman Conquest? If so, then we're mostly French."

"Don't be a silly girl. We're getting rid of the riffraff and vermin. Send them back to their own countries or they can go to America. Let *them* worry about foreign revolutionaries trying to usurp the lawful government."

"You are yourself betraying it."

"No, this is the deepest loyalty. There will be initial opposition, hence the need for armed men and certain special allies—I'd like to know how you know about those. But once the scum are removed, there will be work again for our own people and they'll be grateful to have it."

"Have you *ever* read history?"

"Dear girl, my family makes it." This brought forth a ripple of chuckles from the others.

There was no point arguing. He and the rest were fully convinced of the rightness of their cause; logic and historical precedent wouldn't shift them. She'd met their sort before, but never so many together.

"Tell me one thing," she said. "Why did you order the murder of my father?"

Hollifield's eyes flickered again. "Lord Pendlebury's dead?"

"As of early this morning. In my function as a Reader I was called to the scene of a questionable death by Scotland Yard."

"But he's been out of the country for years. How—"

"You knew him as Dr. Kemp."

"I've never met anyone called Kemp. I know your father, a change of name wouldn't change his face."

She'd opened enough to Read him. He was truthful. "Then

someone in your group is ordering murders. I wonder who that could be?" Alex couldn't hope to pick out any single reaction, but a few exuded uncertainty. "Which of you sent one of those trained beasts to break into Dr. Kemp's home in Harley Street? Which of you told it to overwhelm him with ether and then hang him to make it look like suicide?"

"Alex, you're mistaken—"

"Then why else am I here? One of you murdered Lord Gerard Pendlebury. One of you, perhaps more, has acted out of turn. There is dissention in your ranks, Lord Hollifield. Have you a policy for traitors within?"

"We are men of honor. None here would do such a thing."

"You're certain of that? On your life are you absolutely certain? Everyone lies, sir. Whether telling one's wife that a hat suits her face or denying the worst of crimes, everyone lies. You are lying every day to your own brother and to our queen." She raised her voice. "Which of you cowards murdered my father?"

"There are no cowards or murderers here."

"Prove it. Let me do my work and Read them one by one. You can hide your faces, but no one can hide their guilt from a Reader. I've already Read *you*—you had no part in it, you're at least innocent of *that* crime. But as for the rest—can your 'honorable' group endure a lying murderer in their midst? Your lives and fortunes depend on trusting one another, trusting that the man next to you won't arrange to sink a knife in your back should you become inconvenient."

She felt a shift in the emotional air. Doubt and suspicion— never far from such minds as these—quickly spread through their ranks.

Hollifield hesitated, then cast his eye over the crowd. "It would seem that we must face yet another evil necessity. The girl has raised doubts and those must be removed. We cannot be divided in our purpose. The innocent have nothing to fear."

"How will we know *she* will be truthful?" asked a man still anonymous behind his mask.

"Trust, gentlemen," she said, "trust that more than anything I want to look my father's killer in the eye and demand *why*. Who of you would do less?"

None replied.

She broke the thick silence. "While we're asking difficult questions, which of you ordered the assassination of Lord Richard Desmond?"

Lord Hollifield was clearly shocked. "What are you talking about?"

"He's dead, too. Just hours after my father. I was there when a pack of your hooded swine cut him down with air guns. He was unarmed. Who gave them those orders? Which of you will be next?"

"Don't be ridiculous."

Alex pressed forward. "Who of you ordered the attack on the Psychic Service? Bullets flying within steps of Downing Street? But you lost a dozen soldiers in that assault. Lord Hollifield will confirm I brought a captured air gun to him to ask if he knew who had made it. I assumed his shock was from seeing something new. But then with a smiling face he sent me and a companion straight into a death trap."

"I did not!" he snapped. "My orders were for you to be captured unharmed."

"Obviously that did not happen. To whom did you give those orders? That apish brute that murdered Father? I think not. Someone else arranged that, using the beast as a tool. Make no mistake, the traitor is here. Did he present a report on his crimes? Or is he keeping secrets? From you of all people, is he keeping secrets?"

These were men practiced at holding their thoughts and feelings hidden while looking for weaknesses in others, but she could sense her shots were hitting true. Hollifield's bluff features were grim.

"I am a Reader in Her Majesty's Psychic Service," she stated. "No one can lie to *me*. Have these 'honorable' gentlemen present themselves one at a time and I'll tell you who is exceeding his authority—but you already know him, sir."

"That he does." A man standing by the closed door spoke. In one quick sweep he removed his mask and smiled. "My dear cousin, I had no idea you had such a turn for the dramatic."

CHAPTER FOURTEEN

In Which Family Again Proves to Be Inconvenient

You should have chosen the stage," Teddy added. "Mother would have had seven kinds of fits, but that wouldn't have bothered you."

Alex felt ill and angry, but maintained her control. Showing her temper would blast what she'd so carefully built to flinders.

Hollifield was ready to explode, though. He'd gone red and rounded on young Pendlebury. "You dare?"

"Someone had to act. Allow me to explain and all will be forgiven."

Hollifield's glare could have scorched iron, but he'd not reached his place in the world without knowing when to listen. With visible effort he pulled himself in. "Explain, then," he said after a moment.

Teddy's gaze was steady. This man was a stranger to Alex. This was someone accustomed to walking in the corridors of power. He looked older and extremely self-assured. "It was all on Lord Richard Desmond. Using the Ætherics as a frivolous diversion was no longer working, and quite frankly, most of you are not as careful as you should be. A careless word dropped, a little postprandial chat over the port—the man's no fool. You've seen more of him than all of us together, Hollifield. I wouldn't be surprised if he'd taken some clue from you."

"Have a care, boy."

"I did precisely that. I expected him to send spies. They

wouldn't be hoodwinked by Ætheric table-tippers or shocked by those drunken hedonists. Desmond's spies were removed."

"You killed *Englishmen*?"

"Spies, Lord Daniel. Spies who would have ruined everything. But it didn't put off Desmond. He approached my father in the Home Office about opening an inquiry, a series of inquiries, on most of *you*."

The men had been restive but now went still.

"Caught your attention at last? You're all damned lucky I happened to see a paper my dear old sire left on his desk. It was a list of names, every one of them in the Order. That was *yesterday*, gentlemen. Just yesterday. Father would have launched an investigation tomorrow. They would have brought in Readers just like my cousin here, and none of you would have evaded discovery."

Alex disbelieved that; Uncle Leo was never careless with important papers, but it was a plausible lie. This wasn't the time to point the flaw out to this lot, not with Teddy in full flow.

"Action was required. I gathered a few trusty lads to sort things out. With Lord Richard removed, the investigation would be delayed. We set a watch for the next time he went out. Soldiers of the Order executed Lord Richard Desmond early this morning."

Alex listened with her internal senses wide. Their wave of shock was genuine.

"How could you?" someone demanded.

"Unavoidable. We'd have had to do it sooner or later."

"Executed," whispered Hollifield.

"You and all of us here know his dogged devotion to the crown. He'd have been an implacable enemy to our cause. Possibly the one man who could stop us."

"He'd have come around," said a man in the back.

"No." Hollifield shook his head. "I knew him. He'd never . . ."

"Exactly," said Teddy. "The next necessary evil was to take

the teeth out of the Psychic Service. I anticipated his death would put them in disarray. They panicked and called in everyone. Every true psychical talent in London was together in one spot and we could have gotten rid of the lot, but their damned Seer somehow got wind of it and ruined things. I take responsibility for the attack, but not its defeat; that was out of my control."

"You bloody fool!" Hollifield roared. "You've no idea the damage you've done. You've set us back—"

"I've pushed us forward! We are ready *now*! The game's begun. There's no point waiting. Give the word and by New Year's Day the first of the foreign vermin will be on boats heading across the Channel."

"It's impossible. Our own Seer said it's too soon."

"What makes him so reliable? He's so damned busy blocking theirs, you can't get sense from him. He was half mad to start with, then he got pushed the rest of the way when you began the abyss experiments."

"He volunteered. He was the one who discovered—" Hollifield stopped short. "Damn your eyes! You should be thrashed within an inch of your life for this."

"Deal with me after the year turns, your lordship, if you still think it necessary. Every man here has his duty to perform, none with a greater will for it than myself."

Hollifield snorted.

The masked man who'd spoken earlier stepped forward. "We've been ready for over a year. Time to grasp the nettle, have done with it. We know the cost. I've a brother who will never forgive me, but yours *will* come around, and through him the queen."

Alex raised her voice and put a solid measure of contempt into it. "You know better than that, Lord Hollifield. My godmother's temper is not easily roused, but it is legendary. Particularly where disloyalty is concerned. As of this moment there's no solid proof of your treason. That changes if you and these *honorable* gentlemen listen to my fool of a cousin. You must be aware he's manipulating you. He was a sneaking little tick as a boy and only got worse as a man. He's not told you everything. Ask him what happened tonight at the air gun factory by the river to the men who worked there. They're all dead."

"Chess moves," said Teddy. "A few pawns."

"Murdered by your own knight. Lord Hollifield, Teddy sent that beast to kill me and my companion. Instead, it killed the men who were in the factory, cut them down in cold blood with an air gun. But the Psychic Service prevailed and is even now going through the records there, and those will lead us to—"

"Really, Alex, do you think that's our only arms factory?"

That was interesting news. "Have you so many you can afford to lose one? And what of that beast? How many of those strange allies can you afford to lose? That one is dead. I blew its brains out myself."

Teddy continued to show a confident front, but she knew him well enough to recognize her volley had struck square and struck hard. "You're lying."

"Explain how I'm still alive, then. Was it a special pet? You can't have many like that. Eight foot tall, red eyes, useful with an air gun—sound familiar?" She fixed his drained face with a cold eye, then turned back to Hollifield. "The game is not begun, your lordship. The game is *over*. The traitor in your midst usurped the board. He's lost."

Alex was unsure of the hierarchy of the Order, whether decisions were made by a vote of equals or if it was set up like the military with generals at the top. Either way, she'd gotten them to pause and sown doubt. Above all, she was using up time. An hour must have passed by now. Even if James and Hamish hadn't gotten clear, help would come. Any minute Lord Richard and his flying squad would burst in. The longer she kept this lot here, the better.

Hollifield seemed about to speak, but Teddy interrupted. "Your lordship? A private word first. If you please."

Something in Teddy's expression . . . There was a subtle change in him that made Alex's flesh creep. Hollifield grumbled, but crossed to the door to confer. Their murmurings were beyond her hearing. When they returned, a very long minute later, Hollifield was dead white with a sheen of sweat on his brow. He stared at Teddy like murder personified but frozen in action.

He mastered himself and stood at the head of the table. "Gentlemen, we will proceed. Disregard our earlier session. We'll go over what's to be done now in the face of these changes. Let us indeed grasp the nettle. However much it stings, it is for the good of our land and the queen we all love and serve. Thank God we had everything in place. It won't be as smooth, and some of you will be short-staffed because of the holiday, but I trust you will be able to compensate and fulfill your several tasks."

Alex opened her mouth to interrupt again, but Teddy was suddenly next to her, a hand on her arm and pulling her up. "None of that, Cousin. Allow me to escort you elsewhere. These lads have work to do."

A short man in a full mask and hooded cloak preceded them to the door and opened it. Two other, much larger, cloaked men followed them out, carrying lanterns.

"You dealt with that with exceptional acumen," said Teddy, taking her down the hall, away from the main gathering room and its noise. He tried to pull her hand onto his arm in a friendly manner, but she savagely shook him off. The violence of her reaction surprised her, but it served to keep him at a distance.

Members of the waitstaff threaded to and fro around their party, paying them no mind. She glanced back the way they'd come, but there was no sign of intrusion from Lord Richard's people. Their three guards paced behind like a living wall.

They passed the chamber with the opium and hemp smokers, and then the T-intersection with its ridiculous warning sign. Alex was relieved to see that tunnel was still dark, so their intrusion was undiscovered. Now where the devil was Lord Richard?

"I admit my surprise," continued Teddy. "Some females are capable of overcoming the limits of their sex, and you're one of them. You likely won't do well under the coming changes."

"You won't let me live. You don't dare."

"Actually, I can. I've no wish to harm family, whatever the provocation. You'll be kept under house arrest in a safe place. It will be comfortable enough, but your nature will chafe unless you come to accept it. I suggest you do so. For your own sake."

"Is that where you're taking me?"

"The first leg of it, a nice waiting room. I've arranged discreet transportation."

She could imagine the rest. "What did you say to Hollifield to bring him to heel?"

"That was me being clever. I knew the old boy would kick. He's been delaying things for months. I let him know that unless he cooperated his good lady would get a visit from one of our brutish allies tonight and that she would neither enjoy nor survive the experience. Likewise, his daughters would—"

Alex forced a stop and turned on him. "You sick bastard."

"Oh! Finally, a show of passion from the cold queen of the wide world. Calm yourself. His lordship showed sense, nothing will happen."

"Until the next time he balks."

"Yes. He figured that out. He's a canny fellow, good at hiding the brains under the bluff, cheerful bulldog front. Had you fooled, didn't he? And you a Reader. But he misstepped on a few things. Our large allies are a dubious weapon. They're good at some types of work for a few years, but once fully grown, they are not as submissive about taking orders, then they become a danger to all. Have to be put down. You did us a favor removing that particular one. He was beginning to show signs of independence."

"What are they? Where do they come from?"

"No one's entirely sure, but they will be the subjects of considerable study once things are reorganized. We can put the Ministry of Science on it. Come along now. You look dreadfully done in. Time you had a rest."

"Not until you tell me why you killed Father."

"I expect because he infiltrated the Ætherics more deeply than was good for him. He'd befriended a lady who had made herself useful to the cause by having a talent for numbers. At least that's all the lady would admit before she went into hysterics. The mere sight of one of our allies was exceedingly distressing to her. With the meeting tonight I had no time for more questioning. You said Uncle Gerard was going by the name of Kemp? He should have come as himself. They'd have welcomed another Pendlebury, and he would not have died. One point: I didn't order him killed. Family, y'know."

She expected denial, but not for the denial to be grounded in truth. "Who did?"

"Haven't the faintest. It's not my section. Some chap protective of the cause must have seen to it. Rather elaborate, though. Hanging? Usually we arrange for an accident and a delay for finding the remains. Fewer questions, nothing for a Reader to grasp. I am truly sorry, Alex. You have my word that when I discover who was responsible they will be dealt with in an appropriate fashion. I liked Uncle Gerard. I really did. He was day to my father's night. Believe what you will about me, but I draw the line at harming relatives. We'll have disagreements, but in the end, family is all we've got in the world."

God in heaven, he's absolutely sincere.

Alex shifted her gaze to the short guard who stood quietly apart from the others. "Do you agree with him, Andrina?"

She removed her mask and pushed back the hood. "There are some relatives who should just disappear and the world would be much improved."

Teddy was amused. "I told you that disguise wouldn't deceive a Reader."

"I'll be happy to change as soon as possible. These shoes are impossible."

"The price you must pay if you want to attend meetings."

"There should be an exception for me."

"I'll see about it after the New Year, but you'll still have to be in a mask. You don't want them knowing who you are. The smarter ones will guess, but they'll know it's in their best interest to keep silent."

"How can you be part of this vileness?" Alex demanded.

"How can I not?" Andrina snapped back. "Foreign revolutionaries spew poison on every corner. Instead of land owners of substance, every oaf of a certain age has a vote and they're swilling the poison like gin. With the way things are going there will be no monarchy left in ten years. I'm doing all I can to protect the queen."

Teddy misinterpreted Alex's expression. "Oh, don't worry, females will still have their vote, but only those who own land or are connected by marriage or family to land. It's the only sensible compromise."

Alex sensed the sincere righteousness from them both and it made her sick.

Family, bloody family.

Disgusted and abruptly tired, Alex swayed and stumbled, her long delayed weariness finally asserting itself. One of the guards reached for her. She weakly batted him away, but he grasped her arm and held her up.

Through the gloves he wore, through the fabric of her dress, through the impotent fury roiling in her, his emotions intruded like a clarion. She caught her breath and focused on him.

"It's all right, miss," said Brook through the mask. "Steady now."

"That's Lady Pendlebury to you," Teddy lightly admonished. "Do you want him to carry you, Alex?"

She shook off Brook's hand the same as she might for a real guard. New strength surged into her. "I'm fine. How much farther?"

"Not long now."

They'd left the activity of the waiting staff far behind. This was no longer a hall branching to rooms, but a dank, silent tunnel with a much lower ceiling. The bricks were older, crumbling, with a path trodden through fallen debris on the floor. It led to an aged stairway, the wood gone black, the treads slippery and worn in the middle. She counted steps and worked out that they were back up to street level. That was a relief. The oppressive darkness had pressed on her heart more than she cared to admit.

The last landing was in good order with gas lighting. A single sconce burned steadily, the hiss a welcome sound of modern life after the century-old murk below. Teddy unlatched a plain door and they entered a well-appointed study. The door supported a bookcase on its other side and, when closed, it matched another such case a few feet away. Substantial furniture, masterly paintings of hunting scenes, trophies, sporting equipment, and weapons were on display, all jarringly familiar. Many an evening after a shooting competition she'd come here with the Hollifields for a sherry before dining. It was his lordship's retreat from the rest of the vast house.

"We're at Berkeley Square," she said in astonishment, at the same time passing the information to Brook.

"Hollifield is rather proud of the tunnel system," said Teddy, moving toward a drinks cabinet. "It's been there for ages. They knew how to build during the Regency. Made things to last. You look in need of a refreshment. Whiskey?"

"Where is Lady Hollifield?"

"Probably still at Buck House with her royal in-laws. Holiday dinners do drag on."

"And the beast you used as a threat against her?"

"There's one in a closed coach with its keepers making slow circles of this area."

"How many of those have you?"

"Enough."

"There must be a timetable for this treason."

"Not your concern."

"You won't remain in a subordinate position to any of those men."

Teddy smiled, offering a short wide glass with a generous portion of whiskey. She accepted it but did not drink. He passed another to Andrina. "I'm sure they each think the same of themselves. The problem in dealing with such fellows is that they all want to be the king of the hill. That's how they got into positions of power and influence in the first place. Their loyalty to the crown is an exploitable weakness, though. They'll stop short of visiting harm on the royal family."

"And you won't?"

"No one is more concerned for their safety than I, especially that of our queen's charming granddaughter Charlotte. The girl is of marriageable age, and she's heard nothing but good things about me." He smiled and tilted his glass toward his sister.

Andrina was pleased. "As a trusted lady-in-waiting I have had considerable influence."

"And instrumental in achieving many helpful goals. Andrina would like nothing better than a tangible connection to the royal family. How happy to be sister-in-law to the heir to the throne. An encounter between myself and Princess Charlotte earlier this month at a ball went off very well. I cut an appealing figure. Nice of her grandmother to set a precedent by marrying a peer for love. Dear me, Cousin, you show disdain."

"I know Charlotte. She's no fool."

"I know her better," said Andrina, sinking into a chair. "Teddy struck just the right notes. She speaks of no one else."

"Girls in love are always fools," he said. "Show the right kind of attention and they fall in love in an instant. Be she a princess in a gilded tower or a violet seller in the street, let a female think she's the center of a man's life and she'll gallop down the aisle like a derby favorite when the tapes go up. No use curling your lip, Alex, it's how they're made. You're the exception, but then you've always been odd."

"A fact I delight in."

Teddy opened a window with a view of Berkeley Square, lighted a lamp, and put it on the sill. A freezing draught stirred the curtains.

"Why, that—that's one of my gowns!" Andrina found her feet and stalked over.

Alex almost laughed. Of all the things to fix upon. "Thank you for the loan. It fit me perfectly."

"You ruined it, you-you gutter drab! How dare you? What else did you steal?"

The petty rage was refreshing. "Your peace of mind."

"W-what? What do you mean?"

"I went through every wardrobe in your rooms, every drawer, every box."

Andrina's face underwent a disturbing transformation, her skin going sickly green, then flushing red with fury, eyes wide, teeth bared. She lunged at Alex but Teddy got there first and half carried her back to the chair and dropped her in it. She abruptly subsided, glaring like Medusa.

Alex's internal armor was solidly in place. A look like that might not kill, but the emotion behind it could knock her right over.

"You girls," said Teddy, exasperated. "Nothing changes."

Andrina continued to glare. Alex matched it. Her cousin's reaction seemed out of proportion to the crime. Considering the emptiness of her life, the outer trappings she acquired to conceal it would be of greater importance to her than to another woman. To Alex, it was just a dress; to Andrina it was part of her soul.

Alex remembered the pity she'd felt for her cousin after picking up on the layers of emotions coating that old treasure box. It impossible to feel the same with Andrina just steps away looking ready to spit acid.

Teddy seemed to sense it. "Andrina, show a little control. You won't ever see her again. That should give you some satisfaction. Your old feud is over. You've won."

"I'll have won when she's dead."

The venom in that statement made him look twice. "Don't lower yourself to her level. She's nothing. There are more important matters to think about. Did you cover your absence from the palace tonight?"

"Yes, it's fine. No one questions a digestive upset. I'll be back tomorrow right as rain. You should come. Wear your new morning suit."

"Dazzling young Charlotte will have to wait. I must keep things moving as scheduled and make sure Hollifield behaves."

"Then go. I can look after this baggage."

He shook his head. "I should stay. If you two start up again it'll raise the house. I've a bit of a free hand with the servants, but prefer not to press things. Oh, Alex, don't take that as an invitation to scream and make a scene. I have a most convincing story prepared about dipsomania. Your disheveled appearance will add to its credibility."

"Let's leave, then. I'm sick of the sight of you."

"No need to be rude. We're waiting for transport. You'll be in a coach with one of the beasts; you won't like it, but I'll be certain you'll get there. Don't bother thinking of escape. They don't know their own strength and could hurt you without even trying. I wouldn't mention you killed one of its own, either. They understand a good deal more than one would imagine."

"How intelligent are they?"

"They're very bright, able to carry out complex tasks better than some humans."

"Why do they serve you?"

"Why does a dog serve its master? I suggest you avoid staring. They can take that as a challenge. Don't meet its eye and you should get on splendidly. Just how did you manage to kill one?"

She shook her head. The less Teddy knew about airships, flying squads, and rakshasas, the better.

"I'm not sure I believe you; it's difficult to picture. They seem to set off some people. Is that what happened to you? Lose control, did you? Wish I'd been there to see. Your warders will need to know. Can't have you surprising them." He peered through the curtains when the sound of wheels and clopping hooves drifted in on the quiet air. "Here we are."

She stood next to him and slumped at the sight of the closed coach. "Damn you, Teddy. . . ."

He looked down. "There, now, it won't be too awful—"

She threw the whiskey into his eyes and slammed an elbow strike just under his breastbone with all the force she could muster. He gasped and grunted, lashing blindly out, the back of his hand whipping past just short of her head as she dodged.

Brook instantly engaged the other guard, and they proceeded to make a deal of noise and cause breakage.

Alex kicked sideways to break Teddy's knee, but caught only his shin with her heel, and the blow lacked strength. Her dress was too cumbersome for wide moves. He was much taller with a longer reach and twice her weight. She didn't dare risk getting struck, and fought defensively, backing when he lunged, slamming sharp, fast deflecting blows when he tried to grab. A cricket bat on a wall display proved to be a temporary deterrent, but when he wrenched it from her hands she seized a golf club from a bag by the door.

Andrina kept her distance, but flung a vase. She yipped and dove behind a chair when Alex started for her. It was a feint; Alex reversed and swung hard at Teddy.

He went low, grasped a handful of her skirts, and pulled hard, hanging on even when she brought the driver down on his near shoulder with a bone-bruising thump. He grunted, but kept pulling. Her instinct was to resist and back away, but she turned his ploy against him. She let herself be drawn, pushing off as though diving into water. He turned his head aside, but got a palm slap square in his ear, then a fist in his throat. He gagged and fell over backward, with Alex on top.

She didn't let up, drilling her knuckles into the nerve points of his arms and elbows. Master Shan taught that fighting fairly in the English way was not fighting to win and live. Another strike under the rib cage, and a knee driven into a very vulnerable spot indeed put Teddy past movement. He lay curled in agony, wheezing and moaning.

A thrown book pelted Alex, catching her in the midsection. It was a light volume, causing more surprise than damage. Andrina wasn't strong enough to shift anything heavy.

She bolted for the study door and escape, but did not reach it. Dress and all, Alex got in between and tackled her like a rugby player, lifting her from the floor, then down they went. Andrina clawed and slapped but with no more effect now than ten years earlier when they'd fought. Two swift knuckle jabs and she went limp.

Alex pushed off her, catching her own ragged breath and vowing never to wear anything but trousers and the most minimal of corsets ever again.

Mr. Brook had achieved equal success with his opponent, though not without acquiring permanent damage to his habiliments and wrecking half the room. With two grown men thrashing for their lives in a limited space, it was only to be expected. Their masks were gone, flung away in the first seconds so they could better see. His nose was bloodied, but his head unbowed.

"You are unhurt, Miss Pendlebury?"

"Yourself, Mr. Brook?"

He wiped blood from his upper lip, further ruining a once-white evening glove. "I may have another black eye."

The Hollifield butler, with two footmen and some frightened maids to lend support, opened the door that was not disguised as a bookcase. Shocked gaping ensued until the man found his voice.

"Lady Pendlebury? May I inquire as to what is going on here?"

"Sebbings, thank God! His lordship asked me to do an errand for his royal sister-in-law and these bounders"—she indicated the human debris on the floor—"attacked us. My colleague and I were forced to defend ourselves."

"But, your ladyship, how did you get inside?"

"How do you think?" She had a sharp watch on his reaction. His gaze did not go to the bookcase, but the open window, his eyes widening. He must not know of the secret entry. "The front door, of course. Lord Hollifield gave me a key, but heaven knows where it is now. These three must have come in by the window and were waiting for us."

"Why did you not ring the bell?"

"Lord Hollifield wanted discretion and still does. Please send a man to summon the police. These criminals must be taken into custody before worse happens."

The mention of the police reassured him. A moment later a footman was outside, blowing a whistle and making the devil's own racket with a police rattle. The sinister coach with its covered windows began moving. She caught no sight of any bestial occupant within.

"They're getting away," murmured Brook.

"For now. I've a feeling we've been exceedingly lucky in our encounters with those things, and it's better to err on the side of caution and let this one depart."

"Lady Pendlebury," said the horrified Sebbings, "this is a fearful mess."

"I'll apologize to his lordship when next I see him. If you want to clear things up, please do so, but keep away from those three. Have you any rope in the house?"

"Rope? Some twine, perhaps. Perhaps in the mews . . ."

"Never mind. I require a knife."

"Indeed?" he said, a touch alarmed.

"Nothing desperate, I assure you."

"There should be one in the desk."

She rummaged in the center drawer and found a more suitable tool: some very sharp scissors. Alex attacked the hampering skirts of her gown, cutting the heavy silk from waist to hem into a strip half a foot wide. She tossed it to Brook.

"Twist that a bit and secure that one first, would you?" She indicated Teddy, who was sweating from pain but trying to get up.

"That will be my very great pleasure, Miss Pendlebury."

The maids left to fetch brooms and dustpans. Sebbings made a cautious circuit, righting tables and chairs and *tch-tch*ing at the damage.

Alex cut two more strips, which served as a blindfold and gag. It would not do to have Sebbings recognize one of Lord Hollifield's cronies. She quietly asked, "Lieutenant, why did you leave us without a word?"

Brook grimaced. "It's hard to explain. I just knew I had to not be there. It was important that I be someplace else; I was overwhelmed by the feeling."

She paused. "Your precognitive ability?"

"It's never taken me like that before. Other times I've not been aware, only after the fact, but this was so strong I hardly knew what I was doing. The next thing I knew I was outside that meeting room. It occurred to me that someone in a mask might emerge sooner or later. I could cosh him and take his place with no one the wiser. Which I did. I was mistaken about the meeting being boring. I learned a great deal of interesting information while standing in the background."

"You couldn't have left me a note?"

"The feeling was overwhelming, as I said. If I'm unable to control the ability, I'm not fit for duty in the field."

"Lieutenant, you avoided capture and saved me no end of bother and danger by being in the right place at the right time, however awkward things were initially. Have you any idea whether James and Dr. Hamish got out?"

"No. But they would be hampered by those crowds and all the stairs."

"Unless they were captured, too. We must get back. Fingate and Benedict are prisoners."

He finished the last knot. Their captives were trussed hand and foot in mauve silk, blind, gagged, and unable to move.

Little was left of Alex's skirt but the lining, which was rather shredded due to her haste with the scissors. The petticoat beneath showed through in spots. She felt extraordinarily proud of the damage.

When a policeman arrived he was not overawed by Brook's Service credentials, and looked ready to arrest everyone and let a judge sort things in the morning. Sebbings vouched for Lady Pendlebury, and Alex dropped the names of several detectives she'd worked with on cases, including Inspector Lennon.

"You know 'im?" asked the representative of the law, fixing her with a suspicious glare. "So do I. Peaky lad with a moustache."

"No, he's a great bear of a man with a voice and temper like the wrath of God. He'd as soon throw you through a wall as buy you a pint."

"Huh. You *do* know 'im," he stated with certainty, then began considering the removal of the prisoners.

"Does your station have a telegraph with a line to Psychic Service headquarters?" she inquired.

"You know we do."

"I should say, have you an operator on duty?"

"Always."

"Then I've an urgent message about these three that must be sent immediately—"

"That will wait, Alex."

She whipped around.

Lord Hollifield stood before the open bookcase door. He had a pistol in hand, not one of the air gun models, but no less deadly.

"Lord 'ollifield," said the policeman, straightening to attention, goggling along with the servants at the trick door.

"Yes. These intruders have taken liberties with my hospitality. I must ask you to place them under arrest for trespassing."

"But those two are with the Psychic Service, your lordship."

"They are imposters with forged identification. You need not be troubled; they took me in, as well."

Sebbings, startled at this unexpected appearance of his master along with the untrue statements, opened his mouth but snapped it shut again. Contradicting a peer as well as his employer was not the done thing. He glanced at Alex, but her attention was on Hollifield.

"You're mistaken, Lord Daniel," she said steadily. "If you look closely, you'll see the man who was so unforgivably boorish toward you and Lady Lindsey has been dealt with. He poses no further menace to you—or to her."

Hollifield looked closely. "I see," he said at length. "I stand corrected, but this is a . . . complicated situation."

"Not at all. It's as simple as the divide between black and white and which side you choose to stand upon."

"You oversimplify."

"As have you. You are in place to make history, sir. What kind remains to be determined. You can induce a change, but you know in your heart it's not right, else you would have acted sooner. This evening your control was usurped by a lesser man. There will always more where he came from."

"It's begun. It's too late to stop."

"I do not believe that. Inform your order of the threat held over your head. If they truly are honorable men, they will understand."

"You're a witch with words, girl, but it's out of my hands. They've left to do what must be done. You removed a viper from our midst, and I am deeply grateful, but things must and will proceed."

"What does her ladyship think of this? Does she approve? Does she know people have died and that more will follow? That families will be torn from their homes and cast into the cold to starve? That's what happens in revolutions."

He shook his head. "It's the price that must be paid."

"She will pay, too. Your name is *her* name. It is not you alone. This is also Lady Lindsey and your children. They share in *all* you do. The blame and shame will haunt them and their children down through history."

"There is no shame in this!" he bellowed.

"Sir . . ." she answered firmly, "you know better. I saw your face when Teddy threatened her. You are her protector, first and foremost. You are the center of her world. Will you rip that from her? Is this what a loving husband and father does to his family?"

"It will turn out all right in the end."

"Not for you. Not for her. She's a woman of honor, too. Will she ever look on your face again with loving eyes? With eyes that see her husband rather than a traitor to all she holds dear? She will see the man who betrayed and shamed her children and grandchildren. This will kill her and you know it."

He dropped his gaze, shaking his head, but kept the pistol aimed toward Alex and Brook. "You don't understand."

"But I do. Most clearly. One of your order murdered my father without a second's thought. It was not a necessity of war, but a foul and vicious act. Those are the people you are aligned with: murderers and traitors. If Lady Lindsey got in their way, they'd serve her the same."

"That won't happen."

"You can't know that. You are an honest man, sir. You expect people to be as honest as you are. That makes it hard to determine when they lie to you. As a Reader I always know when someone lies. I always know their true feelings. You should know what I learned from just a few minutes in that room. There was fear, envy, and greed for more power. They claim loyalty to England, but the rot is just under the surface. No mask can hide that from me."

"They can be controlled."

"That is *exactly* what they believe about *you*." Alex held her breath. Popular myth held that Readers could pick up thoughts. She would have given much to have that ability right now.

He raised his head, eyes kindling with anger. "They wouldn't dare."

"You know they would. England won't be defended by the British lion, but torn apart by carrion crows. It is the way of such men. England deserves better. So does your wife, your family."

"I do this for them!"

"They won't thank you for it. Given a choice between you and England, they will always pick you first. What is *your* choice, sir?"

He kept the internal agony from his features, but she felt it cutting him like sharp knife. "I have no choice. It's over. It's done."

"Would you undo it if you could?"

"Yes." His voice cracked. "A thousand times yes." He lowered the pistol.

Sebbings and the policeman, though they couldn't have much of an idea of what was going on, each relaxed and breathed again as did Alex and Brook. On the floor, Teddy gave a disgusted groan.

A tall masked form burst from the shadows of the bookcase door. Head to toe in black, topped by a hooded cloak, he was as alarming a sight as any Alex had beheld that evening, including the beast in the mirror room.

Hollifield gave a start and turned, raising the gun toward the intruder, but the man moved incredibly fast. His lordship's pistol was plucked away in a blink.

The man swept toward Alex, who stumbled backward, bumping into something. His hand shot out, keeping her from falling. As he steadied her, she felt emotions not her own: anger, relief, and an odd, swift spark of amusement, then her barriers came up and halted the flood.

She glimpsed ice blue eyes behind the mask. One of them winked at her.

She began to speak, but he raised one finger for silence.

Lord Richard was apparently not ready to return from the dead just yet.

He turned the pistol over to a startled Alex, strode to the bookcase, and gave a whistle. Two flying squad men clattered in, followed by James, Fingate, and Benedict. They were battered, covered in grime and dust, and smelled of black powder. There was no shortage of weapons among them.

Nonplussed and outraged, Hollifield began to bluster as any man might toward strangers invading his home. Lord Richard towered over him and again raised one finger.

Hollifield stuttered to a halt, then demanded, "Who are you?"

James put himself forward. "Doesn't matter. You made the correct choice in the end. You owe your life to our Alex."

"W-what?"

"That is to say, our friend here has had a bead on the back of your head at point-blank range for the last five minutes. We're delighted he didn't have to shoot you."

Benedict was paper pale and with help from Fingate sought out the nearest chair, folding into it without a word and closing his eyes.

"Those stairs were a trial for him, Lady Drina," explained Fingate. "We should have a doctor in."

"I say there." James was peeved. "*I* am a doctor."

"Sorry, sir, I forgot."

"I'm going to have to grow a great hooting moustache and carry a large black bag with 'doctor' printed on it in gold before anyone takes me seriously."

At that point the policeman blew his whistle, catching everyone on the hop. It had the effect of making him the focus of attention.

"The lot of you settle in one spot and inform me wot is goin' on 'ere," he ordered. He pointed the whistle at the squad men. "You—put those pistols down this instant or I'll 'ave you in irons."

They looked at Lord Richard, who gave one nod, then

obeyed, slotting the weapons into their shoulder harness holsters. He gestured and the men went to stand behind Hollifield.

"You! In the fancy togs! I wants that mask orf an' an explanation—"

Lord Richard produced a heavy folded paper and extended it toward the policeman, who accepted and read it with suspicion. His eyes widened. "Is this . . . ? Truth an' all?"

The masked apparition pointed authoritatively at Alex. He took the paper, passed it to her, and then turned on his heel, departing the way he'd come, pulling the bookcase door shut with a *snick*.

"They should have him in Parliament," said James. "They'd get more work done with less noise. What is that?"

Alex recognized the seals and her godmother's signature under the brief and neatly written statement. The onus it placed on her inspired equal parts of satisfaction and exasperation.

"It means," she said wearily, "that until and unless a senior agent arrives—and I think it unlikely—I'm in charge."

James barked a single laugh. "You should love that, little cousin."

To be entrusted with the responsibility for the state of affairs in Lord Hollifield's study was the last thing Alex wanted, but it had its benefits. She immediately ordered tea.

Sebbings looked to his master for a cue. Hollifield nodded and gave a weary wave, then retired to the chair at his desk. His crisis of conscience over, he seemed uninterested in further participation.

While the squad men stood over the prisoners, Alex wrote a brief telegraph message for Mrs. Woodwake. Owing to the need for secrecy, it had to be vague, but she'd know Alex was returning with prisoners. The policeman was dispatched to the station with mysterious instructions to avoid contact with any closed coaches that might put themselves in his way.

Tea arrived, along with biscuits and other edibles from that day's reception. Fingate helped distribute the refreshment.

Benedict roused enough accept a cup, which he had to hold in both hands. After the first bracing gulp he looked around uneasily.

"Are there mirrors here?" he asked in a sharp tone.

"No, sir," said Fingate. "It's quite safe."

"No place is safe. Besides, *he's* here." He glared at Lord Hollifield.

His lordship looked away. "I'm sorry, lad. Truly I am."

Benedict scowled. "A bit late for that. What you've opened and unleashed—"

"You volunteered!"

"And when things went wrong you left me to rot in the dark with those damned nightmares!"

"I did no such—"

"*Oi!*" Alex's loud interjection cut short the exchange. Instructive as it might be, she was certain it would lead to things the Hollifield servants did not need to hear. "Fingate, how did you two escape?"

"We didn't. They locked us up. Not sure for how long, but things got noisy. Whistles blowing, people shouting, screaming, and thumping around . . ."

"That would be the forces of law and order making a vigorous inquiry about the odd goings-on at number twenty-five," said James. "The guests lost all sense of proper deportment, in fact, most went into a bit of a blind panic, which was not in the least helpful. Then those masked johnnies tried to leg it out by way of the tunnels."

Hollifield lifted his head. "What happened?"

"They were sorely disappointed to find the exits blocked. The tall fellow who left? He knew all about those. Most of the johnnies didn't make it."

"Dead?" he choked out, going gray.

James's normally cheerful expression turned somber. "Some fools began shooting. Couldn't hear their guns, but by God they heard ours. It was over in seconds. A narrow tunnel is a poor place to stage a battle. The men in front fall first, you can't advance, more bodies pile up, and then you can't breathe or see for the powder smoke choking the air." He looked at Alex. "That's where Hamish is, seeing to the wounded. I should be there, but I wanted to make sure you weren't in a bad spot."

"Thank you," she said. "I take it you got the lady out."

"We were met halfway by a rescue party led by that tall fellow. We presented our credentials, mentioned your name, and she was passed to safe and caring hands. Then Hamish and I led them to the secret doings. I won't be shocked if my hair's turned white from some of what I saw in the private rooms. We did have a jolly time breaking through doors and terrifying people. That's how we found Fingate and that poor devil." He cast a look at Benedict, who was now eagerly demolishing a plate of biscuits.

"Our large companion was looking for you. Determined fellow. He loped off into that infernal maze with a couple of men, and I loped after them with Fingate in tow. From some of what was muttered in passing I had the idea we were also tracking the general in charge of the works and had to be cautious. Didn't know for sure it would lead to you, but I should have guessed you'd turn up. You have a talent for ticking off people at the top."

"Really, James—"

"You're right, let me correct that. You've a talent for ticking off people everywhere. I hope you won't stop, as it's no end entertaining for me. I'd be obliged if you'd explain those unfortunates on the rug. One of 'em seems familiar."

"You met him at the swimming race today."

"You're joking."

"Sadly, not."

James bent for a closer scrutiny of Teddy. "What the devil is—"

"Let's keep names out of it for the present. We're all

going to Service headquarters and statements will be taken there."

"How boring. Might I be excused? Oh, well. Nothing for it but to do my duty and all that, however inconvenient. Good heavens, is that a woman you've got tied up?"

CHAPTER FIFTEEN

In Which Miss Pendlebury Deals with a Private Matter

L ittle cousin," said James, looking out the study window at the unusual quantity of traffic in the square, "you've inserted yourself into history. No mistake about it."

"Bother that," snapped Alex.

"It's true. The Grosvenor Square raid promises to have greater repercussions than anything since Guy Fawkes was found strolling under Parliament with a pocketful of matches. Looks like hundreds are being arrested."

Alex had no mind for her place in history, being distracted by the need to acquire immediate transportation to Service headquarters. Every conveyance from half the stations in the city were being used to transport prisoners. Omnibuses were commandeered, even open carts from tradesmen were sent in.

She finally ordered Lord Hollifield's coach made ready, her authority backed up by the queen's carte blanche letter. Alex liked this level of command, but understood a disproportionate amount of responsibility came with it. She gladly anticipated turning the paper and her charges over to Mrs. Woodwake as soon as humanly possible.

As a grudging concession to James, who was more of a gentleman than Alex was a lady, she allowed him to place Andrina on a settee and remove her blindfold. She'd returned to her full senses and chewed at her gag, attempting to talk. It would have been comical, but Alex was certain those bursts of frustrated sounds were not fit to hear. The gag remained in place.

"Andrina, you'll be given the chance to speak as much as you'd like soon enough. Until then, you may want to consider what sort of apologies to write to our godmother and in particular to Princess Charlotte. After tonight you won't be allowed within miles of the palace ever again."

Fingate, poor fellow, looked moderately appalled, not at Andrina's fate, but at Alex's obvious satisfaction over it.

Alex realized that she was not the ingenuous fledgling he'd known ten years ago, but she refused to feel badly about that. Where Andrina was concerned, it was impossible to conceal the pleasure of finally having the last word.

Lord Hollifield remained quiet. He'd made use of pen, ink, and paper, composing a letter to his wife. Alex read it to make sure it wasn't a coded message to another member of the Order of the Black Sun. She apologized for intruding and gave it to Sebbings to hand deliver. Though a traitor, his lordship was royally connected and would require delicate handling for the time being.

Brook, with an abstracted expression, strode across to the desk, opened the top right drawer, took something from under a sheaf of papers there, and returned to where he'd been standing by the bookcase door.

With a dreadful face, Hollifield gave a short groan of misery and slumped.

"Mr. Brook?"

"Yes, Miss Pendlebury?"

"Were you aware of what you've just done?"

It took him a moment to work out how he'd acquired the derringer in his hand. "Oh. Well."

"You could not have known that was in the desk."

"I've never been in this room before," he admitted.

"Your talent is certainly manifesting itself in useful ways today. Bravo." She turned to Hollifield. "You are not taking the gentleman's way out to avoid accountability, sir. Remember your family. Causing harm to yourself harms them."

"What of your family, Alex? What untold harm have you

done to them this night?" He shot a pointed look at Teddy and Andrina.

"They brought it on themselves, but I dread giving the news to their parents. My uncle and aunt won't thank me for it, but better from me than a stranger. I'll have no friends on the Pendlebury side, and the crimes committed will taint my name as well. Uncle will resign in disgrace, Aunt will—well, never mind. What comes will come."

The coach arrived, much to Alex's relief. She wanted to leave before Lady Lindsey returned from her royal dinner.

Lord Hollifield now seemed stoically resigned to accept the consequences of his actions in the best public school manner.

Seemed. Alex sensed he had a small gem of bright hope deeply hidden. What it might be she could not say, but it had to be removed. There was a moment of scandalized distress from others when she ordered his hands restrained behind him by police darbies. They were to be left on indefinitely.

"Really, Alex, must you?" asked James.

She shot him a bleak look. "I don't . . . I don't want the man hanging himself later."

That took James aback. He looked ill, but nodded and said nothing more on the subject.

Alex briefly touched Hollifield's arm as he was helped into the coach. The bright little gem was gone, replaced by bleak darkness.

The ride to headquarters was silent. She was tired to the bone and welcomed the respite, however short. Duty called again when they were stopped at Whitehall by armed men from the Horse Guards. Barricades were up, blocking the street. The queen's letter got them through.

Lights burned in every window of the Service building, and just across Richmond Terrace, New Scotland Yard was active as a knocked-over anthill. Horse Guards and soldiers on foot were everywhere. Some were even posted on roofs overlooking Downing Street. She'd never seen such a thing before.

When they rolled through the gates into the courtyard Alex

picked up the excitement in the air. Her telegram to Wood-wake had prepared the way for the prisoners. Hollifield, Teddy, Andrina, and the hapless guard (still groggy from his fight with Brook) were swept off to hidden regions to eventually be questioned by Readers. Alex wondered if the rules might be set aside to include her in the process, since she could offer insight to her cousins' reactions. Time would tell.

Mrs. Woodwake was busy elsewhere, though. Interviews would have to wait. Instead of a meeting room or even the dining hall, their party was escorted up to a large parlor on the fourth floor. It looked less like a ministry office and more like a private home.

A cheery fire burned, the rugs were thick and mellow in color and some exceedingly fine landscape paintings drew the eye beyond the limits of the walls. Windows looked out over Whitehall and the length of Downing Street. During the day a slice of St. James's Park would be visible beyond.

Bullet holes marred the glass from the attack that afternoon. Rags had been stuffed in to halt draughts. Corresponding holes in the ceiling attested to the velocity and force of the air gun bullets. The great black rectangles of night made Alex uncomfortable, as though invisible things were staring in on them. She pulled the heavy brocade curtains together.

Benedict, blown again from having to climb stairs, balked at the door, pointing in alarm at what hung over the fireplace.

"Mirror! Get me away! Get me away!"

He blundered backward into the hall. Brook and James caught him and Alex promised to remove the offending décor. That calmed him, but he remained rigid as a corpse until two of their staff escorts lifted the framed glass from its hooks and took it elsewhere.

Fingate had apparently appointed himself the poor man's unofficial keeper, and with soothing words got him settled close to the fire. Benedict shut his eyes and hummed to himself, his fingers tapping the chair arms. Alex thought she recognized Bach.

Her exhausted little company spread themselves among the furnishings. Even the indefatigable Brook sprawled in a chair, his long legs stretched out. She knew if she shut her eyes she'd never get them open again. Besides, the damned corset pinched too much. She went to the hall, looking for and finding a necessary room.

Tiled from floor to ceiling in greens and blues with winking highlights of topaz-colored glass, it was the most remarkable and beautiful one she'd ever seen. The walls gave the impression of being in a fairy forest of vines and flowers, dazzling even by gaslight.

Alex quit the water closet to find Sybil waiting on a settee by the bathing tub, a bright smile on her mad face. She wore a purple dressing gown and brilliant red carpet slippers.

"Hallo, traveler's daughter! I'm glad you broke the mirrors. My head's cooler now."

Alex had to smile back. "Pleased to have been of help."

"Dreadful things in those mirrors."

"Yes. There were."

"Are. Still there. Can't let more get through."

"Do you know how many are here?"

"No, how many?" She tucked her lips, waiting for an answer.

"I'd hoped you might say."

Sybil tapped her head. "Doesn't work like that. What comes, comes, and others decide what's important. I gave that up ages ago, too distracting. You look terrible."

"I'm sure I do. Would you mind helping me loosen this corset?"

"I won't know until I try. What a pretty dress!"

"It was some hours ago. Who else is else about? That companion of yours?"

"She's having a nap. I exhaust people. I don't mean to, but there it is. Here—this came, or maybe I had it brought up. Sometimes I forget what I ask for, but these wanted to be in here and they aren't my size. They should trim you up." She gestured at a blouse and a walking skirt neatly laid out on a chair. "Are the colors all right?"

The blouse had blue and brown stripes and the skirt was a slightly darker brown with sky-blue braiding for trim.

Normally Alex would have avoided such a garish and unlikely combination, but anything was better than the rags of Andrina's vanity. "They're beautiful. Thank you."

Sybil gave a breathy giggle, rocking back and forth. "I love color-color-colors. They don't always go together and then suddenly they do. Such a surprise, like rainbows in a mud puddle."

She assisted with the corset and Alex took what seemed to be her first deep breath in days. "Do you live here?"

"All the time. It keeps me safe. Hardly ever have guests. I'm supposed to be in bed, but I like you. Had to say hallo. Do you like my sitting room?"

"It's lovely."

"But so quiet. One day after another with the big clock up the road striking away the hours. Dickie promised to find a better place for me, but there won't be time, things are going to get dreadfully busy for him."

"In what way?"

"He'll find out. I *think* he'll find out. I don't know. I might never know. Or I'll know too much and it gets stopped up trying to get out. I've just the one head and a thousand thoughts a minute, all of them right and all of them wrong and somebody always wants me to pick just one. But I leave that to others."

"Quite right," Alex said supportively, buttoning the blouse. The blue and brown stripes should not have cooperated, yet did. "This is delightful."

Another pleased giggle. "I like getting things right. Makes up for the other times." She ran water in the washing basin and soaked a fresh towel in it. "For the handsome one's eyes."

"Lieutenant Brook?"

"I don't know. There's a handsome man with bruises and

he's keen on you. Be keen right back." She thrust the towel into Alex's hands.

"That's not something I'm able to—"

"Piffle. Be keen." She made shooing gestures, and there was no answer but to leave.

In Alex's absence the fire had been built up with more coal, making the room pleasantly warm for all its size. James, stretched on a long couch, snored gently. Brook began to rise. She waved him down.

"Put your head back," she said.

He obeyed, watching from his blooming bruises. He did have such nice eyes. She eased the cold towel on, and he gave a small sigh. As she started to turn, his hand somehow caught hers. Neither so gently that she could pull away nor so firmly that it would hurt, he held fast. He was insistent about it.

The emotions from that contact . . .

Her instinctive reaction was always to slam her internal armor in place.

This time, she did not.

What flooded in was . . . nice.

His feelings were like chords of music. Sweet. Warm. Boundless. Waves of it, lifting, lilting, strong.

She knew *she* was the source of its creation in him.

Which was a little frightening.

He released her hand. She expected him to move the towel so he could gauge her reaction, but he left it in place. He'd wanted only for her to *know*. What she would do with the knowledge was her choice.

She gulped, seized by a hectic urge to run, which was foiled by a calm curiosity to stay and see what might happen.

"Lady Drina?"

Fingate. Dear, wonderful Fingate saved her from making a decision. She gave her full attention to him as she might grant to a life preserver flung her way on a stormy sea.

"I must speak with you," he said. "A private matter. Family."

Something to do with her father. "The hall, then."

He followed her out and they settled on two chairs beneath a lighted gas sconce.

"I've a small favor to ask, Mr. Fingate. I prefer to be called Alex, or if you must, Miss Alex or Miss Pendlebury. I'm used to it, now. After tonight the less connection I have with that side of the family the better. I've no use for titles in the Service."

His expression was unusually distressed. "Very well. Something . . . I don't know how to say it. This beyond unspeakable if it's true. I hope to God it is not, that I just made a mistake."

"About what?"

"You said earlier today that you live on Baker Street?"

"What of it?"

"And Dr. Fonteyn told me that you've been with the Psychic Service for several years."

"Yes. . . ."

"If that's true, then why is it that—"

Alex found the carte blanche letter almost murderously helpful at clearing obstacles. It enabled her to walk unchallenged out of Service headquarters, to commandeer a coach, and to get through the Horse Guards. She had an errand that would not wait, even if she was dismissed in disgrace as a result.

She stormed up to the door of Pendlebury House and, having lost her key, rang the bell until someone let her in. It might have been Mabrey, she was in no state to notice.

She pushed past, fetched what she wanted, and departed without a word. If her aunt and uncle were back from whatever social demand had taken them away, she didn't know or care. In her present mood she'd have set fire to the whole damnable place and felt only satisfaction.

Fingate had told her much, and Alex worked out the rest.

The coach was barely stopped before the Service building when she burst forth and charged into the front reception area. Mrs. George was not on duty, but the older man at the desk readily provided the number of the room she wanted.

Below street level were the most secure and quiet rooms, used for Readings. Now it was as noisy as an East End public house on New Year's Eve.

Certain select occupants from the Grosvenor Square raid were confined in the small locked rooms here. She recognized a number of grim-faced men in disheveled evening dress being escorted to and fro. Some were silent with shock, others fought and bellowed commands, which were ignored. They'd be questioned by Readers, each in turn, the interviews taken down in shorthand. Of course, they could choose not to speak. That was their right, but there was likely to be other evidence to bring against them. They were in for it.

Alex made her way through the turmoil, her armor firmly in place. She conjured a pleasant fancy about her godmother reviving the custom of putting the heads of traitors on pikes for the amusement and instruction of the populace.

No guard was on the door she sought. A bolt was enough to keep the occupant locked in. Alex peered through the sliding peephole, threw the bolt, and went in, leaving the door open behind her.

Cousin Andrina, still in disheveled male attire, rose from the wooden bench on the far wall. She saw what Alex carried. Instead of showing shame, her chin went up in defiance.

Alex raised high the treasure box bearing their shared name.

Her cousin blanched and cowered back with a scream, hands up to ward off the coming blow.

But Alex smashed the box as hard as she could against the stone floor. The corners burst. It seemed to explode apart. The contents, packet after packet of envelopes tied up in cords, bounded from their captivity and scattered.

There were ten packets in all, one for each year since

Father had waved to her from a dock in Hong Kong. Ten years of letters for A.V. Pendlebury, residing at 16 Wilton Crescent, London.

It would never have occurred to Father that Andrina, also christened with the queen's name, might receive Alex's mail instead.

Perhaps the first delivery had been a mistake on the part of a servant. Perhaps Andrina saw her name on an envelope in a stack on the hall table and opened it.

How she must have laughed all those months as Alex waited in vain for word to come from her father. What an excellent joke on the hated interloper.

Alex found the oldest and thinnest packet and slipped off the ribbon. The first letter was dated on the day of her departure from Hong Kong. Her father sent warm and loving greetings along with the bad news that he would be out of touch for a number of months. Duty compelled him to travel through difficult and dangerous country and he trusted that she would understand he could not discuss details. Foremost in his heart was her safety and well-being. He knew she would be strong and apply herself to become a part of his brother's family until such time as they could meet again.

The next letter was dated months later from Siam. Again, warm and loving greetings and he begged her to write to him care of the embassy there.

That must have been when Andrina replied, perhaps a short note imitating Alex's hand, just to see if she could get away with it.

Four months later Gerard was in Melbourne, assuring her any letters to Siam would be forwarded. He was pleased that her studies in Latin and German were progressing since she'd not been as interested in them before as she was in French and Cantonese. . . .

The whole of the vicious deception was clear and brutally cruel. Andrina imposed her accomplishments onto Alex's life,

getting two things she craved like drink: revenge and paternal love.

Leo's regard for his daughter was distant and cool, bestowed
out of duty, not affection.

Gerard was the better father. Even secondhand and based
on a lie, Andrina fed on his approval, hoarding the letters more
carefully than any miser his gold.

It was brilliant, and at the same time irrationally stupid.
The whole sham could have been revealed at any time. A letter from Gerard to Leo, a note to mutual friends, even a mis-
sive to the queen proudly mentioning his daughter the
lady-in-waiting, and it would have ended.

Yet Andrina kept it going. Long after Alex came of age
and moved to Baker Street, Andrina continued the ruse.

But when Gerard at last returned to England, her decade-
long trick would be exposed.

"You saw Father at one of the Black Dawn meetings," said
Alex. "You recognized him, but he did not know you. The
last time he'd seen you, you were a child in ruffled dresses and
white stockings, your face sticky from stolen candy."

Andrina had her back to a wall, with as much distance between herself and Alex as could be managed in the small room.
Her gaze flicked to the open door and the activity there. The
people without were busy with their own concerns. A Reader
interviewing someone was not worth notice.

"Never mind that a lady-in-waiting to Princess Charlotte
was involved with anything as wretched as a pack of traitors,
you were in a panic that he would turn up at Wilton Crescent
looking for me. It would all come out then. You couldn't tell
Teddy, that would give him something to hold over you. This
had to be dealt with quietly and alone. The Black Dawn had the
means to remove inconvenient people, particularly spies."

"That would have taken too long." Andrina's voice was
thick. "It takes more than one member to issue a death order.
They hold a trial first. A quorum of five goes over the evidence.

It always ends the same, but they're so proud of having things right and proper. That takes days. I had hours."

Alex picked up the packets of letters and put them in order on the bench. She untied the cording on some and threaded the lengths through her fingers. Silk. Silk was very strong.

"How did you speed things?"

"I signed Teddy's name to an order with the date of the last quorum. We had 'Dr. Kemp's' address. He was a spy; they would have removed him anyway. I'd have been forgiven for taking action. Teddy would have protected me. He needs—needed—me to help with his courtship of Charlotte."

"And then you had Father murdered. Brutally, coldly, without remorse. Only relief." Alex played with the cording and stared and stared at her. It was a standard ploy for Readers. Wait long enough and some subjects spoke of their own accord.

"I'm not without heart," said Andrina. "I directed that Uncle Gerard be rendered insensible and then hanged. It was peaceful and painless. He didn't feel anything. The beast's handler assured me it was well able to carry out complex tasks."

"Was my name on the same death order?"

"It had to be. You'd have found out everything. But that fool of a keeper heard the row going on at the other end of Baker Street, saw that our men were routed, and lost his nerve. He left. It was my bad luck that Teddy set his hounds loose to go after Desmond on the same night."

"What a nasty surprise to have me appear on the doorstep in need of a safe place to stay." Alex would ask Mrs. Woodwake if she'd had any inkling of what a bad idea that had been.

"But I covered it. You're not clever. A few insults and you can't wait to leave any room I'm in."

"Well played. What about the next attempt with the beast? I didn't see you at Hollifield House."

"I wasn't there. When the message came to have you kidnapped, the beast's keeper took it as an opportunity to complete his orders to kill you. They're all frightfully dedicated to the cause, and no one with secrets ever wants a Reader around.

"My death wouldn't matter. You'd have still been dis-covered."

"Not at all. I'd have burned the letters."

"It was inevitable. You overlooked Fingate. Father always let him know what you wrote."

"Who'd believe a servant over me?"

Alex shook her head. "What a self-centered witling you are. What a supreme dunce."

"He has no standing. No one would belie—"

"I say again: you are a *dunce*. A bookless donkey."

"Name-calling? If you're reduced to that then you've lost the argument."

"It never once occurred to you that Father would have kept all of 'my' letters as safely as you kept his?"

Andrina's mouth snapped shut. The Medusan glare returned.

"They're in a strongbox at his bankers' with other impor-tant papers. Fingate told me about them. Had you killed me, the game would have still been over. That box would have gone to his brother, who would have found those letters. Unlike you, Uncle Leo is no fool. He'd have worked it out with or without Fingate dropping a word in his ear. He'd have kept it in the family, of course, but he would have *known*. There'd be no disowning of you—can't have that sort of scandal—but Leo would have seen to your removal from the palace. Mustn't have murderers and liars hanging about the royal heirs.

"Your father may be cold, but he's a man of honor. He would have resigned and removed everyone from London. He'll still resign. The family won't survive what you and Teddy have done to it.

"I should be pleased to let Teddy know all that you've achieved. If you'd not acted, his plan for the Black Dawn to press forward might have worked. But whatever the outcome, you'd have lost."

"You won't get those years back," said Andrina. "All those years your father praised *me*, not you. Those are *mine*. He was proud of *me*, not you. I've won."

"Convince yourself of that in the times to come when you sit alone in a cell not nearly as pleasant as this."

"There's no proof connecting me to Gerard's death. It's all on Teddy. No one can prove I forged his name, and I will deny everything. I will put on a most convincing show. Not even a Reader will get past it. You and your ilk may detect lies, but you can't force people to speak. You'll get no admissions from me."

The memory of Lord Richard questioning the captured Black Dawn fanatic was fresh and sharp. Alex had no doubt that whatever talent had been in play then would be used on Andrina later. Alex smiled. "Then you've a terrible surprise ahead. I won't spoil it for you."

"Are you finished? I'm tired. I want tea and food and a proper room. Send someone to bring me a change of clothes. I'll make a list for my maid."

"Witling," Alex repeated. "That life is *ended*. This is your life now—while it lasts. I'll have to look up what's done to traitors these days. I don't know if they're hanged or beheaded. If the latter, then we might have to send for one of those French machines."

Andrina laughed once and sat on the bench. "That won't happen. They won't execute a woman, and they certainly won't execute a goddaughter of the queen. She'll never allow it."

"She may have no choice. She's sworn to support the laws of the realm. But I like our godmother. There are ways of sparing her from such a decision—"

Andrina's shriek for help was cut short when Alex whipped the silk cordings around her throat, pulling them tight like a thuggee sacrificing to Kali. Andrina clawed and beat at her.

Alex let her armor down and felt the rage, the fear, the panic, and then the stubborn disbelief. Andrina *knew* she wouldn't die, not really. Her struggles faltered.

But that wasn't the point.

Alex whispered in her ear. "*This* is what happened to Father. This is how it feels. This is what you brought upon him. You *are* going to die, Cousin. Your tongue bulging and black, your eyes bloodshot, your face purple. What an ugly corpse you'll make."

Andrina suddenly found fresh strength to fight, trying to pull the strangling silk away.

Alex pulled it a fraction tighter and waited until the certainty of survival faded. She felt the raw instant when her cousin realized it was over. The horrified panic returned and it was devastating. Alex slammed her defenses between them to avoid that wailing despair, counted to ten, then let go.

Her cousin fell and lay like a dead thing. After a moment, Andrina twitched, then began wheezing. First short, ineffective gasps, then coughing, then whoops as she struggled to fill her lungs. Alex was reminded of her own near-drowning.

"Was it peaceful for you? Was it painless?" she asked.

Andrina seemed not to hear.

Alex gathered the letters and kicked the debris of the box outside the door. She went back and knelt close to Andrina, looking into her eyes, into her bloodshot and terrified eyes.

"You're going to remember this. When the light fades each night you will *always* feel that tightness about your throat. You will dream about it and wake from nightmares about dying. You will remember what you did to deserve it. This will haunt you forever; each time you take a breath in the dark, you will remember this. You won't be able to help yourself."

Alex rose and walked out, bolting the door.

She made it halfway down the corridor before her knees gave way. The blackness struck her like a club.

Strangely, the floor was a soft and yielding thing. It held her close, rocking and protecting her.

It felt like music.

The peaty taste of whiskey pulled her back. She cleared her throat and shot fully awake.

To her chagrin, Mr. Brook was on the floor, holding her cradled in his arms. She started to rise, but after the first feeble effort decided it might be better to rest for a moment.

It was quite ridiculous. Wholly unprofessional.

But . . . exceedingly pleasant.

Other Service members walked around them, glancing down with concern, but Brook smiled and waved them off, letting them know the situation was well in hand.

"You heard all that?" she asked.

"Some of it. You are a frightening woman, Miss Pendlebury."

Yet he held her. His feelings for her were the same.

"You shouldn't know such things about me."

"Why not? You know everything about me at any given moment. No one can hide aught from a Reader, or so I've been told. Several times."

"Did your talent bring you here?" she asked.

"No, that would be Sybil. She popped in just as Mrs. Woodwake was asking where the devil you'd gotten to. Sybil suggested that I look for you here and wait outside. She was adamant that I not interrupt."

"For all you knew I was killing Andrina."

"The Seer's name is Sybil, not Cassandra. If Colonel Mourne takes what she says seriously, then so will I. Now, I won't say I wasn't worried, but it was your family matter to settle, not mine." She felt his disquiet, but it flared and vanished.

"I said some terrible things."

"You were provoked. She stole something irreplaceable and cut short an innocent life. In the end you took the right path. I don't know that I'd have been as wise or restrained."

"Families," she groaned. "They can be quite dreadful."

"Or your best refuge."

"Not that one. *This* is my family, my home. The Service isn't perfect, but I can be myself here. They understand me. But the days to come . . . I'll have to make arrangements, somehow speak to my uncle and aunt, then go through Father's letters. . . ."

"Mr. Fingate will help. So will I. So will James. You won't be alone."

"It will still be awful."

"And it can wait," he said firmly. "Put it from your mind, at least for now."

"Pendleburys. Damn the Pendleburys. I'd change my name if I could."

"Indeed?"

The blazing soaring uplift of spirit in him was unmistakable: hope.

Oh, God, he can't be thinking of that. *It's absurd. Absolutely absurd.*

And yet . . .

His warmth surged. Enveloping her.

She floated on it.